DONE RUBBED OUT

Reightman & Bailey Book One

Jeffery Craig

This is a work of fiction. All of the characters, organizations, and events portrayed in this novel are either the product of the author's imagination, or are used fictitiously. Any resemblance to individuals living or dead is entirely coincidental and the product of the author's imagination.

Cover design by LaLima Design
Cover images© Artophoto|Dreamstime and ©Bortn66|Dreamstime
Author Photo by Clayton P. King

Library of Congress Control Number: 2016905144
CreateSpace Independent Publishing Platform, North Charleston, SC
ISBN – 13: 978-1530470129
ISBN – 10: 1530470129

BOOKS BY JEFFERY CRAIG

Done Rubbed Out: Reightman & Bailey Book One

Hard Job: Reightman & Bailey Book Two*

Skin Puppet: Reightman & Bailey Book Three*

*Forthcoming

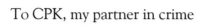

To CPK, my partner in crime

ONE NIGHT IN AUGUST

THE FIRST THING Toby Bailey remembered thinking when he turned on the lights and stepped into the larger of the two treatment rooms was, "Oh shit!" Nothing else. No other reaction. Just one, simple, two word expletive phrase. The second thing he remembered thinking was that he'd never get all the blood out of the new Italian white suede loafers, on which he'd blown his non-existent shoe budget for the next several months.

The blood in question pooled in large, sticky puddles on the neutral bamboo floors, embellished by random, lurid accent spatters on the matte light café mocha walls and the strategically placed lush tropical plants. It wasn't a good look for the room which had previously been his favorite in the Time Out Spa.

Toby stood in place; one hand still slapped against the brushed chrome switch plate, and took in the gore. Three glistening puddles of diminishing size were linked by bloody streams, leading his gaze to a massage table and the body arranged on top of a pile of blood soaked, sky blue sheets. The only sound was the gentle, but steady rhythm of blood dripping from the table's edge to join the rest on the floor. He didn't even hear himself breathe. He eventually realized he was, in fact, holding his breath.

He inhaled, and then exhaled. "Jeez-us!" he exclaimed, catching the metallic smell of blood, bodily fluids, and, something else. Fear maybe. He'd read somewhere that fear had an actual smell.

Toby considered rushing to the body on the table. After all, his shoes were beyond help. However, he stayed frozen in place. There was no need to rush. He could tell from where he stood the dead man on the table was already beyond help – ruined, just like the white suede on his feet.

"Stop thinking about the shoes, Toby!" he told himself. *"Focus!"*

Even from across the room, he could easily identify the body. Geraldo Guzman – or Geri, as he liked to be called – was laid out in well-toned, naked splendor, with a shock of black hair falling against his now ivory cheek and jaw. His green eyes stared directly at Toby, vacant and empty, and light reflected off the single diamond stud in his left ear and the silver Star of David hanging from the thick chain on his neck. He looked peaceful, if you ignored the stark, angry gashes scattered across his body, the slowly trickling blood, and the open eyes.

The third thing Toby remembered thinking was he'd better call the police.

He took a deep breath, and carefully bracing himself against the doorframe, lifted first his right foot, and then his left, out of his ridiculously expensive footwear. He turned carefully to make his way to the phone by the reception desk in the front room, shocked and disturbed by what he'd discovered. He hadn't yet allowed himself to remember the worst thing of all. He hadn't let himself remember the feeling of grief.

CHAPTER ONE

HOMICIDE DETECTIVE Melba Reightman was tired, disheveled, and more than a little cranky, and to make matters worse, her blouse was stuck to her skin from a combination of the August heat and her own out of whack internal system. Summer in the South was sometimes hard to take.

She'd driven herself home after a long hellish Wednesday, and had been looking forward to catching up on the mindless, but entertaining slew of shows she recorded for just such opportunities. She felt she was deserving of a do-nothing night after the day she'd just finished. It had been a long week already and there were still days to go. Digging through piles of paper work, spending way to many hours on the phone with city paper-pushers and unreliable witnesses, and trying to wrap up the string of burglaries which had finally been solved when the perp accidently locked himself in a master bathroom and had been unable to extract himself before the police arrived. She was officially the senior member of the Homicide team, but it had been a slow several weeks in her line of work. Even though it was the State Capitol, the city didn't have many homicides, other than occasional incidents related to domestic violence, bar brawls and robberies. Those were usually pretty cut and dried, and frankly, weren't much of a challenge. She should be grateful, but sometimes she wished for more excitement. When her mind wandered down those paths, she sternly reminded herself murder was never a good thing, and tried to be grateful for the relatively peaceful nature of the city. These days, budget cuts had depleted the ranks, and she was often assigned wherever there was an urgent need for someone to pitch in and pick up the slack. Not that she minded. It kept her from dwelling on other things, mostly things dealing with her personal life – a personal life totally in the toilet, which depressed her more than she'd ever anticipated.

After letting herself into the bland, nondescript two bedroom/two bath condo acquired after her recent acrimonious divorce from Stan, her ass of a cheating husband, she turned down the thermostat to do battle with her cursed state of menopause and slumped against the door, savoring the cool air wafting from the vent. As the air washed across her over-heated body, Melba surveyed her domain. Boring and cluttered with still unpacked boxes and junk mail, its worn carpet and bedraggled mini-blinds were a far cry from the comfortable suburban house where she'd clung to her role of wife and mother for far too long. After her daughter moved out to attend college, she'd thrown herself into her work, putting up with long hours, the good ol' boy network, and mind numbing interdepartmental bull crap until finally making detective. One month later, she found out she was soon to be a grandmother.

Her daughter Abby had married young – too young in Melba's mind. But head over heels in love and dismissing Melba's concerns, Abby had walked down the aisle with Stan by her side, and started her married life.

After the birth of one child less than a year into the marriage and another eighteen months later, Abby had arrived home from a frantic milk and cereal run to discover that her no account husband had moved out of the rundown house they'd shared since their marriage. Melba bit her tongue to keep from saying what she thought about the situation as daughter, with kids in tow, returned to the family home. Abby divorced the deadbeat for abandonment, pulled herself together and enrolled in community college. Now five years later, she was relocated to the upstate where she was happily employed with a growing technology firm.

After her daughter's move, the suburban house lost its appeal. Melba had been surprised to find that she missed the grandkids with their noise and mess, and nonstop animated musicals playing on any device available. She loved those grandbabies. She'd thrown herself back into her work, putting in extra time even when she didn't have to, just to feel engaged and useful. God knows she didn't feel useful at home. Stan was immersed in his own career as an executive at a local accounting firm, with his golf game, and with whatever sport was televised and streamed onto the fifty-four inch state-of-the-art widescreen parked in the place of honor in the den. He barely even noticed when she came home and she only knew that he still lived there from the dirty dishes in the sink, empty beer or wine bottles lined up on the kitchen counter, and overflowing trash bins. She'd faithfully load the dishwasher, stack the empties in the recycling bin, and haul out the trash. She convinced herself everything was normal and just the way things were at this stage of game. She sometimes wondered how they had fallen into the rut they found themselves in, but she simply carried on, trying to avoid any semblance of self-pity. After all, things could always be worse.

On Valentine's Day this year she'd received the obligatory dozen roses with an attached white card imprinted with the generic message "For someone very special to me on this special day." Handwritten underneath the printing was a sappy message totally uncharacteristic of Stan, and obviously in his secretary's handwriting. Melba consoled herself with the thought that at least someone had sent her flowers, even though she recognized the bouquet as the "$39.99 for a dozen" special from a local florist located a block from Stan's office.

Three days later, she stopped by the house unexpectedly to drop off some of Stan's dry cleaning and discovered him on the super-sized leather couch in the den with his Dockers around his ankles, straining and heaving on top of Gina, the aforementioned secretary. Melba later rationalized it must have been shock which caused her to start singing the lyrics to Creedence Clearwater Revival's "Bad Moon Rising" at the top of her lungs. She choked with laughter at the look on Stan's face, and took great satisfaction in watching a mortified Gina scramble to retrieve her lavender lace push up bra from beneath the coffee table. Melba especially enjoyed the sight of the bleached blonde bimbo banging her head of over processed hair as she flailed about under the table searching for her matching panties.

Melba calmly draped Stan's freshly cleaned and pressed shirts and khakis on a bar stool by the breakfast bar, placed an empty wine bottle in the blue recycling bin and hefted her heavy big purse onto her shoulder. She made her way to the side door that opened into the garage, and turned to launch a parting shot: "I guess there was more than one $39.99 special in town this week, Stan! Thanks for the flowers, Gina." Melba savored the look of concentration on Girl Friday's face as she tried to figure out the hidden meaning in the words. Melba howled all the way downtown, knowing the dumb-as-a-rock piece of trash tramp probably never figured it out.

Once at her desk, she quickly googled "Divorce Attorneys" and called the first one she found. Not quite twenty-four hours later, she collected the few things she wanted to keep and moved into this slightly run-down rental. She didn't like it much, but tried to live by the adage "be it ever so humble, there's no place like home." At least she didn't have to wash anyone's grubby dishes but her own.

Melba shuffled her way around a few as yet unpacked boxes, and unholstered and stored her revolver in the gun safe in her closet. She unclipped her badge, took off her shoes, removed her sticking polyester blouse, and changed into a loose and comfy t-shirt and a pair of sweatpants. She gave her shoulder length hair a few licks with a brush, noting the increasing number of silver strands in her dark, unruly curls. Finally, she slipped her swollen middle-aged feet into her favorite pair of fuzzy slippers, and poured herself a glass of boxed zinfandel. Melba sunk down gratefully onto her sagging, secondhand couch and sighed in relief.

After catching up on the first recorded episode of the popular new miniseries featuring her favorite British sleuth and flipping through the mail piled high on the coffee table, she poured herself another glass of wine and started thinking about dinner. She stood in front of the refrigerator enjoying the cold blast of air while debating between a frozen pizza, and a slightly old, but still probably digestible takeout carton of leftover sesame noodles. She was in the process of putting the noodles in the microwave when her phone rang. Melba glanced at the Caller ID and knew it wasn't good news.

"Detective Reightman?"

"Speaking." She glanced at the time display on the microwave and noticed it was just after 9:30 PM. She sighed and walked over to the couch to retrieve her just-poured drink.

As Melba listened to the dispatcher, she set her wine down on the counter next to a framed picture of her daughter and grandchildren. She considered the full glass for a moment, but decided she couldn't take a single sip more with the night she feared was ahead of her. If she took another sip she might decide to just stay home in her loose t-shirt and faded blue sweats. She spied the envelope from the power company peeking out from under her purse and sadly acknowledged staying home wouldn't keep the bills paid. She listened to the voice on the line while searching for a notepad and ballpoint pen from her overflowing bag perched on the breakfast bar.

"1217 Capital Street – downtown," she repeated back to dispatch as she wrote down the address. "Got it," she confirmed and ended the call. Melba took another look at the glass on the counter and sighed with pure regret as she poured the wine down the sink, watching the pinkish liquid swirl down the drain. Her plans for the evening had certainly changed for the worse. Besides, boxed wine didn't keep for very long once it was poured. "What a waste," she said sadly, while shaking her head and gathering up her things. She thought about changing clothes and decided she just didn't care. Reconsidering, she pulled on the jacket she'd removed just two hours earlier. It was hot, but she appreciated the pockets. She picked up the huge purse which served double duty as her catchall security blanket and went out the door. She was getting too damned old for this routine. Maybe she needed to find some other way to make a living. *"Yeah, right! Who else would hire a short, fifty-three year old female cop with a broken internal thermostat and a sometimes iffy temper?"*

Twenty minutes later Detective Melba Reightman pulled up at the address she'd been given and hauled herself and her big stuffed bag out of the car. She fanned her face with one hand, longing for an end to summer and its unrelenting humidity. Her whacky hormones just added to her discomfort.

"Not a bad area of town," she observed, and then looked more carefully. She revised her opinion. *"But, it's not great either."* This block was too eclectic and quirky to fit in with the rest of the downtown district.

The Time Out Spa was situated on the outer edge of the downtown boundary, which was currently undergoing a renaissance of sorts. Situated slightly off center on a block that had seen better days, but still had a certain funky appeal, the spa was bordered on the left by a bookstore with a collection of crystals and sun catchers in the front window. Sharing window space with the honest-to-god rainbow colored unicorn figurine was a diverse selection of books with catchy titles. *Birth NEW Color Into Your Life* and *Healing Poems of the Elven Bards* were her personal favorites among several other equally mystifying selections.

Reightman almost snorted, but controlled herself. Far be it for her to judge what people wanted to read. It took all kinds to keep the big wheel turnin'.

To the right of the spa was a vintage clothing store christened with the name "Passed Around" stenciled in loud psychedelic colors on the front window. After briefly considering the merchandise on display, Reightman decided it was probably a totally appropriate name for the business. On the corner of the block was a coffee small cafe called "Earth Fruits," which claimed in brightly lit neon to have "Best Vegan" – whatever that meant. *"You're really out of touch, Reightman."*

Across the street were two empty store fronts with 'For Rent or Lease' signs. Wedged between them was a Martial Arts studio, flanked on one side by a shop called "Green Dragon" which, according to the signage, sold Chinese medicinal herbs and teas and had – surprisingly – a hand lettered sign in the lower corner of the front window which read "Affordable Legal Services." Located on the far corner of the block was a small parking lot, advertising "Convenient Downtown Parking ONLY $7!"

The only other items of interest were the dozens of campaign posters squeezed and poked into every available piece of public right-of-way in an effort to gain the support of yet undecided voters. *"Don't you just love local elections? Full of promises and heartbreak at every turn."* This time, she didn't even try to control her snort.

All the shops on both sides of the street were currently closed for business, and their dusty windows reflected the red and blue lights of the police cruisers now at the scene. There was no sign of the coroner's wagon yet, although a lone ambulance occupied the handicapped space near the spa entrance. A few late night joggers and folks returning from various bars and restaurants in the area had gathered across the street and were talking among themselves – speculating about all the excitement. There was no sign of the news stations yet, which was odd. Usually, they were on the scene faster than flies on honey.

Two officers were positioned on either side of the spa entrance and through the illuminated windows she could see her partner, Sam Jackson, talking to a youngish, fairly tall, but slightly built man seated on one of the spa's reception couches. She supposed he was the business owner and he looked young – maybe mid-to-late twenties. From this distance, he struck her as being frail and fragile.

"Might as well get this show on the road," she said under her breath while moving her t-shirt away from her perspiring skin and hitching her heavy purse higher on her shoulder. She made her way to the door, moving her mismatched and rumpled jacket aside to show the ID clipped to her sweatpants to the uniformed officer on the right. She had to look up to meet his eyes. She suspected Officer Helliman was delighted that he was taller than she. Since she was only five feet, four inches, almost everyone on the force was taller than she. Reightman suppressed a sigh.

She'd learned many things over her years on the force about the types of men common in these parts, and Helliman certainly fit the profile.

"Detective Reightman," she identified herself, which was technically unnecessary. Everyone on the scene knew her or at least, knew of her.

"Yes, ma'am," he drawled with a pronounced southern accent, and eventually moved aside so she could enter the crime scene. Helliman didn't actually smirk as he scanned her wrinkled, navy jacket and faded blue sweatpants, but she knew he wanted to. Men could be such chauvinistic, judgmental asses, even when their own bellies hung several inches over their belts. There were rednecks like him everywhere, unfortunately for all womankind.

Reightman edged past him and stopped just inside the reception area, taking it in. Directly across from the door was a check-in counter, made out of light brown wood with a photo hanging behind the reception desk. The huge, soft focus black and white picture captured the image of a young, pouting child positioned on a straight-backed wooden chair, with arms crossed defiantly across his tiny chest. Over the photo hung brushed chrome letters which spelled "Time Out Spa." The walls were painted in soft, almost-beige-but not beige colors, and the floors were a glossy brown.

The chairs were plush and well-padded and Melba had an urge to take a seat and test them out. On second thought, the small, low armed sofas in various shades of light blue and green might be a better choice. They not only looked inviting, but reminded her of the 70's. They were scattered around the space, along with a couple of small glass topped tables. There was a small wall fountain made out of stone on a small accent wall. The fountain was off. *"It's all very Zen."* Reightman turned to the right of the reception desk, where an additional uniformed officer was stationed by the door leading into what she assumed was a hallway.

"Just like home," she told herself cynically, *"all brown and blue and green,"* although she knew the colors and textures here were nothing like the dreary walls and faded, worn plaids she experienced in her own dull living room. *"The air conditioning is nice though,"* she acknowledged gratefully as she continued her inspection. This place looked upscale, inviting and relaxing – very classy for a city like this. She turned and caught her partner's attention.

"Jackson?"

He walked over, gave her a quick glance and winced. "Glad you dressed up for the occasion, Reightman. You look flushed."

She grunted at him. "I'm also hot and cranky, Jackson – just to let you know. Glad you like the outfit. I made an effort, and I'm glad you noticed."

"I always notice, Reightman."

Sam was dressed in a nice pair of blue jeans and a linen blend jacket, neat and pulled together even at this hour. The jeans suggested he'd been home settled in for the evening when he'd received his call, but Jackson would never appear in public wearing sweatpants. He maintained a professional image, regardless of the time, day or night. He took another gander at her clothing and then winked, before ushering her over to the furthest sofa where the young man was hunched.

"This is Mr. Toby Bailey, the owner of the business. He found the body and called it in."

"Mr. Bailey." She extended her hand.

The young man rose to his feet and cautiously reached out a hand. She studied him carefully, revising her earlier impression. He stood just under six foot, she guessed, with light brown hair that flopped awkwardly onto his forehead and almost hid one eye. *"Some fancy stylist would probably call that color ash blond,"* she decided.

His eyes were a light icy blue, ringed in darker blue – almost black. They were unusual, but striking and appealing. They reminded her of those Alaskan husky dogs popular up north. He was somewhat thin, in-line with her earlier observation, but after getting up close and personal during their handshake, she decided there was nothing fragile about him.

Underneath the short-sleeved shirt and slim-fitting black slacks he wore, his body looked fit and strong. In contrast with the tentative offering of his hand, his grip was firm and confident, although his palms were slightly damp. He was very pale under his summer tan. Covertly wiping her hand on her sweatpants to remove the damp, she glanced down and noticed his slim feet were bare and slightly pink around the edges.

"Do you always run around barefooted, Mr. Bailey?"

Her question startled the young man. He looked down at his feet and squenched-up his toes.

Jackson cleared his throat, "Mr. Bailey's footwear is currently in one of the adjoining rooms. The room where the body was found," he added meaningfully.

"Okay." She raised an eyebrow in his direction. "Maybe I'd better go take a look." She turned to the young man. "Mr. Bailey, why don't you sit back down for a bit? You look kind of shaky. Jackson, stay here with him. I'll be back shortly."

At her partner's nod, Reightman made her way to the door where the young uniformed officer stood. He was fairly new to the force she thought, not immediately able to put a name with the face. As she passed by him into the short hall leading to what she presumed was a spa room, she looked up at him and inquired, "This way?"

"Yes, ma'am," he replied, motioning down the hall.

She started forward, but he did something which surprised her: He reached out and lightly touched her arm.

"Ma'am?"

"Yes?" she asked, and after reading the nameplate on his uniform to remind her of his name, added "Officer Mitchell." She stared down at the hand resting on her arm.

The officer quickly dropped his hand and looked her in the eye. "It's pretty bad back there, ma'am."

"It usually is when I get called out this time of night, Officer Mitchell." He probably thought she was some kind of delicate southern flower who couldn't handle seeing anything bad, even though she was a seasoned cop and the senior detective on the force. The thought made her irritable. She started down the hall but stopped about halfway. *"Oh, hell! Maybe chivalry ain't dead after all. The kid's just trying to be nice."* Reightman looked back with a tentative smile, "Thanks, Mitchell – I appreciate the warning."

The hall she entered was maybe ten feet long, and ended at an open door through which she could see a couple of familiar crime techs. Halfway down the hall was another door to the left, which was also open, and one to the right, which was closed. There was no one in the room on the left, although the lights were on. She took a quick look, but passed it by, continuing to the threshold at the end of the hall. There she stopped and took her first look at the scene.

Like the front reception area, this room had been done in soft brown colors accented with silvery brushed metal storage cabinets with frosted glass fronts and stone surface counter tops. The beigey walls in this room were also decorated with tasteful black and white photos, but in this room the images were of lush foliage echoing the leafy texture of the large green plants placed around the room. Just inside the door sat a pair of shoes, made of white plushy leather. *"Well, those are ruined,"* she thought, recalling the young man's bare feet. *"What a damn shame for Mr. Bailey."*

In the center of the room was a wide, padded massage table on some sort of mechanical lift. The table currently held a nest of blue sheets. *"Those sheets almost finish off the color scheme."* Reightman allowed herself a moment of sarcastic self-congratulation. *"You're finally getting the hang of this decorating stuff."* Then she saw the body.

Carefully placed in the pile of blood stained sheets was a young, extremely well-built man whose glazed green eyes stared toward her as she stood in the door. She gave the victim a careful once over, noting all the details, including the fact he was completely naked, and his chest and neck were decorated with several cuts and slashes. She turned to view the room again. From the ceiling above the table hung two shiny bars with padding wrapped around their centers. She didn't even want to think about how those might be used by the spa staff. Melba noticed the ceiling needed to be touched up – there were a couple of scrape marks spoiling the otherwise pristinely painted ceiling tiles. Dismissing them, she continued her inspection. Other than the body, the only obviously jarring thing in the room was the massive amount of blood. Stab scenes always included a lot of blood, it seemed, but it looked horribly out of place in this calm, soothing room. *"But then, blood usually looks out of place."*

"Laurie, Tom," she greeted the crime techs. "Is it okay for me to come in?" Tom Anderson, the unit's senior tech, absolutely hated when a crime scene was disturbed before his team was done.

"Sure, Detective, we're almost all finished in this room. We just have a couple more things to check. We're waiting on the coroner before we wrap up in here and start working the rest of the building," Anderson replied. "Be careful though; those puddles of blood are everywhere."

"Yeah. Good thing you told me, I probably would've missed them," she quipped sarcastically, earning a smile from the tech. *"Sometimes,"* she reminded herself, *"the only way to get through nights like this is to make light of the situation, even when the humor's obvious. Otherwise, death becomes overwhelmingly real."*

She pulled a set of gloves and a pair of plastic booties out of the boxes by the door and put them on. "What do we know so far?" Careful to avoid as much of the gore as possible, Reightman made her way toward the table and the reclining victim laid out on the sheets.

It was Laurie Nelson who responded, moving to join Reightman at the table's edge. "The victim is Geraldo Guzman, and he appears to be in great shape." Laurie reconsidered her comment. "I mean, he appears to have been in great shape, well, before this happened." At Reightman's encouraging nod, the young tech continued. "He works – I mean worked here in the spa as a masseur, or as Mr. Bailey described him, as a body worker." Reightman could almost visualize the air quotes, and remembered the female tech was fairly new to her job.

"He is – I mean was – a part-owner of the business, or at least that's what Detective Jackson told me." Laurie stopped her recitation of the facts and gave it some thought. "Frankly, Detective, other than those basics, we don't know a whole lot more. There's no sign of a struggle and no obvious footprints. We've dusted for prints, but all the brushed stainless surfaces on the cabinets and counters are really clean. That kind of material doesn't take prints well, even under ideal circumstances. I guess that's one of the reasons people choose it." Laurie looked down at the body on the table, considering the situation before looking back up again. "As you can see, Detective, it's pretty clear he was stabbed several times and probably bled out." That did seem obvious, but Reightman withheld comment.

Laurie tilted her head toward the man on the table "The vic looks like he was gently placed on the table and arranged like that. It looks very peaceful and…"

"And what?"

"Well, it almost looks like he's lying there exhausted after having really great sex." The young tech quickly looked away, embarrassed at her observation.

Reightman cut her a break and changed the subject. "Any thought on how someone made it in and out of here without leaving more of a trace?"

"No, ma'am, but we're working on it."

Laurie waited while the detective shifted her eyes slowly around the room. "Any sign of a murder weapon, Laurie?"

"No ma'am, nothing so far. We haven't checked the rest of the building yet, but there's nothing here."

"Okay, but we need to get on with that as soon as possible. Any guess as to the time of death?"

"No, ma'am. As Anderson said, the coroner hasn't made it in yet, and the details are waiting on him. He should be here any minute though." Laurie pushed up the trendy tortoise shell glasses that were beginning to slip down the bridge of her shiny mahogany-skinned nose. "The call to him went out well over an hour ago."

The two women shared a cynical look which spoke of shared history with the city's coroner. For Laurie to already be sharing in the cynicism spoke volumes about the doctor.

"Some things never change, Laurie. We all know that Doctor Lieberman operates on his own timetable, so there's no reason why things should be different tonight. Is there anything else you can think of? Anything that strikes you as off?"

"Well…"

Reightman waited for the tech to continue, and then gave her verbal nudge. "What are you thinking, Laurie?"

Laurie shot a glance toward the senior tech, indicating he should answer. "Well, Detective," Anderson replied, "the thing is, we've got a body, and we've got a lot of blood. We've even got a pair of fancy white shoes by the door. But as Laurie said, we haven't found a weapon, and we don't know yet how the killer made it in or out of the room. There are no distinct footprints, just a couple of small markings that might be from the edge of a shoe – an athletic shoe, I'd guess."

"Any sign of a shoe around here that might be a match?"

"Nope, not yet anyway. The other thing that's weird is how clean this scene is. For someone to get in and out of this room without leaving a trace would be almost impossible, given all the mess on the floor. We'll spray it all down and hit it with the lights to see if we can find anything, but right now we don't have much to go on."

"I understand. Is anything else is bothering you?"

"Well, I guess the other thing we don't have, is clothes."

Reightman frowned and rubbed her forehead, feeling perspiration. "Clothes?"

"Yes, Detective. We don't seem to have any clothes in here for the dead naked man laid out over there on that table."

She looked at the body and into the staring green eyes. "Well, isn't that interesting?"

"Yes, ma'am," the senior tech agreed. "I'd say it was."

A noise from the front of the building drew her attention. Looking through the door, she saw Doctor Benjamin Lieberman, the eagerly awaited coroner, lumbering down the hall and talking under his breath, followed by Dr. Riley, his harried young intern and the current assistant coroner. Dr. Lieberman was pulled up short by a hand on his sleeve as Riley tried to keep him from bursting into the room. Before Lieberman could castigate the young man for the imagined affront to his dignity,

Reightman held up a hand. "Doctor, I realize you're running late and anxious to get to work, but remember, this is an active crime scene. Put on some of that gear by the door before you screw up any evidence. The rest of the team's already been here for over an hour, patiently waiting on you. A few seconds more won't make any difference."

The coroner flushed red at her reference to his delay, but bit back any harsh comment he thought about making, either to her, or to poor Riley. He snapped on some gloves, pulled on a pair of footies and huffed past her into the room. Riley followed suit, offering her a polite, apologetic "Excuse me, ma'am," as he made his way past her.

Reightman nodded, and stepped out of the way. She noticed that Lieberman stopped abruptly as he neared the table and saw him glance back her way. When he met her eyes, he flushed again, and after another slight hesitation, he finally stepped up to the body. "*You're nothing but a no good, better-late-than-never SOB.*" After fixing the scene in her mind, she started back down the hall to the calm, serene reception area, and Mr. Toby Bailey. She had a whole lot of questions that needed answers, and he might be just the man who had some.

Toby, in the meantime, curled himself up into a ball on one of the small sofas, with his bare feet tucked up underneath him. He was tired and cold. "*It's probably from the shock,*" he told himself. He'd heard that a severe shock made people feel really tired, and really cold. Someone had thrust a cup of hot tea with an awful lot of sugar at him not too long ago, telling him it would help. He'd drunk it down, but it hadn't helped at all.

He occupied himself by keeping trying to keep completely still, and stared vacantly into space even though his eyes were feeling heavy. "*Maybe if I don't move too much I'll feel warmer,*" he reasoned. "*Besides, every time I close my eyes, I see Geri laid out on that table.*" After a couple of replays of *that* horror show, he decided the best thing to do was to just keep his eyes open, no matter how tired he was feeling.

Toby had no idea how long he'd been curled up on the sofa. There weren't any clocks in the reception area. He felt a lack of clocks made for a more restful ambiance. He didn't wear a watch himself and *somewhere* this evening he had laid down his cell phone. That's what had brought him back to the spa after grabbing a quick dinner to at one of the neighborhood joints. He'd thought maybe it could be in one of the treatment rooms, but given his record of laying his phone down in unlikely places and forgetting about it, the phone could be anywhere.

It wouldn't do him any good to call the number. He always turned the ringer off so the noise wouldn't disrupt a session with a client and ruin the vibe. One of the rules of the spa was everyone had to keep their ringers turned off – no exceptions.

When he'd made it back here, he untangled the ring of keys from his right front pocket, selected the one for the front door, and put it in the lock. He tried to unlock the door, but the key wouldn't turn. Puzzled, he tried again and achieved the same result. Removing the key, he'd pulled on the handle and to his surprise, the door opened. After some consideration Toby decided that maybe SaraJune, the afternoon receptionist, just forgot to lock up. *"But wait, I was the last one to leave."* He remembered SaraJune calling out that she was headed home. He'd decided to catch-up on some paperwork and to finish the weekly supply order. He remembered to throw a load of towels into the washer. There was always more laundry to do than he'd ever anticipated in this business. Although the spa was doing pretty well, he didn't think they could afford a service yet.

He wrapped up at about 7:30 or so, and after putting the towels in the dryer and starting a load of sheets, he tidied up his desk in the small back office, stuffing some things in his satchel to read over dinner. Then he turned off the lights, set the alarm, and left. He *had* locked the door. He was sure he remembered pulling the handle just to make sure.

"So, why is the door unlocked? And why is the alarm turned off?"

He walked in the door, already knowing something wasn't right. He laid his satchel on a chair, and made his way to the bank of switches by the reception desk. After checking the front room, he turned the lights on in the hall, and checked the smaller treatment room, his own small office, and the breakroom. The washing machine was still going, which was weird, but the dryer had stopped. After discovering nothing out of place, he crossed the few steps to the larger room at the end of the hall, stepped into the room, slapped the switch to turn on the lights and...

"Oh shit!" he remembered thinking. *"Oh shit!"*

Toby curled up tighter on the sofa and – forgetting his earlier resolution – he closed his eyes. He saw Geri on the table and heard the sound of blood dripping to the floor. He struggled to open his eyes, but was so tired and cold. It must be the shock...his eyes were really heavy...must be the shock...he'd heard that shock could...

"Mr. Bailey?"

"Mr. Bailey?" This time, the voice was louder. "Mr. Bailey! Wake up, please. I need to talk to you."

With great effort, Toby blinked his eyes open and looked up at the woman towering over him. *"Well, she's not really towering. She's not tall enough to tower. And what is that outfit she's wearing?"* He made an effort to sit up straighter, and eventually recognized the detective who'd arrived after the others.

"Umm …yeah…sorry about that." His mouth felt like sandpaper. He propped himself up with a partially numb arm, and uncurled his feet from beneath him.

Reightman studied him for a minute, giving him a couple of seconds to pull himself together. "I have a few questions for you, Mr. Bailey."

"Okay," Toby yawned, "but I already told Officer Jackson everything I know."

"Detective."

"What?"

"It's Detective Jackson." She'd learned the hard way that it was important to establish a certain level of respect between the person reporting a crime and the person responding to the report.

"Oh…right. I've already told *Detective* Jackson everything I know."

Reightman frowned slightly. Had there been an emphasis on the word detective? The last thing she needed tonight was sarcasm, unless it was her own. "I know you've already spoken to Detective Jackson, Mr. Bailey, but I need you to go over it again with me. I want to make sure that I have my own understanding of what occurred here tonight, and I need to get some additional background information." Reightman waited for her words to sink in. "Why don't you sit up, start at the beginning, and talk me through your evening right up to the point where you discovered Mr. Guzman?"

For a minute, Reightman thought he was going to refuse to say anything more. He just sat on the edge of the couch, hugging his arms across his chest and staring up at her. For some reason, she was reminded of the photograph hanging on the wall behind her. She glanced over her shoulder to look at it again.

"That's me."

"Pardon me?"

"That's me – I mean, it's a picture of me. My mom took it a couple of years before she died."

Reightman wasn't sure how to respond. "It's a very nice picture, Mr. Bailey."

Toby gave a small shrug, and tried to stifle another yawn. "I guess so. She called it "Time Out." She took it one day when I'd been behaving badly. She made me sit in that old chair and said I had to stay there until I found a better mood to get into. She always used to say stuff like that. It was just her way and I guess it runs in the family. I remember her laughing after she developed it, and she told me one day I'd appreciate it as it deserved to be appreciated when I had kids of my own. She said to remember that pouting or throwing a big ol' fit never did anyone any good." He sat silently, contemplating the photograph, before adding, "She always told me that usually the only things that do any real good are pulling your pants up, uncrossing your arms, and getting on with what needs to be done, no matter how bad, or boring, or hard it is..." He trailed off. His odd blue eyes met hers. "Sorry for rambling, Detective."

Reightman nodded and pulled one of the arm chairs closer to the sofa. She unslung her monster purse and hooked it over the back and took a seat with a sigh. Her feet hurt. She reached into the purse and dug out her notebook and pen. "Mr. Bailey, I know this is hard. I know it's been a big shock to you. I can't imagine what you must be feeling right now. But, I need your help. The most important thing you can do right now is walk me through what happened."

Toby glanced back up at the big portrait and then back at her. "I'll try." He cleared his throat and she readied her pen. He cleared his throat again. "Water."

"Water?"

"Yeah. Can I... I mean... I need some water. My mouth and throat are really dry."

"Certainly. You have some here?"

"Yes, in the fridge in the break area."

"Jackson," she called over her shoulder. "Can you grab us a couple of bottles of water from the break room? Mr. Bailey says there should be some in the refrigerator."

"Sure thing, Reightman."

She waited until the water was retrieved and handed a bottle to the young man, keeping one for herself. She noticed it was bottled with the name of the spa on the label. *"Funny the things people will pay for these days."* She set the bottle down on one of the small glass tables and wiped her damp hands on the legs of her sweatpants. She picked up her pad and pen and waved her hand in front of his face to catch his attention. Once he focused back on her, she started from the top.

"Alright, Mr. Bailey, why don't you start by describing your evening for me?"

"It's Toby."

"What?"

"It's Toby. "Mr. Bailey" sounds like someone's dad. I never knew my dad so, please, I'd appreciate it if you'd just call me Toby."

"I'm not sure that's appropriate," She intended to keep the boundaries between them firmly drawn, but then she caught the kid's disappointed expression. *"Would it really hurt anything to play along?"* she wondered as she looked into his face. "Alright then…Toby. Tell me about your evening."

Reightman observed him carefully as she took notes. He described the events of the evening, from the point when the receptionist left for the day to the time he discovered the victim and called the police. Every once in a while, she'd glance over to her partner for confirmation, and every time, Sam gave her a nod in return. So far, the events being described appeared to align with the story he'd given her partner. That was a good start. She placed her notebook on her lap and just studied him for a minute, trying to decide where to head next. "How old was Mr. Guzman, Toby?"

"He was about to turn twenty-eight, in November."

"And how long had he worked for you?"

"Geri's been here ever since we opened, about six months ago. He didn't just work here, he was my business partner."

Reightman nodded at the clarification and continued. "Had he worked in another spa in the area?"

She noticed the question made him hesitate for a moment. *"That's interesting,"* she decided. *"Maybe there's something to dig into here."*

"No. No, he didn't," Toby finally answered.

From his voice, she knew she was onto something. His hesitation was a dead giveaway and experience had taught her to recognize the signs. Reightman settled an expression of polite disbelief over her features. "You hired someone with no previous experience to work in a place like this? I find that very hard to believe."

"He had experience, just not in another spa. He had his state license. We both did…I mean, do…I mean…" He looked down at the floor and she noticed his cheeks were flushed.

"Toby?"

He refused to look up, and the floppy hair hid his eyes. "He did private work," he answered, sounding both sad and hurt for some reason.

"Private work?" You mean he had personal clients?"

"Yes." He still hadn't looked up at her.

"What kind of personal clients?"

"You know, the *very* private, personal kind," he answered with a touch of bitterness.

"I see." She was, for some reason, almost embarrassed as she considered the implications. *"So, Geri Guzman had a little side business."* She could feel a thin trickle of sweat underneath her bra and shifted a bit to try and get comfortable. "Did Mr. Guzman often visit the premises in the evening?"

"No, not anymore. I mean, he did a couple of times before, but when I found out, I asked him not to do it again. I don't like people here late at night. Besides, he wasn't good at using the alarm. I'd always get a call from the company and have to come and turn it off."

"Toby, how long have you known Mr. Guzman?

The boy kept his eyed glued to the glossy floor. Now she knew she was getting somewhere. "Toby?"

He stayed silent, but his hands were gripping his knees so tightly his knuckles were white.

"Toby?" Reightman tried again, on the edge of losing her patience. "Mr. Bailey!" she snapped. "Exactly how long have you known the victim? You need to answer the question."

His silence combined with her own discomfort was wearing on her last nerve. She rose to her feet and looked down at him. "How long had you known Mr. Guzman?"

"Years," he whispered to the floor. He looked up at her with his unusual eyes and answered, "Ever since the summer, right after I graduated high school. Ever since he moved to my hometown."

"So, there's a story here and I was right after all." She settled back down into one of the cushy chairs. "Tell me about your relationship." She picked up her pen and started to write, careful to show no expression as he answered all the questions she could think to ask.

❖ ❖ ❖

Melba Reightman paced the floor, her agitation plain to anyone observing. She was pretty sure *everyone* in the vicinity was observing. After all, four months of her change in life irritability had already provided every cop in the city tons of amusement. *"Funny how the start of my irritability coincided nicely with my divorce."*

She halted in mid stride, flicking her eyes up to catch the quickly hidden grins of amusement around the room. She really didn't give a damn. Her cheeks were flushed, her breathing was a little heavy, and she was overheated, again. Every once in a while she stopped, read from the notes she held clutched in her hand, and swore under her breath before starting to pace again. Her feet really hurt now.

Mr. Toby Bailey had just been escorted to the small office in the back of the building and was there now, with an officer stationed at the door.

Reightman paced some more, thinking about her interview with the young man. She finally came to a stop in front of the portrait of the little boy in the chair. She looked up at it and gave a disgusted snort. She could barely restrain herself from shaking a finger sternly at the photo.

"Melba, I know you're frustrated, but you need to simmer down. You're frightening the children," Sam waved to the observing officers. She caught his referral to the slogan on a coffee cup he'd given her a couple of months ago following a particularly grumpy and vocal day.

Not at all amused by his banter, she wheeled around and shot him a glare. "Frustrated, Sam? You think I'm frustrated? I am *not* frustrated. For your information, I passed frustrated quite a while back, and right this minute I am about just a half a mile from plain pissed off!"

"Why are you so upset, Melba?"

"I don't know." She deflated a little while she tried to figure out what was causing her agitation. "It's the heat I guess, and this situation. Plus, you know my temper is a little jumpy these days."

"Yes. I do know, Melba. Now that you mention it, I recognize all the signs."

"Don't be a smart ass, Sam. You wouldn't be nearly so glib if the good Lord had plumbed *you* differently."

"I'm perfectly happy with my plumbing, and I thank the Lord for it every day."

"From what I hear, Mrs. Jackson is pretty happy with it, too."

"Oh, she is. She surely is."

Reightman finally grinned, and rubbed the back of her neck. "Sam, I hate to admit it, but I find myself more than a little bit embarrassed by

Mr. Bailey's outline of his relationship and history with Geraldo Guzman. Being embarrassed pisses me off even more. I didn't realize I could even be embarrassed anymore." Sam wisely didn't say a word. "Dammit, Sam! This murder is one of the worst we've had on our hands in the last few years and there's a lot of unanswered questions back in that room." She met his calm brown eyes before turning back to contemplate the photo. She finally shook her head and sighed. "At least I finally got somewhere with Mr. Bailey, although it took a while to get the whole story. This…this kid…young man – whatever – and his good friend, Geraldo Guzman, worked their way through vocational school by way of the usual run of part-time college jobs. Nothing unusual about that, right?" Sam shook his head in agreement. "While doing so, they hope and dream and plan for the future. Somewhere early on, they engage in a little romance with each other and I got the distinct impression it was pretty hot and heavy for a while. Don't ask me how I know – just woman's intuition, I guess. Somewhere along the way, they decide to just be friends, although Mr. Bailey wasn't real informative about that part of his story, no matter how hard I pushed. I have the impression their split occurred not too long ago. I have to get to the bottom of that, and I'm probably going to get embarrassed again. Just thinking about it makes me flushed, and Lord knows I'm not a prude."

Reightman took a couple more calming breathes and ordered her thoughts. "They work an assortment of odd jobs for a couple of years, until for some reason – maybe job loss and tight funds – Guzman engages in some off-the-grid activity offering private *massage services* to some very well-heeled clients. Guzman indulged in this money making activity more than Bailey. In fact, I'm not sure Mr. Bailey much to do with it. I need to get more clarity around that as well. Anyway, they successfully graduate, pass the state boards, get licensed, and so forth. Bailey works in a couple of other spas – similar, but less fancy than this place – to gain practical experience. Through it all, the two of them stick together and pool their resources to eventually open this place."

Sam indicates he's taking it all in, makes a couple of notes on his ever present pocket notebook, and motions for her to continue.

"Mr. Bailey apparently had some money stashed away from his deceased mother's insurance and from the sale of her house, and Guzman contributed from…some other source I guess – I'm going to have to dig around some more to get to the bottom of that." Reightman paused to appreciate the cool colors of the room and, more importantly, the cool air blowing from the vents. "Less than nine months after opening this place, they have a pretty impressive clientele, made up of some of the most socially prominent and powerful men and women in the city. In spite of the almost, but not quite questionable neighborhood, all indications are they're even turning a profit. A small one I grant you, but a profit, nonetheless. How often does that happen in real life, Sam? Tell me, in what kind of fairy tale does that happen? And no, there was no pun intended in that last bit."

She ran her fingers through her frizzy curls, figuring it wouldn't make much difference since her head probably looked like a rat's nest anyway. She retraced her thoughts and continued, "Then one hot August night – tonight in fact – Mr. Bailey locks up, goes to grab some grub, realizes he's lost his cell phone, returns here at 8:45 PM and steps in it. Literally. He puts his white leather shoes, which probably cost more than the monthly rent on my apartment, right in a big, nasty puddle of blood – blood belonging to his friend, former lover, and current business partner."

The rattle of gurney wheels sounded down the hall, interrupting her train of thought. Reightman turned and caught sight of the heavy, sweating coroner and his assistant steering the bagged body. At the sight of Dr. Lieberman, some unformed idea pinged in the back of her brain, but didn't quite make it to the front. "Dammit!" She hated it when that happened. She pursed her lips for a moment and tried to get back on track, tugging on the straps of her damp bra. "We now have one well-built Hispanic, part-time hustler, former lover and current business partner of the young Mr. Bailey, murdered in one of the most violent ways we've seen in years and all we have are more questions."

"And you know what else we have, Sam?" she asked as she watched Lieberman. "We have a wormy coroner who shows up late to the scene, although that's getting to be the norm. He's also acting kind of weird." She looked out the front window onto the street and gestured at the small mob gathered outside. "We have half the residents of the downtown neighborhoods lined up to view the latest entertainment. They're like a flock of vultures, bless their hearts." Sam dutifully acknowledged her assessment of the crowd as she continued, "But you know what we don't have?"

"No, Melba. What don't we have?"

"We don't have any footprints or visible means of entry into the crime scene, in spite of all the blood in the room. We don't have a murder weapon. We don't have a clear motive, even considering Misters Bailey's and Guzman's past relationship. And you're thinking I'm frustrated? Frustrated my middle-aged menopausal ass! At least we don't have what passes for the press up in our business yet."

She looked toward the door as a smug looking Officer Helliman stepped inside. "Detectives, I thought you should know that the press has arrived."

"Thanks so much, Officer Helliman. That's just great." For some reason, she had the impulse to snarl right into his ugly face, just for the satisfaction, but Sam's steady hand on her shoulder helped her to maintain some decorum. She'd never liked Helliman, but had never been able to pinpoint the reason. *"Probably because he's a big, pain-in- the-ass, red-necked jerk."* She watched as – with another headache inducing rattle – the gurney was wheeled through the open door into the bright camera lights waiting outside.

"Now my evening is absolutely and perfectly complete," she said, shaking her head and rubbing her temples. "Either this job is starting to get old or I am."

Sam snorted at her comment, proving the old adage that partners started to pick up each other's mannerisms after a while. "You gonna' bring Mr. Bailey in, Melba?"

"I can't decide. I probably should, at least to hold him a while until we get some more answers. But you know what?" She grinned sheepishly at her partner, "No matter how frustrated I am at him and this situation, I really don't think he did it. Mr. Bailey has done absolutely everything he should as an upright citizen and friend or – or whatever, of the deceased. He didn't disturb the scene, he kept his head and he called us. He's cooperated so far, even though it took longer than it should have to get the story out of him." Reightman thought through everything she'd learned up to this point, and shook her head. "I just don't like him as a suspect. Maybe I'm wrong, but without a motive or a murder weapon tied to him, it's probably fine to let him go home for the night and come into the station tomorrow."

"You mean later today, pard'ner."

She looked at her watch and grimaced. "God, it's late. I'll go cut him loose and have him drop by the station in the morning. Make sure to assign a couple of officers to stay here for the night." She gave him an evil little grin. "Make sure Helliman's one of them."

Sam chuckled, but shook his head at her suggestion. "It's not like you to hold a grudge, Melba."

"Sure it is, Sam. In case you haven't noticed, I'm a changed woman these days."

Reightman turned to make her way down the hall and noticed her feet were splashing in the foamy puddle forming on the polished brown floor. "What the hell?"

Tom Anderson hurried through the door to the hall. She noticed the bottoms of his pant legs were drenched, and had frothy, white bubbles clinging to them. "Detectives, you better come see what we found."

"What is it, Anderson? And where is all of this damned sudsy water coming from?" She grabbed her purse off the back of the chair and slung it over her shoulder.

"From the washing machine."

"What washing machine?" she asked as they slogged their way through the pink-tinted water.

"The one in the break area. It started backing up a few minutes ago. We got it stopped, and opened the lid to see what was going on."

"And?"

"Well, the thing was crammed clear to the top with stuff. Everything was all just wedged in. It overbalanced, which probably caused the overflow problem."

"What was in it?" she asked, sure she didn't really want to know.

"Come on back and see for yourself. It'll be easier to show you than to try to explain it."

They all crowded into the room where Laurie was in the middle of photographing a sizable pile of wet material. Reightman plunked her purse down on the small breakroom table, propping it up carefully so it didn't fall over. They all just looked at the pile of wet stuff. Reightman looked at Jackson, and then looked at Laurie and Tom. Laurie and Tom kept on looking at the things on the floor. She found herself getting fidgety, and right when she couldn't stand it anymore, Jackson piped up.

"What's all of that mess, Laurie?"

"It's a bunch of towels, Detective Jackson, and a couple of sheets. And a pair of tennis shoes – which may match the partial print on the floor. And, some clothes."

"Clothes?" Reightman recalled a similar conversation from about an hour earlier, and started to get a very bad feeling about where things were headed.

"Yes, ma'am. We think they must be the dead man's clothes."

"Why were they in the washer?"

"Probably to get the blood out."

She should've known better than to ask. "Probably so," she agreed. Her night didn't seem likely to end anytime soon. She looked around the small room and indicated the other appliance. "Anything in the dryer?"

"No, ma'am, but Laurie did find something else."

Laurie glanced up at Tom and then back at Reightman with a tiny, proud smile. "Yes, I sure did," she said, indicating the first big find of her career. Reightman's eyes drifted to where the finger pointed, and saw a long-bladed knife lying in the mess of wet towels and clothing. It looked like a hunting knife of some sort. The name 'TOBY' was engraved on the hilt in capital letters. Jackson carefully knelt down, trying to avoid wetting his slacks. He took a good long look and whistled through his teeth. "Looks like we have the murder weapon, Reightman."

"Yes indeed, Jackson, I think we do." She pointed at the hilt, careful not to touch it. "Look here. It's telling us plain as day who it belongs to. Lucky us." She rubbed her tired face and straightened her messy wrinkled jacket. Her shoes were soaked.

"Officer Mitchell?' she called out to the cop who had warned her it was going to be a bad night. He'd been right, after all.

"Yes, ma'am?"

"Let's go round up Mr. Bailey. We'll be taking him to the station."

"Yes, ma'am."

She nodded to Jackson and the two techs, and took a last look at the pile of wet towels, sheets, athletic shoes and clothes. She considered the knife gleaming from the wet mess, and at the engraved and incriminating name on its hilt. She watched the pink liquid, already starting to swirl around and down the small drain set in the floor. "What a waste," she said.

Reightman turned, hoisted her big heavy purse unto her shoulder, and sloshed through the small puddles down the hall to arrest Mr. Toby Bailey on suspicion of murder. *"It's a shame,"* she told herself. *"For some reason, I kind of liked him."*

She hitched up the bottoms of her soaking wet sweat pants, and as she passed the large photograph in the reception room, she recalled Mr. Bailey's words from earlier in the evening. "Sometimes the only things that do any good are pulling your pants up, uncrossing your arms, and getting on with what needs to be done, no matter how bad, or boring, or hard it is."

"*Indeed*," she thought. "*Yes, indeed.*" She savored the cool, air-conditioned air for a moment longer, and then headed down the hall to take Mr. Toby Bailey into police custody.

CHAPTER TWO

TOBY'S EVENING WENT from bad to worse. *"They actually locked me up* in a cell. In a real, *honest to goodness cell – like a criminal!"* Toby looked around the tiny room with its two utilitarian metal cots, small sink and – heaven help him – a not anywhere near to spotless toilet exposed for anyone to see. He shuddered. *"No matter what, I'm not going to use that – I'll pee in the sink first."*

After being cuffed, read his rights, and escorted to the waiting squad car under a barrage of harsh light and shouted questions, Toby found himself in a situation he'd never really thought he might be in. It rapidly went from bad to worse. Once at the station, they removed the cuffs. Then they fingerprinted him, snapped photos, and confiscated his belt, his keys, the few bills and coins in his pockets, and finally, his wallet. His shoes were presumably still back at the spa, and the police had retained his satchel. He signed a form acknowledging their receipt of his belongings, and the police asked if he wanted to make a call.

Of course he wanted to make a call.

Problem was – he wasn't sure who he *could* call. He did realize he should probably get a lawyer since things were looking pretty bad. He really didn't know a criminal attorney since he'd never needed one before. He did know a lawyer though – one he thought was pretty good. But he didn't know the number. He hoped there was a phonebook he could borrow.

After being steered to the phone, he discovered there wasn't a phonebook. He looked at the escorting officer.

"Problem?" the officer grunted.

"Uh...yes. I don't know the number."

"You don't know the number?"

"*Jeeze, is this guy deaf?*" As politely as he could manage, he tried again. "No, I'm afraid not, and there doesn't seem to be a phonebook anywhere."

The officer looked at the small attached shelf underneath the wall-mounted phone and then scratched his head. "There isn't a phonebook."

Toby took a slow, deep breath. "Yes sir, that's right."

When the officer didn't respond, Toby took another breath. "I think I might have a card with the number on it in my wallet."

It took the officer a minute to process the new information, but he finally nodded his head and hitched up his pants. "Okay. Come with me."

Toby followed the cop back to the collection station where, after a lengthy explanation and a search of the surrounding area, the bored clerk stared blankly back at him and shrugged.

"It's right there on the desk behind you," Toby pointed at the wallet, apparently surprising both the officer and the clerk standing behind the glass-enclosed intake area. Both of them took a step back and eyed him suspiciously. Was it his imagination, or had the uniformed officer moved his hand closer to his weapon? He lowered his arm and briefly closed his eyes. Slowly and calmly he explained, "I can see it right over there. It's the black tri-fold right by the big stack of files."

The clerk turned around, ever so slowly, and walked over to the desk. "This one?" she asked.

"Yes, that's it."

She picked up the wallet in question, turning it over a couple of times as if she'd never seen a wallet before. After looking at his escorting officer for confirmation, the clerk pushed it, ever so slowly, through the small cut-out depression at the bottom of the window.

The officer was watching him intently, so Toby opened the wallet, slowly, and extracted the card. He held it up between his thumb and index finger, so they could both see it. "This is the card I need," he enunciated carefully. Toby turned to walk back to the phone alcove.

"Stop!"

He froze, and then turned back around to face the officer. "Yes, sir?" he asked, feeling sweat trickling down his back. He really needed a shower.

"Let me see that!" the officer demanded, holding out his hand.

"Uhhh…sure." Toby handed the card to the officer. He took it and as Toby had learned to expect at this point, very slowly read it, moving his lips while mentally sounding out the words. He eventually finished and looked back at Toby. "You have to leave the card here."

"But, I need the number."

"You have to leave the card here." When Toby didn't respond, the officer looked at the clerk and at his nod, she slowly pushed a single post it note through the opening and then, very, very slowly, pushed through a short, stubby pencil with a dull lead. They watched him as if the two objects were potentially dangerous weapons. Toby retrieved them and the officer placed the card on the small ledge in front of the window. Toby positioned the small piece of paper and picked up the pencil. He looked at the card and started to turn it over. Both the officer and the clerk reacted immediately and stepped closer. He raised both hands, one still holding on to the stub of a pencil, and said very softly, "The number is on the other side." The officer reluctantly nodded and stepped back. The clerk continued to watch him suspiciously.

Toby quickly turned the card over and wrote down the number, checking it twice to make sure he had it correct. He carefully placed the pencil and the card back through the small opening. The clerk picked them both up grudgingly – and slowly – and placed the card back in the wallet. She put it in the wrong place, but Toby decided it was better not to comment. He held up the post-it note so the officer could see it. The officer reached out, took the paper and read the numbers written there. He then handed the paper back to Toby and escorted him to the phone.

Toby positioned the slip of paper carefully on the shelf, lifted the receiver and dialed. He waited for the call to go through, but nothing happened. He placed the receiver back in the cradle, and turned to the waiting officer. "The phone isn't working."

The officer gave a mournful sigh. "You have to dial nine first."

"Thanks." Toby lifted the receiver again, dialed nine, and then the number he'd written down. The phone on the other end rang. And rang again. And again. A voice he recognized as a recording announced, "You are reaching Green Dragon. All lines busy. Or maybe no one here. Or we sleep. Leave message after beep and we call back."

"Now isn't this just great?" Toby asked himself, wiping away a trickle of sweat from his neck. He left a message as instructed. "Yes...this is...ah...this is Toby Bailey from across the street. You helped me do all the paper work for the spa. I need help. I'm in...in j-jail." He hated it when he stuttered. "They think I killed Geri." He paused while trying to think of what else to say. "Please come when you get this...thanks." He

placed the receiver back in the cradle and turned toward the officer who stared him down for a minute and then nodded toward small shelf.

Toby picked up the post-it note and placed it into the officer's waiting hand. The officer examined it for a minute, wadded it into a tight little ball, and with very careful aim, threw it toward a small metal trashcan in the corner. It sailed through the air and, with a small ping, it hit the rim, bouncing once before dropping into the receptacle.

"Two points!" the clerk cheered.

"Score!" exclaimed the officer with a happy grin. Then he frowned and hitched up his pants again, before escorting Toby to his cell.

And there, Toby sat with nothing to do. After a while, the lights were turned off, except for one in the hall. He lay down on his back and pulled the rough, thin blanket over himself, trying to get comfortable. He wondered what was going to happen. He hoped that someone would come to help him. He wiggled around, trying to find a position which would keep the cot slats from digging into his shoulder blades. He rolled over onto his side and thought about meeting Geri that first summer.

School was out, graduation was past, and the summer beckoned. Sure, he still had to figure out what he was going to do with the rest of his life, but he had three whole months to worry about that. Right this minute the only thing Toby was worried about was getting out into the sun and getting a start on his tan.

He tugged a pair of bright yellow board-shorts over his narrow hips, toed on an old pair of sneakers and slung a beach towel over shoulder. With a flourish, he snagged his sunglasses off of the dresser and regarded himself in the mirror. "Looking good!" he grinned, and arranged a stray lock of hair. He grabbed a bag containing his sunscreen and a few magazines and headed to the kitchen.

"I'm going to the pool, Grams. Time to work on my tan!"

His grandmother was drying dishes, and turned around, wiping her hands on her apron. "Honey, don't you look spiffy! Got your sunscreen? You know you can't be too careful."

"Yes ma'am, I sure do. I don't want to get all wrinkly like some people I know!

She snatched the dishtowel off the edge of the white porcelain sink and swatted his behind. "I don't know what you're talking about young man. The only wrinkles here are on those shorts of yours. Don't you ever iron 'em?"

"Grams, how many times to I have to tell you swimming shorts aren't supposed to be ironed? When they get wet, the wrinkles just fall out."

"Don't give me any of your sass! What time do you think you'll be back?"

"I'm not sure, but I shouldn't be too late. What are you fixin' for dinner?"

She grinned at him and put her hands on her ample hips. "What makes you think I'm fixing anything for dinner, Toby? I seem to remember that it's your night to cook." Ever since his grandfather had passed away they took turns cooking, although during the school week Grams usually did more than her fair share.

"Um…I thought maybe fried chicken would be good."

"Toby Bailey! You couldn't fry up a chicken if your life depended on it. Last time you tried I thought you were gonna' burn down the kitchen. When you finally wrestled that poor burnt-skinned bird onto the platter and we cut into it, it was raw! I never did figure out how you managed that!"

Toby laughed, remembering that disaster. "Well then, we'll have tuna casserole. I do that pretty good."

"Tuna casserole it is. Your culinary skills are about up to that. I look forward to it with utmost anticipation." She smiled up at him with love and then swatted him again. "Now get on out of here!" she commanded as she turned back to the sink. "I've got things to get done and want to get in some beauty rest before I eat the fancy dinner you'll be making."

"Grams, you're already beautiful!" Toby gave her a big hug and headed to the pool.

"Dang it's hot!" He worked some more lotion into his arms and checked his color. It was about time to turn over. He dug through his bag and pulled out another magazine. After flipping through and dog-earring a few pages, he checked the position of the sun. Deciding it was time to rotate a little, he readjusted his beach towel, scooched the recliner some, adjusted the incline and turned over. He decided to face the pool, just in case something worth looking at happened along. It wasn't likely, but still, it was worth a try. The pool was mostly filled with screaming kids splashing water at each other. Most anyone he secretly found attractive was probably out on the lake or starting summer jobs. Not that he'd be obvious about looking – he knew better than that.

He laid the magazine down after determining there wasn't a comfortable way to read it while on his stomach, and closed his eyes. When he opened them again, he noticed the sun had changed position, and the pool had emptied out. He must have fallen asleep. He quickly rolled off the chair to check his shoulders and the backs of his legs. Thankfully, they didn't look too red. A bad sunburn on the first day of summer would be a drag. He turned around to adjust the chair and spotted someone in a lounge chair two down from his. "Wow!" he thought after catching the view. "Maybe things are looking up!"

The guy in the chair looked a little older than Toby – maybe even as old as twenty. Definitely not just out of high school. He had dark, longish hair and *smooth, tanned skin. Like Toby, he had on board-shorts, but he'd hitched them up to bare his really nice legs. "He looks like he works out," Toby observed as he eyed the smooth chest glistening with warm oil. He suddenly realized what he was doing, and sat down quickly, picking up his magazine. He knew he was blushing, so he held it up to his face.*

"It's okay to look."

Toby ignored him.

"I said, it's okay to look," the man said again.

Toby glanced around to see if anyone had heard, and hissed back, "I wasn't looking!"

"Sure you were," the man said with confidence. Before Toby could think of a single thing to say, the guy gathered up his towel and a bottle of tanning oil and moved to the lounger next to him." My name's Jerry," the guy said, holding out a hand.

Jeeze! This dude had the whitest teeth Toby had ever seen outside of a toothpaste commercial. He put down his magazine and shook his hand, which he noticed was scraped across the knuckles. He made sure to keep his grip firm. "Hey. My name's Toby."

"Heya', Toby. Cool name."

"Jerry's a cool name too."

"It's short for Geraldo. With a 'G' at the front and an 'I' on the end. Geraldo reminds me of that investigative guy on TV. I prefer Geri."

"Um...okay." Toby watched spellbound as Geri proceeded to squeeze some oil into the palm of his hand and rub it onto his smooth, muscled chest. The hand moved in slow circles and occasionally grazed first one bronze nipple and then another. Toby couldn't help noticing that both nipples were getting hard as the hand caressed them. Geri hummed quietly under his breath. "OMG! This is just like porn," Toby thought, although he'd never seen any porn. Until now. He suddenly realized his mouth was hanging open and he closed it with a snap. He swallowed down the lump in his throat, and then carefully adjusted the magazine on his lap. It didn't lie as flat as it should. He covertly adjusted things in his shorts and looked around again before turning back to Geri. "I...uh...I haven't seen you here before."

"Well, I just got into town a few weeks ago. Moved up from Florida. I'm staying with my cousin through the summer."

The hand finished with the chest, lingered for a minute on the hard, ripped stomach and reached down to the right foot. Geri rubbed the oil onto his foot, slowing smoothing it between each of his toes. The hand moved up the shin and around to the calf. Geri coaxed some more oil out of the bottle with a gentle up and down motion and a slow squeeze, and started oiling his knee and working up one hard thigh. Tiny hairs lay flat against the tanned skin and glimmered in the sun. Geri pulled the leg of his shorts up a little higher, and worked the oil in, humming and occasionally reaching up under the fabric to the inner part of his thigh, stroking rhythmically. Then he switched legs and repeated the entire process. Toby thought he was going to cum in his pants, and his cock and balls were beginning to throb under the magazine.

Finished with the slow intricate application of oil, Geri carefully wiped his hands on his towel. He turned directly to Toby and took off his sunglasses. He had the greenest irises Toby had ever seen. Looking right into Toby's eyes he said, "So, Toby…you want to hang out this summer?" Geri slowly licked his full, slick lips, and at that exact moment, Toby shot his load.

The next morning, Toby groaned at the stiffness in his back and shoulders. He stretched, rubbed the sleep from his eyes and looked around. On the floor of his cell near the bars were a small paper sack and a tiny, white foam cup with a lid. He retrieved both and took them back to his cot. The bag contained a cold, greasy breakfast sandwich with some kind of unidentifiable meat. He wrinkled his nose and put it to the side. The last thing he wanted was food, especially *this* food. He opened the lid of the cup and looked at the murky brown liquid inside. He took a cautious sniff. It *kind* of smelled like coffee. He took a sip and grimaced. At least it was hot. That was about the best that could be said.

He set the cup on the floor, and went to the sink in the corner. He washed his face, splashing the tepid water that trickled from the faucet up from his cupped hands. He shook his hands over the sink, and after taking a quick look around the room, he unzipped his fly. As he had vowed the night before, he rose up on his toes and peed in the sink. He almost cried in relief as he emptied his bladder. He ran more water, washing the urine down the drain. He washed his hands, and discovered there were no paper towels. He wiped his hands on his pants, thankful the slacks were black. He went back to the cot, sat down and picked up the now lukewarm coffee. He finished it. Then he placed the empty cup on the floor and waited.

About an hour or so later, he heard someone walking down the hall. He heard the jiggle of keys. A new officer stopped by his cell. "Bailey?"

"Yes, that's me."

"You're supposed to come along with me." The officer unlocked the cell door and held it open as Toby exited. Together they walked down the hall and through another door. The officer escorted him to a small room. Inside were a metal table and four chairs made of orange molded plastic.

"Take a seat," he was instructed.

Toby seated himself in the chair opposite the door as officer left the room. Toby studied the space; ugly gray walls, awful chairs and no pictures. Not even a calendar. One large mirrored glass window was positioned on the left wall. *"Probably an observation room,"* he decided. He folded his arms on the table and waited.

A few minutes later, the door opened and Detectives Reightman and Jackson entered. Detective Reightman was wearing a dull pantsuit made of some sort of stretchy fabric over a pale yellow top. Neither did anything to flatter her sallow complexion or her gray streaked, curly dark hair. Toby, of course, kept that observation to his self. She fanned herself with a pad of yellow legal paper as if she were hot, then tossed it on the table and laid a ballpoint pen on top. Toby noticed the cap looked like it had been chewed. She placed her hands on the back of one of the orange chairs and stared at him. The other detective, in a nice navy blue suit, leaned up against the wall, cradling a cup of coffee in his hands.

She finally nodded. "Mr. Bailey."

Toby nodded back and cleared his throat. "Detective."

Detective Jackson moved from his station against the wall and walked to the table. "We've been informed that your attorney should be here shortly," he said. "When she arrives, we'll do introductions and give the two of you a few minutes alone. In the meantime, can I get you a cup of coffee?"

"Thanks, but no thanks. I already had some of that this morning."

"Well now you know just how awful the coffee around is around here! It only takes a couple of swallows. How 'bout a bottle of water instead?"

"Sure. That would be great." Toby was a little confused about why the Detective was being so nice, but then caught on. *"He's going to be the good cop."*

"Be right back."

Reightman still hadn't said a word, beyond her initial greeting. Toby looked down at the table and fiddled with a hangnail. He needed a manicure.

After a minute or two, Jackson returned with a few bottles of water. He placed them down on the table and handed one to Toby. As he reached to take it, Reightman finally spoke. "I hope you aren't disappointed Mr. Bailey. The water around here is not as fancy as you're used to."

"Huh?"

She nodded toward the bottle. "It isn't fancy like the stuff you have over at your spa." She sounded bitchy, even to herself, and compounded the bitchiness by making quotes in the air with her fingers. "It's just plain stuff without a fancy label. Although, I don't think a label saying 'City Jail' would be real attractive. It wouldn't improve the taste, but would triple the price."

Before Toby could think of a reply there was a knock and Jackson crossed the room and opened the door.

In walked a tiny Asian woman of advanced age, taking small, careful steps. She was wearing flat soled slipper-like shoes and white nylon socks. Her black cotton slacks were too short, and the dusty green tunic had obviously been mended many times. Perched on her small nose was a pair of heavy round-rimmed glasses which magnified her black, piercing eyes. Her white hair was bunched into an untidy bun on the back of her neck and secured with a plastic clip. She carried an immense, smartly designed bag with brass hardware. She looked around the room and gave a small bow to Detective Jackson.

"Thank you for getting door. It very heavy," she said. She walked over to the table and deposited the bag on top. She turned to Toby and crossed her arms. "Well?"

Toby stood up and gave her a big smile, transforming his tired, worried face. "Madame Zhou," he said, giving her a small bow. "Thank goodness you came!"

"Yes yes yes I come. You need – I come. I get message very early this morning." She turned to the two detectives. "Well?"

Reightman removed her hands from the back of the chair. *"Are you believing this?"* she mentally telegraphed to Jackson. "You're here to represent Mr. Bailey?" she asked the tiny woman.

"Yes yes yes. I am attorney," Madame Zhou said proudly. She opened her bag and rummaged around a bit, removing several items and placing them on the scratched and worn tabletop. Out came a small folding umbrella, a box of tissues, a clear plastic rain hat, a huge ring full of keys, and a bottle of pepper spray. She rummaged some more and pulled out a bulging wallet, a few packets of green tea, and a cell phone with a pink and silver Hello Kitty cover. Hello Kitty's eyes which moved from side to side.

She dug around once more, and found a brightly enameled card case with a green Asian dragon on the front. The card case had a red, unwrapped cough drop stuck to it. She picked off the cough drop, held it up to her glasses and then nodded and exclaimed, "That where you were!" She dropped it back into the bag. She opened the case and removed a single business card. Holding it in both hands, she bowed and presented it to Detective Reightman. "See? Says right here."

Reightman took the card which was imprinted across the top with the words "Green Dragon." Underneath, it read "Martial Arts", "Best Chinese Herbs and Teas", and at the bottom in smaller print, "Madame Zhou Li, Attorney-at-Law: Affordable Legal Services." *"What a coincidence,"* Reightman thought, remembering the shop across the street from Mr. Bailey's business.

"I am Madame Zhou Li."

Melba remembered enough of her cultural training to know that the last name was often listed first – especially among the older Chinese population. She listened carefully to the pronunciation and then handed the card to Jackson, who read it and placed it on the table next to the legal pad.

"Ms. Zhou, I am Detective Reightman and this is my partner Detective Jackson."

The little woman scowled. "Madame."

"Excuse me?" said Reightman.

The attorney shook her head, slightly dislodging her glasses. "No no no. Not a Miz. I am Madame. I like older forms. Shows more respect."

"Of course, Madame Zhou," Jackson smoothly interjected. "Shall we all have a seat"?

"Oh yes yes yes," she nodded and gave a small enthusiastic clap.

Everyone moved to their respective orange plastic chair and took a seat – except for Madame Zhou. She looked pointedly at her chair and then to Reightman, Jackson and Toby. Realizing what was amiss, Toby stood and pulled back her chair. She nodded and gave his cheek a single pat, and then proceeded to thoroughly examine her chair. "Nasty," she finally said, and reached for the box of tissue she'd placed on the table.

She extracted three individual sheets and placed them in the seat, arranging them until they completely covered the orange plastic. She took another from the box, and dusted the chair back. Then she eased herself into the chair, supporting herself with her small hands laid flat against the table. When she was seated, she examined her palms and gave another disgusted frown. She took another tissue and carefully wiped her hands while giving Reightman and Jackson a reproachful glare. "Well?"

Jackson looked at Reightman and Reightman looked at Jackson. *"Is this for real?"* she silently asked her partner with a single raised eyebrow. He shrugged his shoulders and suppressed a grin.

Reightman cleared her throat and proceeded to explain what would happen. "Detective Jackson will explain the current situation and then we'll leave you alone with Mr. Bailey for a few minutes. When we return, we have a lot of information to go over. Your client is in serious trouble, Madame." When Madame Zhou gave a curt half-bow to signal she understood, Melba indicated that Jackson should proceed, and settled back in her chair.

While her partner spoke, Reightman's eyes traveled over the collection of items the diminutive attorney had placed on the table, and then came to rest on the bag itself. It was a remarkable bag. Best one she'd ever seen. She marveled that it could hold all those items, and probably more, while looking so sophisticated. She'd love to have something like that instead of her own huge, misshapen purse. Reightman continued her private reverie, listing in her head all of the things she could carry in such a wonderful bag, until suddenly she realized the room was silent. She gave herself a little shake and looked up. Jackson was eyeing her with concern, and Toby Bailey had a guarded expression on his face which gave no clue to his thoughts. Madame Zhou studied her with open curiosity from behind her enormous old fashioned glasses. She looked from Reightman to her elegant bag, and the back to Reightman. She smiled. "Kelly," she said with pride.

Reightman was confused and somewhat embarrassed she'd been caught practically salivating over someone else's purse. "Kelly?" she eventually croaked. Her neck began to perspire.

"Yes yes yes! It a Kelly." The old lady patted the bag with affection. "Genuine Kelly." She emphasized the work genuine, as if she enjoyed the taste. "Vintage original. Moon find for me."

Reightman was now totally confused and felt herself getting a wee bit cranky again, thinking the woman was pulling her leg. "The moon found it for you?" she asked in amused disbelief. *"Is this old lady just plain whacky?"*

"No no no! That silly! Moon from Passed Around find for me. Was best gift ever."

Reightman was somewhat mollified by the explanation. "Moon owns the vintage store on the same block as Mr. Bailey's business?"

"Yes yes yes," Madame Zhou confirmed, smiling widely and baring perfect tiny teeth to show she was very pleased everyone understood things so well.

Jackson cleared his throat, and inclined his head toward the door. Reightman picked up on his cue and rose from her chair. "We'll just leave you two alone for a while. I'm sure you have a lot to talk over with your client. Will twenty minutes be sufficient?"

Madame Zhou fluttered with nervous agitation. "Oh no no no! Be better to give thirty minute. Lot to talk over, like you say. Much to study. Much much. And I old – not do this for long long time."

Melba nodded her agreement, with a sinking feeling the old woman had probably never had a case like this one. She knew she couldn't afford to spare too much sympathy for Mr. Bailey because of the odd representation he'd engaged, so she motioned to Jackson and moved to leave the room. Before she reached the door, Reightman turned, walked back to the table with a mumbled, "Sorry," and picked up the business card sitting next to the legal pad. She slipped it into her pocket and left.

The moment the door closed, Madame Zhou stood and crossed behind Toby, positioning her back to the observation window. Then in perfect English with just a hint of gentile, well-bred southern accent, she quietly spoke. "Well, Toby Bailey, I probably shouldn't ask, but I will. Did you kill that man?"

"No, Madame. I didn't."

She considered his earnest face for a moment and looked deep into his pale blue eyes. Then she nodded her head once, in approval. "Good. I didn't think so."

Zhou Li retrieved a leather covered memo pad from her bag, along with a gold fountain pen. She crumpled up the tissues from the seat of her chair and placed them on the table. She rearranged her chair to keep her back to the mirrored glass on the wall. After seating herself firmly, she brandished the gleaming pen in like a miniature sword. "Let's get started then," she said. "We have a whole lot of work to do and not much time to cover everything we need to discuss. Start by telling me what happened."

Toby began to talk. His day was looking up. Madame Zhou had arrived to help him, and now, there might be some hope after all. He was already feeling better.

❖ ❖ ❖

Reightman and Jackson walked down the hall, made a couple of right hand turns, and soon found themselves standing outside the office of Chief of Police Ernest Kelly. By the time they arrived, Reightman was feeling hot and she could tell her skin was flushed. Seated at a giant desk right outside the door, Nancy Peach, the Chief's admin, was rapidly typing on her keyboard with her brightly lacquered nails and smacking on a huge wad of gum. Nancy told everyone who'd listen that she was trying to quit her two pack a day smoking habit. So far, the rumor mill reported her efforts were in vain. A big diet soda with a lid and a lipstick marked straw was perched on a folded paper towel next to the monitor. In the partially opened drawer on the left side of the desk Melba could see an opened baggy of rice cakes – Nancy was on another diet – several packs of assorted flavor sugar-free gum, and the distinctive packaging of a popular brand of menthol 100's. "Looks like the rumor mill's right," Reightman murmured to her partner. "Hey, Nancy, is the Chief available?"

Nancy answered without looking up from her typing. "Sure is, Melba. Been waiting on you and Sam to get your asses over here."

"Well, it's been that kind of a morning. Okay if we go on in?"

From behind the partially cracked office door a voice rumbled, "That you, Reightman? Is Jackson with you? You two get your butts in here right now!"

At the sound of Kelly's voice, Nancy stood up and thrust a bulging folder at Reightman. "Fair warning, Melba, he's in a mood today. Give him this while you're in there and tell him it all needs to be signed. All of it – today." She reached over to grab a quick drink of her cola, and then promptly returned to her typing and chewing.

Reightman clenched the folder with both hands, struggling to keep any of the papers from falling out. When she had it under control, she handed it off to Jackson. "You give it to him."

"Why do I have to?"

"I figure since you play golf him every Saturday he's least likely to throw this monster at your head while yelling four letter words, that's why. So stop your whining, and just do it."

Jackson rolled his eyes and grinned. The Chief yelled through the door, "I heard that, Reightman. I ain't fuckin' deaf!"

Chief Kelly gave them both the once over when they entered. "It's about damn time!" He reluctantly took the folder from Jackson, grimacing when he felt its hefty weight, and then stacked it on top of the already overflowing in-box. He pointed at the two heavy, pleather covered chairs in front of his desk. "Park your sorry selves there."

They removed several piles of folders from the seats and stacked them carefully on the floor. Once she was seated, Reightman pulled her sticking blouse away from her neck and used one of the file folders to fan herself. Chief Kelly studied them for a minute from under his bushy brows while chewing on the inside of his cheek. He rolled his neck from side to side, causing a couple of vertebrae to crack.

"Feeling warm, Reightman?"

"A little, Chief."

Kelly grunted at her comment and then started in. "This is one fine hell of a mess. Detectives, as I'm sure you're well aware. Already this morning – before I even had my second cup of crappy coffee – I've had calls from the Mayor, the DA, and some piss-ant reporter from the paper.

"Sorry, Chief."

"Hold on to your horses, Reightman. It gets better." Chief Kelly eased his chair back into a more comfortable position. "As you might imagine, the Mayor and the DA are concerned about the murder and the associated publicity. As a result, so am I. You'd best bring me up to date on where we are with this thing."

Reightman and Jackson exchanged one of those looks partners exchange when they're in the hot seat.

"Well, Detectives?"

Jackson set up a little straighter in his chair and filled the Chief in on the events of the night before, stopping to clarify the occasional question. Every once in a while the Chief would hold up a large hand indicating he should stop talking, and chewed on the inside of his cheek thoughtfully. Finally, Jackson wrapped up the briefing.

"Where's Mr. Bailey now? Sitting in a cell?"

"Right now he's in the interview room with his attorney. While I'm thinking about it, have they notified Mr. Guzman's next of kin?"

Jackson answered, "As far as we have been able to tell, Reightman, there are no next of kin. Mr. Bailey says there never have been, at least any he knew of. There was one cousin Guzman stayed with several years ago, but he moved away some time ago and Bailey doesn't know how to reach him. He seems to be the only person who was close to Guzman for a number of years. We can ask again during the interview, just to make sure."

"Speaking of that, Jackson, we should probably be getting back, although the crazy little Asian lady will likely be grateful for any extra time. She doesn't really seem to be capable of –" Reightman stopped short when the Chief sprung straight up out of his chair.

"What crazy little Asian lady?"

"Toby Bailey's attorney, sir."

"Toby Bailey's attorney?" It was unlike the Chief to repeat things. Usually he caught on the first time.

"Yes, sir." Melba looked at him expectantly, and thought he was looking a little worried. "Sir, is something wrong?"

The Chief sat back down in his protesting desk chair. "Detective Reightman what, pray tell and the Savior help us, is the name of the attorney representing Mr. Bailey?"

Reightman wrangled the business card from her pocket, and handed it across the desk. When he didn't take it, she put it down in front of him. He reluctantly picked it up, and read it before dropping it back down. "Things are going to be getting mighty complicated."

"Why do you say that, Chief?"

Kelly pointed to the card. "Because of her."

"Because of Madame Zhou?" When Kelly nodded in the affirmative, she shot a glance toward Jackson, and ran her fingers through her already tangled hair. "Chief, I know this case looks messy right now, but we've had less than a day to work it. We already have the suspect in custody, and we're working on tying up what are, admittedly, a lot of loose ends. But you know Jackson and I are really good at our jobs, Chief." Reightman continued in what she hoped was a confident tone, "Frankly, I think we have more things to worry about than some old, doughty lady who seems barely capable of defending anyone, much less a suspected murderer. I mean, she has to be almost ninety, and she really doesn't seem to have much experience. Sure, she's a really fussy and maybe a little demanding, but I don't think she'll give us much trouble. I'm more concerned she won't be able to adequately represent Mr. Bailey, although I suppose technically that's none of my business."

"Not give us much trouble, Reightman?"

She didn't care for the Chief's tone of voice, or for the expression on his face. "I don't think so, Chief."

Kelly leaned forward and slammed his hands down on the desk. The big file folder slid from its perch on top of his in-box and dropped to the floor, scattering dozens of sheets of paper across the grey linoleum. He stood and glared at her. "Let me tell you something, Ms. Hot-Shot Detective. That old, fussy, doughty lady who seems barely capable of defending anyone is one of the best legal minds in the entire state, if not the entire country!" He aggressively poked the card on the desk. "I'll have you know, she graduated in the top of her class from Harvard Law. For the past forty years she's caused every opposing attorney, and a few federal judges, to break out in cold sweats just by walking into the courtroom. Really fussy? A little demanding? You, Ms. Know-It-All, have absolutely no idea just how fussy and demanding she can be."

Reightman was starting to feel queasy and shifted in her chair as a little trail of perspiration trickled down her side underneath her blouse. "But, Chief –" She didn't get a chance to finish before Kelly started in again.

"She may be getting old, but you better damn well believe she's fully capable of mounting a defense for her client and having us for breakfast at the same time. She can do both with one dainty hand tied behind her scrawny old back. On top of which, she's one of the best connected women in this city." The Chief stopped his rant to mop his forehead with a handkerchief. "To further edify you two," the Chief grimly continued, "she also owns about twenty-five percent of the entire downtown business district. If she decides to fight dirty, believe you me, Reightman, we'll be covered head-to-toe in mud before that old dragon is done with us. "

In the dead silence following the Chief's revelation, Reightman could feel herself beginning to sweat profusely. She felt very warm and wondered if maybe her blood sugar was dropping. Her hands were balled up into tightly clamped fists on her lap. She stared fixedly down at them and bit her lip almost hard enough to make it bleed. That hurt...and so did her feet. She glanced at Jackson and saw him give a cautioning shake of his head. She relaxed her hands, and then involuntarily clamped them tight again. *"What the heck is wrong with me?"* She reached up to check the back of her neck and discovered it felt hot and flushed, as did her cheeks. *"Why doesn't Kelly turn on the air?"* She reached for the file folder and began fanning herself. She considered her body's reaction some more, and then nodded to herself, slowly at first and then faster. Yep. She knew what was wrong. The old lady had played her, and now Reightman was totally, absolutely pissed off. She leaped out of her chair. "Why, that sneaky old…"

"Detective Reightman!" She looked at the Chief and noticed his hard glare. "Sit your butt back down."

"Melba, get yourself under control – please." Sam almost never used that tone with her.

She felt a vein throbbing in her forehead. "How dare she pull some stunt like that? How can that manipulating old…old…"

"Detective, I said to sit down!"

Her left eye started to twitch. She started to snap out another remark, but reconsidered and shut her mouth. She looked at Jackson and then at Chief Kelly and felt behind her for the chair. She sat.

The Chief glared across his desk. "Detective Reightman, you just sit there for a minute and simmer down." He picked up the Green Dragon card and turned it over in his hands a few times. "I know you're upset by her antics. Hell, just the thought of her gets under my skin. But what we need to do now is get our shit together and act like professionals. I damned well know this is not the first time you've had to deal with some sneaky-assed legal eagle, and I expect better of you."

"You have got to be kidding me!"

"No, Reightman, I'm not kidding. You're old enough to know better than to get yourself worked up. Now, you sit there for a minute with your mouth shut. Understood?" He held her eyes for a minute more. "Reightman, do you understand?"

She jerked her head in his direction. "Yes, sir."

"Good. Now here's what's gonna' happen. You, Detective Jackson, are going to walk down to the interview room and inform Mr. Bailey and his legal counsel you've been detained, and that you felt it courteous to inform them so they could continue their little pow-wow. Tell them it'll likely be thirty minutes or so before you'll join them. That should make Madame Zhou happy, and if we are lucky, she might worry about what's going on. Then call the forensics team and see if they've turned up anything new. Call down to the morgue as well. It is probably too early for anything solid, but it's worth a shot. Anything would help. We sure as hell can't afford to be caught cold footed this early in the game." The Chief shifted his attention to Reightman. "Reightman, you're going to walk yourself down to the ladies room and splash some water on your face. Then you are going to take yourself down the street and get yourself a cup of coffee, or a soda – or whatever the hell you drink – and you're going to sit yourself down for a few minutes and cool off. You're going to meet up with Jackson, in say 20 minutes or so, at which point he will bring you up to date on any new information. Then, you're both going into that interview room to start the questioning. There will not be an outburst. There will not be any yelling. You, Reightman, will not let whatever's been affecting you the last couple of months get the better of you today. Don't play into Zhou's hands. Just gather the information you need to move this case forward. I'll be in the observation area with a rep from the DA's office in about thirty. Understood?"

"How dare he talk to me like I'm a small child? I know how to do my damned job!" She caught Sam's calm, encouraging nod out of the corner of her eye. "Understood, Sir."

"Good," he responded tersely. "Dismissed." They both got to their feet. As they opened the office door the Chief stopped them. "One more thing, Detectives." They turned back toward the big desk. "I'm hoping like hell you're both as good at your jobs as Reightman says. Otherwise, we could all be in for a world of hurt." He held their eyes until they nodded their understanding. "Oh, and send Nancy in here. She's gonna' have to help me get all of this damned paper back in order." They shut the door behind them.

After leaving Kelly's office, Jackson and Reightman parted ways; Sam heading to his desk and Melba making her way to the ladies room. Melba walked to one of the sinks and splashed cold water onto her hot, red face. She looked in the flaking mirror. After a minute, she dug around in her bag for a tube of lipstick and added a little color. She considered her reflection and decided the color didn't help much. She returned the lipstick, and walked to the beat-up wooden bench by the door. She dropped the bag and took a seat. She slipped off her too tight shoes and rubbed her aching feet. She checked her bag to make sure she had a few bucks handy and transferred the bills to her jacket pocket. She wedged on her shoes and stood up, shouldering the heavy bag.

She walked down the hall, and went out the glass doors on the side of the building, noticing the glass was dirty and needed a good cleaning. Melba looked up and blinked. The sky seemed very bright today. Her eyes hurt, so she sat down on the steps and opened her bag again, pulling out a pair of dark glasses and putting them on. Better. She stood up, walked down the four steps leading to the sidewalk and strolled distractedly down to the corner coffee shop.

Melba perused the menu hanging behind the register while waiting in the short line and politely greeting a couple of people she knew. She ordered a sweet tea, dug money out of her pocket and picked up her drink from the barista. She left a couple of quarters as a tip. She located an empty booth and sat down, placing the tea on the table. She took a sip, and then rested the cool plastic cup against her hot forehead. She pulled a paper napkin out of the dispenser and blotted her skin. Then, she slowly and methodically tore it into tiny, irregular pieces. She sipped some tea and stacked the little pieces into three separate stacks, making sure they were all the same size. She adjusted one of the stacks by removing a few pieces and placed them carefully on an adjacent pile. Satisfied with her work, she finished her tea and got up. She went out the door and up the sidewalk and the steps, and entered the same door she'd exited fifteen minutes earlier. Sam was waiting in the small side entry lobby.

"I had a sweet tea."

"That's good. It had to have been better than the crappy coffee here."

"Yeah, it was, and I feel better now. I think I have myself under control."

"Good:" He gave he a thorough looking over. "Melba?"

"Yeah, Sam?"

"What's with the sunglasses?"

She reached up with her left hand and touched the rims. "It's bright outside."

Sam looked at her and then out the glass doors. "Looks pretty cloudy out there to me."

Reightman pulled off the glasses and looked out the glass doors. "Yeah, you're right. Silly me." She unzipped her bag and jammed the sunglasses back inside the purse. She zippered the top shut, struggling because the bag was full. "Anything new from Tom, or the folks in the morgue?"

"No, not much. The forensics team said they've confirmed the blood on the wet clothes matched the victim. Said there wasn't as much on them as they'd expect if he'd been wearing them when he was stabbed. They said to check with the morgue to see if there was any fabric fiber inside the wounds, and to have them determine if the slashes line up with the wounds on the body. They also confirmed there were no figure prints on the weapon. They finished processing the scene early this morning. Nothing else showed up and the only prints they found on premise probably belong to the regular staff, but they'll confirm that today. I called down to the morgue, but Lieberman hasn't made it in yet. Riley said he called in this morning saying he wasn't feeling well and wouldn't be in until later today. Riley said he really didn't sound too good."

Melba might have snorted and Sam was immensely pleased with her return to normality. "That's about it."

"Figures," she shrugged. "You ready to get this show on the road?"

"Yep. How about you? Am I gonna' have to kick your lazy butt all the way down the hall?"

"As if." She looked down the hall they needed to traverse to get to the interview room, and squared her shoulders. "I guess I'm as ready as I'll ever be."

"That's the ticket, Ms. Ready-As-I'll-Ever-Be."

This time, she definitely snorted. "Thanks for putting up with me, Sam."

"Always will, Melba." They made their way down the hall, taking the required left hand turns to the interview room.

She knocked once and opened the door. Bailey and Zhou Li were sitting at the table. There were a couple of opened take-out cartons on the top, along with all of the items Madame Zhou had removed from her bag earlier. There were a couple of new additions to the clutter in the form of a memo pad with a gold fountain pen on top.

Bailey was wiping mustard off his chin with a paper napkin. "The Police Chief sent his secretary down with a couple of sandwiches a while ago," he explained.

Jackson nodded and smiled. "That's nice."

"Oh yes, Chief very considerate. We get very hungry." Zhou Li clapped her small hands in delight.

Reightman walked around the table to an empty chair, never taking her eyes off the old lady. She sat down, placing her bag in the chair beside her. She glanced toward the observation window. She knew she had to be careful, but also had to prove she couldn't be steamrolled. More importantly, she needed to show Kelly that she had herself under control. However, she wasn't about to take the kind of bull Zhou Li had dished out for a single minute more. "Let's just cut the crap, counselor."

"What you mean?"

"I mean, cut the crap. Stop with the fussy old lady act and can the pigeon English. I've been informed of your rather formidable reputation, your high-priced law school degree, and your impressive connections. So you can stop the games."

Toby Bailey looked confused. He knew Madame Zhou was far sharper than she acted sometimes, but the rest of her qualifications and credentials surprised him. Jackson stood against the wall watching the scene with his usual perfect calm.

Zhou Li folded her tiny hands on the table and regarded Reightman thoughtfully. She gave a single nod. "All right, Detective. I agree there's no further need for subterfuge." Zhou uncapped her fountain pen and opened her memo pad. "Since we've finished our thoughtfully provided lunch, shall we start?"

Reightman shook her head. "Not quite yet. I have a couple of things to say first, if you don't mind. Even if you do mind, I'm going to say them." Zhou arched a single brow at Reightman's cool, firm tone. "I'll start by stating I resent that fact you lead me to assume you were less competent and experienced than you obviously are. I find it unprofessional and frankly, insulting."

Zhou Li replaced the cap of her pen and placed it once again on the notebook in front of her. "I can see your point, and I apologize. Sometimes, I get carried away trying to gain an advantage. However, I take no responsibility for any assumptions you might have made."

"I beg your pardon?" Reightman could feel her eye beginning to twitch again.

The old lady warmed up to her topic. "Any assumptions made were entirely your own. Surely you are trained to *see*, Detective? Trained to look past the surface to discover what is underneath." She settled her tiny body further back in the chair. "You allowed yourself to form a strong opinion of me and my capabilities based on first impressions, without taking the time to discover the truth for yourself. I find myself quite disappointed in your lack of perception, and can only hope you will use your abilities more carefully until this unfortunate case is concluded. In fact, I must demand that you do so."

"Demand?"

"Yes, Detective, demand. I absolutely require such care from you, and from Detective Jackson, in order to best serve my client," she inclined her head toward Toby. "Surely you understand?"

"What I understand is that you sauntered in here this morning wearing the guise of an old and foolish woman who spoke much less perfect English than you've been speaking for the last few minutes. I was actually feeling sorry for your client, which is probably exactly what you intended. You reinforced that impression by unloading all of these," she gestured to the table, "oddly assorted items from your bag. What's up with this junk anyway? A yellow umbrella, a rain hat, a used cough drop, an absolutely unbelievable cellphone cover, and all the other stuff? And covering your chair with tissues? Which, by the way, you also unloaded from that bag and are now crumpled up on the table. That was the crowning touch. Well done, Madame Zhou! This farce was a ridiculous waste of my time, and the time of this department."

Zhou took a moment to respond. "The bit with the tissues *was* over the top, although these chairs are very dirty. I would have expected things to be a little cleaner, but I suppose budget cuts are impacting all city services in some way or another. As for the other items, let us tick them off now, shall we?"

She surveyed the items on the table. "The umbrella and the rain hat are here because it is cloudy outside and I dislike the possibility of getting wet; the unwieldy set of keys belongs to various properties I own around town and I never know when they might be needed; the cherry flavored cough drop came from a small child who offered it to me in church last week. Rather than hurt his feelings, I thanked him and simply dropped it into my bag. I hadn't been able to find it to remove until this morning; I carry green tea because I don't like coffee, and the sweet stuff they insist on serving everywhere is not acceptable to me, regardless of the season. The cell phone cover? It is indeed unbelievably awful, and I assure you it does not reflect my personal taste. However, it was a birthday gift from my eleven year old great grand-niece, who absolutely adores Hello Kitty. I love *her*, so I choose to use it. It makes her happy, and *that* makes me happy. Perhaps you have children, Detective? Or maybe even grandchildren?"

Reightman wasn't pleased with the familiarity Zhou Li was trying to establish between them, but had to admit it was probably a fair question under the circumstance. Grudgingly she allowed, "A daughter and two grandchildren."

Zhou Li offered a tiny smile. "So, you understand about Hello Kitty."

Remembering the endless sound of animated cartoons playing in her former home, Reightman had to agree. "I suppose I do. But, what about that…that get-up you're wearing?" She indicated the odd clothing the attorney wore.

"Well, Detective, if you really must know, I was doing a bit of gardening this morning and I am afraid I ran short on time. And before you ask, I choose to be called Madame, rather than Miz, because it is a custom in my family – a custom of long standing. In old cultures, such a title shows respect to me and for my position, just as occasional bowing shows the respect I have for a person or occasion. I know it's terribly old-fashioned, but I have retained those customs because it is how I was raised in my parent's household. I have never married, so addressing me as 'missus' would not be correct. If I had married, I would have considered the adoption of that salutation. Now, is there anything else for which you require an answer?'

Accepting the many contrasts of the difficult morning, Reightman shook her head no.

"Good," Zhou Li nodded in approval. "I am glad we have so successfully settled the first set of questions today. I am optimistic this bodes well for the resolution of this case. I am certain you have many more questions to ask, so I suggest we get started. Detective Jackson, why don't you join us here at the table instead of lurking from your current position against that wall? It will be more pleasant, although the evident lack of comfort provided by these hideous chairs might cause me to regret that statement before the day is done."

Reightman almost smiled, because she absolutely agreed the chairs were hideous and uncomfortable. However, she reminded herself she was still miffed at Zhou Li.

Jackson made his way to the table. "There seems to be a purse in my chair."

Reightman sighed, and removed the offending bag, placing it on the floor at her feet. She fanned herself with her notepad as Jackson took his seat. Toby Bailey looked from each of the people around the table with a slightly wide-eyed gaze.

Madame Zhou Li uncapped her gold pen, and gave an encouraging smile to her client. "We are ready when you are, Detectives."

Reightman took a minute to collect her thoughts. She aligned the yellow legal pad at her right hand and uncapped her ballpoint. She knew it wasn't as impressive as the one Zhou Li held in her own hand, but it worked, and it made her feel more confident to have it at the ready. She cleared her throat and started, "Mr. Bailey, I'm going to be asking a serious of questions about your involvement in the death of Geraldo Guzman."

Zhou Li interjected immediately. "Detective Reightman, I must protest your characterization. My client had no involvement in the unfortunate murder of Mr. Guzman."

Reightman had anticipated the objection and was ready to rephrase. "Mr. Bailey, I am going to ask you a series of questions which will, hopefully, help me understand the events leading up to and surrounding Mr. Guzman's murder." She paused for any new objections, and when none were forthcoming, she continued. "You've been arrested as a suspect in this murder. Do you understand that this is a serious charge?"

The young man swallowed and looked to Zhou Li. After a receiving her small nod, he answered. "Yes."

Reightman made note of his shaky voice before she continued. "According to the statement you made last evening, you returned to the Time Out Spa at around 8:45 PM, at which time you discovered the door unlocked and the alarm off. Is that correct?"

Toby Bailey turned to his attorney and Zhou Li indicated Toby should answer. "Yes, that is correct."

"Did you find those discoveries surprising at the time?"

Again, Toby looked to Zhou Li for direction. She started to nod, but raised her hand instead. "Toby, you need to answer the questions without looking for my approval every time. You may trust me to interject if I have an issue with the question, or if I wish to advise you not to answer. Do you understand? "

"Yes, Madame Zhou." He bestowed a trusting smile on her and then turned to Reightman. "Yes. I did find it unusual, because I knew I'd locked the door and set the alarm before I left."

"Were you worried about what you might find when you entered the building?"

Toby thought back to the previous night. "No, not at first. I was more confused than afraid or worried."

"Did you go directly to the back room of the building after you had entered the premises?"

"No, I didn't. I turned on the lights in the front room and checked each room as I worked my way down the hall. The room where I found...where I found Geri was the last room I checked."

Jackson looked up from his notes and asked the next question. "Mr. Bailey, what did you do when you discovered the body?"

"I didn't do anything."

"What do you mean you didn't do anything? Didn't you want to help your friend?"

"Of course I wanted to help him! But, I knew it was too late. I could tell by the way his eyes were open and staring off into space. I knew he was already dead. I could tell, somehow. He just wasn't there any more, you know?"

"Of course, Mr. Bailey." Jackson gave him a minute to recover. "What did you do next?"

"I called the police."

"You called the police at about 8:55 PM, is that correct?"

"I guess. I'm not really sure. There aren't any regular clocks at the spa and I don't have a watch. I usually just check my cell phone when I need to know the time."

"And did you check your cell phone?

"No. I didn't have it with me. I lost it somewhere earlier."

"That's right. Last night you indicated the reason you returned there was to search for your phone. Did you find it?"

"I didn't look. After...after I found Geri, I couldn't do much of anything. "

"Mr. Bailey, what did you do between the time you called the police, and the time the first officers arrived on the scene?"

Toby tried to recall how he'd occupied the time. He didn't remember what he'd done after he'd found Geri's body. "I don't know."

"You don't remember?"

"No."

Jackson tapped his pen on the small notebook he held in his hands. "Do you forget things a lot?"

"No, not usually."

"Yet, last night you forgot your phone, and you forgot what you were doing before the police arrived. That makes me think maybe you do have a habit of forgetting things."

"I don't forget things. I *do* put my phone down sometimes and then have to hunt around for it. But, I don't forget other stuff."

Jackson studied the young man's face and pursed his lip. Finally, he nodded. "Alright, Mr. Bailey." He wrote down a couple of notes, and then handed off to Reightman.

"Mr. Bailey," she asked, "did you start the washing machine in the break room before you left the premises?"

"Yes. I threw in a load while I was there. We go through a lot of towels and sheets and it's hard to keep up with all the laundry. I'm always starting a load of something."

"Did you load the washer yourself?"

"Yes, I did."

"What did you put in the washer?"

"Last night it was towels first, and after they were finished, I moved them to the dryer. Then I started a load of sheets."

Jackson stood up and walked around the table. He grabbed a bottle of water and twisted of the top. "Would you like another bottle of water, Mr. Bailey?"

"Yes, please."

Jackson picked up another bottle of water and walked over to the young man seated at the end of the table. Reightman longed for a bottle too, by Jackson hadn't offered. She watched her partner carefully, knowing what he intended. They'd used this approach many times before. As he handed the water to the young man, Jackson asked casually "Why did you put the knife in the washer, Toby? "

Toby Bailey lost his grip the bottle and fumbled to set it upright. "I didn't put the knife in the washer – just towels and then the sheets."

"How about the clothes? Geri's clothes, with all the blood on them."

Zhou Li frowned, but didn't object to Jackson's questioning.

"I didn't do anything with any clothes. The only things I put in the wash were towels and sheets." When he realized they weren't buying his story, he looked frantically around the table. "You have to believe me!"

Jackson leaned closer to the boy. "How long did you wait before calling the police? Did you go and grab a bite while your buddy was bleeding to death?" Jackson leaned even closer, until he was crowding the young man. "How long, Bailey?"

The young man was on his feet in a flash and his face was red. He held his hands balled up at his side and he started to cry. "I didn't kill him! I told you that already. I didn't kill him!"

"How long, Toby Bailey? How many times? How many times did you stab him?"

"Stop saying that! I didn't do it." The young man covered his face and turned away sobbing.

Jackson maneuvered to face him. "Why did you do it?" he asked gently. "Tell us and maybe we can help you."

"Madame Zhou!" The boy was now almost wild with grief and fear. "Help me. You said you would help me! Make them stop – I can't take this!" Zhou Li didn't respond. "I didn't kill Geri. I could never do that. I loved him. Madame Zhou, you know that true…you said you believed me." Reightman was suddenly very sad for Toby Bailey.

Zhou Li finally had enough. She stood and threw her notebook onto the tabletop. "Detective! This is out of bounds! I insist you stop this at once."

"Your client is a cold blooded murderer, counselor. The sooner he admits it, the better things will be."

She slapped her hands down on the table with surprising force. The sound echoed in the room. "My client hasn't killed anyone, Detective Jackson!"

Jackson was unfazed by her show of anger. "It's time to get your client to talk. Maybe the DA will agree to a deal. Right now, things are looking pretty bad for your client. We have the murder weapon and it's directly linked to him. Pretty soon, the time of death will be established. Then it's just a matter of time before we find a motive. There's bound to be one, given their relationship. After that, we'll place Mr. Toby Bailey at the scene."

"I don't think you will." The old lady sounded harsh and very certain of herself. "I think this has just been a very dramatic fishing expedition." She regarded Jackson with steady black eyes. "I understand the need to pressure and traumatize this young man – it's part of the routine in cases like this, which is why I let it continue. But I have now had enough of the cheap theatrics! It is time to face facts. Shall I outline the hurdles ahead of you, Detective?" She ticked off the items on her fingers. "Number one: there are no prints of any kind on the knife, much less prints belonging to my client. Number two: any prints of Mr. Bailey's you find on premises are perfectly explainable as he owns the establishment, and has a perfect right to handle or touch anything he desires in the entire building. Number three: within the next fifteen minutes, I expect the private detective I hired this morning will have established Mr. Bailey's whereabouts for the evening, and will have also confirmed an alibi covering the majority of time – if not all of the time – which lapsed between the moment he left the office and the moment he returned. Toby is well-known in the area, and not only will the bistro staff confirm the time he spent over dinner, but you can rest assured people of the neighborhood will verify his path to and from. As for number four, you have nothing – and I repeat – nothing to tie the weapon to my client. Any evidence you have is entirely circumstantial and will never be anything more than that because my client did not kill Geraldo Guzman. You made a poor decision and arrested my client not only prematurely, but wrongly."

Reightman stood up from her chair and gazed steadily at Zhou. "The weapon in custody clearly belongs to Mr. Bailey. It has his name engraved on it."

Zhou Li shook her head disappointedly. "Detective Reightman, I warned you earlier about the need to look beyond your assumptions. What proof do you have the knife belongs to my client? You claim it has had his name on it. So what? Does it have his full first and last name engraved on its hilt, or does it simply read 'Toby'? How many men in this city, this state, or this country might be called 'Toby'? How many of them might have conceivably owned a knife of this sort over the last thirty years? Hazard a guess for me, Detectives. Or, perhaps someone unknown simply found it somewhere and thought it might be nice to have. Do you have any written or photographic proof the weapon belonged to *this* Toby? Do you even have the smallest anecdotal account of my client possessing such an item?" Zhou Li considered the Detectives for a long moment, waiting on a response. When she was satisfied she'd made her point, she continued in a softer voice, "Detectives, have you ever even considered that someone may have used that specific knife in order to frame my client?"

Reightman met her stare for stare, resisting the urge to pull her blouse away from her sweating skin. The old woman had raised some valid points and enough doubts that Reightman found herself worried. And she was feeling so damned overheated.

Zhou Li turned and walked to the mirrored observation window. Facing it she bowed, without any irony whatsoever, and spoke very formally. "I am sure behind this glass there are observers. I have had many, many years of experience in rooms such as this so I would be highly surprised if no one of importance is listening. It is procedure. This, I understand and respect as a tool to find evidence and establish guilt. I would venture one of the observers is the Chief of Police, Ernest Kelly. I would venture there is at least one more observer, perhaps someone from the office of the District Attorney. I will say this to those listening and observing: you and this team have made a grave error. You have acted in haste, and allowed others to act without full and irrefutable evidence of wrong doing. I appeal to you to see past the surface and to think!"

"If you do so, my client will cooperate in any way he is capable to help find the killer of his friend, Geri Guzman. Of course, out of pride and conceit, you may choose to act differently. You may choose to continue to wrongly hold Mr. Bailey. You have that right, at least for a short time, and even with a complete lack of evidence. If you choose that path, I *promise* you I will be in front of a judge before another hour has past. You should believe I can, and will, do what I say. I will secure my client's immediate release, and then, I will sue this department, this city and every official involved in this travesty for enormous sums of money. And, I will be successful – have no doubt." Zhou Li looked at the watch on her wrist. "You have ten minutes to make your choice." She bowed again and walked to her seat. She sat in the hard plastic chair and calmly closed her eyes.

Three minutes later, there was a knock on the door. A uniformed officer brought a closed file folder to Madame Zhou. She thanked him politely and opened the file. She scanned it quickly and handed it across the table to Reightman. "As I anticipated, Mr. Bailey has a firmly established alibi, and this report details and confirms how he spent his time last evening before discovering Geraldo Guzman."

As soon as Zhou Li finished speaking, the lights on the observation room were turned on and Reightman could clearly see Chief Kelly and one of the assistant district attorneys through the no longer reflective glass. She felt sick to her stomach as she watched the Chief leave the observation room, followed by the ADA. A moment later the interview room door opened and they entered the room. "Mr. Bailey, you're free to go," the Chief informed the young man. "Detective Jackson will escort you to get your belongings."

Kelly turned and left the room without once looking at Reightman or acknowledging her presence in any way. The ADA left as well. Jackson gathered up the empty water bottles and put them in the corner wastebasket.

She watched Toby embrace Madame Zhou Li, while the old lady gently patted him on the back. Wiping away his remaining tears, Toby left the room with Jackson.

Reightman approached the small, old, and very shrewd woman. "Congratulations, Madame."

Zhou radiated extreme disapproval. "Detective, we both know there are no congratulations warranted. My client is free, that is true. But so is the person who committed this terrible act. A man is dead and there is much work to do to see justice served. As I have promised, we will cooperate fully and if we work together, we will prevail. Of that, I am sure." She crossed to the table and began to gather her belongings. Before putting a single item back into her bag, she dug down to the bottom and retrieved the sticky red cough drop. She placed it in the exact center of the table.

Zhou picked up the umbrella, the rain hat, the ring of keys, the green tea, and the box of tissue, her cell phone with the Hello Kitty case, her notebook and the fountain pen. She placed each item carefully down into the bag, each in its own place. She opened the enameled card case and removed a single engraved card and placed it next to the cough drop. She snapped the card case shut and placed it in the bag, before closing the vintage Kelly and lifting it with both of her small hands. The tiny lady walked with great dignity to the door, then turned and lifted a hand. "I will expect your call tomorrow, Detective." Walking carefully and with a perfectly straight spine, she left the room.

Melba Reightman was immobile. It had been a very bad day, perhaps the worst ever. She was exhausted and hot and felt old, tired and pretty damned useless. She still had to face Chief Kelly and her feet hurt. She sighed, and it felt good. She walked to the table and picked up Zhou's card and tucked it in her pocket. She picked up her yellow legal pad and the cheap, ratty-ended ball point and crammed them into her purse. Then, recalling the old woman's dignified exit, she straightened her own spine and marched out to pay the piper.

She left the cough drop sitting on the table, slightly damp and all alone. She'd bet Sam it would still be there tomorrow. She'd win.

CHAPTER THREE

IF HE HAD any energy, Toby would have sprinted up the stairs. Instead he trudged up them, putting one foot in front of the other until he reached the top. For a moment, he regretted that he lived on the third floor, until he remembered that living at the top of the building gave him a pretty decent view, and a lot of privacy. He unlocked the door and dropped his keys on the small entry table. Before he went any further, he toed off the too big shoes they'd loaned him at the station. He'd carry them outside later. For now, he just wanted them off his feet. He locked the door and secured the safety chain, then made his way through the living area and into the small modern kitchen. He grabbed a handful of vitamins and a couple of extra strength aspirin and dry swallowed them. He filled a glass of water from the water dispenser and downed it. He filled the glass again, and finished that as well. Next, he pulled off his shirt, removed his belt and set it on the counter, and quickly took off his slacks and underwear. He bagged all the discarded clothes in a white plastic trash bag, then knotted the bag and sat it by the stainless trashcan. He stood naked in the kitchen and took several deep, cleansing breaths. He then walked directly to the bathroom and turned on the shower, adjusting the water until it was very hot. When steam started to filled the shower, he stepped in.

He scrubbed his body twice, and started on his hair. He worked the herbal scented shampoo into lather, then rinsed and shampooed it again. Once he finished, he sat on the small wooden bench and started in on his feet. They were filthy, but at least the pink stains from the blood were almost gone. After they were clean, he stood up and turned off the water.

He squeezed the water out of his hair and, reaching over the door, he grabbed the plush towel off the hook and dried off.

He stepped out of the shower and moved to the sink. He wiped the steam off the mirror and regarded his reflection. He didn't look much different than he usually did. More tired perhaps, and his hair was standing on end. He grabbed a comb and ran it through the wet strands a couple of times, before wrapping the towel around his waist and walking into the bedroom. He pulled back the drapes and looked out over the city. In the darkening evening light, he watched a couple of joggers pound their way down the street. He wasn't worried about being seen – people almost never looked up. They didn't have much experience with danger coming from above. When the joggers rounded the corner, he moved his gaze to the group of buildings across the street, until it rested on his spa. He liked living across the street. If he worked late or if something came up, he was just a few steps away. The cop cars were gone, but he knew there'd be a policeman or two stationed inside the door. He'd deal with everything *that* represented tomorrow. He was too tired to think about it anymore tonight.

He took one last, lingering look at the street below and walked to the bed. He untied the towel and let it drop to the floor. He folded down the comforter and pulled back the sheets, then climbed in and closed his eyes. He was home, and safe. Soon, he started to cry, and great aching sobs racked his chest. He hurt like never before. He cried for Geri, and he cried for himself. He hugged a pillow tightly to his chest, willing the tears to stop. Eventually, his breathing slowed, and he slept, and dreamed.

Toby found himself back in his old room at Grams' house, grabbing for the ringing phone.

"I'm off work today. You want to go to the pool later?" Geri asked over the cell. "Weather's supposed to be pretty good."

The ceiling in the room melted away, showing him the promised blue skies. As he looked up, the sky vanished and the ceiling was once more overhead.

"No, I can't. I promised Grams I'd help her around the house and the yard today. She has a list a mile and a half long!"

"Need some help?"

"Why the heck would you want to help with my chores? Don't you have anything better to do?"

"Not really. I don't mind helping."

Toby thought about the day ahead and how much he'd enjoy his friend's company. "Sure, that'd be great! I bet Grams would even feed us dinner…maybe even fried chicken."

"You'd introduce me to your Grandmother?"

"Of course! She loves feeding strays!" Toby's room transformed into the kitchen as the phone disappeared from his hand.

"Hey, old lady! What's cooking?"

"Ain't nothing cooking, and there isn't going be if you don't watch your smart mouth!" Even though she was facing the sink snapping pole beans into a colander, Toby could tell by her voice she was smiling. She complained about his smart-alec sass, but he knew she liked the banter. It reminded her of his grandfather, who'd dished out loving, fun-filled grief every minute of the day. "Pour yourself a bowl of cereal and take a seat," she instructed. "We can talk about what needs to get done today."

Before he knew it, Toby was seated on top of the counter with a bowl of cereal in his hands. They were just the way he liked them – liberally coated with sugar. He crunched down the cornflakes. Grams turned around from the sink and gave him her special look. "When I said for you to take a seat, I didn't mean for you to sit your fanny on my clean countertops. Now get on down from there!"

Toby kept his perch and swung his legs, letting the back of his sneakers hit the fronts of the cabinets. His heels made a sound like thunder. Grams filled a glass of milk and flew to the counter, settling herself down gently. She swung her feet and the thunder grew louder. She tilted back the milk and drank it down. It took her a couple of tries. Then she sat the glass down and smiled a milk mustache smile.

"I got some good news," he said from his place up on the counter.

"Oh, you do?"

"Yep. I rounded us up an additional pair of hands for the day."

"Is that right?"

"Yes, ma'am. Friend of mine named Geri. He's nice. Said he'd be happy to help us out for the right fee."

"Oh he did, did he?"

"Yes, ma'am."

"And just what might that fee be, Toby?"

"Dinner."

"Well, that sounds more than fair. We've got plenty of pole beans."

"Yeah, you know I love those! There's only one catch."

"I figured there would be. With you, there 'bout always is. What might this catch involve?

"Well, you see, I'm sure he'll like the beans a lot. But the thing is, he only eats one kind of meat." She raised her eyebrows, but motioned for him to continue. "It is because of some really rare medical condition." She waited. "He can only eat fried chicken."

With a flash of light she was down off the counter. "Toby H. Bailey! You know I don't have time to be making fried chicken today. We've got a ton of yardwork to get done!"

Toby smiled down at her. "He'll a good worker Grams! That'll free you up from most of the hard stuff. And about that 'Toby H. Bailey' thing, you know I don't have a middle name."

"You do now! The 'H' is for hellion!

That set them both to laughing. "So is it a deal?" he wheedled.

"We'll see how it goes and how tired I'm feeling. Your friend is more than welcome to stay for dinner, especially if he's helping with chores. However, I won't be making any promises about what I might be dishing up, other than that it'll taste good. Now, get yourself down off that cabinet so you can get started on the first of your many chores for today."

"What might that be?" he hopped down.

"Well, you're going to get down and retrieve a rag and the cleaning spray from under the sink. Then you are going to get our heel marks off those cabinet fronts."

Geri appeared out of nowhere, and he and Grams exchanged a series of small, formal bows – almost like a dance. Grams waved her arms and he and Geri were weeding flower beds which changed into vegetable gardens. The screen flew off the door, headed their way. Toby reached out a hand and grabbed it, and placed it back where it belonged. Geri grabbed a garden hose, and soon Toby was wet with the water and covered in soapy lather. Geri was wet as well and hollering like it was the best thing ever. They cut the lawn, taking turns with the old push mower. They were hot and sweaty and Toby felt happier than he ever had, even though he knew he was dreaming about doing chores. They drank from a huge glass of cold sweet tea, holding each other high in the air so they could reach the straw. Then instantly, they were cleaned and scrubbed and sitting at the big kitchen table with all kinds of good things. There was a big bowl of beans, a fresh cool cucumber and tomato salad, biscuits, and in the place of honor, a big platter of crispy chicken.

"Told ya!" Toby cried out in happiness as he danced with Grams, and then with Geri around the big table. He hugged his Grams and whispered, "You're the best."

They all laughed and joked, and wore funny hats, like it was someone's birthday. "He's a nice boy," Grams informed him as she pointed to Geri, "And he's the first guest you've ever brought home."

"Man-oh-man! This was the best dinner ever!" Toby stretched and touched the ceiling, which was now the evening sky.

"Yes, ma'am. It was great, Mrs. Bailey." Geri gave Grams a courtly bow and she curtsied in return. "I've never had anything as good as that chicken. And the cobbler was terrific! If I had to choose a last meal, this is what it would be." Geri laughed in delight at the thought of having a last meal, when he had his whole life ahead of him.

Grams shared his laughter, and then looked at the giant clock on the wall. "My goodness, look at the time!" She frowned and all three of them looked at the giant clock. Its hands went round and round, spinning faster with each turn. Toby desperately wanted to stop it, but he didn't know how. He knew that if the clock kept turning, something bad would happen. "Well, it's getting late boys, and I'm sure we are all tired." Grams turned to Tony and waved her towel. "Toby, why don't run up and get Geri's bag and then you can walk him out?"

"Sure thing." Toby ran down the hall to retrieve Geri's things and spied on them through the walls. He saw Geri hold out his hand to shake with Grams. "Thanks again for dinner, Mrs. Bailey." Grams took his hand in both of hers. "You're welcome, Geri. I'm glad Toby has a good friend like you – one that'll do the chores and all the things that need to be done." As Toby watched, Grams grew taller until she almost didn't fit in the room. She leaned down over Geri and picked him up in her hand, lifting him up until she could look him in the eye. "Toby is my whole world, young man, and I want him to be happy. He laughed a lot today and it did me good to hear it. As long as you stay nice and helpful, and keep making my grandson laugh, it'll be a pleasure to have you around here anytime. Consider this your home, home, home." She put him back on the floor, and shrunk back down to her normal size.

Toby could tell Geri felt tightness in his throat, but his friend nodded respectfully. "I'll do my best, Mrs. Bailey."

"I trust you will, Geri. I trust you will. I trust you. I trust you." Toby saw the clock hands spin faster. "One more thing…"

"Yes, ma'am?"

"If I'm going to be seeing a lot of you around here, it seems best for you to call me Grams…call me Grams…call me Grams."

The wall became solid again and Toby couldn't see them anymore.

Soon, Toby was back with Geri's things and they all danced in a spinning circle, until they reached they door. Grams fluttered her tea towel and Geri was borne away on the wind she made. She turned back around, and waved the towel again, and the kitchen was clean and sparkling.

"Toby, come up here with me and we'll spin a while."

"Sure, Grams." Toby climbed on the carousel horse next to the one Grams rode, and they revolved around the big table.

"Your friend Geri seems very nice, Toby."

"I think he is. He sure did like your cooking!" He grinned at her sitting high on her steed.

"Toby, I'm glad you have a good friend. I know it hasn't always been easy for you. After your momma died, you were just the saddest thing. We were all devastated of course, but while your grandfather and I eventually made our peace with it, it took you a long time. I guess that's only natural, knowing how close you two were." Grams looked behind her and motioned to him. "Look, Toby, your mother's here now." Toby turned and saw his mother on another painted steed, far behind their own. Her pony was gray and black and white, instead of the beautiful colors they rode. "Smile, Toby!" she said as she pointed her camera at him. With a flash! she was gone, and Toby was very sad. The carousel stopped, and Grams climbed down, motioning for Toby to follow. He noticed the clock hands, spinning out of control. When he stepped to the ground…

….he woke.

Toby went to the bathroom and splashed water on his face. He dried it off and looked into the mirror as he tried to recall the dream. He thought back to that day, and that summer evening. In a way, what he dreamed was very like the way things had been. He remembered the talk he and Grams had that night after Geri had gone.

"Toby, today I heard you laugh more than I have heard you laugh since you've lived in this house. You sass me all the time, but sometimes I think that's more for me than for you." She paused for a minute, thinking about how she wanted to say what was on her mind. "You know how much I miss your grandfather. I hope one day you'll find someone you would miss as much as I miss him." She stopped his fidgety hand and gripped his fingers. "Do you understand what I am saying to you?"

"I think so…"

"I think right now you'd miss this Geri very much if he left and you weren't able to see him again. I realize I don't know him well, but I do know people, and I think he'd miss you too, even though you boys just met a few weeks ago. Now, I want to ask you something important and I want you to answer me truthfully. Do you like this boy?"

"What do you mean, Grams?"

"You know what I mean! I'm not blind and you aren't stupid. Do you like – I mean really like – this boy? Maybe even enough to love him a little one day?

Toby's heart hammered in his chest, but he'd promised he'd answer truthfully. *"I think I might…like him. A lot. I'm not sure about loving…"* He was a little bit afraid, and a little bit heart-busting happy at the admission. He was afraid to look at her.

"I think you will be, Toby. I think you will be sure one day."

He looked up her and saw her wiping tears from her eyes. *"Grams, I'm…I'm sorry!"* he was horrified at what he'd caused. *"I didn't mean to make you upset. I'll quit liking him, I swear! Just don't be mad. I didn't mean to make you ashamed of me."*

She gave a little laugh, which sounded more like a sigh, and brushed the tears out of her wise, old eyes. *"Toby-boy, I'm not one bit mad. And, you better darn well know nothing you can say or do could make me truly ashamed of you. I might get mad as a hatter, but I love you, child. Did you think I didn't know, or at least hadn't suspected, your nature? Your Gramps loved you and he wouldn't be ashamed either if he were sitting with us right now. And you know your momma wouldn't be ashamed. You'll learn soon enough you can't just stop the kind of feelings, and longings you're beginning to have."*

"Then, why are you crying, Grams?

"Toby, I'm crying because my heart is split and that causes it to hurt like nothing you can yet imagine. One side is so very happy you're discovering the joys of love and life, and that you have a special friend. The whole wide world is waiting for you right now. The other side is grieving; because it knows the way that same world works. The plain truth is, the world isn't always very loving or accepting, and people are hard and judgmental, even those who know better. There are dangers and temptations and threats everywhere, Toby; some of them you've likely learned about it school, and some we've talked about. There'll be bad days, but if you're strong and brave, and careful and clever and learn to be just a little bit wise – and learn not to sass so much," she gave him a wink *"you'll be fine."* She stood up and gave him a hug. *"It's time for us to call an end to the day, young man. I'm tired, and based on all the planning going on*

over dinner, you have a big day ahead of you. I only have one more thing to say."

"Yes, ma'am?"

"You be careful, Toby, of your heart, your mind and your body." He nodded. *"And, for Heaven's sake, use protection!"*

Toby laughed, although he was embarrassed, and then stood and looked at her – really looked at her – like a man looks at the woman who has raised him, and loved him, and scolded him and pushed him, and accepted him because he was who he was and, most of all, because he was a child, dear to her heart, in all the ways possible.

"Good night, Grams. I love you."

"I love you too, Toby."

Toby brushed away his own tears and walked through the living room and opened the French doors. He stepped out on the terrace, remembering what came next.

The next day he met Geri at the pool. Under the mid-summer sun, they splashed in the water, shared their ideas and dreams while sitting on the lounge chairs, and they napped in heat. Geri grinned with his very white teeth and reached for his towel. His hand brushed Toby's hand. Looking into Geri's green eyes, and knowing it was alright if he did, Toby Bailey fell in love.

He looked up at the stars, and saw one bright light trailing across the sky. "Is that you, Geri?" After a while, he went inside and eventually fell back to sleep. If he dreamed again that night, Toby didn't remember.

At the same time Toby let himself into his apartment, Reightman and Jackson were headed down to their boss's office. Both expected to get their ass thoroughly chewed by Chief Kelly.

Nancy had tracked them down earlier and had matter-of-factly informed them that the Chief would see them at 6 PM on the dot. She popped her gum. "And don't be late. I've got kids to feed and a diet club meeting to get to." She then turned on her heels and left.

They arrived at precisely 5:59 PM. They slunk into the office and positioned themselves in front of the big desk, hands clasped behind their backs. Reightman was uncomfortably reminded of her one and only visit to the principal's office back in her elementary school days. She hadn't liked the chewing she got then, and suspected she really wasn't going to like it any better now.

The Chief was seated in his rolling swivel chair, head down, working his way through the huge folder of paper and forms needing his signature. "Well." He said, looking up at them from underneath his bushy brows. "That went to hell in a handbasket."

Reightman decided she'd best agree. "Yes, sir, it did."

"The old lady was right about the knife, and the alibi. We jumped the gun, and but good."

"Yes sir, we did." Jackson was going to take his beating like a man, right beside her.

Kelly leaned back and Reightman winced when the chair gave a small squeak. "We're all to blame here –there's plenty to go around. We all saw what we expected to see. You two did, and so did I. Even the DA's office failed to raise a fuss during their review. We all formed a conclusion and didn't think it through. She was right about that too." Reightman let out a little of the breath she was holding, as the Chief continued, "We haven't had a murder like this in a long time. Now I grant you, we've had the occasional shooting, and a bar fight or two which got out of hand. Usually, when someone gets killed it's a case of domestic violence or a family squabble. Sometimes it's a drug deal gone bad, or an attempted robbery that got out of hand. Plenty of witnesses and evidence to wrap things up, nice and neat. This here situation is different, and we are going to up our game and put in some serious work." He looked at her from across his desk and drummed his fingers. "Reightman?"

"Yes, sir?"

"I'd like you to summarize where we are now." He waited for her to speak, and then snapped impatiently, "For God's sake, both of you stop standing there like kids caught stealing candy, and put your butts in a seat. This may take a while."

Reightman and Jackson settled their asses on vinyl. "Sir, here's the current situation: We have a victim, presumably killed by multiple stab wounds to the neck and chest, which resulted in extreme blood loss."

Kelly held up a hand to stop her. "You said it's presumed the stab wounds were cause of death. Why presumed?"

"The coroner hasn't signed off on official cause of death yet, sir."

"What the hell has Lieberman been doing? Playing with himself?"

Jackson jumped in, "Coroner's been out all day, Chief. Riley said he'd be in later today when I called and checked this morning. I followed up a few minutes ago and was told Lieberman called in sick for the rest of the day. Stomach virus or something." Reightman's look of disbelief caused him to add, "The man's entitled to sick leave, Reightman – city policy, and all."

"Sick leave, my ass," Kelly muttered under his breath, "Recovering from a late night binge, more likely."

When Kelly cleared his throat and looked at her expectantly. Reightman continued. "The victim was a partner in the Time Out Spa. Mr. Toby Bailey is the other partner. The stabbing was accomplished with a large knife – a hunting knife, I believe – currently in custody. There's an identifying name on the case. It's been established the knife doesn't likely to belong to Mr. Bailey."

"Do you think the knife is his, Reightman?"

She chose her words carefully. "I'm going to work under the assumption it isn't until proven otherwise."

"Good enough. Continue."

"We know that there's a lot of history between Mr. Bailey and the victim. I got the thumbnail sketch during my initial interview with Mr. Bailey. I have a feeling there's more to the story, but the relationship appears to have been stable, and there's no indication there were any hard feelings between the two of them. Certainly on the surface there's nothing to indicate motive for murder, but I intend to dig deeper to be sure." When neither the Chief nor Jackson interrupted, Reightman finished up, "The techs have finished with the crime scene, and we've placed an officer on premises for the time being. At this juncture, we have no idea how the killer entered or exited the room. No motive's been established. There are no current leads or additional suspects." She looked to her partner. "Feel free to add anything you'd like, Jackson."

"I think you've summed it up pretty well." He pulled out his notebook and reviewed what they knew. "We may be working with an angry customer, although it seems unlikely. Not many folks kill someone because they didn't like their hot stone massage or seaweed wrap. There may be a financial motive, but we haven't even started digging through the business files."

"Where are the files now, Jackson?"

"Still at the scene, sir." The Chief frowned at that, so Jackson reassured him. "We have officers in the building round the clock. They've been there since last night."

"Alright. That should suffice, but we need to get to those files sooner rather than later." Kelly rubbed his chin, and the stubble rasped against his hand. "So to summarize your summary, Detective Reightman, we have a dead man who was killed somehow, although death by blood loss due to multiple stab wounds is the front runner right now. We have a murder weapon with no proven owner. We have a crime scene with no clues as to how the murderer made it into or out of the room. We have no identified, or suspected, motive. We have no leads at this time. Sound about right?

"Sounds about right, sir."

"Then we've got a hell of a lot of work to do and we need to make some progress ASAP. The Mayor and the DA aren't exactly happy right now. We haven't been hammered by the news teams yet, but that's bound to change; especially now the suspect's been released. What kind of resources do you figure you're going to need, Reightman? Things are pretty tight in terms of departmental headcount, but I might be able to free up a couple warm bodies from somewhere."

"Chief, if you could find a person or two to help analyze the files it would be a big help, and it would be extremely useful if we could get the final reports from the coroner. I just hope Lieberman gets back to work soon and confirms cause of death."

"Lieberman will be in bright and early tomorrow morning if I have to go pick him up and drive him here myself." Lieberman was not on Kelly's list of favorite people either. "Do you think Mr. Bailey will cause us any problems? He doesn't have much reason to be feeling warm and fuzzy towards any of us right now."

"No, he doesn't, sir," Reightman agreed. "However, his attorney has assured me of Bailey's full cooperation. I'm supposed to call her tomorrow morning to set things up." She had a sudden thought, but hesitated to bring it to his attention. After thinking it through, she decided it couldn't hurt. "Sir, do you think we can arrange to get official assistance from her and Bailey?" To her surprise, the Chief didn't immediately shoot her down.

"Why do you ask?"

"Well," Reightman spoke carefully, not wanting to set him off until he heard her out. "As you've said, sir, Zhou Li is well connected and she's incredibly shrewd. I'd rather have her working with us instead of putting roadblocks up at every opportunity." She also thought Zhou Li would enjoy being in the thick of things and might end up being a powerful resource, but didn't mention that part of her thinking. "As for Bailey, bringing him inside the tent, so to speak, might also be helpful when it comes to getting information from the rest of the spa staff. He knows the business and the client list better than anyone and can probably help us make progress faster than if we tried to shift through those files on our own."

"Not a bad idea, but I'll have to get approval from up the chain. I'll try to get you a decision first thing in the morning."

"Thanks, Chief."

After a small amount of additional logistical discussion they wrapped up. Reightman and Jackson stood to leave. "Jackson, I need a few additional words with your partner. She'll catch up with you when we are done here. Close the door on your way out." The Chief couldn't have given a clearer dismissal if he tried. After Jackson left the room, the Chief addressed her. "Reightman, you lost it earlier today when you figured out the game Zhou Li was playing. However, you pulled it together and handled yourself well during the interview." He held up one finger to forestall her objection. "Yes, the interview went to the crapper, but you didn't let the old bat push you around. Tomorrow, you need to be a focused, capable Detective, regardless of what's going on with you right now. Hell, I've got a feeling before this is done you'll need to be the best detective this city has ever seen, bar one." He studied her for a minute more before dismissing her and turning back to the stack of files.

On her way to the door she stopped and turned back to him. "You said, bar one. Who was the one, Chief?"

He leaned back in the chair and put his big hands behind his graying head of hair. The chair groaned. "The best Detective this city has ever seen, bar none, is sitting on his lard ass in this here chair, right now."

She gently closed the door.

When she got back to her desk, she gave Sam a quick update and then gathered her things and left for the day. She started up her car and pulled out of the lot. She took a quick look at her watch and decided to stop at the grocery store on her way back home. She was almost certain the carton of old leftovers in the fridge had passed the safe-to-eat date. She parked and quickly made a mental list of supplies as she rushed toward the automatic doors. While looking down to dig out her wallet, she collided with a shopper exiting with the store. She lost her footing and fell right on her butt, breaking a heel off her shoe in the process.

"Dammit!" She scrambled around on the concrete on her hands and knees frantically gathering up her scattered belongings.

"You better watch your step, Detective," a voice whispered. "You might be headed for a fall if you miss a clue." She started to turn, but a foot shoved her flat on her face. Disoriented, she blinked her eyes, focusing on the shiny row of silvery shopping carts. She lifted her head and turned to identify the source of the words. The voice sounded scared and seemed almost familiar. She picked herself up off the concrete and looked around. The only people in sight were an elderly couple struggling to return a buggy with a wobbling wheel, and a young woman towing two small toddlers into the store.

A store employee knelt down to help gather the last of her things, joined by a few concerned onlookers. "Are you okay, ma'am?"

"Yes, I'm fine." She bent down and began shoving items haphazardly into the purse. "Did you see who ran into me?" She felt a hint of moisture on her check, and reached up to check. She hissed as her fingers made contact with a pretty good scrape.

The young woman handed her the broken heel and pulled a mostly clean paper napkin from her store apron and handed it to her while shaking her head. "No ma'am, I didn't. Are you sure you're alright? I probably should take you over to customer service to file an accident report."

Melba daubed at her face, figuring all the employees had been trained to try to get any slip and falls on the record to avoid unpleasantness later. "I'm perfectly alright. The only thing hurt is my dignity." "*And my butt and my face*," she thought, "*and my shoe*." "Thanks for your help. I think I'll do my shopping another time." Melba hobbled back to her car, tossing the broken heel onto the passenger seat. "*That was really weird*." She backed out of her space and headed home, never noticing the worried man watching her from across the street, hidden in the dark interior of his car.

The morning sun shining through the window inched its way across the bedroom and until it shown directly on Toby's face. He woke, blinking at the bright, shimmery glare. He closed his eyes for a minute more and lay in the warm nest of covers, thinking about the day ahead. He sat up and stretched and then padded his way across the wooden floors to the bathroom to take care of his morning business. A few minutes later, coffee in hand, he opened one of the French doors and stepped on onto his rooftop terrace. The patio had been one of the apartment's strong selling points, along with its proximity to his business, and the very reasonable lease terms. It wasn't huge, but was plenty big enough for a small table and chairs, a couple of sun loungers and a few big pots of plants. An enclosed privacy railing encircled the space, cutting most heavy wind and screening any curious eyes in the area. Not that there was anyone to see him up here, three stories above the ground. His was the tallest building in the immediate area, with the exception of the units across the roof from Madame Zhou's shop. He occasionally saw the drapes move in one of them, but had no idea who lived there. If they wanted to spy on whatever he was doing, he hoped they enjoyed the show.

Toby sat in the sun, sipping his coffee and enjoying a temporary, peaceful moment. Soon, it would be time to start the day, and the first unpleasant task awaiting him was calling Grams. He regretted the sorrow and horror he'd have to share with her as he relayed the news and circumstances of Geri's death. She'd be devastated. She'd grown to love Geri too. He reached for his phone and realized he still hadn't found it. *"Add another thing to the list for today."* He grabbed his empty cup and went inside to call from the apartment phone. She picked up on the third ring and he could tell by her breathing that she must have raced to the phone.

"Grams?"

"Toby Bailey, you'd better be calling to tell me you're alright! And why am I just now hearing your voice?"

"I'm fine, Grams," he replied, although he wasn't. "It was late when I got home and I was really out of it."

"What happened, hon?" she asked him quietly.

He told her how he'd found a man murdered in the spa, and about the events that led to his arrest. He didn't go into much detail, hoping to spare her any unnecessary upset. Then he came to the hard part. "Grams?" his voice was very quiet and soft. "The man who was killed, was Geri." The phone was silent except for a quick intake of breath, and the sound of her breathing. "Grams?"

"I'm heard you, Toby. I'm just trying to take it in." Her voice was very sad. "My heart is breaking for that poor, sweet misguided boy."

"Mine is too, Grams." And it was, although the breaking had started a year ago. He could hear her sniffling and could picture her wiping her eyes with a kitchen towel, or maybe her apron.

"When's the burial, Toby? She asked after a moment.

Toby went silent, shocked by the question. "I haven't even thought about it. I'm not even sure when they'll release his body. How could I not know that?"

"Honey, it's alright. You've had quite an upset and more than a few other things to deal with." When he didn't respond, she prodded him gently. "Toby Bailey, please don't go quiet on me. I know you're sitting there convincing yourself you're an awful person and you need to stop that right now. It's not going to do anyone any good whatsoever, and it isn't true."

"Grams, what am I going to do?"

"You'll do what needs to be done. The Lord knows the poor boy doesn't have anyone else in this world that will." The phone was silent for a moment and then she told him, "Bring him home, Toby. Bring him home. This was his home for a while, as much as anywhere. What better place for him to be, than here, where he was and always will be loved?" After a quiet moment, she continued, her mind turning to things needing to be done, rather than to her own grief. "We've a whole big empty row of cemetery plots down here. Your Gramps always figured someone would need 'em. Might as well put one of them to good use – the ground's just sitting there waiting."

"But, Grams…"

"No buts about it, Toby! It's what I want, and what your mamma and your Gramps would want if they knew the situation. Although, I suspect they do, up where they are now." She waited and then added, "When they release his body, bring Geri home."

He thought over her words while tears ran down his cheeks. "Grams, I will. I'll bring him home, when they let me."

"Good. I'll call down to Goodwin's and get them started on the arrangements. You have any idea what you want?"

Her pragmatic tone of voice helped him collect himself and soon he was able to answer. "I think something simple, Grams. Other than that, I just don't know."

"Honey, simple is often the best. The dead don't much care anyway." She knew he was hurt and grieving, and probably sadder than he even knew, but she'd never been a person who coddled others along and she wasn't going to start now. "It's only those of us who are left behind that care, Toby. I'll give them a call and they'll be ready when it's time. Now, do you need me to come up there?"

"No, ma'am, I don't think so. I've got a lot of things to take care of, so that'll keep my mind occupied. I don't even know when I'll be able to open yet, and I need to call the staff and the customers who've made appointments. If I have any left."

"Oh, you'll have customers left, Toby, even if they reschedule just out of morbid curiosity. That's one of the bitter truths of the world. Folks always flock to where there's been trouble. Just don't let them get to you – no matter what nonsense tumbles out of their mouths. You hear?"

"Yes, ma'am."

"That's my boy. I'll take care of things on this end and you'd better get started on things there. I know it's going to be really hard, but don't wallow around in doubts or recriminations. It doesn't help, and it often hurts. I speak from experience, so you listen and take my advice."

"Yes, Grams. I'll will. Love you." He ended the call and set the phone down. He poured himself another cup of coffee and went to track down some clothes, and another pair of shoes.

CHAPTER FOUR

MELBA FLAILED ABOUT in her double bed, struggling to find the button to silence the blaring alarm, and knocked over a glass of water in the process. "Dammit!" She flung back the tangled sheets and covers and sat up on the edge of the bed, breathing heavily. She'd slept deeply, probably due to the three glasses of zinfandel she'd finished – along with the too old carton of sesame noodles – when she returned from her aborted attempt at grocery shopping. She gently touched her scraped cheek, noticing it was still tender from its short, but meaningful contact with concrete. She allowed herself a moment of worry about the events of last evening, and then shook it off. *"Probably just some nutcase,"* she told herself, although the whispered warning echoed in her mind. It bothered her more than she cared to admit. She shuffled to the bathroom, took care of business, and applied some generic-brand antibiotic ointment on her cheek. "Aren't you pretty?" she asked the mirror as she ran a brush through her bedraggled hair.

After starting the coffee, she turned on her small television. That was a mistake. The news stations had been late in covering the story, but were making up for it now.

"...and here we see Mr. Toby Bailey, one of the proprietors of the well-known Time Out Spa, being escorted downtown for booking," announced the suave, over-groomed news anchor as the video clip played. "Mr. Bailey was arrested late Wednesday evening for the suspected murder of a yet unnamed victim, but has since been released. All charges have been dropped following yesterday's interrogation by senior homicide Detective Melba Reightman and her partner, Detective Sam Jackson."

The station flashed an unflattering photo of her – and a pretty good picture of Sam – up on the screen. "Long time City Police Chief, Ernest Kelly, in an off camera interview earlier this morning, confirmed Mr. Bailey is no longer a person of interest in the investigation. News 7's repeated calls to the office of the District Attorney have not been returned. However, insiders have told News 7 reporters this is one of the most brutal murder the city has seen in several years. Currently, no additional suspects have been identified."

Melba aggressively pointed the controller at the set, and changed the channel. News 39 and News 14 had more of the same. She punched the 'off' button on the remote, and tossed it toward the coffee table. It landed in her mug. So far, her day was off to a great start, and it was past time to hit the shower.

She emerged thirty minutes later, prepared for her day. She moved on to the next item on her list. *"Time to call the diabolically clever Madame Zhou Li,"* she decided and reached for her purse. After digging around for her cell phone, she simply gave up, and upended the bag over the kitchen counter. She reached into the jumbled mess to grab her phone, but stopped mid-motion. Lying in the middle of the pile was not one, but two, phones. She fished out the phone she recognized as hers and moved it to the side. She started to pick up the other, but stopped herself for some reason. Recalling her training, she bent down and pulled a pair of yellow dish gloves from underneath the sink and pulled them on. She then picked up the strange phone.

It was one of the newer smart phones, encased in a brushed silver-toned case, which had no identifying marks. She turned the phone over in her hands, examining it carefully. Satisfied with her inspection, she pressed the power button with one plastic covered finger. Nothing happened. She pushed again. When the screen failed to light up, she decided the battery was dead. "Where did you come from?"

She put the phone back on the counter and threw the motley collection of items back into her purse while reviewing her last twenty four hours. "How *did* you get in my purse?" she glanced at the phone. It gave back a silvery gleam – communicating with her somehow. She frowned, her brain picking up on a clue which evaporated as quickly as it'd manifested. "Come on Melba, think!" She shut her eyes and concentrated, thinking back to the night before. Deciding to buy a few groceries...finding a great parking place...hurrying into the store, colliding with someone and then falling to the ground...disoriented

…she'd focused her eyes and had seen…shopping carts, gleaming silver in the store lights…her stuff scattered on the ground, and a lot of hands helping her to place things back in her purse…hands putting things in her purse…

She tried to remember the faces of the people who'd helped, but she couldn't – other than the face of the concerned store employee. She closed her eyes for a few seconds, trying to remember, before finally giving up. She had a pretty good idea of when, and how, the phone had been placed in her purse, but the rest was a total mystery. She added it to the list.

She pulled out a plastic sandwich baggy and placed the phone inside, sealing it before placing it in her purse. Then she picked up her phone and dialed Zhou Li.

Madame Zhou suggested they meet for a mid-morning conversation over a cup of tea. From the remarks made yesterday, Reightman knew she wouldn't be treated to a tall cold glass of southern sweet tea, but beyond that, she had no idea what to expect. Probably some straw-like, bagged herbal variety served in an upscale bistro or coffee shop. At least their meeting would held be on neutral ground.

"Where would you like to meet?" she asked, reaching for something on which to write down the address.

"Why, Detective, we will meet at Green Dragon, of course. It will be much nicer than any of the local establishments and will give us the added benefit of privacy while we get to know one another better. I assume that you are familiar with the address?" Reightman suppressed a shiver at the thought of a private tete-a-tete with Zhou Li, but indicated she was indeed, familiar with the location.

"Excellent. I will expect you promptly at 10. I am looking forward to it, Detective."

Melba took a quick inventory of her appearance; dark blue jacket and slacks, beige blouse and sensible, low-heeled footwear. Remembering the old lady's eccentric appearance the day before, she decided it was good enough. Besides, her limited wardrobe could only accomplish so much. As a newly divorced woman, she didn't have much extra cash for nice clothes and a detective's salary didn't stretch very far these days. She added a touch of lipstick and after taking a quick glance in the mirror she decided the shade really didn't do her any favors. Good thing she wasn't aiming to be included on anyone's best dressed list. She grabbed her things and locked up the condo.

She made a quick call to the Chief to fill him in on her plans for the morning, and he relayed the official permission to involve Bailey and Zhou in the case, in a limited capacity. Fifteen minutes later, she pulled into a space directly in front of Green Dragon.

A small set of bells attached to the door chimed softly as she made her way inside. Reightman stopped just inside the shop entrance, surveying her surroundings. The shop interior was painted a cool, calm green, very similar to colors used across the street in the spa. There was a deep red accent wall at the back of the shop behind an old fashioned dark wood counter. An intricately embroidered scroll of a rearing green oriental dragon was hung in the center of the wall, and a huge brass scale of some sort set square on the counter. Melba identified it as an apothecary scale and decided it was probably older than she was. Simple wooden shelves hugged the walls on the two longer sides, displaying pristine glass jars filled with unknown herbs, and groupings of teapots and small cups without handles. A couple of large rocks were placed here and there along the shelf, their striations and coloring reminding her of wind-swept beaches or desert sand dunes. There was a closed door on the right-hand wall, positioned between the wooden shelves, presumably leading into the vacant storefront next door. Recalling the Chief's mention of Zhou's substantial real estate holdings, she decided Zhou Li must own the entire building. An open doorway to the back of the shop was screened with intricately carved wooden beads.

Music played softly, made up of some unknown instruments – perhaps some sort of flute accompanied by the occasional plucking of almost discordant strings. All-in-all, the space was clean and elegant, not at all what she'd expected. As she finished taking in her surroundings, a voice called from behind the beaded curtain. "Come on back, Detective, I'm through here."

Reightman parted the curtain, causing the beads to clash gently together with a rustling, wooden sound. She turned back, attempting to still them with her hands. "Don't worry about that, Detective. Those beads are nothing but a nuisance. I should have replaced them ages ago, but they've been here forever. I suppose I just don't give their rattle much thought anymore." Zhou Li came forward from the middle of the room to great her.

Gone was the deceptively harmless old Asian woman of yesterday. Madame Zhou was dressed in an impeccable pair of dark gray linen pants, with a dark green silk blouse. She wore a strand of the biggest, dark gray pearls Reightman had ever seen – not that she'd seen many. Matching pearl earrings the size of a bird egg were tightly screwed to her ear lobes. Her tiny feet were encased in a pair of elegant dark green leather flats. *"Crocodile,"* Reightman identified the material, *"and you probably hunted, killed it, ate it and cobbled those shoes out of the hide before I had my first cup of coffee."* She felt shabby in her own ensemble and tugged at her jacket. At least polyester didn't wrinkle too badly.

Madame Zhou stepped closer to her, peered through her huge, thick lensed glasses and extended her small hand. "Thank you for coming, Detective Reightman. I'm sorry I didn't greet you when you came in, but I was puttering around back here and must not have heard the bells on the door."

Reightman reached out her own hand. *"I bet you didn't hear them. You were probably crouched back here like a spider waiting for an unsuspecting fly."* She fixed a pleasant smile on her face. "That wasn't a problem at all, Madame Zhou. I enjoyed looking over your shop. You have some very interesting things."

"Thank you, Detective, I enjoy collecting things." Zhou Li gave Reightman's hand a little pat. "Shall we?" she gestured gracefully to the seating area in the middle of the dimly lit back room.

Compared to the front of the shop, this room was a treasure trove. Reightman had always heard dragons were famous for their hoards, and tended to guard their things jealously. This was exactly the kind of setting she'd imagine a dragon would find comfortable.

A multitude of knick-knacks were scattered throughout the room, placed on small pedestals and tables along with several silver framed black and white photos. Multiple painted scrolls hung from the walls, and shelves held a profusion of leather-bound books, some of which appeared to be quite old. Everywhere she looked, something gleamed, glittered or beckoned.

Zhou Li carefully picked her way through the room to a grouping of four low armchairs clustered around a carved stone tea table. The table's glass surface was held aloft by eight intricately carved green dragons, their five fingered claws outstretched to support the thick top. In the center of the glass sat a ceramic tea set on a lacquered wooden tray. The tray was inlaid with mother-of-pearl which picked up the room's light, and reflected back a soft rainbow of colors.

Zhou Li seated herself in an armchair and indicated Reightman should do the same. "Now, isn't this more pleasant than meeting in some public establishment?" she asked rhetorically. "We can be cozy and comfortable while we get to know one another and will not have to worry about any over-eager ears."

At Reightman's hesitant nod, the little lady lifted the teapot and began to pour the tea. A sweet, delicious scent of some exotic flower permeated the air. Reightman thought it might be jasmine. As she watched Zhou steady the pot with her hands, she noticed the entire tip of one of the lady's pinky fingers was missing. Strange that she'd not noticed it yesterday, but then again, she'd been focused on other things.

Zhou Li followed the detective's gaze, and gave a small shrug. "A reminder of a singularly unpleasant incident from my childhood, Detective, nothing more. Thankfully, it is long past passed." Reightman noticed Zhou made no attempt to hide the remnants of the finger as handed her one of the small cups. Following the example of her hostess, she blew gently across the pale golden liquid and took a sip. She looked up, surprised. The tea tasted like the most wonderful spring evening. "My own blend," Zhou said, catching the look on Melba's face. "I'll be happy to package some for you when we are through here."

"Thank you, Madame. That would be very nice.'" Reightman wondered how much the tea would set her back, but after taking another sip, she decided she didn't care.

Zhou Li nodded and sat her own cup on the dragon table, and folded her hands on her lap. Reightman was eager to move immediately into a discussion about the case, but intuited it would not be viewed favorably. Zhou Li had asked her here for a reason, and was obviously not going to spill the beans until she was good and ready.

Reightman decided she had nothing to lose if she played along. "Have you owned this shop for a long time, Madame Zhou?"

"For quite some time, Detective. My father opened it shortly after he moved the family here in the 1950s." She set completely still, waiting for the Detective to respond.

"That long?" Reightman was surprised she'd never noticed the shop before. "Did your family come from China?"

"Not directly. My family came from Sarasota, Florida." Zhou Li gave her a tiny smile, indication the conversational ball was back in Reightman's court.

"I've heard Sarasota is very nice."

"It was, at one time, and I believe it's striving to be so again."

Reightman was beginning to feel a little sticky. She tried to arrange herself more comfortably in the chair. "Had your family lived in Florida for a long time?"

"Yes, Detective. My grandfather immigrated there in the final days of the nineteenth century." Zhou picked up her cup, taking a small sip. "Unlike many of the Chinese who came to the United States of America, he came with considerable wealth. And, unlike so many others, he decided to settle here, in the southeastern part of the country, instead of California." She placed the teacup on the table and waited.

Reightman took a sip from her own cup. "Was he an attorney as well?"

"No. He was what might be called an entrepreneur. He acquired significant holdings in the area around Sarasota after arriving in this country. The area was starting to become quite popular as a winter resort. There was a lot of opportunity there at the time. Many well-known individuals settled there, including John and Charles Ringling. I believe my grandfather knew them, and many others of their ilk, quite well."

"That must have been an exciting and interesting time."

"Indeed, I believe it was. Fortunes were made and lost in those early days. But it was also a time of sorrow and danger from sickness and crime. My grandfather's children all died during a severe influenza outbreak. Thankfully, a few years later my father was born. He was the only child of my grandparent's to live to adulthood. He grew up in privileged environment, acquired a good education, spent some time wandering the world and even visited China in the late 1920s. He returned home, and went to medical school, eventually obtaining his medical degree. He became one of the early pioneers in combining traditional Chinese medicine with western practice. He made quite a name for himself in some circles, but my grandfather did not approve of his vocation."

Reightman was puzzled. "But why? Surely being a doctor was considered a prestigious profession."

"To many, it would have been. However, my grandfather was very traditional. He disapproved of my father working at all. There was no need for him to work. There was plenty of money."

Reightman started to respond, but was interrupted by Zhou's raised hand. "My grandfather came from a very different world, Detective, the world of the last days of Imperial China. His family, and even he for a time, were courtiers or mandarins and had been for over two hundred years. The family was favored by the last dynasty. In fact, a not too distant ancestor was granted permission to own and display carvings and wall hangings of the five-toed Imperial dragon, although never allowed to possess any in the color yellow. Only the Emperor, Empress or their immediate family were allowed dragons of that color."

Reightman glanced down at the table in front of her, and at the dragons holding their five-toed paws in the air. Zhou noticed and nodded toward the table. "The table in front of you was brought here from China by my grandfather, along with a few other things which I have on display here and in my apartment. Mostly, he brought a large amount of gold, which proved to be more useful, although there are now many museums which would be delighted to have any of these objects. He wasn't able to bring much with him, you see, and so he brought only the very best. He had to leave rather quickly."

"Oh?" Reightman was now listening to the story with interest and found it all rather fantastic.

"Yes. There was something he did that incurred the old Dowager Empress's anger. It was some incident involving British gunboats, cannons, and opium, I believe." Zhou lifted her tea and drank.

"What an incredible story. You must have had a wonderful childhood, growing up in such a household."

"I suppose many parts of it were wonderful, but there were parts which were quite the opposite. Would you care for more tea, Detective?" Zhou inquired, resting her hand on the pale green pot.

Melba was surprised to find that she would. "Yes, please."

Madame Zhou filled Melba's cup and then her own. "As I mentioned, those days were filled with both sorrow and with danger. There were many prejudices to overcome, especially for foreigners. I was born in 1930, Detective, and attitudes were more rigid then. Our family's wealth insolated us somewhat from unpleasantness, but I still remember the rudeness my mother experienced from other woman and from certain shopkeepers. 'Chinks,' they called us – used in much the same way they referred to the black Americans by hateful, racial slurs. It didn't help that my grandfather, and other members of the household, wore the traditional Chinese garments of his youth. My mother and father were more modern in their outlook and in spite of my grandfather's disapproval, dressed in the height of fashion. However, we were obviously different from others in the area. There was also a huge amount of crime in those days."

Reightman was feeling uncomfortable, but wasn't sure why. She tried to discreetly pull her blouse away from her skin. "Crime of what sort?" she finally asked.

"Much the same sorts as we experience today. However, violent crime in those days was in some ways made more violent by the prohibition movement. I was very young in the last days of prohibition and don't remember much. However, my grandfather ran afoul of a group of criminals which made money off of the illegal sale of alcohol, and I was part of the price he paid for his action. You see, he joined in efforts to reduce illegal bootlegging, and applied his considerable financial resources to frustrate criminal efforts to control more of the city, and city leaders. Quite simply, the bootlegging ring retaliated. I was three years old, give or take a few weeks, when they abducted me while I was out with my nurse. They held me for ransom and demanded as a condition of my release that my grandfather stop all efforts to inconvenience them."

Reightman suddenly felt herself flush with heat.

Zhou Li raised her left hand. "Along with the first ransom demand, they sent my grandfather a part of my little finger." Interrupting Reightman's gasp, she quickly added, "That was a long time ago, Detective, far in the past, although I have never forgotten I was once a small, frightened little girl from an immigrant family. I promised myself I would never be unable to protect myself, or those I cared about, ever again. Whenever I feel my resolve falter, or become depressed and maudlin, I look at my disfigured hand and buck up. We all carry scars, whether they are seen or not. It is pain, and how we deal with it, which defines our character." The old lady folded her hands on her lap again.

"To conclude a rather long story, I was returned to my family, grew up, and went to school where I did very well. When I was about ten years old, my mother gave birth to my younger sister, Zhou Mei. Following the additional unpleasantness Asian Americans experienced following the events leading to the United States' involvement in second World War, and the toxic environment fueled by Senator McCarthy, I eventually attended college up North, were prejudicial attitudes weren't as strongly held. I did well there also, and eventually was accepted to Harvard Law. I graduated with honors and returned to the family home in Florida. My grandfather had long since passed away, and many of the traditional strictures had eased. I practiced my profession as a member of a small firm in Florida until I moved here with my father in the mid 1970's. Sarasota was in the middle of a very difficult time during those years, and my father felt there was better opportunity for us here. He refused to move further north knowing he would find the winter temperatures hard to bear. I have lived here in this building ever since."

"Did you never marry?"

"No. I never married. I did fancy myself in love once, later in life, but the gentleman was killed during the early days of the Vietnam War. I never found anyone else I could conceive of marrying. I became too set in my ways I suppose, and too accustomed to doing things my own way." Madame Zhou leaned forward in her chair. "My sister's brood is quite large though, and her children have given me much pleasure over the years. You might remember my very special phone case." Zhou smiled wryly and folded her hands again. "That is enough about me, Detective. Please tell me about yourself."

Reightman shifted in her seat. She'd never liked to talk about herself or her background. "There's really not much to tell."

"Nonsense!" Zhou Li exclaimed. "We all have stories which are important to tell. Sharing experiences, and the resulting perspectives, are what form the human connections. They in turn, establish and foster relationships."

"I guess I've never been comfortable talking about myself." Since Zhou continued to look expectantly from across the carved table, Reightman forced herself to start. "I have a daughter and two wonderful grandchildren. They live in the upstate." Madame gave her an encouraging nod. "I grew up in a small town about an hour away, and went to the university here. I majored in criminal justice. I always knew I wanted to be a police Detective. I guess I grew up watching too many television shows where the very sophisticated and glamorous Detective always solved the crime within an hour and got his, or her, man. The real world is very different from what we imagine in our youth."

"Yes, Detective, it certainly is," Zhou agreed. "And your husband?"

"Is out of the picture, thank God! He discovered the joys of having his own very personnel secretary. I happened to interrupt an out-of-office consultation between them which was taking place on the couch in our den. It wasn't an amicable separation, to say the least. It was actually quite bitter and hurtful and I still have bruised feelings over it all. The day I walked in on his little rendezvous with the office help, I just walked out the door. Looking back on it now, it was the best thing I ever did for myself." Reightman felt her skin flush again, and perspiration beginning to form on her forehead. She tried to pull her arms out of her jacket. "Excuse me, Madame Zhou, but is it unusually warm in here?"

"I don't think it is particularly warm, Detective. However, it is hard to tell at my age. I find I am chilled more often than not." Zhou watched her struggle with the jacket, and her forehead creased with concern. "Are you quite alright?"

"Yeah, I think so." Reightman freed herself from the jacket and unbuttoned the top of her now moist blouse. She pulled the fabric from her skin and sighed in relief. "I'll be fine now my jacket is off."

Zhou Li regarded her intently through the lenses of her glasses. "How old are you, Detective?"

"Excuse me?"

"I asked how old you are. It is a simple enough question. I know it is considered impolite to ask one's age, but in this case I have a suspicion I would like to verify. Please, Detective, answer my question."

Reightman mumbled a number under her breath. It was pretty close to the truth, give or take a couple of years.

"Yes, it makes perfect sense." At Reightman's questioning look, she continued, "I believe you are experiencing what is euphemistically referred to as 'that time of life', Detective. I think I may have something that will help. Come through to the front with me and we can finish our chat while I prepare something for you."

"That's really not necessary, Madame Zhou."

"Of course it is, Detective. You need to be at your very best to solve this murder, and it is not an inconvenience for me to help." The small lady rose from her seat and walked briskly through the beaded curtain. Reightman gathered up her jacket and ever present purse and followed. Zhou Li pulled on a frayed cotton jacket, like those worn by doctors or pharmacists.

"What?" Zhou Li asked, noticing Reightman's quizzical look. "I don't want to get anything on my clothes. I have a luncheon appointment and would hate to have to change." Madame Zhou Li moved quickly from shelf to shelf, occasionally removing a glass jar lid and placing a carefully measured amount of the contents into the small pottery bowl she carried in her hands. "I had a call from Chief Kelly this morning," she said as she climbed up a small two stepped ladder to reach the jar that she needed. Reightman watched in trepidation lest the woman fall. "He indicated he had received permission for Mr. Bailey and me to participate in the investigation, if needed. I know his Aunt quite well, you know. Ernest

Kelly was an interesting boy, very sharp, although a bit impatient. He could also be somewhat of a bully." Once she gathered all of the ingredients she needed, Zhou Li moved behind the counter and pulled a mortar and pestle from beneath the counter. She expertly pounded and mixed the herbs, punctuating her efforts with a comment or two. "I assured him I would be delighted to help, and Mr. Bailey would be anxious to assist as well." Fascinated by watching Zhou work the pestle in her small capable hands, Reightman was reluctant to interrupt. "I told him I would send you over to Toby as soon as we had talked, so you could work things out." Eventually, Zhou was satisfied with her efforts and separated the mixture into tiny individual mounds, wrapping each into small cotton mesh bags. She wrote something on a small white card, and then wrapped it with the bags in crisp red paper, which she tied with twine. She pulled out an additional prewrapped bundle of green from beneath the counter. "Here, Detective – that should do it."

"Do what?"

"Why, help with the hot flashes, of course. It is my father's original formulation. He made it for my mother himself and claimed it cooled her humors and sweetened her temper, although he never made any observation about her temper when she could hear. My father was a very wise man."

Reightman took the packet into her hands and looked at it dubiously.

"Not to worry, Detective. I used this same mixture during my middle years. It helped with the sudden feeling of heat and the sweating, although I, of course, never really needed help with my temper. " Zhou leaned back her head and laughed. It sounded remarkably like the bells on the door.

Melba didn't bother to even try to suppress the grin she felt forming on her face. "Thank you."

"Certainly, it is my pleasure." Zhou nodded with a pleased nod. "Oh here, I almost forgot." She handed Melba the green bundle. "This green bundle is the tea we shared earlier. Brew and drink one of the packets in the red bundle three times a day, morning, noon and before sleeping. It should begin to make a difference in a day or so. Brew and drink one of the packets in the green bundle whenever you want something comforting to drink. Don't confuse the two."

"I won't. How much so I owe you, Madame Zhou?"

"I won't take money from you, Detective. Consider the jasmine tea a gift to remind you of our time together and the things we discussed.

Consider the red packets another sort of gift – one to make partial amends for my deception yesterday. As I said, I can get carried away."

"But I can't accept these," Melba protested.

"You can, and you will. You don't want to upset a poor, defenseless old woman, do you?" Zhou Li smiled.

Melba considered her gleaming white teeth. They were probably sharper than they looked. "Thank you again then."

"When you run low, come back and I will mix you another batch. I will charge you for it next time. I am after all, a business woman. Now get on over there, and talk to Mr. Bailey. As I mentioned earlier, I have a luncheon appointment, and I fear I am running late. Punctuality is a courtesy, Detective."

As Reightman headed to the door, she turned and asked "Madame Zhou, who owns the building across the street? Where the spa is located?"

"I do, Detective. As well as the apartment unit next door where Toby resides. He is not aware I am his landlord for either premise. He leases both through a management company. Please don't mention it to him. " She fixed Reightman with a gimlet eye.

"I won't, Madame. But, may I ask why?"

"I have two reasons for my hesitation to let Mr. Bailey know he lives and works in my buildings: The first is simply he will likely feel beholden to me, since I have helped him with this unpleasant business, and will continue to do so. I want to avoid any feeling of unnecessary obligation, if possible. He has more than enough on his mind."

"And the second reason?" Reightman could have sworn that the lady blushed.

"The second reason…well… the second reason is my apartment windows overlook Mr. Bailey's terrace. On warm sunny days Mr. Bailey enjoys taking in the sun, without wearing even a single item of clothing. I …I occasionally – very occasionally mind you – peek out my window and…well…I enjoy the view."

"Madame Zhou!"

"Well, I do! I may be ancient, but I am not yet dead. My father always taught me to have due appreciation for good art. And in this case – how shall I put it? The art is very impressive, even at rest, if you catch my meaning." She winked and opened the door, causing the little bells to chime. "Good day, Detective."

"Good day, Madame Zhou." Cradling the packets of tea in her arms, Melba suppressed her laughter until she walked out the door. *"Some fairy tales are right,"* she decided. *"Dragons are unpredictable and very, very interesting. Once in a while, they will even help out a mere mortal."* She looked across the street toward the Time Out Spa, where Toby Bailey waited. *"Or two."*

Toby slowly paced the sidewalk outside the big windows in front of the spa, trying to work up the nerve to open the door and go inside. *"Just do it!"* he told himself. *"The worst thing you could've ever imagined has already happened."* After a couple more nervous passes, he stopped in front of the door and did the one thing he didn't want to do – he took out his keys, unlocked the door, opened it and walked inside. As the door shut, he took a deep breath, trying to calm his rapidly beating heart. He closed his eyes for a minute, and gathered his courage before squaring his shoulders and crossing through the front room. He didn't even notice the lights were on, until his progress was halted by the appearance of a uniformed officer.

"You're not supposed to be in here," the officer growled. "Place is on lockdown."

Toby recognized the condescending cop who'd been on premises the night of the murder. He wasn't sure how to react to the statement, until he remembered that Zhou Li had already taken care of the problem. Still, he wasn't prepared for an outright confrontation. He nervously cleared his throat. "I have permission to be here, Officer. My attorney cleared it with the Police Chief yesterday."

The cop eyed him for a minute, running his eyes from the top of Toby's head down to his sneakers. After completing his once over, the officer eventually replied, "I have to call this in and verify your claim." Toby seated himself on one of the reception area chairs while the cop stepped a few feet away, turning his back and speaking into his hand-held. After a hurried conversation the officer turned around and approached Toby. He came a bit too close, right on the edge of Toby's personal space, fully expecting to claim the dominant position. To the cop's surprise, Toby stood and faced him, with feet planted. The cop's eyes widened slightly. He'd expected Toby to stay seated in the chair, weak and uncertain, and forced to look up at him. The officer's eyes narrowed slightly at the change in expectations. "You're cleared to be here." He said it grudgingly. "You have to stay out of the back room and the break area. They're still sealed and marked with tape, so stay out. Don't make me tell you again. Clear?"

Toby stared at the officer until he reluctantly took a step back. "That's clear, Officer. I'll be in the office if you need me for anything." The officer continued to block his path, clearly unwilling to let him pass. "Do we have a problem Officer…Helliman?" Toby read from the name badge.

The cop's face reddened slightly and Toby saw his nostrils flare. Helliman gave him a small sneer. "Didn't think you'd come back. Thought you'd stay away for sure. Your type usually doesn't have the guts to face something like this." The contempt and loathing was clear in the officer's voice.

Toby just wanted to get to his office without any more hassle, but it was clear the belligerent cop had other plans. He reached the end of his patience. "What type are you referring to, Officer Helliman?"

The cop's eyes widened at the obvious challenge. This wasn't going the way he'd planned. The now angry Helliman clenched his hands into fists, ready to strike the man in front of him. He pulled back his arm, but before he could carry through, a cold voice interjected "Yes, Officer Helliman – fill us in. I'm curious how you are planning to respond to Mr. Bailey's question." Detective Reightman stepped to Toby's side. "In addition, I'm sure you're going to explain why you were about to haul off and hit Mr. Bailey." Helliman glared at them both for a moment and then dropped his hands, and his gaze. He didn't respond to Reightman's inquiry so she turned up the heat. "Helliman, I'm waiting, and if you have any brains at all you'll answer me before I have to ask you again."

The cop shot her a look of pure loathing. "It wasn't nothing. We're just having little conversation – that's all. Isn't that right, Mr. Bailey?" He eyes dared Toby to denounce him to Reightman, like the pansy Helliman knew him to be.

"That's right, Officer – just a little conversation." Toby's eyes never wavered from the man.

Reightman alternated her gaze between the two and then settled her eyes on Helliman. "I'm glad that's the case." She considered Helliman a second or two more. "That will be all, Officer Helliman."

"I'm on assigned duty here."

"I'm on assigned duty here – what?" The man clenched his jaw and refused to meet her eyes. "Helliman?" Reightman took a step closer to the officer and stood absolutely still, her face set in stone. She waited while the cop had time to realize his options were now severely limited.

Helliman licked his lips nervously. "I am on assigned duty here – Ma'am."

"No, Helliman. You *were* on assigned duty here inside, where it's nice and comfy and cool. You're now assigned duty by the door. Outside – by the door." She waited, feeling tension building in her neck and shoulders while she maintained eye contact. Helliman flushed a deep angry red and looked down at his shoes. Eventually he hitched up his pants and stalked to the door. Reightman watched him until he'd exited, before releasing her pent-up breath.

"Whoa…" Toby looked at her with something akin to awe. "You're one badass detective, Detective."

"Helliman's a bully and like most bullies, he doesn't know how to react when he is directly confronted by someone meaner and smarter than him. I knew he'd back down." Privately she hadn't been sure he would – she'd thought for a moment she was going to have to deck him. That would've hurt, but she would've gladly taken him down and nursed her bruised knuckles later. "Let me offer my apologies for his outdated attitude."

"No apologies needed, Detective. He just doesn't like faggots."

Reightman's eyebrows shot up to her forehead. "Please don't use that word to refer to yourself, Mr. Bailey."

Toby considered her closely, trying to garner some hint of what she was thinking. When he was unable to read her expression, he shrugged. "He just doesn't like good looking, successful gay men who happen to own their own businesses." He thought he saw one corner of her mouth twitch. "Is that better?"

"Much better, Mr. Bailey."

"It's Toby."

"Pardon me?"

He couldn't tell if she was irritated or simply confused, but pressed the point anyway. "My name is Toby. We had this conversation a couple of days ago, Detective. I recall the time and place very clearly."

Reightman regarded the young man. His odd eyes looked right into hers. *"Something about him is changed,"* she thought. *"He looks older and harder, and he stood his ground and didn't back down from Helliman."* She considered his face, so very young, but showing the strain of the last couple of days. She knew she was going to need his help to get through all of the work piling up on this case, and at this point it couldn't hurt to strengthen their relationship a little. "Alright then, Toby, if you're sure. Given the circumstances of the last couple of days I wasn't sure you'd want anything to do with me or the department."

"Save it, Detective. You were just doing your job. I mean, I was pissed and all, but I've thought about it. You had a job to do, and you did it. I wish things hadn't happened the way they did. But, there's no point holding misplaced grudges in light of everything else. I promise, I don't have any hard feelings. Besides, you backed down Officer Bigot."

"It's Officer Helliman, Toby. He may be a bigot, and a cretin, but he's still an officer of the law. As long as he wears a badge, he deserves respect, because the law deserves respect."

Toby guessed he could accept her positon, if it allowed him to get to his office. "Okay, Detective, whatever you say. But I still think he's a jerk."

Reightman tried to keep from smiling, and failed. "Don't get me wrong, Toby. I absolutely hate his guts." After a moment, Toby returned her grin. They were in complete understanding. "I spoke with Madame Zhou this morning. She said you'd be expecting me to drop by, and if possible, you'd make time to go over a few things. Is now a good time?"

"Yeah, she mentioned it to me. She gave me a rather firm talking to, and told me – in no uncertain terms – that I was to cooperate. I would have anyway." He considered how he'd really felt after his visit to the city jail, and then added, "Probably." He winced as he remembered some of his attorney's choice commentary regarding the dangers of continuing to hold a grudge under the current circumstances. "After having her chew on me for a while, I didn't have much choice. She's a badass too."

"Yes, she is a badass. I've seen her in action and even fell victim to her methods myself, if you remember." Reightman indicated the passageway in front of them. "If I recall, you have a comfortable office back there somewhere, correct?"

"Yeah, although I don't know how comfortable it is. I spent most of my available time, money and effort on the rest of the place."

"Does it have a couple good chairs, four walls, a door, and air conditioning?"

Toby was puzzled by the question, since he figured every office had those things. "Yes, I guess it does."

Reightman shared another grin. "Well then, it has three more things than my digs down at police headquarters. I can only claim air conditioning. It even works – most days."

Toby smiled. "In that case, the next time I bitch about feeling cramped, I'll think of you and feel fortunate instead. Come on, let's go on back."

Reightman followed him as he led the way through the hallway door, noticing he made a visible effort not to look toward the break room with the lurid yellow tape across the doorway. Nor did he spare a single glance toward the room at the end of the hall where he'd discovered Guzman's body. He opened the office door and motioned her to take a seat.

She claimed a chair in front of the desk and looked around the small room. Toby's office didn't have the sophistication of the rest of the rooms. It was plain and fairly utilitarian, but didn't lack personality. There were some humorous cut-out cartoons on a bulletin board, and multiple framed pictures on the desk and on the wall. Several were candid shots of Toby and Geri Guzman, and a larger photo of Toby and a much older woman, hugging each other and laughing together. "Who's the lady in picture with you?"

"That's my grandmother," Toby replied, with love and affection in his voice. "I call her Grams. She and Gramps – my grandfather – raised me after my mother died."

"She looks like a lady who enjoys life. I bet she can give you a run for your money."

"Yeah, she's a pistol and you're right; she's always busting my chops about something." A chirp sounded and Toby pulled his cell phone out of his back trouser pocket. "Excuse me while I get this." Melba sat back in her chair, listening to his side of the conversation.

"Hello? Oh hey, SarahJune, yes…yes…thanks, I appreciate it…no I'm not sure yet. Well, if you don't mind, can I send you a list of appointments to reschedule…Yeah, I know we do – let me check." Toby moved the phone away from his mouth and turned to her. "Detective, do you have any idea when you'll be through here? I need to get this place open as soon as possible and we need to start trying to reschedule the customers."

Reightman knew the crime team had finished their work and all the rooms had already been photographed and plotted, but hedged to be safe. "We'll probably only need a few more days, Toby."

"Thanks." He turned back to the phone to continue the conversation. "SarahJune? Yeah – sorry. Detective Reightman thinks they'll finish up in a couple of days. Yeah, but – SarahJune, I know! I was about to tell you we're going to have to get someone in to clean...to clean the back room where...." His voice broke as he remembered the last time he'd see the room where Geri died. "....clean the room where...." Toby felt a surge of grief rise up in the center of his chest. He tried to swallow it down, but knew he couldn't. "SarahJune? Hang on a sec..." He put the phone down, and rubbed his eyes with both hands. *"I won't cry!"* he told himself, and struggled to get himself under control. After a few seconds, he took a deep breath and picked up the phone again. "SarahJune, you still there? Yeah, I'm okay. I just needed a minute. I'll send you a list of client names and appointments in a little while so you can make the calls. Yes, I know where the appointment book is... Yeah...Okay, I'll call you if I have any problems....thanks, SarahJune...Bye." He hung up the phone. "Whew," he exhaled. "That was intense for a minute."

Reightman knew he was still struggling with his emotions, but understood he was also determined to move on with everything that needed to be done. "You handled it though. You did a lot better than many people would have."

Toby made the effort to give her a smile of acknowledgement and ran his hands through his hair a couple of times before sitting a little straighter in his chair. "It's just hard – you know? You forget for a second and then...then suddenly, it all comes slamming back and hits you right here," he touched his chest above his heart, and hung his head.

Reightman couldn't think of anything helpful to say. After a moment he took a couple of deep breaths and lifted his head. As he moved the phone to one side of his desk, she ventured, "I see that you found your phone."

"Huh?" He looked at the phone and then back at her. "No, it never showed up. Who knows where it is? This morning, I bought a new one." Toby held up his phone. "It's the same model and everything. It even has the same case, except the old one had a big scratch on the back." The brushed silver finish shone faintly under the office light. "It's going to take forever to get my contact list and calendar under control. Without my old SIM card, they couldn't transfer much of anything to this one. Sometimes, I really hate technology!"

Reightman whole heartedly agreed with him about the evil nature of technology, and they shared a few horror stories of their relative ineptness. She enjoyed the banter, but knew it was time to get back to the business at hand.

Before she could redirect the conversation, Toby did. "Detective?"

She sensed, rather than heard, the pain behind his question. "Yes?"

"When will they release him? Geri, I mean. When will they release his body?"

Reightman couldn't even begin to imagine what he must be feeling, and there was no way her answer was going to help. "I don't know, Toby. I'm sorry to have to admit that, but they haven't finished with it – I mean him – yet." He blue eyes begin to cloud again. "I'll do my best to find out and let you know later today, or tomorrow at the latest. I'll try to drop by his personal affects, too. You'll have to sign for them, but I can bring the form along so you don't have to make a trip to collect them."

"Thanks, I'd appreciate it. Grams and I are trying to make plans. For his burial, you know?"

The sad note in his voice was hard for her to hear. "I promise I'll do my best, Toby. "

"I know you will." He looked away for a moment, and wiped a drop of moisture from the corner of one eye. When he turned back around, it was clear that he wanted to change the subject. "So, I guess we'd better determine how I can help, or Madame Zhou will want to know why. I don't want to have her on my case again so I'd just as soon get started."

Reightman appreciated the effort it took him to confront all of the challenges ahead. They talked for a while, agreeing on a plan for the next couple of days. They decided Toby could help most by helping them work through the client records and the spa's financial reports. Reightman arranged a time to meet him the following day and indicated she might be bringing a couple of additional hands. Hopefully, the Chief had been able to free up some help. As she stood to shake his hand, she had a thought. "Toby, I'm sure Geri had a phone, but I don't remember it being found at the scene."

"Yeah, he did. It was the same as mine. The exact same make and model and he even had the same case, except his was scratch-free. We were always getting them mixed up, before…before we didn't spend as much time together. Is there a reason you're looking for it?"

"No, it's just another loose end I need to tie up." She gathered up her purse and turned to leave.

"Detective?"

She looked back at him over her shoulder. "Yes?"

"Well, I was wondering – what do I call you?"

"What do you mean?" Reightman didn't understand the question.

"Since I finally have you calling me Toby, I thought we should settle on something for me to call you."

"Oh." She wondered where the kid was headed. "What's wrong with Detective Reightman?"

Toby wrinkled his nose. "That sounds very uptight."

"Really? You think so?"

"Yep, I do. I was thinking maybe something like…Detective Melba." She frowned at the suggestion, not sure she cared for the informality. He picked up on her indecision and quickly added, "Just when we're alone, and there's no one else around."

Reightman rolled her eyes at his hopeful expression. "Don't push your luck, Mr. Bailey." As his face fell. She thought it over some more and shrugged. "We'll see. Ask me tomorrow."

Pushing through the front door, she stepped outside and checked on Helliman. "Sure is hot outside!" she yelled his way. He didn't even look at her. She snorted at his sweat-soaked shirt and then felt the perspiration running down her neck and her own shirt sticking to her skin. She hoped Madame Zhou's tea worked – this was getting to be ridiculous. She walked to her car and her mind kept turning to the extra phone stashed in her purse. Maybe she should have told Toby about it. Then again, maybe she was right to have kept it to herself. It was probably better to get it checked out first. She stepped onto the hot asphalt of the parking lot. *"Detective Melba, huh?"* She climbed in her car, getting rid of the heavy bag on her shoulder and stowing it on the passenger seat. She started the car and rolled down the windows to let the hot air escape, and then turned the air conditioner on high. As the cool air worked its magic, she picked up the broken shoe heel and held it in her hand for a minute. She ran an internal check of her system and thought through the events of the last couple of days. She realized, with surprise, she didn't even feel cranky. She tossed the heel out the window. *"Detective Melba…I think…I might kind of like it."*

CHAPTER FIVE

THE HONORABLE SUTTON DAMERON, member of the City Council and local politician on the rise, stood in front of the huge mirror in his master bathroom in his white cotton briefs, with a plush towel slung over his shoulder.

He smiled at himself broadly, checking out the results of his latest teeth whitening session. He viewed his 5'7" frame appreciatively as he turned first one way, and then another. He puffed out his chest and pulled in his stomach, lightly slapping his belly. He frowned and slapped again, mentally adding an additional hundred crunches to his workout routine. He turned and twisted to check out his ass. *"Not too bad Dameron!"* He slapped the ass as well. He turned and faced the mirror again and wiped the last traces of shaving gel off of his face with the towel, and leaned in to check for any signs of dark circles or bags under the eyes.

"Shit!" He hurriedly dug through Christina's vanity drawers. *"She has to have some concealer in here!"* After digging through several drawers and disarranging their contents, he finally located what he needed. He carefully daubed a little of the concealer underneath his slightly blood-shoot eyes, applying it with the ring finger of his left hand, as he'd watched his wife do many times. She said the ring finger of the left hand was the weakest, and therefore, the gentlest and best finger to use to avoid bruising the skin around the eyes. He didn't want any bruising.

Once his application was complete, he leaned in and checked out his reflection again. The concealer didn't match. Christina's skin was a shade or two darker than his, and now he looked like a fuckin' raccoon. He grabbed a damp washcloth and washed it off. *"Maybe some eye-drops?"* He located a small bottle and tilted back his head and gently squeezed, blinking rapidly after each drop. He wiped away the trails of moisture running down his face, and checked the mirror again. "*That's better.*" He tilted his head under the lights, checking to make sure no trace of the concealer remained, and caught sight of a gleam of bare skin underneath his bright auburn hair. "*Dammit!*"

He grabbed a comb and made the required adjustment. Then, carefully trying not dislodge his handiwork, he lifted a bottle of Christina's pump-action hairspray and applied a fine mist. He tapped his foot impatiently waiting for the spray to dry. After a moment's consideration, he picked up his wife's blow-dryer and swished it around his head a couple of times to see if the precisely placed and spayed hair moved in the simulated breeze. Satisfied, he turned off the dryer and padded to his mirror again, where he repeated the entire inspection routine.

Pleased with what he saw, he reached his right hand underneath the waistband of his briefs and adjusted himself. He removed his hand and checked out his reflection. He frowned and inserted his hand again, closing his eyes as he fondled himself. He ran his fingers underneath his ball sack and then across the head of his dick a couple of times, until he felt the beginning of modest growth. He quickly re-tucked and looked down, thrusting his hips slightly forward while gazing in the mirror. "*That's my big 'ole monster.*" He smiled and gave his package an appreciative pat before heading to his closet.

He dressed quickly and efficiently. Christina had carefully grouped different combinations of appropriate business wear together so he didn't have to decide for himself what looked good. "*She's a pretty good wife,*" he acknowledged, "*always focused on how to best present the image of a successful and ideal American family.*" She'd been difficult during the last campaign, questioning both his motives and his actions, but now she was even more driven that he was, and aggressively worked to make sure their carefully constructed life was viewed to its best advantage. She served on the best community boards, and was an active member of the Disciples Circle at their conservative, old-line church. All-in-all, she was handling her role with exemplary dedication. "*She's still quite a looker, and she's incredibly flexible,*" he thought with smug satisfaction, recalling past examples of her marital gymnastics. "*Must be all her childhood training, and her weekly workout regimen.*" Whatever it was, he wasn't complaining, although, sometimes a little variety was nice. Sutton grimaced when he thought about the short leash she had him on, insisting that was the only way to avoid any unpleasant surprises during the campaign.

Sutton considered his selection of ties. Christina still left that choice to him, but after checking his appearance for the day, she often made him select an alternate. He reached for a dark blue silk tie he thought would go well with the rest of his ensemble, but it didn't feel quite right. It didn't send exactly the right message for today. After flipping through the selection a few more times, he finally settled on a buttery yellow tie, knowing it was the new preferred shade for power ties. Today, he wanted to appear very powerful. He knotted it carefully and pulled it tight, adjusting the folds until it was perfect.

Christina Dameron was seated in front of her laptop at the big table in the newly remodeled kitchen of their historical downtown home. Her fingers moved rapidly over the keyboard, and she ignored her tension headache as she replied to numerous campaign related questions and fired off a few suggestions of her own. In a few minutes, after Sutton left for his day, she'd begin the process of dressing herself.

Today was the press conference her husband had called. He'd given her very little advanced notice, and there'd been a ton of unexpected complications to handle. The stress was getting to her, and she knew it was important for them all to be at their very best today. She kept the children home from their private church-affiliated school to make sure they were perfectly turned out and looking adorable as they stood by her side, with one of her gentle, loving hands on each one's shoulder. They would all gaze adoringly up at their father, as coached, while Sutton delivered his speech in front of reporters from the city's newspapers and local news stations. "*Who knows?*" she speculated. "*Today a modest, supportive councilman's wife and soon – a United States Congressman's socially powerful spouse.*" She'd worked hard for her position and had sacrificed so many things, including most of her principles, and would to do whatever she needed to ensure their joint ambitions bore fruit.

She took a sip of her coffee and evaluated their chances. "*If it all goes well today, we'll be perfectly positioned.*" Sutton's message of moral steadfastness, coupled with his call for a stronger, more conservative city government should play well, especially when contrasted with the Mayor's recent policies and the ineptness of the City's Police Department in recent days. However, now was not the ideal time to go too far out on a limb, and she hoped the reporters didn't ask too many difficult questions. Sutton was a fair orator when working from prepared and rehearsed materials, but when confronted with uncomfortable questions he rambled, sounding vague and unclear. She'd rehearsed every possible scenario with him over the last two evenings, but one never knew what to expect. She tapped one manicured fingernail against the side of her coffee cup. Sutton had experienced stumbles during this past term, and they'd added up. His frequent vacillations on positions important to his constituency had damaged his credibility, but was nothing compared to his debacle with the new zoning measures he'd proposed and championed, only to see them defeated by some behind-the-scenes political maneuvering. Somehow, he never understood that he was on dangerous ground until it was too late.

If the opposition could garner enough groundswell support, they might hurt the campaign significantly. However, local area voters were notoriously complacent, and Sutton's fund raising efforts were far more successful than any of the other candidates. "It's a damn good thing," she mused. "Our personal financial situation is very tight right now, given so many unexpected expenses." Fortunately, Sutton had the financial and political support of many of the city's more conservative factions, which counted for a lot in a southern community. But she did worry about the increasingly liberal attitude emerging among the voting public, and was even more concerned about the city's new non-discrimination policy. She wasn't sure how either would impact the campaign, but she knew that today, Sutton had to come across as articulate, decisive and morally self-assured or they'd be in trouble. She's done all she could to prepare him and it was now out of her hands.

Sutton came into the kitchen and she got up from her chair to pour him a fresh cup of coffee. She handed it to him, noting with approval the clothing he'd selected. When he took the cup and sloshed a little coffee onto the counter, she frowned. "Tuck in your tie."

"What?"

"Tuck in your tie, Sutton. It will protect it against spills. Coffee almost never comes out of silk." He put his cup on the counter and dutifully tucked the tie underneath the button placket on his French blue shirt. "Are you ready?" she asked.

"Of course I am ready. I'm always ready," he smirked. "I've never been more prepared." He noticed she didn't immediately praise his self-confidence, and she was looking tired and drawn. It must be stress.

"Do you want to go over your speech again?" she asked tiredly "We've got a few minutes before you need to leave."

"No, I don't think so. I don't want it to seem too ~~perfect~~ right now." He took a gulp of hot coffee, glancing ~~over~~ rim of his mug. "You look like hell, Christina. Is something w~~rong~~"

"No, nothing's wrong. The last few days have been really stre~~ssful~~ the incident with…." she broke off at the sharp concerned look he ~~threw~~ her way. She took a resigned breath, knowing nothing must ruffle his ow~~n~~ composure. "No, everything's just fine, Sutton. You know I have complete faith in you." She turned and reclaimed her seat at the table, looking out the bay window into the backyard. *If he fumbles things this time, I don't think I can take care of it like I have in the past.* She gave a small almost imperceptible shake of her head.

"Christina, honey, I'm concerned. It's not like you to be so tense, and you seem distracted. You never mumble to yourself, but you've been doing it a lot over the last four or five days. You need to pull it together. I need you beside me – beautiful and confident."

"I said nothing was wrong. I'm just thinking about all I have to get done this morning before the press conference, that's all."

"The children will be there?" he asked unnecessarily, since she'd assured him multiple times they would be in attendance to witness their father's big moment.

"Of course they'll be there," she snapped. "I've told you a hundred times I had it under control, and you know I kept them home today."

Sutton looked away from her irritated expression and set down his coffee cup. "I knew I could count on you." He checked his cell phone, seeing two missed calls from Lieberman, but no indication of a message. Lieberman was a fat, disgusting dick-wad, but he'd been useful, so he'd call him back later. Right now he had more important things to worry about. He put the phone in the breast pocket of his jacket. "I've really got to run. I have a meeting downtown in a few minutes and don't want to be late." Sutton leaned over and gave her a perfunctory kiss.

"Okay. We'll see you there, Sutton."

"Wish me luck?" he asked, hoping for a sign that she was going to be alright today.

She directed a strained, but sunny smile at him, reaching up from her seat to untuck and smooth down his tie. "Sutton, you don't need any luck. As you said, you've got this." He gave her a satisfied nod, picked up his sleek brief case and his keys, and left, leaving her alone in the kitchen.

Christina collected his empty cup and rinsed it out before placing it in the dishwasher. She leaned against her carefully chosen granite counter

hearsed. I think it's
t at her over the
ong?"

sful and
shot

DONE RUBBED OUT ❖ 99

You better not fuck things up. After the
ry here, you'd better not fuck it up now."
:, turned it on and then hurried upstairs
.y.

❖ ❖ ❖

/eral uninterrupted hours at home Sunday
.ught up on her laundry. She'd feel a little
loɪ、,   ʌing clothes baskets surrounding her bed like
watchful guaɪ˰   ʌe would enjoy the luxury of not having to
search for clean underwˑar for a few days. She'd even done some much
needed grocery shopping, and no longer had to depend on whatever was
lurking and waiting to spoil in the fridge. The refrigerator was now full of
more salad fixings and fresh fruit than it had probably held in its entire
existence. *"I'm almost living like a real human being for a change."* She'd
dutifully prepared and drank the packets of medicinal tea prepared for
her by Zhou. She wasn't certain, but she thought maybe it was helping.
The uncomfortable flashes of heat hadn't been as frequent or as severe
over the last couple of day, but she still was undecided if the tea had
helped her temper. Much to her surprise, she'd also cut out her zinfandel
habit, preferring instead to savor the delicate jasmine tea she'd been
given.

In contrast with her Sunday, the Guzman murder case wasn't going as
well. It wasn't going badly. It just wasn't going anywhere and that
bothered her. Usually, in cases like these, something broke open in the
first couple of day. But, four full days had passed and she had more
questions than answers.

As she began to get dressed Monday morning, she thought it over:
*"Item one; mystery cell phone found in my purse after the super market
incident."* She pulled a blouse from the closet and tried to shake out a few
wrinkles. She'd done her laundry, but there was no way in hell she was
going to ruin a Sunday by ironing. As she pulled it on, she recalled her
conversation with Tom Anderson when she'd dropped off the phone on
Friday.

"What do we have here Detective Reightman?" he asked as she placed
the phone enveloped in its protective sandwich bag on his desk.

"It's a cell phone, Tom."

"I can see it's a cell phone. Where did it come from?" She explained the chain of events that led to the phone being discovered in her purse. "Ouch! That must have hurt." He studied the item through the clear plastic, turning it this way and that. "Do you think it might be connected to the case?"

"I don't know, but I thought it was too much of a coincidence to not bring it in."

"Alright, fair enough. I guess it's better to be safe now, than sorry later. I'll run some prints and get back to you as soon as I can. I'm going to have to squeeze it into the line-up of very important things already on my overfull plate, but I'll do it for you. Don't tell anyone else I'm such a softie or I'll never dig out from under the pile. It'll probably be Monday morning before I can get to it. Will that work?"

"Sure Tom, I know you're swamped."

He finished his initial inspection and jabbed the power button through the plastic covering. He soon gave up, and tossed the phone onto his cluttered desk. "I'll see if I can round up a charger as well – this thing is totally dead. After I check for prints, I'll charge this baby up and we'll see what secrets we can convince it to share. Check with me Monday mid-morning. I should've made some progress by then."

Reightman was relieved to have passed off the problem and could mark another thing off her list. "I appreciate it. Anything else to report?"

He pulled out a folder from the stacking system on the wall. "You know I can't remember anything, Reightman. Thankfully I make outstanding notes. Let me take a look." He quickly reviewed his notes and then tossed the folder on the desk, on top of the phone. "The athletic shoes found in the wash appear to be a tentative match to the marks on the floor. After we sprayed the whole area with chemicals and put it under our super-special-DNA-finding lights, we picked up a few faint footprints. I think the prints mostly likely came from bare feet walking on the floor, lots of different shapes and sizes of bare feet. However, I don't think it's unusual to find those sorts of prints, given the nature of the business. The only other thing to report is we confirmed the blood on the garments belonged to the vic, and there were minute traces of another blood type. Not enough for anything conclusive, but I did note it. It could have come from anywhere. Anything new from the morgue?"

Reightman shook her head in disgust. "No, nothing yet. When Sam checked, Riley informed us that the good doctor was out on sick leave and won't be back until Monday. Riley sent in samples for a toxicology screen, but won't have the results back until the first of the week at the earliest. Too bad it's not like it is on TV. The city budget doesn't make allowances for all kinds of nifty toys and almost everything has to be sent out."

"How well I know, Detective. Some days it seems we don't even have the basics around here."

That pretty much concluded their discussion, and Melba resigned herself to the fact it would be a few days before she had any answers. Bringing her thoughts back to the present, Melba pulled a pair of slacks off a hanger and checked them for wrinkles. They looked pretty good, except for a couple of specks of dryer lint. She picked off what she could and decided no one would notice anyway. She turned her attention back to the case. As of right now, she had nothing except a few minor findings from the crime techs and she was still waiting on Lieberman. Hopefully at least the mystery of the phone would be solved today, so she moved on to the next item.

"Item two: review of all client files and financial records of the Time Out Spa." Melba, Sam and an additional headcount scared up by the Chief had worked through the records over the last couple of days, assisted by Toby. The client list included movers and shakers from across the city and the surrounding area. They'd sorted the list by name, address and profession but so far nothing unusual had popped up, unless you counted the name of some of the customers combined with the variety and nature of the services requested. When she reviewed the initial findings, her eyebrows had shot straight up to her hairline a couple of times. She didn't even want to think about people she knew or saw on a frequent basis getting their backs waxed, or having themselves slathered in Dead Sea clay. And heavens, visualizing a couple of them getting something described as a Total Brazilian would scar her for life. She'd never be able to look them in the eye again.

The financial records told a similar story. Again, she'd been surprised at the amounts of money people paid for things like hot stone massages. The single anomaly was the number of large deposit transactions made over the last couple of months. The transactions simply identified the deposits as cash, and hadn't provided any additional information. Since Geri Guzman had handled most of the banking, Toby wasn't able to offer much insight. He'd have to go down to the bank on Monday and have them pull copies of the actual deposit slips. At least he had offered some explanation why the deposits might be so large. The spa staff often preformed outcalls, and those services were always paid in cash. Apparently, all the full-time and a few part time spa technicians and body workers took on extra offsite appointments. Toby split the payment with them generously, with the spa keeping 70 percent of the earnings and the technician keeping the remainder, plus any tips. According to Toby, the tips were often quite large. The cash was turned in the next morning and included with the day's bank deposit. If the services were provided on Friday after close of business or over the weekend, the deposit was made on Monday. The process made sense to her, but the irregular, large amounts of cash deposited appeared to be excessive.

Melba stood in the open closet door and perused her limited wardrobe choices, trying to decide what jacket to wear. It was going to be hot as blazes today, but still, she liked the extra pockets a jacket gave her. She flipped through the hanging clothes with a sigh. She really needed some new things, but didn't know how she would stretch her dollars. She finally decided to just wear the navy jacket that went with the slacks since finding something else to coordinate seems like too much effort. As she dug out a pair of shoes from the floor of her closet, she realized she'd just reviewed all she had. Nothing else was in process, waiting on tests, needing additional examination or follow-up. There was nothing else to go on. She was in trouble, and desperately needed something to break.

When Reightman reached the office, she stashed her purse in the bottom desk drawer and headed to the breakroom to grab a cup of hot water. She spied Sam hovering near the coffee pot with a couple of others as they waited for the brew to finish. There was a half empty box of donuts on the small table against the wall. "Junkies," she commented, gesturing to the now sputtering machine.

"Pour you a cup, Reightman?" Jackson held up the pot expectantly. He looked crisp and well turned out, as he always did. Some days she hated Sam.

"Nope, I'm just getting some hot water."

"You sick or something?" He poured himself a mug and put the pot back down on the extra burner. He yanked out the brewing basket, emptied the old grounds and reloaded. Coffee went fast around here, even though it was pretty awful. "You usually don't turn down a cup, if it's fresh," he observed. "And this is fresh. I just made it myself."

"Thanks, but no thanks. I'm just getting some hot water." She reached around him to fill her cup from the spigot attached to the hot water reservoir. "I'll pass on that sludge."

"You implying I don't make a good cup of 'joe'?"

"Not implying a thing, Jackson. You make the worst coffee in the entire southeastern part of the United States."

"Do not."

"Do too." Her cup was full. She pulled a teabag out of her jacket pocket and dunked it in the cup, holding the string with one hand. Immediately, the delicious jasmine scent filled the air. Everyone in the room turned her way, sniffing. It sounded like a room full of pug dogs.

"What the hell is that?" asked Jones from his place in line. "Smells like some fancy perfume. Got a hot date tonight, Reightman?" he grinned.

She grinned back – she liked Detective Vince Jones. "Hotter than anything you'll ever handle, Jones." Amid the hoots and hollers that followed, Nancy entered the room, teetering in on unbelievably high platform shoes. She catwalked to the refrigerator to stow her lunch. "What's that smell? Did somebody get flowers?"

"Reightman did, from the hot Monday night date she has lined up." Detective Jones sometimes didn't know when to stop.

"I don't have a date." That set the room off again, because the thought of Reightman having a romantic evening out was hilarious. She ignored them all and dunked the bag a couple of times. "It's tea."

"Tea?" Nancy asked.

"Tea," answered Reightman.

"Tea?" asked about a half dozen of the cops in the room, in tones ranging from disbelief to outright horror.

"Tea," Reightman answered again. "Tea that was given to me by a friend. It has jasmine in it. "

Now, the comments flew fast and furious around the room. "Oh la la." "Fancy pant-cee." "What kind of friend, Reightman? "A 'special' friend?" "Hey, do you put out on first dates, Reightman?" Cops could be such juvenile asses.

She caught Sam's grin from across the room and rolled her eyes in disgust. He just laughed at her expression. Deciding to just ignore them, she turned to Kelly's admin. "Nancy, does the Chief have any time this morning?"

"I'm not sure, Melba. I'll check his calendar when I get to my desk and try to find you a spare couple of minutes if I can, and give you a ring." She smacked her gum. "I stopped here first to drop of my lunch. I didn't want the yogurt to get warm." The room started up again, discussing just how awful yogurt must be. Some of the comparisons were pretty gross. Nancy faced the room and slowly shot the group a finger before striding out of the breakroom on her towering shoes, not giving the wolf whistles any notice. She did glance longingly at the donuts though. This might be a bad week for the diet.

Reightman pulled her teabag out of the cup and tossed it in the trash. "Come on, Jackson. We've got better things to do than hang out with the kids." The room reacted with a few good natured jokes and a couple of smart-ass remarks as she made her way out of room, followed by Jackson.

"When did you take up tea, Melba?" Sam asked as they settled into their desks.

Melba picked up her cup. "Umm...Friday, I think. Zhou gave it to me."

Sam snorted coffee out of his nose. Brushing off his shirt with a napkin, he looked quizzically across the table. "Are you referring to a certain Madame Zhou Li, the old, harmless looking attorney who chewed us up and spit us out last week?" At Melba's nod, he leaned back in his chair and folded his arms across his chest. "When did you two get to the gift giving stage, Reightman?"

"We're not at the gift giving stage, Jackson." When her partner gestured towards her still steeping tea, she added, "It's not like that, Sam. She asked me to stop by for a chat. I did. We discussed things. She assured me of her cooperation and that of Toby Bailey – who you have to admit has been helpful."

"Yes. Mr. Bailey's been very helpful. Still, I can't see you getting all buddy-buddy with old lady Zhou."

"She was just looking out for her client, Sam, and did a damn fine job. I've decided she's..." Melba hated to say it. "She's not *too* bad."

Sam sat up in his chair. "Now I know you're sick."

She picked up the stack of messages on the corner of the desk. "I'm just trying to be fair." She crumpled up a couple of pink slips and dropped them into her trash can. "I wonder if Lieberman made it in today."

"I know he did, Melba – bright and early. A little bird told me the Chief ran into him on the golf course this weekend." Sam tapped the side of his nose. "Word is he bit him right on the ass, and you know the Chief bites hard."

"I do indeed. Wonder when they'll be done with Guzman?"

"I have no idea. Want me to call and see if I can find out?"

"No, I'll do it. Riley owes me a couple of favors."

"My great-aunt Louise, who was four times widowed under somewhat questionable circumstances, always did say it was good when a coroner owed you favors."

"You're a nutcase, Sam. You didn't have a great-aunt Louise," she said good-naturedly as she picked up the phone. "And besides, it's the assistant coroner who owes me favors. The actual coroner hates my guts." She quickly dialed the interoffice number to the morgue. The extension rang several times. Frowning, she hit the release button and tried again.

This time it only rang twice before it was picked up. "City morgue, Assistant Coroner Riley speaking." He sounded out of breath.

"Hey, Riley – it's Reightman. How's it going?"

"Okay, I guess." Riley didn't sound too sure. "Are you alright, Detective?" he asked in a hushed voice.

That was weird. "Yes, I'm perfectly fine. Why wouldn't I be?"

Riley gave a relieved sigh, and then caught himself. "I...I was just being polite.

"You sound a little frazzled this morning. Is Lieberman giving you shit?" Reightman heard him catch his breath.

"How'd you guess?" he asked after a second.

"I know Lieberman, Riley. Don't let him get to you."

"I try not to, but man! He's on a tear today. He wasn't happy about me sending the Guzman samples out for toxicology reports. He's been on my ass all morning about absolutely everything."

"Just let it roll off your back if you can. It won't last."

"That's what I usually tell myself...Good morning, City Morgue. What can I help you with, Detective Reightman?" His voice was suddenly very formal. Lieberman must have walked in on the call.

Reightman played along. "I was calling to check on the status of the Guzman autopsy. Any idea when the coroner will be done?"

"Not for sure, ma'am. I think we should be finished by the end of the day."

"That would be good. I've had inquiries related to the release of the body, and I wanted to provide an update. You think you'll be wrapped up and able to release it in the next day or so?

"That should be fine, Detective."

"He still listening?"

"Yes, ma'am. I'll tell him that you called." She heard him sigh with relief. Lieberman must have gone. "Detective Reightman, he is being really, really weird."

"Weird how, Riley?"

He hesitated. "I'm not sure. He's jumpy and really secretive. He's keeping all information related to this autopsy really close to his chest. He's even sending me off on stupid errands when I should be helping. He's not letting me do my job."

Reightman was silent, thinking about what that might mean. Lieberman was always a pain in the ass, but at least she didn't have to deal with him on a daily basis. "It's probably nothing, Riley. He's been out sick for a day or so. Maybe he's just not feeling well."

"That's not it! I think he's – Yes, ma'am." He switched back into professional mode again. "Yes, we'll call you as soon as we're through, and have the results ready. It should be sometime later this afternoon. I'll give you a call." Riley hung up without even a goodbye.

"What's up, Melba?" Jackson asked when he noticed the crease in her forehead.

"I don't know. Things seem a little tense down in the morgue." She tapped a pen against the edge of her desk.

"Things are always tense down in the morgue, Melba. All those dead people don't make for a restful work environment. "

"You'd think they would, wouldn't you? After all, being dead, they don't talk all the time. Unlike you."

Jackson shook his head sadly at her feeble attempt to bait him. "Just finish your tea, Detective." As Melba tilted the cup back and drained it, he asked, "What's on the to-do list for today?"

"Well, since I haven't heard from Nancy yet, I have to assume the Chief is swamped and won't be able to fit us in this morning. We could head down to Capital Street and interview the other shop owners. It's a long shot, but they might have seen something." She looked at him across the table. "We just can't sit here working crossword puzzles all day."

Jackson put the puzzle book in his top desk drawer. "It's Sudoku."

"Whatever." She stood up, checked her weapon and pulled her purse out of the desk drawer. "Ready?"

"Ready when you are," Jackson confirmed as he pulled his jacket off of the back of his chair and slung it over his shoulder.

As they made their way through the maze of hallways leading out of the building and to the parking lot, they happened upon Lieberman in the middle of a hushed and hurried conversation with Helliman. Both men looked up at their approach and Helliman scurried away, leaving Lieberman alone in the hall. The coroner didn't look too good.

"Doctor," said Jackson. "Good to see you back at work. Hope you're feeling better."

Reightman watched the fleshy doctor closely. A few drops of sweat were popping out on his forehead. She knew the feeling.

"I'm fine, Detective Jackson." He didn't look fine, he looked a wreck. "If you'll excuse me, I need to get back to work. I've got a lot to catch up on."

"Yes, you do, Doctor," Reightman decided to sharply remind him exactly how much he had to do today. "I'm anxiously awaiting your findings on the Guzman case, and I'd appreciate them sooner, rather than later. I can't accept any further delays."

The doctor's red face paled at her strident tone. "Well...yes – I'd better get back downstairs then. Excuse me."

They watched as he plodded down the hall. Sam grunted. "I think he's scared of you, Reightman, but that doesn't surprise me." Sam shook his head slowly as he watched the coroner move down the hall. "Something makes me really hate that guy, Melba. Not sure why, but I just can't stand him."

"I know what you mean, Sam. Something about him just rubs me the wrong way." Reightman snorted in disgust. "Hey, I just remembered something. I need to pick up Guzman's personal affects. I told Mr. Bailey I'd drop them by."

"Good thing you remembered before we left. I wouldn't want to turn around again and come back for them. I don't know if I could stand your driving for that long."

"Sam, you...are...an...ass. Besides, my driving's not that bad."

"If you say so, Melba."

"I do say so, Sam. So shut up and come on."

About fifteen minutes after the two detectives left the building, a uniformed desk officer laid a white sealed envelope on Reightman's desk, right on top of the remaining pink message slips.

CHAPTER SIX

O N MONDAY MORNING, Toby slept in. He hadn't been sleeping well. He'd toss and turn, and when he finally did sleep, he'd wake a few hours later from a bad dream or maybe just restless energy. Sunday night he'd only been able to drift down into sleep sometime after two in the morning. He was still asleep – dreaming of the past.

"Keep your eyes shut, Toby Bailey."

"But I'm blindfolded. I couldn't see even if I did open 'em," Toby protested.

"Well, be that as it may...don't let me catch you peaking!" Gram admonished as Geri led him by the hand, laughing at Toby's awkward progress. He kept his eyes shut, even though he didn't care for surprises. But, to make his Grams happy, he'd play along.

Geri carefully pulled him along, telling him when there was a rock or uneven patch in the gravel driveway and keeping him from stumbling too badly. Finally, after what seemed a long time, they stopped. He felt Geri's hands on his shoulders, turning him around.

"Alright Toby Bailey, you can take the blindfold off!" Grams called out, giving him permission to look.

He carefully slipped the knotted dish towel from his eyes and pulled it over his nose and down around his neck. He opened his eyes, blinking in the sudden brightness of the afternoon sunlight. He focused his eyes and then stared at what was in front of him.

"Don't you like it? Grams asked him after a minute, sounding worried. "If you don't, you can blame Geri here, since he helped pick it out."

Sitting at the end of the gravel driveway right in front of the detached garage where Grams parked her car, was...his car?

Toby walked over to the four-door sedan, running his hands down the metallic silver sides. He walked all the way around before he looked back at Grams and Geri. "Is this for me?"

"Of course it is, Toby!" After a moment had passed where he didn't say anything, Grams added "It's a used car. Didn't see any point in buying a brand new one. Besides, your Gramps wouldn't have approved. He always said a low mileage used car was a better deal, because it had already proven its worth, plus the tags didn't cost as much. It's pretty nice though. It'll do what's needed."

"What do you mean, Grams?" he asked, not understanding.

"It will take you away when it's time for you to go, and bring you back again whenever you need to be here, at home. Even just for a little bit…"

…and the dream shifted…

"What do you want to do for a living Geri? I mean, when the summer is over." They were sitting at a picnic table under a big pin oak tree in the city park. Geri twirled a leafy twig in his hands.

"Don't know. I guess I haven't thought about it much."

"Don't you think it is time to think about it? It's gonna' be August in another ten days. Summer is more than half over."

"Yeah, I know."

"Are you planning to go back to Florida?" Toby asked, afraid to know, but having to know all at the same time.

"No!" Geri threw down the twig with force. A few of the narrow dark green leaves flew off the now broken twig and lay in the dirt. "I'll never go back there." He jumped out of his seat and took off towards the pond.

Toby stood up and brushed off his shorts. He made his way slowly down to the water's edge, where Geri sat on a rock pitching pebbles into the water. Each time a pebble hit with a 'plonk' little ripples of water ran across the pond's surface. Geri waited until the water stilled before throwing in another. Toby crouched down near the water and scooped up a hand of pebbles for himself. He joined his friend in tossing a pebble and then watching the ripples.

"You want to talk about it?" he asked without looking at Geri. "About why you won't ever go back there."

"No." Plonk. Ripple. "Well, maybe." Geri picked up a few more small rocks. "There's nothing for me back there."

Plonk.

"My mom doesn't want me – never really did," he said dejectedly, keeping his face turned toward the pond. "The man she's been with for the last six years is a mean bastard. Unlike her, he wants me too much ...if you know what I mean."

Plonk. Ripple…plonk.

"He started to get more insistent a few months ago, making suggestive comments and touching me all the time. One night when my mom was out scoring a hit of something, I was trying to fix some dinner, and he…came up behind me. Before I knew it, he managed to grab my arms and twisted me down to the floor. He held me down on the scuffed linoleum floor and he….."

Plonk.

Toby sat very quietly, holding his pebbles tightly in his hand, afraid to move or look up at his friend.

"I fought him, Toby – I did! I got a couple of good licks in, but he was a lot bigger and stronger – he smelled like cheap beer and dirty sweat." Toby looked up at him, but still didn't say a word. Geri was crying, and the tears running down his face broke Toby's heart. "I'll never let anyone have power over me again, Toby. I'll be bigger and stronger and meaner and smarter than they are. I'll be prepared for bad things." Geri brushed his eyes with a trembling angry hand. "I'll never go back to Florida again."

"Why didn't you tell me?" Toby threw his handful of rocks and a dozen pebbles hit the water one at a time.

Geri stood up and looked down to where Toby sat. "I was afraid you wouldn't–" his voice broke, "wouldn't want to be around me anymore. You can do better."

Toby stood up and faced him. "Maybe I can – maybe I can't. I don't know anything except I don't want to do any better right now. Not unless you decide you don't want me as your friend and maybe… maybe more one of these days." He held Geri's eyes steady with his pale blue ones, and Geri finally smiled.

Toby reached out his hand for another pebble, and after a minute, Geri gave him one. Now, they each held a single pebble in their hands. They turned and flung their final stones into the water, watching as they hit the pond's surface and broke the sky's reflection into a million shimmering pieces. The ripples merged and soon Toby couldn't tell where one started and the other ended.

"Let's go home Geri." Toby said and…

…the dream changed again.

They were all seated at the big kitchen table: he and Geri and Grams.

"…and I'm telling you, Toby H. Bailey, you're not going off to some fly-by-night massage school in Lord-knows-where, and that's final!"

"But, Grams, you know that's what I want to do. If I'm going to open a fancy spa one day, I need to learn." He'd finally shared his dream with the two of them, shyly bringing out the notebook where he had taped and pasted in the pictures and articles of high-end resorts and spas that he'd cut out and collected for years. He'd carefully explained to both of them what he was thinking. He hadn't expected her reaction.

"There's more than one way to do most things, Toby." She got up and went to her sink. "Let me think on it a minute." She started drying and putting away the few dishes that were sitting in the drainer. Toby and Geri sat at the table looking down at the open notebook.

After she finished up she dried her hands on a towel and turned around. "I really want you to get an education. I want you to go to a real school." As he started to repeat his argument that college wasn't for him, she held up a hand. "Let me finish." She poured a cup of coffee from the pot and joined them at the table, sighing as she sat down. "I know you say that you don't want to go to a four year school, and that's fine if it's what you really mean. But how can you know until you've tried it?" When she got no response from her grandson, she tried a different approach. "I think the best thing would be to start with a two-year school. You can get a good grounding in the basics and take some business courses, which you'll need if this," she tapped her closed fist on the notebook, "is what you really want to do. You can take your massage classes at the same time, as long as you keep your grades up."

"I rather stay here than go away to some college."

"You can't stay here, Toby."

He looked up at her, shocked. "But, Grams–!"

"Toby Bailey," she reached for his hand and held it tight. "I love you more than I've ever loved a single person, other than your grandfather. You know that, don't you?" She waited until he gave her a small nod, then released his hand, and brushed the hair back from his eyes "But now, it's time for you to go and discover that there's more to the world than this tiny little town can offer. This place will always be here," she said, indicating the kitchen and by association, the house, "when you need it, and so will I for as long as the Lord is willing. But, Toby, you have to go."

"It'll be too expensive, Grams."

She laughed, then got up and left the room. She came back a short time later with a little oblong booklet that he recognized as coming from the local bank. She handed it to him. "This account is in both our names, Toby. It's the money from your momma's insurance and what we got from selling the house you both lived in. Open it."

Toby pulled open the cover and flipped a couple of pages. He looked up at her with his eyes wide and his mouth open. "But Grams, this is a lot of money."

"No, Toby. In today's world it isn't a lot of money, but it will be more than enough to get you started on chasing your dream. That's what it's meant to be used for." He looked down at the account book, trying to take it in all in.

"Toby?" she asked and waited until he looked up. "Tomorrow you and I are going down to the bank and you're going to open an account– separate from the savings account you have had for the last few years. I'm not going to put all of this in it right now – just enough to get things started and give you a little independence. After that, we'll decide what to do together."

"Okay, Grams." He was still a little shell shocked.

Geri looked up from staring at the vinyl table covering. "You have to go Toby. It's important. Don't worry – I'll still be waiting here for whenever you come back on breaks and over the summer."

"No, you won't," Grams corrected him.

"What?" Geri tried to swallow his fear. He was afraid he would no longer be welcome here with Toby away at school.

"You won't be here, Geri. You'll be wherever Toby decides to head."

"But I can't! There's no way I could –"

"You can and you will, Geri Guzman. It doesn't cost much more to educate two instead of one if they live together someplace inexpensive, and," she tapped the bankbook, "there is plenty of resource to do it. I think my grandson would agree." When Toby grinned and nodded across the table in acknowledgement she nodded in approval. "That's what I thought."

"But…" Geri started to protest again.

"Just shut your mouth for a minute, Geraldo H. Guzman!" Grams held up one of her hands until she was sure he was going to let her have her way without further argument. "It's settled." She rose from the table and gave a tired sigh. "I'm worn out and am going to bed. I expect you two to do a little research and pick a couple of places to at least look over by morning. Summer is almost over, and you've both wasted enough time." She kissed them both on the top of their messy heads. "Good night."

Toby and Geri looked at each other across the table. Geri spoke first. "Toby, are you sure about all of this?"

"Yep."

"I feel funny, Toby, about using your money, and everything."

"Don't be a dumb ass, Geri! I didn't even know I had any money until about ten minutes ago. Besides, I really want you to come with me, wherever we decide to go to school."

"If you're sure…"

"I am."

"Okay then." Geri stood. *"I think I'll go on back to my cousin's. It's getting late and I've got some things to think about."* He headed toward the outside door and stood looking out the screen. *"Toby?"*

"Yeah, Geri?"

"I won't let you down – I promise. I'll pull my weight and contribute my fair share. I don't know how, but I will, and I'll keep doing it however I can. That's the only way I can come with you, and stay with you. You understand?"

"Yes. I think you're being silly, but I think I can understand."

"Good." He thought of something and turned around and asked *"Toby, what does the 'H" stand for?*

Toby concentrated for a minute then grinned a big grin. "The 'H' stands for 'hellion' Geri. I think Grams just decided you needed a middle name. It's the same one she gave me."

Geri pushed open the screen door and went out into the night.

Toby set at the big table flipping through the notebook in the quiet kitchen. "H" also stands for home, Geri," he said. As he listened to the June bugs fight to find the light through the window, he thought about the possible future. "H" stands for home," he said again, softly and…

…woke up.

Melba and Sam headed downtown, with Sam insisting he be the one to drive. Melba occasionally mimed holding tight to the handle above her window while placing a hand over her heart. Sam didn't find it very funny. About halfway to their destination Melba's phone rang. She dug it out of her purse and answered, "Detective Reightman."

"Hey, Melba, sorry I didn't call you earlier." Melba could hear Nancy chewing her gum. "Chief's pretty booked and all, but he has a minute now if you want to talk with him."

"Sure, Nancy, Jackson and I are just on our way down to Capital Street."

"Great – I'll put him through," she popped the gum. "Hold on a sec." Reightman listened to the department's version of hold music, while Nancy connected Kelly.

"Reightman, you there?' the Chief's voice interrupted the painful Muzak rendition of a popular eighties hit.

"Yes, Chief. Thanks for finding a minute to talk. Nancy said you were pretty busy today."

"Busy as hell. I've been ass deep working with the city planners on the damned Labor Day festivities. I snatched a minute while the assistant to the assistant city manager takes a bio break.

"I totally forgot this was Labor Day weekend."

"It snuck up on me too. Don't forget we're all on call. The city planners are anticipating record numbers out on the streets and we've got that danged parade to cover. Why anyone thinks it's a good idea to have the high school bands marching in those heavy uniforms in August is beyond me. The powers that be have requested every available officer to be on standby."

"Great! There goes the weekend. Abby and the kids were planning to come down for a visit," she said with disappointment. She'd been looking forward to seeing her grandkids.

"Sorry, Reightman. You'd better give Abby the head's up. Now, what's the reason you requested this cozy little chat?"

"I just wanted to give you an update on where we are with the Guzman murder, Chief." She filled him in on the case and outlined their plan for the day. She mentioned the phone she'd dropped off with Tom Anderson, and her hope that Lieberman would soon be finished with the autopsy.

"He better be finished soon! He needs to get the lard out of his ass. Anything else, Reightman?"

"No, sir, I think that's all."

"Good, because Nancy's signaling through the door that the city flunky is headed back this way. Later."

"Later, sir." Reightman stuffed the phone back into the bag while Jackson parked the car in front of one of the buildings on the block. "That sucks! I forgot about this being Labor Day weekend. I was looking forward to seeing the girls."

"Well, you know what they say."

"What do they say, Sam?"

"They say 'them's the breaks' in this glamourous, highly paid and vastly envied profession."

They cracked the windows, got out of the sedan and headed to the first business on their list. They entered the empty bookstore and looked around, hoping to spot someone. "Hello?" Reightman called out. "Anyone here?"

"Just a second," a high reedy voice answered, before the door leading into the back of the shop opened. A middle-aged man carrying a dusty box of books met them in the middle of the store. "Sorry about that. I'm trying to restock this morning. Monday's are usually slow and I try to get as much done as possible." He sat the box on the counter and brushed some dust off of his hands. "Can I help you with something?"

"I'm Detective Jackson and this is Detective Reightman." Both showed him their badges. "We're hoping to ask you a few questions. Would now be a convenient time?" Jackson's tone clearly indicated that an affirmative response would be the only correct answer.

"Sure, Detectives. Like I said, Monday mornings are pretty slow, so I'll have plenty of time to finish the restocking later. I'll probably be glad of the delay once the afternoon rolls around and I'm searching for something to keep myself busy." He tugged on the long faded red beard that was a shade or two darker than his graying hair. "Can I ask what this is about?"

"Certainly Mr....?'

"I'm Herman the Red, the owner of this place," he gestured expansively with his thin arms to indicate the glory of their surroundings.

"Herman the Red?" asked Jackson, writing notes on the small pad he carried. "Did I hear you correctly?"

Herman looked a little sheepish. "Well, my real name is Herman Jones, but I go by Herman the Red. It seemed to fit the ambiance of the place better." At their questioning looks he shrugged. "The name of this store is "The Colors of Life" and I thought a name with a ...well, with an actual color in it would be better, from a PR standpoint and all. Plus, it goes with the beard." He tugged again then looked at the detectives expectantly. "Get it?"

Jackson was looking a little nonplussed, so Reightman stepped in. "Mr. Red, we wanted to ask a few questions related to the recent murder of Mr. Geraldo Guzman. We're canvasing the street and checking with all of the businesses to see if anyone heard or saw anything unusual that night."

"Yes, I heard the unfortunate news of Geri's death. It's a tragedy a young life was ended so suddenly and in such a violent way." Herman inclined his head and pressed his palms together, apparently giving Guzman's memory a moment of respectful silence. "I was worried the last time I saw him."

"When was that Mr....Red?" Jackson held his pencil at ready.

The proprietor gently stroked his beard and closed one slightly rheumy eye. "It must have been last Tuesday. I was sweeping the front sidewalk to banish negative energy from the entrance and I saw him crossing the street. I always dispel negativity by sweeping on Tuesday afternoons."

Before Jackson could make any sort of comment which might add to the aforementioned negativity, Reightman asked, "Why were you worried?"

"Because of his aura."

"His aura?"

"Yes. His colors were quite muddied. A muddy aura usually signals a soul in turmoil, or one about to face great unpleasantness." Reightman kept her face totally still, making an effort not to show any expression. She saw Jackson give a quick roll of his eyes. Herman the Red noticed. "You may scoff if you like, but I'm very well-known for my aura reading skills. I'm never wrong about the impressions I receive from the guardians of the plane."

Reightman intervened hastily, "Please excuse my partner, Mr. Red. We're not used to this sort of thing. Speaking for both of us, I'm sure you're the best of your kind around." She waited for Mr. Red to accept her apology, and after he thought it over , he grudgingly acquiesced. "Sir, did anything else strike you as unusual?"

Herman the Red shook his head, causing the beard to wobble its way across his thin chest. "No, Detective, I can't. After I saw his disturbed color halo, I stopped my sweeping and came inside to offer a small plea of intercession for him. I'm afraid it took me some time to appropriate the spirits, and when I came back outside there was no one else around."

Jackson carefully replaced the notebook and pencil in his breast pocket. He didn't meet her eye.

"Well, thank you for your help." She handed him her card. "My number is on the card. If you think of anything else I'd appreciate it if you'd give me a call."

"Certainly." He picked up the box of books and headed toward the shelves. As they made their way to the door he called out, "Detectives?"

"Yes, Mr. Red?"

"Can I interest either of you in a healing crystal?" he held out a bowl filled with sparkling purple, pointy-ended stones. "I have a very nice selection and they're half price today. Or, perhaps, an energy pyramid?"

Jackson inched closer to the door. Reightman smiled and replied for both of them, "It's very nice of you to offer, but I don't think we are in the market for either today." She wondered if all of the shop owners on Capital Street were such odd ducks as those she'd already met. She exited the bookstore as Jackson held the door. He didn't say a single word about their interview with Herman the Red, although he did pull out his handkerchief and wipe his brow.

Once outside, they headed down the sidewalk. Toby Bailey was crossing the street to meet them. He carefully looked both ways then broke into a jog. He was wearing only a pair of short nylon shorts and a pair of running shoes and was holding a sports bottle.

"Hey, Detectives," he greeted them and took a drink.

"Good morning Mr. Bailey. You look like you've worked up quite a sweat," answered Reightman, shielding her eyes from the glare, and noticing the sunlight glinting off the fine line of hair that travel downward from his navel. She quickly looked away, embarrassed for some reason. She imagined Zhou Li spying on him from her window and her embarrassment faded. As Zhou said, she wasn't dead yet.

"Yeah, I went for a run. I slept later than expected and was groggy when I woke up. I thought a little exercise might do me good and help me settle my mind."

"It's hot out here already," Jackson commented as he tucked his handkerchief back in his pocket.

"Sure is," Toby agreed. "Detective Reightman, when I saw you guys over here I thought I'd check what time you wanted to meet this afternoon. I have a few errands to run and don't want to keep you waiting."

"We still have a couple places to stop by this morning. We're interviewing all the shop owners on the block to see if any of them have noticed any strange activity over the last couple of weeks. It'll probably take us a while to finish up, and then Detective Jackson and I need to head back to the office for a while. I have a couple of items to take care of and Detective Jackson needs to pick up his own car, so he can follow up on some other things." She calculated how much time that might take, and padded her estimate a little to account for a quick lunch. "Why don't we say three o'clock? That should give us enough time to do everything. Will that be convenient for you?"

"Sure. My schedule's pretty flexible right now until…until we're able to open up again." He looked toward his spa and then back to the Detectives, wiping a small rivulet of water off his face. "Uh! I really should head to the shower and wash off all this sweat. I probably smell disgusting. See you at three." He jogged back across the street toward his apartment. He stopped as Madame Zhou exited her shop. They talked for a minute and Toby pointed them out from across the street before heading up the stairwell. Madame Zhou placed her palm above her eyes to protect them from sunlight and motioned for them to come over.

"We've already seen the wizard so we might as well go talk to the witch," Jackson grumbled.

She jabbed him with her elbow. "Come on, Jackson. Don't be a cowardly lion."

"Whatever you say, Dorothy."

They crossed the street, watching for any traffic. Zhou Li greeted them a cheery "Good morning Detectives! I was wondering if you've already had lunch."

"No, we haven't Madame Zhou." Reightman's stomach growled at the idea of food, and she tried to ignore it. "But we can't stop just yet. We've really got a lot on our plates today, and we need to get in a couple more interviews before we head back to the station."

"It is important to take regular sustenance, Detective Reightman. It helps to properly regulate the body. Joining me will allow you both to have a decent lunch, and to talk to another business owner."

Reightman's stomach growled again, signaling its agreement. "Where were you planning to eat, Madame?"

"Over across the street, of course." She pointed toward Earth Fruits Café. "They serve excellent food, and I think it's always a good idea to support the neighborhood businesses."

After sharing a questioning look with his partner, Jackson lifted one shoulder in a half shrug, resigned to his fate. Reightman looked at her watch and decided it couldn't hurt to indulge her. "I suppose that would be fine. After all, we have to eat sometime."

"Good. Kindly lend me your arm, Detective Jackson. I could use the extra assurance of a strong man's arm. I wouldn't want to fall." Reightman suppressed an involuntary grin. She couldn't decide which she was enjoying more; Zhou Li's charming flirting or Jackson's grave, expressionless courtesy as he offered his arm and slowly escorted the old lady to the corner and then across the street. *"It's kind of cute,"* Reightman decided as she trailed slightly behind. Once they arrived at the eatery of choice, Jackson escorted Zhou Li inside while Reightman held the door for them.

"Good day, my dear," Madame greeted the young woman who met them inside the door. "There will be three of us for lunch. A booth would be nice if there's one available."

"There's one open over by the wall. It's a little close to the TV, but it's the only one free right now."

"That will be acceptable," the old lady replied. They made their way to the booth via a somewhat circuitous path between several filled tables. Once seated, Zhou Li smiled at them across the booth. "Now isn't this nice?"

They both agreed that it was, as they looked around the space.

The Earth Fruits Café was reasonably sized, with several paper covered tables set at angles in the center and a handful of booths lined up against one wall. On each of the tables was an antique glass cola bottle with a few wild flowers poked into its neck. Every table had the expected assortment of salt, pepper, and varieties of hot sauce, placed beside small metal racks holding packets of raw, unrefined sugar. A door led somewhere to the back; presumably the kitchen. There was a small cooler filled with an assortment of unfamiliar beverages and a couple of cake stands filled with pastries and cookies. A wide, flat-screened television hung from a bracket high on the wall to the left of the booth, positioned so that everyone could see it easily. The cash register was positioned near the door on a counter displaying a few items for sale. The décor was enhanced by vintage protest signs and an assortment of old, rusted farm implements.

The TV was tuned to Channel 7's local midday feature, *Lunch with Lydia Larson*. The 'news-ertainment' show, a catchy phrase coined by Lydia herself, offered blended coverage on current fashion trends, local events of importance, a short weather update, and political commentary. Reightman thought it was a random collection of crap, but it was popular with area viewers, and both the show's hostess and lead commentator had inexplicitly received a variety of broadcast awards over the last few years. At least the volume was turned down.

After a short wait, a new server stepped up to their booth and asked, in a bored voice, "What can I get you to drink?" while passing around menus. Jackson asked for an iced tea, while Reightman and Zhou Li both requested mugs of hot water with accompanying glasses of ice water.

"What kind of tea do you want?" the server asked Jackson. She tapped her sock and sandal covered foot impatiently.

He looked confused since no one ordered anything but sweet tea around here. "What kind do you have?"

The girl pointed to the chalkboard hanging near the television. The entire thing was covered in tea listings and was decorated in colored chalk-drawn flowers. The flower faces were accentuated with small round eyes and big curvy smiles.

"Uh…just regular tea I guess."

The server wrote something on a pad of paper and then crammed it down into her apron pocket. "I'll bring the drinks in a minute and then I'll take your food orders."

"Lindsey is such an interesting individual," offered Madame Zhou as she arranged her cutlery to her satisfaction.

"Is Lindsey the owner?"

"No, Detective Jackson. Lindsey is our server. I think she spells it with an 'i' at the end." Reightman and Jackson digested that piece of information. "The owner's name is Bernice Williams. She has been very successful with this place. I believe she learned to cook while she was serving in the Army."

Lindsey, who Sam and Melba now knew was 'Lindsi,' arrived back at the table carrying a tray with their drinks. "Water, hot water, water, hot water, and one *regular* tea," she announced, placing the drinks in their respective places. Zhou Li and Melba both retrieved tea packets from their bags and placed them in their mugs of hot water. Zhou Li nodded approvingly across the table to Melba.

"I'll take your food order now," Lindsi announced tonelessly.

Zhou Li looked at the server and politely ordered. "I'll have today's special, dear."

"And for you, sir?"

Jackson had been hurriedly scanning the menu. "I don't see anything with meat."

Lindsi quickly educated him in a disapproving voice. "We don't serve meat or any animal products. They are *bad* for you. They sit in your gut and rot for days after eating them. We only serve dishes prepared with the freshest fruits and vegetables, harvested sustainably from the earth. We do not serve anything that was living, that will live, or that comes from the living."

"Aren't fruits and vegetable living?"

Lindsi offered him a disgusted sneer. "No. Animals live. Fruits and vegetables grow."

Jackson was thoroughly perplexed now.

"Detective Jackson, perhaps I can help?" Zhou Li offered." Will you allow me to order for you?"

He gave her a hesitant, "Okay."

"Lindsi, dear, this gentleman will have the eggplant filet, a side of crispy kale chips and, hmmm….yes, an order of the delightful carrot slaw Bernice prepares."

Reightman noticed Jackson's eyes were looking kind of wild.

"And for you, ma'am?" Lindsi inquired while raising a single eyebrow and showing off the bright blue piercing that decorated the upper portion of her face.

Reightman closed her menu. "I'll have the special as well."

Lindsi dutifully scribbled some more on her pad and then tucked it into the front of her canvas apron. As the girl turned, Reightman noticed the back of her t-shirt was imprinted with the slogan, "Join the Feral Cat Project." She decided not to ask. They all made small talk, commenting on the heat and offering their opinions about the planned Labor Day festivities, until Lindsi arrived with the food.

"Two daily specials and one eggplant filet with Kale chips and carrot slaw," she announced, placing down the food. "Can I get you anything else?"

"I don't think so, dear," replied Zhou Li, eying her food appreciatively through her thick lensed eyewear. "But, could you please ask Bernice if she would spare us a moment when she has time?"

Lindsi thought it over *completely* before committing herself. "I can do that," she eventually decided, and walked away leaving them to enjoy their meals.

Reightman looked down at her food. There was a bowl of some sort of cool, green soup garnished with what looked like toasted seeds and a single slice of cucumber with dill. To the side of the bowl was a large slice of hearty multi-grained bread with a pale yellow spread. She ventured a bite. "This is really good!" she exclaimed in surprise.

Zhou Li smiled up from her own serving and nodded. "Bernice is really very talented. She is always creating interesting and delicious things. You should taste her chickpea juice meringue. How is your food, Detective Jackson?"

He was staring down at his order, exploring it with a fork. "There are yellow raisins in the slaw."

"Why, yes, there are!" Zhou was delighted with his discovery. "Isn't that a nice touch?"

Reightman watched out of the corner of her eye as Jackson took a hesitant forkful of his meal. He carefully placed it in his mouth and closed his eyes. He chewed slowly, waiting to see if anything chewed back, and then opened his eyes and took another bite. Pretty soon he was eating at a good pace, although he still had a slightly doubtful expression on his face. Conversation lagged as they enjoyed the food. Before they had finished, a woman, who Reightman assumed was the owner, came to their table.

"How's the food?" the sturdy woman asked.

"It is wonderful as always, Bernice. You do such marvelous things with garden vegetables."

"Thanks, Madame Zhou." The woman was obviously pleased at the compliment. "If you like that, you should see what I can do with an apricot and a few kumquats." She pulled an empty chair over from another table and took a seat. "Lindsi said you wanted to see me?"

"Yes. Thank you for making time – I know you're busy. You must be pleased with the success of this place."

"I am," Bernice replied as she bent down to retie the laces of her steel toed boot. "Business has been pretty good."

"I am delighted for you, Bernice. Allow me to make introductions if you will. This, is Detective Reightman," she indicated Melba, "and this, is Detective Jackson. They're both with the City Police Department. Detectives, allow me to introduce Bernice Williams, the proprietress and creator of these wonderful meals." Each nodded to the other, and Reightman wiped her hands on a napkin and shook hands with Bernice. Zhou continued, "They were hoping to ask you a few questions about the days immediately preceding the horrible murder at the spa."

"Poor Toby. I really feel for him. He must be going through a terrible time." Bernice replied, obviously sad for the young business owner from the neighborhood. "I'm happy to answer any questions I can, Detectives."

"Thank you, Ms. Williams." Reightman hesitated a second to allow for any other preferred forms of address to be offered. When none were forthcoming, she continued. "Can you tell us if you've noticed anything unusual or out of the ordinary over the last couple of weeks? "

"Like what?"

"Like any strange people hanging around the area, or things that struck you as odd, especially in the evening hours."

Bernice gave a little chuckle. "There are always strange people hanging around, Detective. Just check out this lunch crowd, not to mention the people that operate businesses on this block. But, I take your meaning." Bernice thought for a moment, running a weathered hand across her brush-cut gray hair. "Can't say I have, but I'm usually pretty wiped out by the end of the day. I try to head out around 4:30 in the afternoon when I'm able. We don't offer dinner, only breakfast and lunch."

Reightman tried not to show her disappointment. She rummaged in her purse and pulled out a card. "If you do think of anything, please give me a call. The number is on the card. Thanks again."

About that time, one of the regulars shouted, "Turn up the tube, Bernice! That little prissy balding guy from the City Council is getting ready to talk. Let's hear what bullshit he spouts today."

"Sure thing, Charlie." Bernice pulled a remote control from her apron and turned and pointed it at the television, pushing the volume button a couple of times. They all adjusted themselves to better view the TV.

"And now, city viewers, we're going live to the steps of City Hall, where Councilman Sutton Dameron will address members of the press!" Lydia Larson's blue eyes widened in joyful anticipation. The cameras cut to a view of City Hall, where a sizable number of people were gathered. A rank of microphones was stationed at the top of the steps, and to one side stood a woman with her arms resting on the shoulders of two children dressed in matching outfits. A gentle breeze ruffled the woman's peach colored linen dress, which hit just below the knee and bared the lady's arms. *"That must be the Councilman's wife,"* Reightman thought, noticing her large, sparkling pendant, which looked like it cost a pretty penny.

Councilman Dameron eventually made his way up the steps, stopping to shake hands and greet supporters. A few held up campaign placards which read "Vote for Sutton Dameron – for HE shall lead the way!" Reaching the top of the steps, the Councilman stepped behind the microphones. Reightman noticed a small step stool partially hidden behind the podium, and grinned when she discovered he was using it to increase his height.

Dameron held up his hands to quiet the cheering and clapping crowd and then cleared his throat a couple of times before starting his address. "Fellow citizens of this great city, and ladies and gentlemen of the press, allow me to express my appreciation for each of you who chose to join Christina," he indicated the woman in the peach dress, "my two wonderful children, and me on this glorious summer afternoon." The crowd applauded enthusiastically until the Councilman motioned for quiet.

"I know that many of you have more important and critical things to do today than to spend this time with me," he gave a tiny self-deprecating smile, "and so I'm humbled and gratified by your attendance. I come to you today as a citizen who finds himself both saddened and inflamed by what I see around me. I am saddened by the poor state of our wonderful city and the deteriorating morality evident in the past decisions made by *some* of our leaders. I'm particularly sad because of the infringement and rending of our city's charter, and the outright desecration made to the guidelines and regulations laid down for us by our founding fathers over one hundred and fifty years ago. It is a sad, but honest truth that recent actions taken by the majority of the council, and endorsed and supported by the Mayor, rip open the very fabric of our society."

He looked into the cameras with a troubled expression. "It is bad enough that we suffer those of weak moral fiber and unsavory life choices to live and prosper among us, endangering our children and our principles, but granting them additional rights through the adoption of dangerous protection policies goes beyond the pale! I know what many of you are thinking. I can see it in your faces." He scanned his audience, and nodded his head sagely. Reightman thought he looked like a parody of some noble, wise statesman. "You say to yourselves, *"Sutton, other cities and states are adopting similar policies."* You ask yourselves, *"Why shouldn't we do the same? Surely it's alright?"* Well, my fellow residents, I'm here to tell you that I believe it's very wrong and nothing more than a direct attack on the biblical teachings and rules of society handed down to guide and govern us. Why should we grant poor misguided and perverted creatures additional rights and protections under the law? Why should we allow them a greater foothold in this city where they'll corrupt our youth, encourage licentiousness and sin, and put us on the road to ruin? I tell you – we should not! For therein rests the seed of destruction and that seed will lead to suffering for all moral and righteous men and women."

Dameron moderated his voice into a more reasonable, edifying tone. "We should instead require that they educate and reprogram themselves to align within the *proper* order. We should instead offer programs to correct their deviant sexual leanings and behaviors. I fear that soon we'll even see a time when members of the opposite sex freely violate the privacy and safety of our small defenseless children through polices that will designate public restrooms as gender neutral territory – a misguided concept – and allow dangerous predators and filthy deviants into those most vulnerable spaces. I know that I fear for my own sweet and innocent babies." Sutton sniffled and wiped a single tear from his eye while gazing tenderly at his children. He visibly firmed his jawline and Reightman noticed after a moment's effort, his eyes held impassioned fire. "My brothers and sisters, concerned and right thinking citizens who I know and believe you are, it's time to take back this city from the degenerates and hold it forever more for those who maintain and uphold the traditions and attitudes of the righteous!" As Dameron shouted his last sentence the crowd applauded and cheered loudly, although as cameras panned around, Reightman noticed clumps of people talking together and shaking their heads in disbelief that they were hearing this type of rhetoric in current times.

Dameron raised his arms again for quiet. "I promise you, that if re-elected, I will do everything in my power to put us once more on the path of moral triumph and that, only *that* my friends – will help alleviate the sadness I feel today." Reightman saw the Councilman look toward the woman in the peach dress, and at her encouraging nod, he continued. "Citizens and supporters, I also come to you today incensed and inflamed. Incensed at the prolific waste I see in our city and incensed at the wasteful programs and initiatives in place. I'm incensed at the crony-ism that is prevalent at every level of our city government, and at the ineptness our critical city departments have shown over the last months. But most of all, I'm inflamed with anger over the latest terrible event. A few short days ago, a horrific murder was committed here in our beautiful city, in the heart of our vibrant and growing downtown district." Reightman and Jackson were now completely riveted to the broadcast. Sutton Dameron continued in the same tone of righteous indignation. "A man was murdered in cold blood, just steps from our homes and workplaces. I can ignore the fact that this horrible action took place in a business owned and operated by one of those misguided and deviant homosexuals I alluded to earlier. I can ignore the fact that the victim was found splayed sinfully naked within a room of that business. But I cannot ignore the fact that nothing is being done to identify, capture and detain the perpetrator of this most heinous crime." The Councilman's voice now rapidly increased in volume and intensity. "I can't ignore the fact that the police department of this city, under the questionable leadership of Police Chief Ernest Kelly, have failed to effectively use the *multitude* of resources provided by the taxpayers of the city. Resources each of us provided through hardship as we shouldered the tax burdens imposed upon us all! We deserve better!" Again, Dameron expertly moderated his tone to keep the attention of the crowd, and the television viewers. "To that end, I call upon the Mayor and the rest of the city leadership to open an investigation to examine and determine how our city police have so woefully mishandled their investigation of this case. Furthermore, I humbly offer myself up to head such an investigation, regardless of the personal sacrifices my family and I must suffer to make this possible. As you know, my friends and supporters, Christina and I feel it is our duty to do whatever necessary to ensure the safety of our children, and all of the other children, families and business owners of moral integrity across our city."

As Dameron once again looked into the cameras, a gust of wind caught a hunk of his hair and lifted it up. The councilman hurriedly smoothed it down and his lips thinned in sad determination. "I fear our city leaders will not take up this challenge. I fear they will refuse to take action and that kind of behavior mustn't be allowed to continue. I stand before you today, sadden and inflamed, and ask for your vote. Vote Sutton Dameron – I *can* lead the way." He took a drink from a bottle of water stowed underneath the podium behind the microphones, glanced at his wife, and then smoothed his tie. The cameras panned over the crowd once again. Some were clapping in approval. Others were looking at him thoughtfully, expressions unreadable. A few were shaking their heads in disgust. "I will now take questions from the ladies and gentlemen of the press," Sutton Dameron offered.

Earth Fruits' lunchtime regulars erupted into an absolute babel of load voices, as if they'd all awakened from the same bad dream. "Turn the blow-hard off, Bernice! I've heard enough and it's not sitting well with my lunch." "That's for damn sure!" "What kind of prissy name is 'Sutton' anyway?"

Bernice pointed her remote at the TV and turned it off. She excused herself and stomped back to kitchen growling. "Who in the hell does he think he is? Probably has a tiny dick to go with his tiny, narrow mind."

The three at the table let out the breath they'd been holding ever since the councilman had ratcheted up his rhetoric and directly attacked the police department and the Chief, while referencing the Guzman case.

Zhou Li summed up her feelings. "I have never liked that self-righteous little man or his wife either."

"You know the Dameron family, Madame Zhou?"

"I know of Sutton Dameron, Detective Reightman, and I don't like what I know. I do have the misfortune of being acquainted with Mrs. Dameron."

"'Oh?'"

"Yes. Her people are from Sarasota. She served briefly on a charity committee for an organization which my sister served as Board Chair. After marrying this Sutton Dameron fellow, she presumed upon her very distant association with my sister, and approached me at a fundraiser. She was overly familiar, which she knew was ill considered. Her parents certainly raised her better." Zhou Li raised her napkin to her face and delicately wiped her mouth.

"You're also acquainted with her parents?"

"Yes, Detective Jackson, I thought I had been clear. Her family was well known in Sarasota and in fact had a small amount of fame at one time."

"Her family is famous?"

"They were, at least in the circus world. They billed themselves as the 'Flying Martellies'. They were a very talented and well regarded circus act specializing in aerial gymnastics and flying routines. The whole family was involved in the act until the 1980's. They opened a flying school sometime later, about 1995 I believe, to cater to the tourist crowd. It has been fairly successful, and they still enjoy a certain level of prestige in some circles, although nothing like in their glory days. I believe Mrs. Dameron participated in the school in a limited fashion before going off to college, where she met her husband." She folded the napkin, creasing each fold separately. "Christina Martelli was certainly raised to have proper manners. I was very disappointed in her."

"What did you expect, Madame Zhou? She's from a circus family."

Zhou Li placed her napkin firmly on the table. "Detective Jackson, your prejudices are at play. In my experience, the offspring of the older circus families are brought up very well. Their profession requires extreme discipline and a lot of hard work. To make it to the top, they must be able to interact perfectly with a wide range of people, from event promoters, to wealthy investors, to their fellow performers, as well as with the media. You may believe me when I tell you that their children are brought up with the highest of expectations. They are very unlike the carnival crowd, although I must admit that I do not, to my knowledge, know any members of that profession. I suspect their number might include some very acceptable people as well."

"My apologies, Madame."

"Apologies accepted, Detective. Now, shall we go? I believe the lunch hour has passed and I have things to do."

"Would you like us to escort you back?" Reightman offered as she gathered up her belongs and picked the check up from the table.

"No need, Detective Reightman. Before going back to the shop, I want to stop in at Passed Around to see if Moon has anything new. Shopping always uplifts my spirits and gives me a new perspective, especially after experiencing unpleasantness such as Councilman Dameron's press conference." She wiggled her body down the booth length, eying Melba's outfit. "Would you like to join me, Detective Reightman?"

Reightman recalled the tacky display in the shop window and declined. Zhou Li gave a disappointed sigh "Please tell me the amount of my portion of the check, Detective."

"There's no need, Madame Zhou. We'll take care of it."

"Thank you. That's an unexpected treat. I'll take care of the tip." Zhou reached into her bag and placed a twenty on the table. "I think I'll check out the items up by the counter." She finished scooting herself to the end of the booth and stood up. Soon she was heading toward the front of the cafe, stopping at a few tables to greet a few fellow diners she knew.

Jackson and Reightman followed. As Melba was settling the check Sam nudged her and pointed out one of the displays on the counter. Melba glanced over to the rack which offered a selection of items marked "Poo-Tea" "Is that for what I think it's for, Reightman?"

Before she could respond, Zhou Li piped in from behind them, "If you are having problems of that nature. Detective Jackson, you may visit me at my shop. I'm certain I have a much more effective blend." As Jackson stammered and tried to think of a reply, Zhou Li waved and headed out the door for her shopping excursion.

Melba finished up the payment transaction. "Ready, Sam?"

"More than."

"Are you sure you don't need a box of that stuff"" Melba pointed at the display. "You're sure full of something."

"Shut up, Reightman. You're the one drinking all those funny teas."

On their way back to the car Melba asked Sam if he wanted to drive.

"You better Melba. You drive faster and I think we need to get back to the station."

"What's the hurry? I think we are pretty much on schedule."

"That's not it. The thing is, the Chief's probably looking for us. I bet he's busted a vessel in his head over that damn press conference. I'm surprised Nancy hasn't already tried to hunt us down."

Since she agreed with his reasoning, Reightman just pointed the car and drove.

Once back at their desks, Reightman picked up the desk phone and dialed Kelly's office.

"Hey, Melba. He's not here," offered Nancy before Reightman could ask.

"Where is he?

"Over at Mayor Clarkson's office. Her secretary called right after Dameron's press conference. Chief Kelly had to calm down quite a bit before he headed over there." Nancy smacked her ever present gum.

"Do you expect him back anytime soon?" Reightman tried to consider all possible implications of a command visit with the Mayor.

"Nope. Said he was going home when he was done. He didn't trust himself not to burn down the building," Nancy said and added happily, "He said I could leave early too if nothing urgent came up. I can probably make it to bingo. I haven't had a night out for a long time so I think I'll just round up some of my girlfriends and make a night of it." Nancy sounded positively giddy. "I'm really excited about it."

"Okay, Nancy. I hope you have fun tonight. Thanks."

"The Chief's not in?" Jackson asked as she put down the phone.

"Nope, he's with the Mayor."

Sam whistled through his teeth. "Bet that won't be pretty. What's next partner?"

"Give me a minute, Sam." Reightman picked up the stack of interoffice mail and messages on the corner of her desk. On top was a white departmental envelop with her name typed on a standard label. "Wonder what this is?" She pulled out the letter and unfolded it. She scanned it which didn't take long. "What the hell…?"

Centered on the page in capital, bold type were the words, "CHECK THE PHONE DETECTIVE." It was odd for Tom to send something like this. Sometimes she just couldn't figure out those crime techs. They were kind of quirky.

"Why don't you head out and canvas the pawn shops and see if they have any recollection of selling a blade matching the murder weapon?"

she suggested as she put it back in the envelope. "It's probably another wild goose chase, but you might as well."

"Okay. What are you going to do?

"I'm going over to see Tom. I think he may have something for me." Jackson gave her thumbs up sign and pulled a mint out of his desk drawer.

"Then I'm doing back over to Capital Street to meet with Toby Bailey."

"You need me to meet you there?"

"No, I don't think so. I'm just going to drop off Guzman's personal belongings and get a signed release. I'll call you if I need something. Otherwise, I'll plan on seeing you tomorrow.

"Sounds good." Jackson stood and took his jacket off of the chair. "Hey, don't forget to call Abby and tell her about the change in plans for Labor Day."

"Thanks for the reminder. I'll see you in the morning."

When she reached Tom's cubicle, she discovered there was no one at his desk.

Laurie poked her head over the divider between the two spaces. "Hi, Detective."

"Hello, Laurie. Tom around here anywhere?"

"Not right now. He had to rush out – something about a sick kid. His wife's on duty at the hospital so he had to pick up the boy from daycare. He said he'd be back as soon as his mom made it to the house to sit with him."

"Any idea of time?"

He said it should be between 3 and 4. Is there anything I can do for you? "

"Thanks, Laurie, but I'd better wait on Tom. He was working on something special for me."

"Okay. I'll tell him you came by."

"Thanks. See you later."

"Sure thing, Detective Reightman." Laurie popped her head back down.

Reightman headed back to her office, trying to think how she could rearrange the afternoon. She dialed Toby. "Hello, Toby. I'm sorry to call at the last minute, but is there any way we can move up our meeting? Something came up here that requires some rearranging." Reightman opened the envelope and looked at the typed message again, wondering what it meant. She was going to give Tom a ration when she saw him later.

"That's no problem, Detective. I have all my errands done, and there's nothing else on my schedule for today. What time works?"

"How about in twenty minutes or so?"

"Sounds good."

She checked her purse to make sure she had Guzman's things. She unfolded, then opened the large manila envelope, and checked through the contents. *"Good thing I checked!"* She picked up the phone to call the clerk in charge of the signing in and out personal affects.

"Hey Doris, this is Detective Reightman.....Yes, thank you. I was wondering if you could check something for me...Sure. Ready? I'm looking for a couple of the items found at the Guzman scene. I have the wallet and a set of keys, but I seem to remember some kind of jewelry. Can you check on it?...Yes, I can hold." This time the muzak was of the classical variety and she appreciated the effort someone was taking to change things up. "Yeah?" Reightman replied when Doris picked up again. "Really? You're sure? ...Scratched through?...Yeah, that is strange...Any ideas?...Okay. If you could keep looking I'd appreciate it. I'll review the crime screen report again, but I'm sure there was some kind of jewelry...Thanks, Doris, you too."

She hung up the phone, and immediately dialed Sam. "Hey, Sam...no – nothing urgent. Let me ask you something. Do you remember Guzman having on any jewelry when we arrived at the scene?" She refastened the envelop brads and folded them back down. "That's what I thought I remembered. A necklace of some sort and some kind of sparkly earring, huh?....Yeah, Doris said there was an entry for Guzman, but two of the items on the list were scratched out and she couldn't read the description... No, she had no idea...Yes, I'll check with them. I'm headed over to meet Bailey now...Yes, I did, but Tom had to go pick up a sick kid....Okay, you too." She sat the phone down in its cradle. She *knew* that she'd remembered some jewelry. Maybe Tom had pulled it for some reason. The mysterious ways of the crime tech team never failed to amaze her. She carefully wedged the envelope back inside her purse while trying to decide about what she would tell Toby about the missing items.

He was very understanding. "I'm sure they'll show up, Detective. Thanks for telling me, although, I don't even remember anything like that. Geri did have a pierced ear, but I don't remember him ever wearing anything that looked like a big diamond. It was probably a hunk of junk."

He sighed and shook his head. "Sometimes he was attracted to shiny things." He opened the envelope she had given him and took out the items, placing them on his desk. He reviewed the form, signed and dated it, and tore off the top copy. He gave the bottom copy to Reightman. "Any news on when they will release his body?"

"I'm not a hundred percent sure, but the assistant coroner thought it would just be another day or two."

Toby covered his eyes with one hand and rubbed his temples. When he looked up again, his face was pinched with strain. "I wasn't prepared for anything like this."

"No one ever is, Toby."

He stood up and held out a hand. "Thanks for bringing these things by, Detective. I appreciate it."

"No problem. I'll track down the other things as soon as possible, I promise. I'll call tomorrow when I have news, and we can talk about finishing up with the files. I think we'll be done with them in the next couple of days which will be a relief to me and to you. It shouldn't be too long before you can get a service in to clean the place and do whatever else you need to do in order to reopen."

He hesitated before answering. "I guess that's good news."

"You don't sound very sure." Reightman picked up her bag and slung it over her shoulder. Her neck ached a little from the weight.

"It just doesn't seem to be much of a dream for me anymore. I used to want a place like this so much and I was excited to be here every day. I just don't know if I'll ever feel that way again."

As they walked to the front door Reightman offered, "Maybe it'll be good to be less invested in this place, Toby. You can focus on having a life."

"I thought I had a life, Detective. At one time I thought I had a good life and a shot at a great one."

Something in his voice made her turn toward him.

"I'm just feeling sorry for myself, Detective," he responded to her sympathetic expression. "I'll talk to you tomorrow." Toby locked the door and headed back to his office. He sat down in his chair and picked up the ring with its few keys he identified as belonging to the spa and to the apartment he'd once shared with Geri. He threw them into a drawer then picked up the wallet and opened it.

Inside, there were a couple of low denomination bills, a few business cards, a debit card and a credit card. He pulled out a little white envelope and felt it. *"It's just another credit card,"* he decided as he pulled it free. He stared down at the card in his hand. It was a silver-gray color with an orange and red bank logo. Embossed on the lower portion of the card were Geri's name, an account name and the expiration date. On the back of the card Geri had signed his full name in green felt tipped marker. Toby held the card to his forehead and cried.

Toby and Geri did as directed by Grams and completed their research. They set off to visit a school in the upstate and returned disappointed. Although they liked the city and the surrounding area, the school didn't fit their needs. There were limited physical therapy classes offered and there wasn't a single massage school in the city that could adequately prepare them for their state certification exams. Dejected, they headed back home. Toby drove while Geri slept in the front seat. "One day wasted," he thought.

They ruled out a school the next state over after talking to the admissions office. The tuition was exorbitantly high because neither of them met the residency requirements. The only remaining viable option was located in the state capital. As they made appointments for their visit to the admissions office and for a discussion and tour with a facility advisor, Grams suggested they make a long weekend of it.

"I know it is not more than an hour and a half away, but it is a shame to go there and not see the sights," she said from her usual place by the kitchen sink. Today she was husking corn from the garden. "There's a lot to see and I'm sure things have changed a lot since you went there on that field trip during your sophomore year. Why don't you boys stay a couple of days? Your appointments are set for Thursday, so you could see the city, take in the sights and be back here Sunday evening in time for dinner."

"Really, Grams?" Toby was warming up to the idea.

"Yes. I think you'd both enjoy it. I'll call around tomorrow and see about making a hotel reservation."

"Thanks, Grams! What time is dinner?"

"I don't know – it's your night to cook. This corn is for tomorrow. What are you planning?'

"To tell you the truth, I kind of forgot." Toby thought for a minute. "How about spaghetti with meat sauce? I think we have all of the stuff."

"Yes we do, and your spaghetti's almost edible." Gram teased.

"You said it was good last time!"

"I was really hungry that night." She turned to the other boy in the kitchen. "Geri, Toby may not be a master chef, but he is very creative with some of his concoctions." They all three had a good laugh at that.

"Yeah, I've had some of his creations at this very table."

Toby crossed his arms and thrust out his lower lip. Catching sight of him, Grams exclaimed. "Toby Bailey, that reminds me of something! You boys wait right here. Geri come and finish up this corn, there are just a couple of ears left to do." Grams hurried from the room and Geri went to the sink to finish the shucking.

"Maybe after dinner we can do a little research about what we want to see this weekend."

"That'd be great, Toby. We just have to watch what we spend though."

"Yeah, I know. We'll do as much free stuff as we can fit in and I'm sure there are plenty of reasonable places to eat since students like to eat cheap." Before Geri could respond, Grams came back into the kitchen carrying a large cardboard tube which she handed to Toby. Geri finished up the last piece of corn and rinsed off his hands.

"Open it, Toby," she instructed.

They all gathered around the table and Toby uncapped the plastic end of the tube. He lifted it up and peered inside. "It looks like some kind of rolled up paper." He reached his fingers inside and slid it out of the tube, laying it in the middle of the table and carefully unrolling it.

As soon as it was flat and its corners were held down with a couple of spoons, Geri started laughing. "That looks just like Toby did a minute ago."

"Yes, it does. That's because it is Toby." Grams looked at her grandson as he bent to examine the photo, hair falling into his eyes. "Your momma took that picture when you were just a little boy. She said it was her favorite picture of you."

"I remember, Grams." Toby's voice was very quiet and his eyes were suspiciously damp. "She said I'd appreciate it one day." He carefully rolled the photo up and placed it back in the tube, replacing the plastic cap. He held it carefully in both arms. "I will appreciate it one day, Grams, the way she would've wanted me to. But until then, will you keep it for me?"

"Yes, I'll be honored to keep it safe for until you want it." She walked to his side and gave his shoulder a little squeeze and then took the tube from him. "I'll just go put this away again."

"You okay, Toby?"

"Yeah Geri. I just wasn't prepared to see that picture again, that's all." Toby rubbed one eye with the back of his hand. "Hey, you ready to learn how to make my world famous spaghetti?"

"Sure. Maybe if I supervise we'll all be able to eat it without getting sick."

The next afternoon Grams announced she'd secured them a hotel reservation and then left on an errand. Toby and Geri spent the afternoon making plans for their trip and making a list of things to pack. Grams got back home around five thirty, and was pleased that one of the boys had remembered to put the casserole she'd made that morning into the oven. She put the corn on to cook and hollered for them to set the table. As she listened to their chatter and the clank of forks and knives and spoons being laid in their proper places, she asked "What time are you boys thinking of leaving in the morning?"

Toby answered from the table where he was putting down the big dinner plates. "I think about 9 in the morning. Right, Geri?"

"Yeah, that's right."

"That should give you plenty of time to make your appointments even if you do get lost," Gram approved. "Everything packed?"

"I'm all packed, except for a few things. Geri can do his when he goes back his cousin's house after dinner." Toby surveyed the table and decided they were done. "Geri, I was thinking I would pick you up at about a quarter 'till. Is that okay?

Grams quickly interjected, "Geri, why don't you come over here around 8 instead? I'll put together a big breakfast to send you boys off properly."

They shared their plans with Grams and cheerfully adjusted them to add a few things she suggested. They'd never thought of the zoo and looked forward to seeing the new gorilla exhibit. The food went down fast, as did the vanilla ice cream from the freezer. Pretty soon the dishes were done and Geri was out the door.

"Need any more help, old woman?" Toby sassed.

"I am not an old woman!"

"You're older than I am."

"Pretty much everybody with a lick of good sense is older than you. Toby Bailey."

"You're right, Grams. Maybe I'll get some sense someday."

"Maybe you will."

Toby gave her a good night kiss and went to check he hadn't forgotten anything he wanted to take. Grams finished up her tidying and looked out of the window over the sink. "You better be careful out there, Toby Bailey," she whispered to the night sky. She folded her towel and hung up her apron, before turning off the lights and going on to bed.

Geri showed up a few minutes before eight the following morning and knocked on the door before opening it. "Good morning."

"Good morning, Geri. Sit that bag down over there. Bacon will be done in a minute."

"Smells good."

"I don't think there is anything in the world that smells as good as bacon frying."

"Good morning, Grams. 'Morning', Geri," Toby said with his voice still full of sleep. He went to the refrigerator and grabbed a pitcher of orange juice. "Anyone besides me want juice?" When they all agreed they did, Geri pulled three small glasses for the cabinet and carried them to the table, where Toby poured a glass for each of them. Grams dished up some eggs and placed the strips of crispy bacon on a dished lined with paper towels, and Toby carried the food to the table. Geri grabbed the plates and forks and soon breakfast was on the table. They all took their seats, and Grams said a simple grace. Then they all dug in.

They weren't as talkative this morning, concentrating on the food and their private thoughts about the day ahead. After breakfast was done, they carried the plates and other table items to the sink where they rinsed them and loaded the dishwasher. Grams wiped down the vinyl tablecloth while they washed the platter and the bowl. Geri reached for a towel, brushing against Toby's chest. Toby looked up, ready to make some remark about how clumsy Geri was, and their eyes caught and locked. Toby felt a shiver go through his entire body.

"Sorry," Geri apologized, whispering for some reason.

"No problem," Toby whispered back, confused by what he was feeling.

"You two about done?"

"I think so, Grams."

"Good, come over here and sit back down at the table."

They dried off their hands, getting in each other's way – which they'd never done before. For some reason, it made Toby nervous.

Once they were seated around the table, Gram asked, "Toby, you got your checkbook packed, along with the rest of your things? And the reservation information for the hotel?"

"Yes, ma'am, I have it all."

"Geri, you got everything you need in that bag?"

"Yes, ma'am."

"Good. Now, I've have one more thing for the both of you." She reached into her apron pocket and withdrew two small rectangular items and laid one in from of the each of them.

"What are these, Grams?"

"Those are credit cards. One for each of you, tied to mine. They're for emergencies only, you hear?"

"But, Grams, we have money. I have my checkbook, that debit card they gave me at the bank, and some cash. I think we're set."

"Listen to me, Toby Bailey. There may be an instance where you need this. One of you might be hurt or stranded. This might be the only way to get out of a jam. I'll rest better knowing you boys have these. Like I said, you shouldn't use them unless needed. The bill will come directly to me and I don't want to have to pay for a lot of unexpected charges at the end of the month. Understand?"

"Yes, ma'am," Toby answered. Grams brushed a lock of hair away from his face. "Go get your stuff, Toby. It's almost time for you to hit the road."

Toby picked up the credit card and put it in his wallet. "Thanks, Grams," he said and kissed her cheek.

As soon as they were alone, Geri pushed the card slowly across the table until it was sitting in front of her. "I can't take this. It wouldn't be right."

Gram sat still in her chair, looking at him intently. "Geri, I want you to listen to me with everything you've got. In all ways that matter, you've become another grandson to me. You matter. Not because of Toby – not wholly – but because of you. This is your home now and don't you forget it. There'll always be a place for you here. Now, you pick that card up and put it in your wallet. If not for yourself, do it for my Toby. He might be in need some time and I have to trust you to see that he never wants for everything because of your pride and hardheadedness. Don't let that happen if you can help it. Do you hear me, son?"

Geri didn't trust himself to speak. He picked the card up and put it into his wallet. He walked over to her and gave her a hug. She held him tight for a second, giving his arms a tight squeeze before letting go. Then she yelled out, "Toby Bailey you're going to be late. Get this show on the road!"

While Geri and Grams were sitting in the kitchen, Toby made a quick check of his bags, making sure he had everything he needed. Thinking back to that moment in the kitchen when he'd thought he was going to shiver apart, he opened his nightstand drawer and pulled out the pack of condoms Grams had placed on his bed earlier in the summer. It hadn't been opened because there'd never a time to even explore much. Besides, he didn't want his first time with someone to be in Grams' house. It didn't seem right.

After a moment's more thought, he unzipped his bag and shoved the box in between some extra clothes and things. "Better to have something not needed, than to need something and not have it," his Gramps had always told him. He lifted up his bag and looked around his room as if saying goodbye to something he couldn't quite name. "I'm on my way!" he shouted when he heard Grams yelling for him to get the show on the road.

They made good time, following the directions on the phone. They only got lost once, when Toby made a wrong turn after stopping to get something to drink. When they pulled into the visitor parking section of Mid State Vocational and Trade School they realized that they were about 30 minutes early.

"I guess we can just walk around and look at things, until our appointments." Toby unbuckled his seat belt and got out of the car. When Geri didn't get move, Toby walked to the other side of the car. He knocked on the window until Geri looked up and opened his door. "What's wrong?"

"Nothing. Just a little jittery I guess."

"I'm jittery too. But I have a good feeling about this. Get out of the car and let's go look around."

They walked around taking in the campus and, after asking for directions, they found the admissions and administration building. They presented themselves right on time and with some help from the admissions clerk, they filled out all of the basic forms. There seemed to be a whole lot of them. The clerk looked the completed forms over and asked if they knew what courses they wanted to take. "Usually first semester students focus on the prerequisites," she advised. "Here's what I'd recommend." She pulled out a double-sided piece of paper and used a yellow highlighter to mark the ones that they had to take some time over the next two years. She helped them complete their selections and Toby wrote at his first big check to pay for their schooling.

"Can you direct us to where we can find Dr. Nelson?"

"Do you have an appointment with him?"

"Yes, ma'am. We're supposed to meet him in about ten minutes," Geri replied after checking the time on his phone.

"Why don't you have a seat over there at the tables and I'll call him and tell him you're here. He can meet you here instead of having you wander all over the place and chance getting lost. Will that work?"

An hour later they had seen about all there was to see. After thanking Dr. Nelson, they headed back to the car. Once they'd buckled up, Geri turned and asked "What did you think Toby?"

"I think I liked it. Everyone seems to be very nice and they went out of their way to be helpful and welcoming."

"Especially Dr. Nelson," laughed Geri. "He thought you were hot. I saw him looking at you like you were something yummy."

"You think so? I didn't notice."

"You dweeb! Sometimes I think you wouldn't notice anything if I wasn't around to point it out. Come on, let's head to the hotel. I'm getting hungry."

Geri plugged the address from the reservation confirmation into his phone and read the directions while Toby drove them to their hotel. Once there and standing in front of the reception desk they discovered that they did in fact, need a credit card.

"But we don't have–" Toby began, but before he could get any further, Geri had fished out the new card.

"Here," he said handing it to desk clerk.

She took it from him and looked it over. She turned it over and handed it back. "You forgot to sign it. You need to do that before I can accept it."

"Do you have a pen I can use?"

"Sure do, Mr. Guzman," she replied, reading his name from the front of the card. She handed him a felt-tipped pen and watched as he signed it in green ink. "It's supposed to be lucky to write in green ink," she informed him as she took back the card and the pen.

"Wow, that was a close call," Toby said as they made their way to the elevators. "Good thing you thought fast and remembered about the card. For a minute there I thought we would have to just go on back home."

"I was just looking out for us, Toby."

The room they had been given was very nice to their young and inexperienced eyes. The beds had bright spreads on them and the bathroom was the most modern either of them had ever seen. They hung up their few shirts and stowed most of the rest of their stuff in the drawers of the dresser which had a TV on top. They put their duffle bags on the little folding stands at the foot of each double bed. Toby flopped on the bed closest to the window. "What do you want to do now?"

"We could go find something to eat. It's been a long time since breakfast!" Geri eyed the basket of candy bars and crackers by the small coffee pot. He picked up the list next to it and scanned it. "You won't believe this, Toby! These candy bars are $5.00 a piece! I could buy five of them for that price back at the gas station at home."

"Whoa – don't eat any of those! That would be like eating pure, solid gold."

After some discussion they decided to go down and ask the front desk clerk where they could find a reasonably priced place to eat. She provided directions to a couple of places within walking distance. They found a place that looked good and had dinner, then walked around and saw some of the sights. They stopped and bought some ice cream, watching in fascination while the shop assistant pounded the scopes out on a marble slab, added some fruit and bits of chocolate, and arranged it in cups.

"This was a good day!" Toby announced as he toed off his shoes back in the room.

"Yeah, it was. You want to shower first, or should I?"

"You go ahead. I'll shower after you're done"

"Okay". Geri gathered up a few things and went into the bathroom, closing the door. Toby stretched out on the bed with his hands behind his head. After a while he heard the shower water running, and then a while later, the sound of Geri brushing his teeth. Geri came out of the steamy room, wearing a bathrobe he had found hanging on a hook. He dropped his dirty clothes on the closet floor and went to the dresser where he pulled out a pair of briefs. Turning his back slightly, he put one foot in then another and pulled them up his strong, muscular legs.

Toby caught a glimpse of his body in the reflection of the closet door mirrors and felt his body respond.

"The shower's great!" Geri informed him as he hung up a wet towel. "There's an adjustable showerhead and there's a lot of white fluffy towels and another robe hanging on a hook. You better go on and wash yourself. You're starting to stink!"

Toby threw a pillow at him and got off the bed. "I do not stink."

Geri sniffed the air. "Something does."

Toby gathered up a few things and went into the bathroom. The room was still steamy so he left the door open a crack. "Geri was right," he thought as he stepped under the spray, "this shower is great." He finished up quickly and brushed his teeth. He knotted his own robe and walked into the bedroom toweling his hair.

"Hey, Toby, what are we going to do tomorrow?"

"We're going to see the sights and maybe look for a place for us to live. That's what we decided."

"Hmmm…okay." Geri reached up and turned off his light.

Toby caught the reflective quality in his friend's voice "What?" he asked as he tied the sting of his drawstring sleeping shorts.

"I was just wondering…"

"What were you wondering?"

"If we're going to be any good at this. I know we have plans and all, but what if we're not good enough?"

"We're going to be great! Between the two of us we'll figure it out. Stop worrying about it and go to sleep." Toby settled into his own bed a few feet away.

They hunkered down on their beds, one young man on his back and one on his side. Geri lay facing the ceiling, thinking about the future and how he was going to pull his weight. Toby hugged his pillow and thought about the glimpse of Geri's bare body he'd seen in the mirror and the tiny goosebumps which had played down his arms at the sight. He wondered if he'd ever work up the nerve to make a move. He should've left the condoms at home after all.

Light from the outside streetlamps filtered through a gap in the drapes, washing them with a gentle glow. As they each thought their own thoughts, they closed their eyes, and eventually, slept.

CHAPTER SEVEN

R EIGHTMAN PICKED UP the phone on her desk and dialed Tom's number.

He answered on the first ring. "Reightman, you'd better come on over ASAP."

"Okay, can do. But, why?

"You'll see when you get here." He hung up without saying goodbye.

"He must have found something on the phone." A couple of minutes later she rounded the corner to his cube and knocked on the side by the opening to his workspace. He was hunched over the phone, connecting to some sort of cable. He looked up briefly, grunted something she didn't make out, and went back to what he was doing. "Tom? How's your son?"

"Puking," he said, still focused on his work.

"I'm sorry, is he going –?"

"Hold on one second," he interrupted. He fiddled with the cable some more and then performed what looked like intricate maneuvers on his computer, watching the screen. After a few seconds, he sat back in his chair and swiveled it to face her, a grim expression on his face.

"I take it from your expression you've found something."

"Yep, I did."

"Care to share?"

"You're either going to really hate it, or really, really like it."

"Why don't you tell me what you found and then I can figure out which one it will be?"

"First, I let me say I did find a couple of prints; one on the phone screen and one on the case. The print from the screen is pretty clean.

The print on the case is not as good, because the finish doesn't hold a very good impression."

"Alright. Have you identified who each belongs to?"

"No. I've loaded them into the database though and hopefully it'll spit something out soon. Sometimes it's quick – sometimes it's not. We'll just have to wait and see."

"When do we get to the good part?"

"Right about now." Tom glanced over to check his computer monitor. "I've verified this phone did belong to Gerald Guzman. I also found some…stuff on it."

"What kind of stuff, Tom?"

"The usual apps and a contact list of names and numbers. Some of the numbers were not tied to a contact. Either they were unknown to Mr. Guzman when the calls came in and he never associated a contact name with them, or they came from burner phones."

"Why would he be getting calls from a burned phone, Tom?"

"It's burner phones, Detective. There are a few numbers on it which indicate this is indeed a burner phone."

"Is this the part I might like, or might hate?"

"Neither. We're not to that part yet."

"When do we get there?"

He glanced up at the computer monitor and made a few more clicks. He leaned forward expectantly. "Now, that's more like it!" A set of files was populating the small box in the center of his screen.

"What's it doing?"

"Reconstructing files. If we are lucky and I'm good, we'll get a look at what else was on Mr. Guzman's phone."

"Can't we just see the stuff directly from his phone?" asked Reightman, mystified by what Tom doing.

"No. You know why?"

"No, Tom, I have no idea why." She finally gave in and asked, "Why?"

"Because, someone tried to delete the files. In most cases, it would have worked, but they didn't count on me getting my grubby little hands on this baby. I'm very good at pulling secrets out of things like phones and laptops."

"Is this why you sent me that note?"

"What note?" he asked as he finished typing in more garble-de-gook.

"The note you sent me through interdepartmental mail this morning."

Tom turned around in his chair, confusion written plainly on his face. "I didn't send you any note, Detective Reightman."

"Tom, you can quit kidding around. I knew the note was from you the minute I opened it."

"I repeat, I did *not* send you a note this morning through interoffice mail, or any other time." He caught himself. "Except for one, a couple of years ago. Now that was a good one!"

"Then who did?" asked Reightman, rubbing her temples

"Don't know." The computer made a series of chiming sounds and Tom quickly turned around to face the monitor and scrolled down the files that had finished populating the window. "Now we're getting somewhere," he said with satisfaction. "Told you I was good! Hmmm, these look like pictures of some sort. Some of the files are damaged, but a few appear to be in good enough shape to view. Let's see what we've got." He double clicked on a file and they both leaned into the monitor, waiting for it to open. "Holy shit!" Tom exclaimed, sitting back quickly. "What the hell?"

It took a minute for Reightman to recover her aplomb. "It looks like... a penis, Tom. A somewhat large, uncircumcised, and very erect penis. Can you make the picture smaller? Not that I mind it that size, but it might be intimidating to *you*, it being so big and all..."

Tom shrank the window and moved it to one side of the screen. "Just so you know," he grinned over his shoulder, "I'm not intimidated. Not...At...All."

"I don't need to know, Tom. Not...At...All." She nudged him with her elbow. "Are you going to sit there comparing yourself, or are you going to open the next one?"

He hovered his mouse over the next icon. "Ready or not – here it comes." He double clicked the icon.

"Now, that's more like it!" he whistled appreciatively at the next picture. It depicted a generously endowed woman of a certain age laying on her back in nude, full spread glory. The woman's identity was hidden by an arm thrown over her face, but there was a single identifying mark; a tattoo of a flower in full bloom near the junction of her thighs. Her other arm was positioned across her left side with her hand reaching down toward her lady parts.

"Looks like she is getting ready to take a walk through her just trimmed summer meadow," observed Tom, in a dreamy voice. Reightman felt her face flush.

"Minimize the picture and move it over by the other one," she directed, hoping that he didn't pick up on her discomfort. "You can enjoy that one later – when you're alone."

He clicked on a couple more pictures, revealing other bodies in various stages of undress, a variety of shapes, colors and degrees of physical fitness, and engaged in a wide range of activities with another body. There seemed to be a fairly equal distribution across genders. In most of the photos, the faces were unidentifiable, although there was always at least one prominent marking such as a mole, birthmark, or in two cases, accentuating hardware in the form of piercings. One body of an in-shape male was turned slightly away from the camera, and had a small tattoo of the word, Alias, in dark blue cursive script on the back of one shoulder.

"Most of the rest are too damaged to view, but this one looks okay." Tom opened the final electronic file.

They both sat in their chairs silently as they contemplated the final photo. They both recognized the subject

Eventually, Reightman spoke, in a grim voice, "Better print me a copy of that one, Tom."

Tom hit his print icon, and selected the nearest departmental printer. Reightman studied the image on the monitor. Doctor Benjamin Lieberman was caught in a reflective mirror in all of his naked, heavily fleshed glory.

"He's sure a big guy," observed Tom. "Except for his little soldier there, standing up and saluting. The little man sure looks perky though."

Reightman was silent, thinking back over the last few days, beginning to understand Lieberman's odd behavior, his absences from the morgue and the lack of progress in finishing the autopsy. Some of Riley's observations suddenly became much more meaningful. She shook herself out of her mental review, and snapped impatiently, "Where's the printer, Tom?"

"Just down the hall. Come on, I'll take you." As they made their way through the cubicles to the hallway, he lamented, "We used to have printers in our area, the next cube over. But with all the budget cuts, the bean counters reduced the number of small printers and centralized into a few central print stations."

Reightman didn't comment. Her mind was occupied with what she needed to do next. When they reached the big printer that served this side of the building, the expected print job wasn't there.

"What the hell? Where's the copy, Tom?"

He checked to make sure there was nothing wrong with the printer and shrugged. "Happens all the time and it chaps my butt, but what can you do? Must be some kind of bug in the system. Come on, we'll print it again."

They returned to Tom's desk and she watched him hit the print icon again. "It'll just take a minute. Should be out by time we get there."

"Tom, you go get the damned thing. I need to let the Chief know what we've found." As Tom headed off to retrieve the incriminating photo, she reached over and picked up his desk phone, dialing the extension she knew by heart.

"Hey, Tom. What's up? Nancy asked, in a sultry voice Reightman had never heard from her before.

"Nancy, it's Reightman, I'm calling from Tom's desk." She chose not to acknowledge Nancy's disappointed sigh. "Is the Chief back?"

"No, Melba. Did you try his cell?"

"No, Nancy, I didn't. My phone is back at my desk. I'm going to need you to track him down."

"But, Melba, I was just getting ready to leave to make myself spiffy for my big night out. Can't it wait?"

"No, Nancy, I'm sorry, but it can't. Find the Chief and then have me paged. I'll call in from wherever I am as soon as I hear it."

"I'm gonna' miss Bingo and my night out with the girls, aren't I?" Nancy asked in a forlorn voice and without even a single pop of gum.

"I'm afraid so, Nancy. Sorry."

"Let me find the Chief," Nancy snapped and hung up abruptly just as Tom rounded the corner.

"Here it is. It printed this time." He handed her the copy of the photo at the same time the computer made a little chiming sound. Tom turned to the computer and checked the monitor. "We've got a hit on one of the prints, Detective. That was pretty fast." He clicked on the indicator box and the screen changed to provide name, last known address, occupation and picture of the owner of the finger print, along with a match probability score. The score indicated the system was certain of the match. The name and picture of the owner was of one Dr. Benjamin Lieberman, City Coroner."

"Shit!" Reightman swore under her breath. Things were falling into place very quickly. "Any status on the other print?"

"No. Sometimes it takes a while, and sometime we never get a match."

She started to respond, but heard her name being announced over the out-of-date paging system. She picked up the phone and dialed Nancy's number.

The admin picked up immediately. "Melba, I've got the Chief – let me connect you." After a brief thread of hold music, the Chief's voice boomed in here ear.

"Reightman, this better be important."

"It is, Chief." She filled him in on the photos and the fingerprint found on the phone.

After he unleashed a string of four-letter words, he gave one command. "Take Jackson and go pick him up, Reightman."

"Jackson's tracking down some other info, Chief. I'll pull someone else from the building. I know better than to try and do this on my own." She hesitated. "Chief, we might need a warrant if Lieberman's not in the building. Can you get a hold of a judge?"

"Old Judge McLarity's probably still in. He hangs around later than most of the others. If he's not, I'll shake someone loose. I'll check back with you after I have it handled. Try to collar Lieberman before he leaves."

"I'll do my best," she said, hanging up the phone and immediately dialing Nancy. "Nancy, can you try and dial either Detective Jones, or… Officer Mitchell?" she quickly decided as she went through the roster of who might be in the building.

"Sure, Melba, since I don't have anything better to do than be your personal secretary!" The admin snapped into the phone.

Reightman sighed and prayed from some patience. "Nancy, I'm sorry. I'd do it myself if I was at my desk. I'll owe you one, Nancy."

"You sure will, Melba. Hold on." Once again music played in her ear, this time, a hit from the seventies.

Less than a minute later, Officer Mitchell spoke into her ear. "Officer Mitchell here, Detective." She'd hoped for Jones, but she'd take what she could get.

"Mitchell, I need you to meet me by the elevator bank. We're going to try and pick up a person of interest in the Guzman case." She heard him swallow hard. "Look, Mitchell, I know this is out of your usual bailiwick, but Jackson's out and I need back-up. I won't lie and say it's not dangerous, but I think it'll be pretty cut and dried."

She only had to wait a split-second for his reply. "I'll meet you at the elevators, Detective. I should be there in a couple of minutes. See you there."

Reightman put down the phone and turned to Tom. "Keep that file handy, Tom. We're going to need it. Can you track down Jackson and fill him in? I hate to ask, but I need to head over to the elevators to meet Mitchell."

"Sure thing, Detective. Be careful."

She checked her weapon and took a breath. "Hey, Tom?"

"Yes, ma'am?"

"I think you can probably call me Melba – at least when we're alone. After all, we just watched the equivalent of porn together. I think that qualifies as being on a first name basis." Sometimes it was good to laugh before heading into a possibly dangerous situation. While he was laughing at her characterization of the last hour, Reightman hurried to the elevator. Mitchell was there, waiting. "Officer Mitchell, I appreciate this." She punched the elevator button.

"Not a problem, Detective." He replied as they stepped into the elevator. "Where we headed?"

She passed the basement button. "To the morgue, Mitchell." As the door opened, she filled him in, sharing only the basics. "I don't think there'll be a problem, but it's best to be ready." They prepared themselves for trouble as they entered the doors to the morgue. "Where's Lieberman?" she asked as they entered the room.

Dr. Riley stood from his chair at the small desk just inside the doors. He looked wide-eyed from her to Mitchell. "He....he just left," he croaked.

"He what?"

"He's gone. He ran out of here a few minutes ago. He just grabbed his stuff and left." Riley was looking a little shaky.

"Did he say anything, Riley?"

"Not to me, but he did shout at the other officer."

"What other officer?" She didn't like what she was beginning to suspect.

"The officer who brought in a photocopy of something a couple of minutes ago. I'm sorry, I didn't see it. "

"Did you recognize the officer?"

"Yes, it was the one who's always strutting around acting cool. His name is Haller, or Herman, or something like that."

"Helliman?" Reightman asked with a sinking feeling in her stomach.

"Yeah, that's the one."

Reightman wanted to punch something, badly. "Anything else, Riley?"

Before he could answer, Tom came racing through the doors. "Detective Reightman, the ID on the other print just came through."

As she watched the assistant coroner's face, somehow she just knew. "Who does it belong to, Tom?"

"To him, Detective. The print belongs to Assistant City Coroner, Peter Riley. His print was in the City employee database."

She watched dispassionately as Riley sunk down into his chair and covered his face with his hands.

"Help Dr. Riley to his feet, Officer Mitchell, and then escort him upstairs. Do you need backup?"

"No, ma'am," Mitchell replied as he helped the shaken man to his feet. "I can handle it."

As they walked to the doors, Riley turned and asked, "Detective, do I need a lawyer?"

"I don't know, Dr. Riley. Do you?"

Reightman's stomach clenched when he answered. "I think I might."

She nodded once and addressed Mitchell. "Officer, please make sure that Dr. Riley is able to reach his attorney, then escort him to one of the interview rooms. I'll be up as soon as I finish checking things down here."

She and Tom went through Lieberman's office. He'd be back later with Laurie to give it a more thorough inspection, but she wanted a quick look while she was here. Nothing immediately jumped out at her, but if there was something here, the techs would find it. In the process of removing their gloves, Reightman stopped at Riley's desk. Pulling the partially removed glove back on, she motioned for Tom to do the same. She opened the top middle drawer and took a quick look. Nothing seemed out of the ordinary. She opened the top drawer to the right and, again found nothing. The next drawer down, Reightman hit pay dirt. There, hidden behind a stack of forms and an extra stapler, was a small box which formerly held paperclips. As she opened the top, a small flash of light caught her eye. She turned it over with a gloved finger and recognized the diamond earring which had previously resided in Geri Guzman's ear. Coiled next to the earring was a substantial silver chain strung through the bale of a six-pointed star, the symbol of the Jewish faith. It matched the necklace that Lieberman was wearing in the picture.

"Tom, do you think Guzman was Jewish?" she asked the tech.

"I'm pretty sure he wasn't."

"What makes you sure?"

"Well…" Tom looked down at the floor and cleared his throat. "He was…I mean – Oh, what the hell? I got a really good look at Mr. Guzman at the murder scene. I'm certain he wasn't Jewish, because he wasn't circumcised."

"Oh," she answered, thinking furiously. She remembered something about circumcision being important to members of that particular faith: A circumcised man wasn't necessarily Jewish, but an uncircumcised man certainly was not. "And the first picture we saw on the computer…?"

"Could be him. Based on what we know so far, it seems likely."

Reightman handed him the small box with its contents. "We need to log this in, Tom."

"Yes, ma'am." He took the box from her hand.

She took one more look around the room. "I need to check with the Chief about a warrant, and then send a car to try and pick up Lieberman. We've also need to find that piece-of-shit, Helliman." She flipped off the lights as they went out the door.

"Why'd you turn off the lights, Detective?"

She shrugged. "The dead don't need them. Might as well save the city a few bucks."

They opened the door and were met by two uniformed officers, trailed by Jackson. "I thought we should button this place up until the team can check it over." Jackson greeted Tom and offered her a grim smile. "You've been a busy girl, Reightman."

"It's about to get busier, Jackson."

"Yes it is. The Chief's waiting on us upstairs." They stood next to the elevator bank, waiting for the door to open. "And I better warn you, Nancy's pretty miffed."

"Is she snapping her gum?"

"Nope. She threw all twelve packs right in the trash. She snatched a pack of menthols out from the back of her drawer and said she was taking a break – right after she stopped and bought a candy bar from the vending machine in the breakroom."

"Oh, man! She's going to hate herself in the morning," Reightman said to no one in particular as the three of them entered the elevator.

He pushed the button for the next floor. "Unless she focuses her blame on you instead." Tom and Sam burst into delighted laughter as the realization dawned.

"I am so screwed," she said, as the elevator door closed.

Benjamin Lieberman drove into his garage and hit the automatic button clipped to the driver's side visor. As the door closed, he sat in the car, trying to catch his breath. Sweat ran down his fat, flushed face and dropped on his drenched shirt. *"You need to calm down, Benny,"* he told himself. *"You could have a heart attack."*

He opened the car door and heaved himself out of the plush leather seat and fumbled with his keys as he unlocked the door to the house. He set his briefcase down on the kitchen table and hurried to his bedroom.

Lieberman flung open the closet door and rushed to a row of hanging clothes hanging on the lower rod, quickly pushing them out of the way. He dropped to the floor, groaning at the pain it caused his knees. He punched a sequence of buttons on the revealed wall safe and waited for the indicator light to turn green. When the small door sprung open, he grabbed handfuls of stacked and bound bills and tossing them on the floor. He took out a small bottle of liquid which preserved something very meaningful to him. He rubbed his hands over it lovingly for a moment and then, remembering his plight, scrambled frantically on the carpet, reaching back behind another set of hanging clothes. He found an old duffle bag and stuffed the cash in its bottom. He pulled himself to his feet and started to cram several things into the bag on top of the bills. He placed the vial of liquid carefully in the bag, nestled between a stack of bills, and closed it.

After looking around one last time, he carried the bag into the kitchen and pulled a different set of keys off of the hook hanging by the door. He was going to the only place where they might not find him. His mother had passed away six month earlier and he hadn't listed her house for sale yet. *"Maybe they won't know about it,"* he hoped as he picked up his briefcase. He opened his car door and removed the garage door opener. He closed the door and waddled over to the car parked next to his. It was an older model sedan, which had also belonged to his mother. He opened the back door and threw in the bag and briefcase and then carefully wedged himself into the front seat. He sat in the dark garage, trying to calm his racing heart. He held his fingers to his wrist, checking his pulse while breathing deeply.

Lieberman leaned over and opened the glove box, rummaging around until he found a bottle of aspirin. He tried to open the cap and panicked when it wouldn't turn. He forced himself to focus, pressing the cap down and around to disengage the child-proof mechanism. He poured the pills into his shaking clammy hand, spilling several onto the seat and down onto the floorboard. He held two in his hand. *"I need some water."* He considered a run back into the house for something to drink, but decided against it and dry swallowed the pills, almost choking. He rubbed his throat trying to help the pills move down, and then collapsed on the seat, exhausted.

"Come on Benny! Pull yourself together. You've got to get out of here." He used the steering wheel to pull himself up in the seat and started the car. He opened the garage door with the controller, and eased the car out. When he cleared the door, he closed it and backed out and drove away. Lieberman avoided the main streets and highways as much as possible. The indirect route took much longer, but he considered it safer. He checked the rear view mirror every minute or so, checking for lights or sirens. *"They're probably looking for you now, Benny."*

Twenty minutes later, he pulled into the driveway of a well maintained ranch style house in an older neighborhood. *"You're almost safe,"* he told himself. He looked around to make sure no one was watching before he opened the car door and hurried to the garage. He inserted a key in the locked door and turned the mechanism. *"I should have bought her an automatic opener,"* he lamented as he struggled with the heavy door. Once he lifted it, he returned to the car and drove it in. He scurried out and quickly lowered the door, wincing as it hit the concrete floor and bounced. He hoped no one had heard the noise. He unloaded the car and unlocked and opened the back door, squinting in the darkness. He fumbled for the switch and turned on a single light. The house smelt musty and it was hot. He walked to the thermostat and adjusted the air down, not worried about the expense. With any luck, he'd be long gone when the bill came due. He checked the blinds then filled a big glass of water. After chugging it down, he waddled past the plastic covered furniture to the recliner in the corner of the living room and collapsed into the plushy softness. *"I need to rest."*

An hour later, Lieberman woke up with a start, confused and disoriented. He blinked and looked around him, trying to determine where he was. *"Oh, no!"* he thought as it all came rushing back. He hauled himself out of the chair and went for another glass of water.

Standing by the sink while he drank, he tried to think of what to do next. He rinsed the glass and put it in the draining rack, just like his mother had taught him.

"We're not dirty people, Benny," she'd say. "We keep things tidy and nice in our home. Rinse your things and don't be a schlep."

He retrieved his briefcase and went back to the comfortable chair. "*I feel better,*" he assured himself after checking his pulse again. Lieberman opened his briefcase and pulled out his phone. There were several missed calls. He remembered if the phone was turned on, they might be able to track him, so he turned it off and stowed it back in his briefcase. He pulled out an alternate phone. There was nothing to connect this phone to him. After it powered up, he opened his text messenger app and laboriously typed:

IN TROUBLE HELP THEY NO

In a few minutes a reply came.

NO???

He needed to type more carefully. He tried again, with shaky fingers.

KNOW ABOUT GUZMAN

There was no reply for several minutes.

WHERE R U

He considered telling, but he was smart enough not to trust the person on the other line.

SAFE

He waited for the reply.

$$$?

He punched in three words:

YES

There was no reply, and after an hour he turned off the phone and stowed it back in the briefcase. He closed the briefcase and carried it to the larger bedroom along with the duffle. He rearranged things and placed an item into his pocket. He then went into his mother's kitchen to find something to eat. "*You need to keep up your strength, Benny.*" He stood at the counter and wolfed down a can of spaghetti and drank several glasses of water from the tap. Once he was finished, he carefully rinsed the plate and the glass and placed them in the drainer. He was not a dirty person.

He made his way back to the chair and checked his pulse again before leaning back the recliner and falling asleep.

❖ ❖ ❖

In a stripper bar a few miles away outside the middle of nowhere, John Brown was stretched out at a table by himself; his booted feet up on the chair next to him. He nursed his twenty-five dollar bourbon while he watched the show. The bourbon wasn't all that good, but that was what even the cheap stuff cost in this dive. He had the place mostly to himself since it was late, and most of the regulars had already pried their eyes off the girls and gone home.

He watched the redhead working the stage, mentally critiquing the goods on offer. *"Tits aren't real,"* he decided. *"No one has real tits as firm and unmoving as that."* The girl bent backward, thrusting her crotch into the air. Her bent legs stretched and spread, providing him a glimpse of a thin swath of the hot pink nylon thong she wore. He was considering moving closer to the stage for a better look when his phone buzzed.

He reached into his pocket and removed it, glancing at the message.
I HAVE A PROBLEM

He considered the text for a while, glancing up occasionally to watch the girl on the stage. As she finally crossed her spread legs and lifted herself from the stage floor he typed back, SOLVE PROBLEM 4 U?

He wasn't worried about who the target was, or who was looking to take out the hit. Only people who'd been pre-screened and vetted had his number. John Brown was a careful and experienced man. He wouldn't have survived in his business if he hadn't been.

In a few minutes, he got an answer. HOW MUCH?
50K

There was no response for several minutes and he considered the current state of his finances. He adjusted his price. 40K

He hated to make cut-rate deals, especially with the bastard he was texting, but a man had to make a living somehow if a regular job didn't quite cut it. After a few more exchanges, the transaction was agreed and the details finalized. He'd start the job in the morning. He put the phone back in his pocket and took a drink.

The girl on stage was now working the pole in the center of the stage. Her ass jiggled a little, just the way he liked 'em. He drained his bourbon and signaled for another as he moved to a seat closer to the stage. He pulled a fifty out of his front shirt pocket and beckoned to the girl with the bill in his hand. She worked her way over to the edge of the stage in front of him and spread her legs widely as she bent down in a provocative pose, giving him a good shot at her goodies. He made a leisurely inspection, discovering she was, as he'd expected, waxed clean as a whistle. He crooked his finger and she leveraged herself closer, putting herself practically in his face. He breathed in her scent and reached out with his hand and tucked the fifty into her thong. She smiled and brushed his finger with her snatch. She was moist. Money did that to girls like her, he knew. As she backed away, he brought the finger up to his mouth and licked it while she watched over her shoulder on her way back to the pole.

When the topless server arrived with the new drink, he whispered in her ear then gave her a very generous tip. Thirty minutes later, he was seated on a zebra-striped sofa in a back room waiting for his lap dance. He figured he'd earned it. He'd done a little business this evening and had a new job ahead of him. The redhead from the stage entered the room and walked over to him on her five inch stilettos. He unbuttoned his shirt and lifted his hips slightly to stuff several fifties down his pants while she watched. He was just making sure that if she wanted them, she'd have to work for them. She smiled, eager to please, and licked her glossy, cherry-red lips as she eyed his crotch.

If he didn't have love, at least he had money. John Brown's night looked like it was going to turn out to be pretty damned good, even if he had to pay for the privilege.

CHAPTER EIGHT

REIGHTMAN AND JACKSON stood outside Chief Kelly's office, waiting for door to open. Reightman could hear the Chief talking on the phone, but she couldn't make out his words. She'd given him a brief thumbnail update via phone about a half an hour earlier, and he'd indicated he had a couple of calls to make before he'd be free to see her and Jackson. Nancy sat at her desk filing away at a chipped nail, and occasionally shooting a baneful glare her way.

"Nancy, I'm really sorry your night was ruined. That's just the way things happen sometime."

The woman shot her another look, then opened a desk drawer, tossed in her nail file and closed the drawer, not quite slamming it shut. The admin turned away pointedly, and focused on her computer. From the movements of the mouse and the sounds coming from the monitor, Reightman guessed that Nancy was playing a game of solitaire. She looked over at Jackson, just in time to see his shit-eating grin. At least one of them was enjoying this snippet of office drama.

After a couple more minutes, the phone on Nancy's desk buzzed and she paused in her solitaire game. "Yeah, okay... Yes, I'll tell them." She placed the handset back in the cradle and turned back to her game. After she made a couple of more moves with the mouse she spoke to no one in particular. "Chief Kelly says you can go on in." She didn't look up as they passed her desk, but Reightman could feel Nancy's eyes, aimed like daggers at her back.

They filed into the office and shut the door. Chief Kelly turned away from his computer monitor. "I was able to reach Judge McLarity. Warrant should be on its way in the next few minutes. There is also an area wide APB out for his arrest. Hopefully, we'll find the sleazy SOB."

"Thank you, sir."

"What tipped Lieberman off, Reightman?"

"Not what, but who, Chief. Helliman snagged the photocopy from the printer and took it down to the morgue."

"Helliman, huh?" the Chief grunted. "I wish I could say I'm surprised, but he's always been a pain in the ass. Where's he now?"

Jackson answered for both of them. "No idea, Chief. He was gone from the building by the time Mitchell escorted Riley upstairs. Reightman and Anderson were occupied with their initial inspection of the morgue area."

The chief picked up his phone and dialed a number. When the call was answered, Kelly barked into the phone, "Find Helliman and bring him in. I want him in my office, now!" Without waiting for a reply, he slammed down the phone and sat back in his chair with his hands folded over the beginnings of a slight paunch. "Where is our Assistant City Coroner now?"

"We're holding him in an interview room," Reightman replied. "He asked for an attorney, who's not yet arrived."

"He thinks he needs one, huh?" The Chief leaned back in the chair, accompanied by its familiar squeals and groans. "Both Lieberman and Riley involved – what are the odds?" he asked the ceiling before looking back at the two detectives. "How tangled up in this mess is Dr. Riley?" He directed the question to Reightman.

"I'm not sure, but it doesn't look good for him right now. We've identified a print belonging to him on Mr. Guzman's phone and found two pieces of Guzman's jewelry hidden in one of his desk drawers. Those items were missing from the deceased's effects, and Doris told me that the corresponding descriptions were scratched out on the evidence log. Tom is on his way to pick it up to see if he can find out anything."

"So, we have a motive tied to Doctor Lieberman, and possible obstruction along with aiding and abetting chalked up for Dr. Riley." The Chief chewed his cheek for a minute, thinking through the new pieces of the puzzle. "Any luck in tracking down where the murder weapon originated?" he finally asked Jackson.

"Some, sir." Jackson pulled out his notebook and flipped a couple of pages. "I made a circuit to the pawn shops downtown this afternoon. I stumbled onto a bit of luck at "Best City Pawn and Loan." The proprietor remembers having a knife matching the description of the murder weapon in his inventory. He said he sold it about a month or so ago, but can't remember who bought it. I showed him a photo of Mr. Bailey and was told it wasn't him. That's about the only thing definitive to come out of our entire conversation. His records are a mess, and he can't see worth a damn either." Jackson glanced down at his notes. "Mr. Goldbleum, the owner, is pretty old and when I asked him why he didn't upgrade his record keeping system, he stated, quote, "I don't hold much with all of this computer crap," end quote. He mostly records everything in old-fashioned ledgers, and for cash transactions of non-regulated items he just writes down the sale amount. "

"Did he have any recollection of where he originally picked up the knife?"

"He thought he got it along with a bunch of other hunting and fishing items at a sale he attended in Tennessee last fall. He is going to check his records, such as they are. I left him my card and asked him to call if he remembers anything about the buyer or saw the person again."

"How about security footage, Jackson?"

"There's none available. Apparently Mr. Goldbleum recycles the tapes. Says it's more economical."

"At least he verified the knife in question didn't belong to Mr. Bailey." The Chief leaned forward and put his big hands on the desktop. He examined the backs of his hands carefully, as if he were looking for answer. "Lieberman may have been involved in some unseemly way with Geraldo Guzman, so he killed him and took his phone. He then roped Riley into the mess somehow, maybe by threating his job or paying him off. Lieberman's pretty well situated financially." Kelly pulled out a pair of nail clippers and took care of a hangnail, putting the small piece of skin contemptuously in the trashcan under his desk before replacing the clippers. Reightman watched impatiently as he finished his inspection of his hands and then turned them over. Just as he started to inspect his palms, Nancy buzzed from her desk.

The Chief picked up the phone. "Chief Kelly," he announced. "Yes, ma'am….thank you….yes…that's good. I appreciate the turn-around. I do have one more which will need the city attorney's review… Yes, ma'am – Officer Helliman…Yes, that's the one. No, ma'am…apparently he tipped off Lieberman…No, ma'am, but we're working on it. Yes, I understand…thank you again…Yes, I will. Goodbye," he concluded as he hung up the phone.

"That was the assistant city manager. Lieberman is officially suspended and so is Doctor Riley. Assuming Riley's not in this up to his neck and has some kind of reasonable explanation for the missing evidence, she may agree to change it to suspension with pay until the investigation is over – if we don't arrest him." The Chief looked tired. "It's a damn shame. I liked Riley. She also confirmed they'll be bringing in an acting Coroner and an assistant for the time being. They should be here by tomorrow afternoon. Given Lieberman's involvement, he'll have to start over with the autopsy to make sure the findings are valid."

"Understood, sir. I'll let Mr. Bailey know there'll be a delay in releasing the body. He's going to be upset."

"There's no other option. He'll just have to understand."

When neither of the two detectives responded, Kelly picked up his phone again. "Nancy, any word from Judge McLarity's clerk?...What?...Why in the blazers didn't you tell me?...Okay, just simmer down…" He turned to them with an astonished look on his face. "She hung up on me. She's really pissed at you, Reightman."

"Yes, sir," she agreed. "I'm aware."

"Buy her something nice. It doesn't even have to be expensive, just bright and colorful. Women love a gift and that'll smooth things right over. Believe me, you don't want Nancy up your butt."

Reightman tried not to react to his chauvinistic comment about women loving gifts, but thought his idea about smoothing things over with Nancy might have merit. "Yes, Chief. Thanks for the advice."

He nodded and stood, rolling his neck. "The warrant's here. One of the Judge's clerks dropped it by about ten or fifteen minutes ago." Reightman winced as a couple of vertebrae were jostled into position by the neck rolling and popped. "The warrant covers Lieberman's arrest, as well as search and seizure within Lieberman's home and of any personal transportation. The office, the morgue and any equipment are already covered under city policy. Keep me informed about your discussion with Riley. I'll be available by cell phone."

"Yes, sir, will do."

"One more thing, Reightman. I've seconded Detective Jones to your team for the remainder of the investigation. I've pulled him off his regular duty in Vice, and he'll report in to you tomorrow morning."

Reightman liked Jones, but she wasn't sure she could stand working with both him and Jackson at the same time. They both dished out a fair share of crap individually, but the two teaming up together was too much to contemplate. However, done was done. "Thank you, Chief. The extra help will be appreciated." She hesitated, and then added, "If I might make a suggestion, sir?" At his nod she continued, "Could I have Mitchell, too?"

"Officer Anthony Mitchell?" the Chief frowned.

"Yes, sir. He stepped up to the plate today. Another body would be helpful right now."

The Chief considered the request, undecided if Mitchell was the right choice. "I'm assuming you want him in plain clothes rather than a uniform."

"Yes, sir."

"That would effectively be a step up for him."

"I understand, but you could make it provisional, sir."

The Chief chewed his cheek for a minute and looked to Jackson. "You agree?"

"Yes, sir. Mitchell's proven to be a good cop and deserves the chance."

"I'd still need him for the weekend."

"Hopefully things will be tied up by then." Reightman hoped they would be, because if not, they'd have a whole different set of problems on their hands.

Kelly considered the request a moment more before giving her a curt nod. "I'll agree, but just until we've wrapped this up. I'll review what might be next for Officer Mitchell after this case is closed. I'll inform him in the morning. If you see him, tell him to drop by here early tomorrow."

"Will do, sir."

They met Officer Mitchell heading toward them as they approached the interview room. "Detectives, you have perfect timing. I was just coming to get you. Dr. Riley's attorney has arrived."

"Thanks, Mitchell"

"You're welcome, Detective Jackson."

"How long ago?" Reightman asked, wondering if Riley had come up with a plausible story yet.

"Fifteen or twenty minutes ago. I thought you were probably with the Chief, but when no one answered over there, I figured I'd just head on down."

"Chief Kelly must have gone home, as well as Nancy. Maybe she'll be over her snit by tomorrow." Reightman doubted it, but decided it didn't hurt to hope for the best. "Good thinking, Mitchell. By the way, Chief Kelly

wants to talk to you in the morning. You'd better make it early, before he gets pulled away for something."

"Did he say why, Detective Reightman?"

"I'm pretty sure it's not about anything bad, Mitchell. You'll find out tomorrow." She thought about telling him the news herself, but the Chief was very protective of his territory, and this was very much his territory.

"It's probably about the weekend assignments," Mitchell decided. "I hate holiday weekends."

"We all do," Jackson commiserated with the young officer. "At least it is supposed to be a little cooler this weekend. I'm past ready for the heat to break".

"Me too, Detective Jackson. It's been pretty brutal." Mitchell looked toward both of them, eager to clock out. "Detectives, if you're through with me…? "

"Sure, Officer. Get on out of here. We'll talk later." Jackson gave him an encouraging smile as the young man turned and hurried down the hall.

"Hey, Mitchell?"

He turned and looked back her way, a little warily. She had that kind of reputation. "Yes, ma'am?"

"Thanks for the assist. You did good today."

He ducked his head a little shyly at her praise. "Thanks, Detective. I'm just glad things didn't end up ass over elbows."

"That makes two of us. Good night."

"Good night, ma'am, and you as well, Detective Jackson," he replied, before making his way to his locker to retrieve his things.

Outside the interview room, they both greeted the officer stationed in the hall. Reightman knocked on the door, announcing their arrival. As she entered the room, she noticed Riley was seated behind the table next to another man, who must be his attorney. Their heads were bent together, and they looked up as they heard the detectives enter. They both stood and Reightman examined Riley's lawyer, noting an uncanny resemblance between the two.

"Dr. Riley," Jackson acknowledged as they all took their seats.

Reightman looked across the table to the other man, waiting. He hesitated as if he wasn't quite sure what to do, then dug a card out of the leather case on the table and presented it to her. He also handed one to Jackson, who looked it over and handed it back. "One will be sufficient, Mr. Riley. But thank you anyway."

"Edmond G. Riley Family Law," Reightman read from the card in her hand. "You're related, I assume?" she asked, looking from one to the other. Two almost identical faces looked back.

"Yes, Detective, we're brothers. Some people think we're twins, but I'm about eighteen months older," Mr. Riley, Esquire answered with an open smile.

"I can see the resemblance." Reightman considered her next words carefully. "Your brother and client, is in what may be a lot of trouble." She indicated his card, "This could end up being a long way out of the ballpark from dealing with your normal Family Law clients."

"I understand. If needed, someone else from my firm will take over from me, but I was the one available tonight and when Peter called, I came."

"Alright, Mr. Riley, why don't we get started then?"

Dr. Peter Riley had watched the exchange intently, obviously worried about the interview ahead. After Mr. Riley, Esquire shot him a stern look, he nodded and his brother faced Reightman and Jackson. "We're ready, Detectives."

"I'm sure your brother…err…client has filled you in on the basics, but I think it'd be best to summarize the mess he is in, just so we're all on the same page," began Jackson. "If that's acceptable?"

"It is."

"Earlier today, Detective Reightman, with the help of one of our crime technicians, Tom Anderson, retrieved photographic information from a phone verified to have belonged to Mr. Gerald Guzman, who was found murdered at the Time Out Spa, located in the downtown district. One piece of this evidence, in addition to a print found and determined to belong to Dr. Benjamin Lieberman, lead Detective Reightman, assisted by Officer Mitchell, to attempt to detain Dr. Lieberman. To accomplish this, they entered the lab at approximately 4:15 PM this afternoon, and discovered Lieberman had been tipped off, and had left the premises before the Detective could apprehend him. The informant was identified by your client, Dr. Riley." Jackson paused and looked toward the attorney. "Does this information align with that provided by your client?"

"It does, Detective. Peter has provided his version of the events, which matches yours exactly."

Jackson nodded. "To continue then, moments after Detective Reightman and Office Mitchell learned they'd be unable to detain Dr. Lieberman, they were joined in the morgue area by Tom Anderson. At that time, they were informed another print on the phone had been identified as belonging to your client." The attorney nodded his agreement with Jackson's summation of events. "Following this disclosure, Dr. Riley was escorted from the area and brought here. He was allowed to make arrangements for representation, which he determined he needed."

Again, Edmond Riley indicated his agreement.

Jackson looked at Reightman and she indicated he should continue. "What you may not yet know, Mr. Riley, is following those events, an inspection was carried out by Detective Reightman and Mr. Anderson. During their search, items were found in one of Dr. Riley's desk drawers. Those items are believed to have belonged to Mr. Guzman and are also believed to be items missing from the logged inventory of his personal affects." Jackson paused again to await their reaction.

Mr. Riley inclined his head toward the Detectives. "Peter warned me such evidence might be found."

Reightman watched Peter Riley closely while his brother spoke. The young man was pale but very composed. *"Aren't they a cool, calm and collected pair?"* She wondered when or if there'd be a break in their composure.

"Perhaps this would be a good time for Detective Reightman to continue?" Jackson suggested.

"Thank you for the summation, Detective Jackson. I think it's time to ask Dr. Riley a couple of key questions – the answers of which will determine how we proceed."

The two Riley's waited across the table.

"Mr. Riley, the questions are very straight forward. My first question relates to the phone which belonged to Mr. Guzman and is a fairly obvious question. Tell me, Dr. Riley, why did the phone have your print on it?"

Edmond nodded to his brother, indicating that he should speak. "Go ahead, Peter."

"It's kind of a long story," the doctor warned.

"We have plenty of time. I don't have anything else planned for tonight." she assured him sardonically, thinking of everything still to be done, including tracking down Lieberman.

"Remember I told you Dr. Lieberman was acting weird?"

"Yes, I do."

"Well, I was watching him very closely. The night we brought in Mr. Guzan's body, he made a call, and I overheard him tell the person on the other end not to worry, because he had the phone."

"Did you, or do you have at this time, have any idea who Dr. Lieberman was speaking with?" asked Jackson.

"No Detective, I didn't then and I don't now."

Jackson made an entry on his notepad. "Please continue, Dr. Riley."

"Well, Dr. Lieberman became increasingly agitated and I overhead him mention the phone a couple of times in conversations he had that evening, and the next morning. I finally asked him which phone he was worried about."

"What did Lieberman say when you asked him that?"

"He blew a gasket, Detective Reightman! He told me to mind my own business and reminded me very harshly that I was his assistant and shouldn't be asking questions of my own superior. He said if I needed to know, I'd be told. Until then, I was to keep my mouth shut." Peter took a drink of water from the bottle in front of him. "Later the next morning, he told me my performance review was coming up, and said he was afraid he'd have to give me a negative rating unless I towed the line. He implied it could seriously impact the completion of my residency, and I might find myself without a job and without a way to complete my certification process."

So, the Chief was right in thinking Lieberman had pressured him. "Why didn't you report him to someone, Riley?"

"I don't know, Detective Reightman. I guess I was just scared."

"Alright. Please continue."

"He made another call that morning, and it got really loud. I heard the word 'phone' again before he shut the door. I could see him through the window but didn't want to get caught looking. Every time I snuck a look, I could see him waving his arms and shouting and he knocked his briefcase off the desk. I couldn't see him anymore for a while. I guess he was on the floor picking stuff up. Pretty soon, he came out of his office with his briefcase and told me he was going home because he wasn't feeling well. I asked if I should continue on with Guzman's autopsy and he nearly bit my head off. He told me it would mean my job if I went anywhere near Guzman. Then he stormed out."

"What happened next, Riley?"

"Detective Reightman, I waited until he was gone. Then I looked in his window and saw something silvery underneath one corner of his desk. I figured it was something from the briefcase and I… well, I was curious."

Jackson looked up from his notetaking, and after a glance at Reightman, nodded for him to continue. Riley took another drink of water. He looked at his brother and cleared his throat. "I opened his office door with the spare set of keys and went in. I got down on my hands and knees and reached under the desk and gave the thing underneath a little push. That's probably when my fingerprint got on it. Anyway, it came scooting out from under the desk and stopped right near my knee. It was a phone, and I thought it might be the phone Lieberman was shouting about."

Riley took another drink and looked down at the table to collect his thoughts. "I started to pick it up, but then I thought about finger prints. I should have thought about that a little sooner, I guess. I went and put on a pair of gloves and picked it up. I turned it on and saw whose it was by the photo and name on screen. I thought I heard someone coming, so I put it in my pocket and locked up the office before I got caught. I didn't know what to do with it then, so I just kept it in my pocket and took it home with me, hoping that I'd come up with some idea. By the time I got home, I was pretty worried and knew I shouldn't have taken it. I didn't know what else to do with it, so I just kept it with me."

Jackson thought over the man's testimony as he reviewed his notes. "If you had the phone with you, Dr. Riley, how did Reightman come to find it in her purse?"

She felt perspiration on the back of her neck for the first time in several days. She answered before Riley could. "Mr. Riley went to the grocery store that night." She looked across the table at the doctor. "Didn't you?" Peter Riley looked down at the table and stared at its battered top. He didn't answer. Reightman thought back to that night at the grocery store and everything that had happened: Falling to the ground after colliding with someone, her disorientation, the push of a foot that sent her face down into the concrete. "Didn't you, Riley?"

He looked up but wouldn't meet her eyes. He started at the wall behind her. "Yes," he finally answered.

"Why?" She didn't have to explain the question. He knew exactly what she wanted to know.

"It just happened. I'd just gone into the store and realized I didn't have my wallet. I started to go back to the car to check if maybe it had slipped out of my pocket. When I turned around, I saw you through the windows, coming from the parking lot. I thought about the phone I still had with me and I panicked." Riley looked over toward his brother and then finally, at her. "I figured if I could somehow pass you the phone, it would be out of my hands. You'd know what to do. I didn't mean to crash into you so hard, Detective. I swear I didn't."

"And when I tried to get up, that was you too, wasn't it? Pushing me back to the concrete with your foot."

"Yes." Riley was flushed now, remembering how he had forced her face down into the pavement. "I couldn't risk you looking up and recognizing me," he admitted. "I dropped the phone in with the rest of the stuff scattered on the ground and then I ran back to my car. I was parked around the corner from the entrance, and I hoped you wouldn't see me once I made the turn." He inhaled a shaky breath. "I got in the car and sped out of the lot."

"I could have been hurt, Riley. I was hurt, a little," she said as she touched her face, feeling the tender skin.

"I know," he said, regretfully. "But, I watched from my car once I made it to the parking lot across the street – the one by the dry cleaners. I saw other people stop and help. I saw you walk back to your car and get in. I watched you drive away..." his voice trailed off as the enormity of what he had done began to sink in.

The room was perfectly silent, except for the sound of Peter Riley's shaky breath. "After you drove away, I went back to the store," he continued. "I looked on the ground by the entrance to see if I could spot the phone. When I didn't see it, I went into the store and asked if anyone had turned a phone in. No one had. I was still worried about you, but I was more relieved the phone was gone."

Reightman viewed him through narrowed eyes until Riley averted his face. Shaken by the pitiless expression on her face, he took another drink of water and worried the plastic cap in his fingers. After taking another deep breath, he forced himself to continue. "When...when you called to check on the status of Guzman's autopsy, I was relieved. I started to ask if you were alright."

"You did ask, Riley," Reightman interrupted as she replayed the last few days in her mind. "You did ask, although it was well after the time your concern would've done me any good. I remembered thinking you were acting weird, but chalked it up to you catching crap from Lieberman." As the events of the last few days came together, another small piece fell into place for her. "You also sent me a note through the interdepartmental mail, didn't you? A note telling me to check the phone. That was you as well, wasn't it?"

He didn't answer until his brother nudged him with his elbow. "Yes," he replied, relieved that the worst was over.

Reightman stood up and walked over to the other side of the table, and looked down at him from a couple of feet away. "I want to just punch you, Peter Riley!" she told him heatedly. "For knocking me to the ground and shoving my face down with your foot. " She watched him shift nervously in his chair and lowered her voice. "Why didn't you just bring the phone to me, or to Detective Jackson? We would've believed you."

"I was afraid," he said simply, as if it explained everything. "It would've been Dr. Lieberman's word against mine." When he couldn't think of anything else, he added, "I just wanted to do the right thing."

"Which you accomplished, in absolutely the worst possible way." Reightman shook her head in disgust. She looked at him with very little pity, and with a great deal of annoyance. "What about the necklace and earring Tom and I found stashed in your desk?"

"When we…right after we had the body back at the morgue, and had removed the earring and the necklace, Lieberman placed them in a little clear bag and laid it to the side. They were eventually logged in with the rest of the victim's things." Riley thought through the events of that night. "He – Dr. Lieberman – wasn't being careful you know? He was kind of rough and …disrespectful I guess, with the way he handled the body. He practically ripped the earring out of the lobe of the ear. He was more careful with the necklace and even polished the pendant a little. It was really weird, because I thought I recognized the star. It looked like something he used to wear. He even kind of played with…with…well, with some of Mr. Guzman's body parts and I think maybe he also cut off…" Riley blinked his eyes rapidly as if he was trying to erase the memory from his mind. "When I realized what some of the things he was doing were, I was appalled, but when Lieberman saw me looking at him, he stopped." Riley took a gulp of the water in front of him and paused to settle his disturbed thoughts before continuing. When he spoke again, he was more composed. "I didn't think any more about the jewelry until a day or so later. That officer, the one that brought down the photocopy, came down a day or so later right after Lieberman returned from being out sick, and handed him something."

"Helliman?" Jackson asked for clarification.

"Yes," Riley confirmed.

"Did anyone else see Officer Helliman come in?"

"No, there wasn't anyone else around. About an hour after Officer Helliman left, I saw Lieberman swinging the pendant around by the chain, kind of like an old-timey hypnotist, and then he put it in his lab coat pocket. After he left for the night, I snagged the coat and found the necklace and the earring as well. I dug around and found a box of paperclips and I emptied them into the top drawer of my desk. I put the jewelry in the box and hid it in the back of the drawer." He shot Reightman a quick glance. "I was going to send it to you, Detective, like I did with the note."

"Why were you going to do that, Riley?"

"I thought that maybe you'd get it back to whoever it belonged to. Someone must have wanted those things to help remember Mr. Guzman."

"Well, you've certainly been a very busy man over the last few days Dr. Riley." Jackson looked up briefly from his notes when he heard the scorn in her voice. The doctor flushed a deep red, but to his credit, didn't look away. The four of them set in silence until Jackson finished with his review of the notes he'd taken throughout the entire interview.

"Did you see anything else? Anything that struck you as odd?" asked Jackson.

Peter Riley took his time, thinking things over carefully before turning toward Jackson. "Nothing else like that, but Lieberman was really strange. Like I said, he wasn't respectful to the body. He made... incisions he didn't need to make, especially around the neck. It was almost like –"

"Like what, Dr. Riley?"

"I'm not sure, Detective Jackson, but it was almost like he was trying to confuse things."

"Confuse things in what way?"

Riley shook his head. "I don't know." He looked toward Reightman. "Remember, Detective, when I said he wasn't letting me do my job or assist with anything? And I told you he was always sending me away?" Reightman nodded. "Well, it was like he didn't want me to see what he was doing. He knew if I was too close, I'd know some of the things he was doing were not only unnecessary, but harmful in terms of preserving evidence. He also seemed to be taking his time with things – delaying almost. Like with the toxicology samples. He was really mad when I went ahead and sent them out for testing."

Jackson flipped back a few pages and read the notes he had taken since the beginning of the interview. He tapped his pen on the paper a few times, looking at Riley intently. "Is there anything else, anything at all, you'd like to add?"

"No, Detective Jackson."

"Alright then." Jackson closed his notebook and stood to address the attorney. "Detective Reightman and I are going to step out into the hall for a minute." Melba and Sam left the room and once in the hall Jackson leaned against the wall. "What do you think?" he asked.

"I think I'm glad Dr. Riley only works on dead bodies and not live ones. I can't believe he was so stupid!"

"I agree he wasn't very smart, but Melba, we have no idea what it must have been like down there with Lieberman."

"But, Sam, he could have come to us! We would have believed him."

"Maybe. But as he said, it would've been his word against that of a more senior, respected professional who's been the City Coroner for several years. Lieberman's also well connected." Sam contemplated his partner as she leaned against the wall, mirroring his own pose. "We might have believed him, but would anyone else? You know how things work, Melba." He regarded her for a minute more and then straightened. "You want to charge him, Reightman?"

"With what, stupidity?" she asked from her slouch against the wall.

Sam chuckled. "Well, we could definitely make that charge stick." Then, more seriously, he suggested, "I was thinking more along the lines of tampering with evidence and assaulting an officer."

Reightman shook her head, "No, Sam, at least not with the assault charge. As for the other, I think we should run it by the Chief. I say we let him go for tonight, but advise him and his attorney brother that we may have further business."

As she straightened from the wall, she shook her head and then rubbed her temples. "It's a shame."

"Yes, it is," Jackson agreed. They both knew they were talking about young Dr. Peter Riley's actions and the probable result those actions would have on a career he'd only just started. Sam held the door open for her as they went back into the interview room.

Jackson was the one who gave him their decision. "Dr. Riley, I think we're done for the present. We will not be pressing charges at this time, although our position may change after review with Police Chief Kelly.

We may also have further questions for you and will expect your cooperation should the need arise."

When both of the Riley brothers signaled their understanding and agreement, Jackson looked toward Reightman with a raised brow. After she gave a curt nod of agreement, he concluded, "I think we are done here for the evening."

The brothers stood and Peter Riley spoke from across the table. "Detective Reightman, I'm really sorry about the night at the grocery store. I'm glad you weren't hurt."

Reightman offered all she could to a former co-worker. "I am as well, Dr. Riley."

"Well, I guess I'll see you around tomorrow, Detective,' he added, hoping to normalize the situation.

She looked him full in the face without speaking for several seconds. Finally, she said, "No, Doctor. I don't think we'll see each other around here again."

As the meaning behind her words became clear, he paled and dropped back down into his chair.

"Mr. Riley," she addressed the brother standing at his side, "We'll be in touch."

"I'll wait for your call, Detective," he acknowledged before gathering his things and ushering his brother from the room.

Sam and Melba followed, and when they reached the door, she flipped off the lights, causing Jackson to arch an eyebrow her way. "Just trying to save the city some money, Sam."

"Why, Melba? You hoping for a raise?"

"Like that will ever happen!"

"Yeah, it sucks to be us, doesn't it?"

"Well, I can only speak for myself, but I guess it sure must suck to be you."

"Not as much as it would suck to be you."

"Sam?" she grinned over to where he was walking by her side.

"Yes, Melba?" he grinned back.

"Just shut up!" They laughed like children and kept it up all the way down the long hall, until turning to make their way, side by side, to their desks.

❖ ❖ ❖

Later that night after a long traffic laden drive home that included a brief update to Chief Kelly, Melba unlocked the door to her apartment, struggling with her purse and a handful of mail. She dropped the mail on the counter and slipped out of her shoes. After removing her weapon and locking it away, she changed into her usual comfy set of sweats and made herself a salad while heating a can of soup. *"It sure beats a five day old carton of take-out,"* she decided with satisfaction as she shoved the vegetable peelings down the disposal and turned it on. She plated her salad and rinsed out the chipped mixing bowl and then poured the warm soup directly from the small sauce pan into a mug. She set them on the bar and took a seat on a stool and ate her dinner while looking through the mail.

After finishing her solitary meal, she dug in her purse and pulled out her phone. She rehearsed a few words to herself as she dialed her daughter. "Hey, Abby," she said when the call was answered.

"Hi, mom. I was just about to call you. I thought you should be home about now."

"Yes, I got in a few minutes ago and just finished dinner. The girls in bed?"

"Yes, finally! I didn't think I'd ever get Emily out of her pretty princess dress and into her PJs. I wish she was easy, like Melissa."

"Emily takes after you, Abby," Melba teased. "Although in your case it was a ballerina dress. You insisted on wearing it every day until it finally fell apart in the wash."

"I *loved* that dress," Abby replied wistfully.

Melba allowed herself a rare moment to reflect back on happier times. "I know you did, Abby." Making an effort to pull away from bittersweet memories, she forced some brisk cheer into her voice. "I was more than ready to see the end of that dress by the time it met with its unfortunate demise."

"Death by washing machine!"

They both laughed, and then caught up on the girl's antics. Abby asked the best way to get grape juice stains out of carpeting. After Melba gave her daughter the best advice she could come up with, she moved to the other reason for her call. "Abby, I wanted to talk about this weekend." she started.

"Ummmm…Mom, would you be terribly upset if we postponed?"

"Postponed?"

"Yes. You see, the thing is, I've met someone. I think I've talked myself into asking him to the company picnic this weekend."

"Sounds promising," Melba replied neutrally.

"I think it *is* promising, mom. He's really nice. I've only been seeing him for a little over a month, but...I think I like him. I mean, I *really* like him."

Melba wondered what kind of life she was leading when she had no idea her daughter had been seeing someone special for over a month.

"Mom?" Abby asked after a pregnant pause.

"Sorry, Abby. I'm here."

"Okay. You're not too upset are you? I know you were looking forward to seeing the girls."

"I was looking forward to that, Abby, and to seeing you as well, but I'm not upset." Melba took a breath and decided that she couldn't let Abby take all of the blame for their postponed weekend. "As a matter of fact, I was calling to ask if we could postpone anyway. When we made plans, I'd forgotten it was Labor Day weekend. The Chief needs everyone on call."

"I think it's terrible you have to work the whole weekend, mom."

"It probably won't be the whole weekend. I just have to be on call in case something comes up."

Abby was silent for a couple of seconds and then brought up the topic they'd both been avoiding. "I saw that awful case on the news, mom – the one where the man was found horribly murdered at that spa." When her mother didn't comment, she asked "Are you working that case?"

"Yes, I am." Melba tried to think of something to add, and settled on, "It's pretty complicated."

"Sounds like it is. I also saw that awful City Councilman on the news. He sounds pretty extreme."

"I think so too, but he has quite a few supporters. This is a very conservative state, Abby."

"You don't have to tell me, Mom. You may be in the state capitol, but I live in conservative central up here. I can't believe some of the attitudes I run into, and how judgmental and narrow minded people can be sometimes. It just amazes me. It wouldn't hurt anyone to just ease up a little, and live and let live."

"Does your new man think the same way?"

"Will. His name is Will Cooper, Mom. And yes, he finds it as stifling as I do. You'll like him."

"I'm sure I will, Abby," Melba replied, although like any mother worth her salt, she'd reserve judgement for a while.

"I know! Since we can't get together this weekend, why don't you plan to come up next weekend? You can stay here and spend time with me and the girls, and you can meet Will. How does that sound?"

"It sounds great. I need to see how the case is going, but if nothing gets in the way it would be terrific. I might be able to get up a day or two early. Lord knows I have the personal time saved up. You just need to know things might change at the last minute."

"Mom, I know how it goes with your job, and how things can change. I understand. I didn't always, but I do now. I won't say anything to the girls until the last minute so they won't be disappointed if things don't work out as planned. Why don't we leave it open, and you can call me in the middle of the week? We can firm things up then."

"As long as you don't mind last-minute notice, Abby."

"Not at all, Mom," assured Abby. "It'll be great." Her daughter was quiet for a moment. "The girls miss you, and so do I."

"I miss you all as well." Melba replied. *"I miss you terribly some days,"* she thought, looking around the dull, shoddy room and wondering how things had worked out in such a way that she was alone. "Abby, I love you a lot."

"I love you too, Mom." There was another moment of thoughtful, loving silence on the phone and then Abby remembered her role as a properly dutiful daughter. "I'll call you after the picnic and let you know how it goes."

"You'd better! I'll be on pins and needles all weekend. Are you taking the girls?"

"Yes, as if there was any doubt! If they knew they'd missed out on a chance to act like little hooligans in public, I'd never hear the end of it. And, they adore Will. He thinks they're pretty special too, although so far they've been on their best behavior around him. Keep your fingers crossed that he'll feel the same way after witnessing one of Emily's famous, dramatic meltdowns, or experiencing a three day stretch of Melissa's sulks. I don't know where they get it from."

Melba thought she just might know where her granddaughters had come by those traits, but kept it to herself. "I can't wait to hear about the weekend, Abby. I'm sure you'll have a lot of fun. Now, before we get off on another tangent, I better get off of the phone. It's getting late and we both have to be at work early in the morning. Kiss the girls for me!"

"Will do, Mom. Goodnight."

"Goodnight Abby. Talk to you soon." Melba ended the call and dropped the phone back in the purse.

She considered pouring a glass of wine, but settled for a cup of the special tea that Zhou Li had given her. She carried it to the ugly plaid couch and curled up, with her sock-covered feet underneath her. As she held the warm cup between her hands, she thought about Abby and the girls. She reflected on the life she'd once had, with a comfortable home in suburbia, and all that came with it. She remembered having extra money to spend on things like a good haircut or a nice blouse or pair of shoes that she really didn't need, but wanted. She took a sip of the tea. *"Stop feeling sorry for yourself, Reightman! That was then. This is now. And it ain't all bad."*

As she sipped her tea she thought about her current case and the people she had met: Toby Bailey, Madame Zhou Li, and the quirky folks operating the businesses on Capital Street. She thought about her partner, Sam. She thought about her daughter and her two precious grandchildren. *"Some of it's interesting, some of it's surprising, and some of it's really good."*

Melba finished her tea, and put the cup on the table by the sofa. She turned off the light and headed to her bedroom. Climbing into her bed and pulling back her sheets, she thought she smelled the lingering perfume of jasmine.

CHAPTER NINE

TUESDAY MORNING, Melba tracked down Sam at his usual place by the coffee pot waiting for the brew to finish. He was catching up on the scuttlebutt with the rest of the gang.

"What's up, Jackson?" she asked as she nodded good morning to the rest of the bodies squeezed into the room waiting on their own cups.

"Well, while you've been catching up on your beauty sleep, the rest of us have been catching up on the news. Greggs is retiring." The Assistant Police Chief had been a fixture in the department for as long as Melba had been on the force.

"Really? When's his last day?" She inched in front of Sam and filled her own cup with hot water.

"In another week or two. Said it was time to hand in his badge and pick up a fishin' pole."

"Good for him. It's about time."

"Yes, it is." Jackson filled his cup and moved away from the pot and reached for a donut. "You thinking about applying for the job?"

"I don't know, Jackson. This is the first I'm hearing of it. How about you? You'd be a great Assistant Chief."

"I don't think I could deal with all the administrative bullshit. Plus, Alice would kill me. She's looking forward to my retirement in a few years and is already making plans for how we're going to spend the time. Some of her ideas are pretty surprising." He wiggled his eyebrows to make sure she got the point. "You should give it some serious thought, though." He sidled over to the table loaded with the daily assortment of pastries. "Want one?" He considered the selection and then picked up the chocolate glazed winner.

"Nope, better not," she answered regretfully. "I might as well just wear a donut taped to my hip." She dunked the tea bag in her cup and waited for the ribbing to start. When it didn't, she looked around the full room and noticed the unnatural silence and the anxious looks on some of the faces. "What else is going on?"

"Helliman's in with the Chief."

"Oh. I guess they rounded him up then."

"Yes, they did. He was pretty out of control when they escorted him to the Chief's office."

Reightman refrained from further comment as they headed to their desks. She'd just stowed her purse when Jones and Mitchell rounded the corner. They pulled up about a foot away from her desk, and Jones clicked his heels together and saluted.

"Detective Vincent Jones reporting for duty, ma'am. Have your way with me, please, ma'am."

She groaned at his salacious smile. "You wish, Jones." She swung around in her chair to face Jackson, "Can you believe this crap?" Sam tried, unsuccessfully, to hide his grin. He was obviously anticipating all the fun ahead. Reightman turned back around to Mitchell. He was dressed in a pair of khakis with an open collared shirt and a navy sports coat. *"He must have received secret dress for success tips from Sam."* He started to copy Jones with the saluting routine, and she quickly cut in before he could finish. She didn't need three smart asses in their new little group. "Don't even think about it, Officer Mitchell."

The young cop gave her a sheepish grin. "Good morning, Detectives," he cheerfully greeted them. "The Chief said I was to report in to you this morning."

Melba nodded and Sam stood to welcome both of new members of the team. "Why don't you both pull up a chair and we can bring you up to speed?" he suggested. "One thing we do know about this case is we can use all of the help we can get."

The two men located a couple of empty chairs and started wheeling them over. Reightman got up from her seat to help Mitchell with a particularly difficult set of wheels right as Helliman stormed into the room.

He was in uniform, but sans badge and service revolver, and he was carrying a packing box. Obviously the Chief had cut him loose, although she wasn't sure if the leave was of a permanent nature. She, for one, hoped it was. When Helliman caught sight of her trying to shepherd the uncooperative chair into place, his face reddened and he headed toward her, crashing into the desks in his path.

"You fucking bitch!" he yelled. "This is all your fucking fault, Reightman!"

Jones moved to intercept the enraged cop as Melba stood bracing her feet, and readying herself for confrontation.

"Just simmer down, Helliman." Jones put a hand on the man's shoulder, trying to calm him down.

"Get out of my way, asshole!" Helliman pushed him out of the way with shoulder and elbow. "Mind your own fucking business, Jones."

Jackson came quickly forward to stand by her side and Mitchell moved the unruly chair out of the way to do the same. "Stand down, Helliman!" Jackson ordered.

The red-faced cop halted about four feet from her. "Afraid to fight your own battles, Reightman?" he sneered. "You're a stupid, fucking bitch and you should have left well enough alone."

"I was doing my job, Helliman, and I did it in spite of your interference."

Helliman started toward her again, but reconsidered when he saw Jackson and Mitchell begin to close ranks. He looked around at the crowd which had gathered and sensed the tension mounting in the room. A couple of cops had their hands on their revolvers, at ready. He licked his lips and leaned slightly forward. "If you did your job so well, Reightman," he hissed into her face, "where is Lieberman?" When Reightman didn't respond to his taunt, he changed tactics. "You'll be sorry, Reightman, you and your faggot friend. Some people are gonna' be real pissed about this." He wiped a little spittle from his lips and regarded her with pure hatred. "If you're not real careful, you'll end up just like that whore, Guzman."

Reightman stepped out from between Jackson and Mitchell, noticing that Jones had moved behind and to the right of Helliman. "Is that a threat?" She watched his hands tighten on the box he carried and saw the sweat break out on his forehead.

He looked around, blinking small mean eyes. "Consider it a friendly warning." Helliman glared at her once more and then turned and bumped past Jones. "I thought I told you to get out of my way, asshole!" He stomped to his desk past the circled bodies, flung a few things in the box and then closed the lid.

He looked her way once more and his lips curved into a small hate-filled smile, before he picked up the box and headed for the hallway. He turned, and blew her a kiss. "Later," he mouthed as he headed out of the room, followed a short distance away by Jones.

She stared across the room until he was no longer in sight and then released the pent-up breath she had been holding. She heard Jackson call out, "Show's over everyone. Get on back to work."

"You okay, Detective Reightman?"

"Yeah, I'm fine, Mitchell."

"I was worried there for a minute."

"Helliman's just a bully. He wasn't going to do anything much with everyone watching." She hoped she sounded more confident than she felt.

Jones walked over to give them an update. "He's left the building, Reightman. I saw him get into his car and pull out of the lot."

"Thanks." She looked at the three faces eyeing her with concern. "Now, where were we?" She forced some confidence into her voice. "Oh yeah, before we were so rudely interrupted, we were just about to sit down and determine how we're going to solve this case." Following Jackson's lead, they pulled up their chairs and got to work.

"The most pressing issue seems to be the whereabouts of Lieberman. Any word yet, Jackson?"

"No, not yet."

"Jones, why don't you take Mitchell and see if you can track down any word about where he might be holed up? Mitchell, follow his lead. I hear he's a pretty good Detective when he is not being a smart ass." Reightman grinned at Jones and continued, "See if you can run down any info about a vacation home or rental property Lieberman might have in the area."

Jones and Mitchell nodded. "Sure thing, Detective," Jones winked at her and tossed the young cop a set of keys. "Come on, Mitchell, you drive."

"Jackson, did the search team uncover anything of interest from his residence?"

"No. They said there's nothing unusual in the house, although looked like he'd been there. His safe was open and his car was in the garage."

"Any material of a sensitive nature on his home computer?"

"There wasn't anything on it except for a few downloaded movies of the adult variety. There was nothing tied to the victim or the case.

They're going to spend time today going through all the files and emails just to make sure."

"I assume there's already a trace out on credit cards as well as tracking in place for his phone."

"Yes, and the warrant for his arrest is out on the wire."

"Okay. I think we've done all we can about the good Doctor for the time being." Reightman mentally ran through the other loose ends and then had an idea. "Sam, can you run a picture of Helliman down to Mr. Goldbleum at the pawnshop? See if he recognizes him as the buyer of the knife."

"Sure, Melba, but do you really think Helliman was involved?"

She played out the different angles as she gathered up some things. "I don't know, Sam. We know he's a dirty cop, and he provided the tip-off to Lieberman. But to murder Guzman? I just can't see it. Geraldo Guzman could have wiped the floor with him. Besides, whoever did it was way smarter than Helliman, given the fact there was so little evidence at the scene."

"Helliman may not be smart, Reightman, but he's cunning. I saw the look in his eyes a minute ago. He was like a boar hog trying to find the best way out of the underbrush while staring down a dog." Jackson hesitated and then added. "Melba, there may be others in on it."

She refused to meet his eyes as she continued sorting through the items on her desk.

"Just think about it. What are the odds that Helliman would have teamed up with Lieberman on his own initiative?" As she started to interrupt he held out a finger and touched the side of his nose. "Don't trust anyone and watch your back."

Not even you, Jackson?"

He didn't say anything for a minute, and then saw the look on her face. "You can trust me." Then more seriously, "You can probably trust the Chief and I think young Officer Mitchell and Detective Jones are okay. But I wouldn't bet on anyone else." He thought for a minute and, in an effort to lighten the mood, added, "And you can trust Nancy – even though she hates your guts right now."

Reightman was glad for the change of mood and for the reminder. "Oh damn! I forgot all about her snit yesterday. I guess I'd better take the Chief's advice and pick up a present or something."

"I always knew you were a woman of uncommonly good sense."

"You can say that again, but, please don't. I might get a big head."

Sam stood and patted his pockets to make sure he had his phone and his notebook before taking his jacket off of the back of his chair. "What's on your agenda for the morning?" he asked.

"I'm headed down to Capital Street to inform Toby Bailey we will not be releasing Guzman's body as hoped. After that cheerful task, I thought I'd close the loop and stop into the one or two stores we haven't hit yet and talk with the owners. That's probably another dead end, but I might as well finish up the legwork." She put a few more things in her purse and slung it over her shoulder. "Once I get back, I am going to march downstairs to the morgue and introduce myself to the new acting coroner, assuming he or she gets here by then. While I'm making nice, I am going to throw myself on my knees and beg them to *please* finish up with Guzman. After all that, we'll see."

"Don't forget your shopping."

"Alright, Sam, I got the hint the first time."

"Seems like a light, restful day, Melba."

"Sam?"

He held up his hands. "I know what you're going to say. You're going to tell me to shut up."

Reightman shook her head. "No, not right now, anyway." She looked up into his face. "I'm going to say thanks, for standing by my side when Helliman went berserk. It helped."

"'Twern't nothing ma'am." he touched two fingers to the imaginary brim of his equally imaginary hat. He looked at her seriously and added, "Just be careful, Melba. Please. I don't know what I'd do if something bad happened to you."

She felt a spot of suspicious moisture in the corner of her eye, and turned away slightly so he wouldn't notice.

"Besides," he added, having seen her expression, "it would take forever to break in a new partner."

"Sam?"

"Yeah?"

"Shut up."

Jackson gave her little salute and headed out to the pawnshop, whistling a *really* irritating tune under his breath.

Thirty minutes later, Reightman pulled up in front of the Time Out Spa. She got out of her car with her ever present purse slung on her shoulder and tried the door to the spa. It was locked. The uniformed detail was no longer in place, having been pulled off to cover other things. She knocked and peered through the glass. After a few more attempts, she pulled out her phone and dialed Toby. The call went to straight to voice mail. She left a short message saying she'd either call or stop back by in an hour or so. After putting the phone back down into the purse, she started down the sidewalk and spotted Madame Zhou tottering across the street – jaywalking. Zhou Li reached her side of the street and stepped up over the curb.

"Good morning, Detective," she greeted Melba brightly. "What brings you down to Capital Street?"

"Good morning, Madame Zhou. I was just in the area and thought I'd see if I could catch Mr. Bailey. He doesn't seem to be here."

"He is probably off on a jog. Now that your plans have been delayed, why don't you come with me, Detective?' Zhou suggested.

"Where are you going? It seems too early for lunch."

"It is too early for lunch, Detective. I had a rather hearty breakfast anyway," Zhou patted her stomach appreciatively. "I'm headed down to discover if Moon has anything wonderful in today. Why don't you join me?"

"You're going to shop at Passed Around?" When Madame Zhou nodded that she was, Reightman decided to join her. "Why not? I was meaning to stop and talk with her this morning anyway."

"Since that's the case, Detective, we will go together."

The two women made their way down the sidewalk until they were in front of the window to the shop. Zhou stopped to look at the window display, giving it her full attention. "Moon has such a flair for display! This window in really something, wouldn't you agree?"

Reightman looked at the window of mannequins, wearing what looked like a rainbow collection of poufy net prom dresses and augmented by a few more dressed in a collection of things only a group of especially slutty cowgirls would wear. "It's really something," she agreed.

Zhou Li continued to peer through the window and soon, the shop door opened and a tall African-American woman glided out from the shop's entrance. The woman's skin was a luminous medium-dark tone, and was glowing in the sunlight. She was wearing a brightly colored print tunic over a pair of black leggings with flat ballet slippers. Her dark hair was cut asymmetrically, with one side just reaching her shoulders and the other hitting just at her jawline. The haircut perfectly accented the strong features of her face. She looked very edgy and very chic.

"Madame Zhou! It is so good to see you!" she exclaimed in a pleasant contralto voice. "Don't you just adore the window?"

"It is perfect as always, my dear," Madame Zhou agreed enthusiastically. "I think it will be just the ticket to bring them in." Zhou Li remembered her manners. "Moon, I would like to introduce you to Detective Reightman. She is working to solve the horrible murder."

Moon quickly assumed a sad, tragic expression and brought a large, thin hand to her heart. "Oh, that poor, dear man. The world has lost one of its great wonders with his unfortunate passing. Toby must be grieving the deep, rending, never ending grief of a man for a former lover."

"Yes, I am sure his death is a great tragedy," Reightman responded to the brief soliloquy and held out her hand, "It's nice to meet you Miz...."

"My name is Moon. Detective, just Moon. Not a first name, nor a last name. Just Moon, like the beautiful gleaming orb that sails through the night sky."

Reightman decided that Moon most probably had a background in theater, or had perhaps learned elocution from a tragic Byronesque poet. "I was wondering if I can ask you a few questions? "

"Most assuredly, Detective. I will happily pledge to assist you in any way which might help Geri's gentle, slain spirit find its just and peaceful rest."

Reightman collected her thoughts with some effort, having been momentarily enthralled by the mournful cadence coming from Moon's scarlet painted mouth. "Can you tell me if you noticed anything out of the ordinary over the last few weeks, especially the days immediately prior to Mr. Guzman's death?"

Moon assumed a classical thoughtful expression, and touched one long exquisitely manicured finger nail to her full lips. The polish on the nail matched, exactly. "Alas, Detective," she exhaled breathlessly, disappointment trembling in her voice, "I fear I've failed to noticed anything or anyone out of the ordinary on any of the past days."

"How about during the evening hours?"

"On what night was the beautiful Geri so dreadfully slain? Please remind me, the days do blend together so."

"Mr. Guzman was murdered last Wednesday night."

"Oh!" Moon gave a startled exclamation as she was reminded how few days had passed since the murder. "Yes, it was just this last week wasn't it, Madame?" When the tiny woman gave her an affirmative nod, Moon whispered, "The fickle inconsistent wings of Time have flown so very swiftly." Moon tapped her finger on her lips and then, without her usual, adjective laden verbosity added, "I remember seeing two mysterious cars in the lot across the street. I thought that it was odd at the time."

"Why did the cars strike you as mysterious, Moon?"

"Because, Detective, they were there!" Moon declaimed with a flourish of her arms. "There are hardly ever cars in the lot during the sultry summer evening hours when all of our wonderful and gloriously unique shops are closed. That there were *two* on the same night was very mysterious."

"I see," Reightman responded slowly, wondering if something in the water on Capital Street had somehow affected every shop keepers in the area. "Could you describe them, or did you by chance write down a license plate number?"

"I'm terribly afraid I failed to do that, Detective. You see, it was inky black with deep and doleful darkness that evening and the moon, the gracious lady of the heavens, had not yet risen to grace the evening sky."

After decoding the response, Reightman deduced Moon was unable to describe the cars and had not written down the plates. "Thank you anyway, Moon. I appreciate the information."

"But of course, Detective. My heart is filled to overflowing with sorrow, knowing I was unable to be of any service." She shook Reightman's hand with a surprising firm grasp and turned to Zhou. "Madame, if you will allow me to mention, I do have a few new items of delectable and irresistible beauty I feel will be of the utmost interest to you, just inside."

"That is wonderful, dear. I'll be in momentarily, just as soon as I finish with the Detective." Moon glided back into her shop and Zhou Li turned to Reightman "I'm sorry she wasn't able to help, Detective, and I know she's disappointed as well. She thinks very fondly of Toby, and always appreciated Geri."

"Appreciated him?"

"She's been one of the spa's regular clients ever since Toby opened. Moon felt Geri Guzman had the most skillful technique of anyone on the staff."

Reightman found herself wondering if Guzman had employed the same skillful techniques he'd apparently offered to others in the city, but quickly dismissed the thought from her mind. "I'm sorry she wasn't able to provide more information as well, Madame Zhou, but I'm really not surprised. It was a long shot anyway."

"Where are you off to now, Detective?"

"Well, I need to do a little shopping." Reightman's tone described exactly how she felt about shopping in general, and this task, in specific. "I need to pick up a small gift for Chief Kelly's administrative assistant. I'm not sure where to go, though."

"Perhaps I can help, Detective. Do you have an idea what you are looking for in the way of a gift?"

"No, not really. I thought maybe I could find a scarf, or a trendy pair of earrings. Something like that."

"It may surprise you, Detective, but you're already in the best place possible. I am sure Moon has a wonderful selection from which you can choose something."

Reightman glanced doubtfully to the window, trying to imagine Nancy's reaction to a pale pink prom dress.

Madame Zhou followed her gaze and said dismissively, "Don't pay any attention to that tawdry stuff, Detective. Moon just drags it out from the basement every year about this time. Several of the local sororities plan themed rush parties right about now. She wouldn't normally be caught with any of that kind of thing, but, regardless of her theatrical demeanor and her somewhat excessive use of words, she is a very shrewd business woman. There are very few people with her innate sense of style and fashion in this city."

"Really?"

"Yes, Detective. Now, lend me your arm please. There's a slight step up at the door and I would appreciate your assistance."

Reightman dutiful escorted Madame Zhou into the shop. As they stepped over the threshold her eyes widened slightly. She had expected piles of dusty clothes displayed on card tables, and stacks of badly worn shoes lined up along the floor. The inside of Passed Around was about as far from that as it was possible for a shop to be.

The deeply polished antique wooden floor was covered by what appeared to be, to Reightman's admittedly untrained eyes, very good quality rugs. Round clothing racks similar to those found in high-end department stores were dotted about the store, filled with clothing arranged by style and size. Recessed shelving lit with small spot lights held shoes and handbags, and there were several shelves filled with accessories of assorted natures and colors. There was also a small locked jewelry case near the counter.

"Oh, Madame Zhou…" Moon came through a door at the back of the shop, carrying a couple of filled garment bags and an immense old fashioned hatbox.

"The Detective is in need of a gift today, Moon, and I assured her this would be a wonderful place to find one."

"You do me too much honor, Madame, in recommending my humble shop." Moon touched her hand to her heart in a show of appreciation and then turned to Melba. "How may I help, Detective?"

"Well, as Madame Zhou mentioned, I'm in need of a small gift for an associate at work. It's for the Police Chief's secretary. I was thinking that either a pair of earrings or a scarf would be nice."

"Could you describe this most worthy personage for me, Detective?"

"Yes, of course." Reightman launched in with a description which took longer than she'd anticipated, because she was required to pause occasionally to answer Moon's many, interjected questions.

Once she'd finished, Moon closed her eyes as if savoring the description with deep appreciation. "That was just wonderful, Detective. I feel that I know her as I know a close and dear friend." After a moment more of silent contemplation, Moon opened her eyes, focused on the task at hand. "I think I know just the thing! One moment, while I get it." Moon went directly to one of the shops many shelves and returned with a small folded bundle. When she reached the counter, she unfurled it for their inspection, causing a considerable length of fabric to flutter gracefully in the air before settling on the counter. The scarf which Moon had retrieved from the shelves was made of some light, cobwebby material the color of the summer sky and was artfully embellished with large, appliqued daisies. One or two large, brightly colored butterflies were embroidered on the material, as if they were flitting from flower to flower. It looked exactly like something Nancy would wear – if she was possessed of good taste.

"It's beautiful." Melba had never seen anything like it before.

"It is indeed, lovely." Zhou Li stroked the fabric with a tiny hand. "The silk is very good quality and the hand-work is excellently executed."

"Yes, isn't it absolutely, unbelievably breathtaking?" Moon gushed. "It is a Paris original from the late 1950s and it is in *perfect* condition. I don't know who the designer was, to my misfortune and regret. Alas, there was not a tag. But it's of exceptionally high quality."

Reightman, having heard the words silk, Paris original and exceptionally high quality, was afraid the scarf was way out of her price range. "I'm afraid to ask, but, how much is it?" Moon walked behind the counter and wrote something down on a small piece of paper. She folded it once and handed it to Melba, who opened the paper and read the number. She blinked in shock. "But this can't be right!"

The scarf was expensive, but much less so than she'd feared. Reightman considered the possibility of enduring the ongoing Wrath of Nancy, and weighed that unpleasantness against two or three boxes of Zinfandel. *"What the heck? After all, you're not drinking much besides your tea these days, and dealing with Nancy's snit fit for any longer than necessary is out of the question."* Melba fingered the silk, and thought about the purchase. "I'll take it," Reightman heard herself say. "Could you just put it in a bag please?"

"I will most absolutely not just put it in a bag, Detective!" Moon objected. "A scarf of this vintage and supreme workmanship deserves the most wonderful wrapping." She excused herself and went through the door at the back of the shop.

"You see, Detective, Moon has the most wonderful things, and most of them are more than reasonably priced," Madame Zhou commented. "That is the beauty of shopping at a reputable resale shop owned by someone like Moon. She never accepts any merchandise but that of the best quality and condition. She usually knows something about the background of every item she sells. And she is very, very discreet. She has clients all over the southeast, both buyers and sellers."

A few minutes later, Moon returned from the back of the shop carrying a dramatically wrapped package. The paper was dark midnight blue, as was the ribbon and bow. From underneath the bow hung a heavy embossed round paper disk about the size of a silver dollar. The disk depicted a stylized smiling moon.

"Thank you, Moon. This is beautiful."

"You're very welcome, Detective. I am happy to have been of some small service to you, at least in this matter," Moon gracefully referred to her earlier failure to provide a description, or license plate information for either of the mysterious cars. "Will there be anything else? Perhaps something as a treat for yourself?"

Reightman suddenly felt dowdy and run-down in her serviceable, but old and very dull suit. Moon however, didn't give the slightest indication, by look or tone, that she found anything objectionable with her attire. Zhou however, was looking at her with hope. "I'm afraid this will be all for today." Reightman replied, catching the disappointed frown forming on Zhou's face. "Although, I'll be back soon to find something for myself." She paid the bill and, after thanking both the smiling shopkeeper and Madame Zhou, she walked out the door of Passed Around. Reightman put the package in the backseat of her car and then dialed Toby Bailey. He answered right away.

"Hey, Detective Melba."

"Hello, Toby." She rolled her eyes at his use of the previously suggested form of address, but since she kind of liked it, she let it pass. "Did you get my message?" She leaned against the hood of the car, and quickly stood up again. The hood was already hot from the morning sun.

"Yes, I was at the gym and then went for a run. I'm all done now, and even freshly showered. You want to meet now?'

"If it works for you. How about here at the spa? I'm right out front."

There was a pause before he answered. "Yeah, sure. That'll be fine. I'll be over in a couple of minutes."

"I'll be the one out front, standing in the hot sun."

Not five minutes later, Toby came out of the stairwell entrance that led up to his apartment. "It's a scorcher out here already," he said by way of greeting. He quickly unlocked the door and ushered her inside to the cool air. "What's up?" he asked as he flipped on a few lights and started toward the hall that led to his office.

"I've got a few things I need to bring you up to date on," she said following him down the hall. "Some of it's not great news, I'm afraid." Toby unlocked the door to his office and opened the door for her. "I don't remember you having a lock on this door."

"I didn't. I had it added yesterday. I thought it would be more secure."

"Probably a good idea," she agreed as he seated himself behind the desk.

"So, what's the bad news, Detective Melba?"

Reightman dropped her bag in one of the chairs in front of his desk, and took a seat in the other. She decided the best way to break the news was to just hit it head-on. "Toby, I'm sorry, but they will not be able to release Mr. Guzman's body as I'd hoped."

"But why not, Detective?"

She noted the clouded, confused look in his eyes as she prepared to share what she knew. "It's a long story, Toby. Bear with me, and I'll try and explain it." She walked him through her discovery of Geraldo Guzman's phone and the surprising find of the prints and the pictures. When she got to their current hunt for Lieberman, he interrupted.

"So, what you are telling me, Detective, is the evidence related to the autopsy results is compromised and the work will have to be redone."

She sat back in the chair, surprised. "Yes. How did you know?"

"I may be a dumb spa jockey, but even I watch TV. I know cop shows on the tube are exaggerated, but I guess in this case they'd be right."

"In this case, they are." He didn't reply but looked down at the top of his desk. "Toby, I really am very sorry. I know how badly you want to get this chapter closed."

He looked up at her with an indecipherable expression. "That's an interesting way to put it – this chapter closed." He fiddled with a pencil on the desk for a few seconds before asking, "What's the *next* chapter, Detective?"

"I don't understand the question. Do you mean, what are the steps to be completed before we can release Geri's remains?"

He regarded her across the desk, his face almost expressionless. "Yes, that's what I'm asking. I'm just trying to come to terms with things."

"I know it's tough to be in this situation, Toby." He dropped his eyes for a minute and then looked up at her, preparing himself to hear what she had to say. "The new acting coroner should be in the office today," Reightman eventually continued. "I assure you, I plan to apply as much pressure as possible to make sure releasing Geri Guzman's remains is the top priority. Even given the nature of the case, and the events that led to us to call in a new acting coroner, I think I'll be successful." After he nodded his understanding, she continued, "As important as releasing Geri's remains are to you, having all the evidence verified and confirmed are, to me, equally important. Short of finding Lieberman, I can't think of anything more important right now."

"What are you hoping they'll find out from the autopsy?"

"I don't know for sure," she admitted, while considering what she could reasonably tell him without crossing the line. Deciding he had the right to know the basics, she laid it out for him. "The autopsy will firstly confirm the cause of death. The coroner will examine the wounds and confirm their match with the suspected murder weapon. He'll then determine if the wounds sustained were indeed the cause of death, or if there was another cause, or set, of contributing causes. I don't know what to expect, but that's where he'll start. He'll also take samples and send them for a toxicology screening, to rule out the presence of drugs or unusual substances. This should have all been completed, but I think you understand why we couldn't trust the results even if it had been. As callous as it sounds, it's a good thing we caught on to Lieberman when we did, and now have a chance to re-verify the evidence. Otherwise, we might have never known who was responsible for your friend's death."

Toby listened to her words, and then asked the question which had been bothering him since she'd first told him about Lieberman's involvement. "Why didn't you tell me you had Geri's phone, Detective?"

Reightman looked at the hands clasped in her lap, feeling a little guilty about her deception. "I couldn't, Toby." She met his eyes." I wasn't sure the phone belonged to Geri. I thought it might have belonged to–"

"Me."

"Yes. I thought there was a remote possibility it might have been yours."

Toby leaned back in his chair and looked at the picture that included his grandmother, Geri and himself. After a long and uncomfortable moment of silence, he straightened his chair. "I understand, Detective. I think it was the smart thing for you to do, all things considered." He leaned forward and folded his arms on the desk. "What's next with Lieberman?"

"Our team is working to find him, along with every other resource the department can spare. There are bulletins out everywhere, and I have two additional officers working directly with Jackson and me. We will find him." Toby didn't respond to her last assurance. Instead, he watched her from across the desk, rolling the pencil in his fingers. She had no idea what was going on behind his blue eyes. After a moment she asked, "Do you ever remember Geri mentioning Lieberman? Did you ever see them together?"

"I don't remember him mentioning anyone by that name," he answered slowly. "And I wouldn't have any way to recognize him."

"Didn't you see him here, the night of the murder?"

"I was somewhat occupied with other things, like being interviewed by you and then locked up for the night in the city jail."

She winced at his pointed reminder about the events of that evening. "So much has happen in the last few days I forgot for a minute. Let me think for a second." After running through a couple of possibilities, she hit on an idea she thought might provide some answers. "Can you pull up the city webpage? There should be a picture of Lieberman on the city directory in the City Coroner's Office section."

"Sure." He turned to his computer and started typing on the keyboard. From her seat in front of the desk, Reightman recognized the City website as it appeared on the screen, and she could see Toby navigating to the appropriate place in the directory. After a while he looked back at her. "He's not in here."

"Are you sure?" She went behind the desk to look over his shoulder.

"Pretty sure." He wiggled the mouse over the space for the coroner's office. In place of Lieberman's name and picture there was a gray box populated with a generic graphic of a person's head. Text underneath the graphic read, "Position currently vacant."

"Dammit! They always pick the most inconvenient times to be efficient. They sure burned rubber to get his picture and bio down." Using his mouse, she scrolled down to the box for the Assistant Coroner, and saw it too had a gray box and similar text.

"What now?"

"I can probably track a picture down from someplace." Reightman thought of the picture of Lieberman that Tom had retrieved from Geri's phone. *"It's a sleazy picture, but it'll do."* She walked back over to the chairs and picked up her purse. "I'll track it down and give you a call in the next day or so, on the off chance you might recognize him."

Toby stood to walk her to the door. As they exited his office, he turned and locked the door.

"You're not staying?"

"No," he said, as he turned the key and checked to make sure the lock had engaged, and then indicated the crime tape placed across the entrances to the other room off the hall. "There's not much point until you guys are done and I can get a crew in to clean. "

"I'm sorry. Toby. We'll be done soon."

"Detective, stop apologizing for things which aren't your fault. It's just the way it is right now – you can't control everything. I do need to get this place open again and I need to do it as soon as possible. But at least some of the spa technicians are working outcalls for a couple of area hotels. That gives them a paycheck of some sort, and brings in a little money for this place. I'll be able to pay the monthly electric bill at least, unless this heat wave continues." Toby hit the lights as they headed toward the doors.

He held the front door open for her and she started to go out, but stopped with a new thought. "Toby, Helliman was kicked off the force today. He made some really ugly comments and a few threats."

He let the door fall closed again. "Isn't Helliman the cop from the other day? The day you went all badass?"

"He's the one." Reightman acknowledged. "Toby, keep your eyes open and look out for him. I don't think he'll try anything, but he's angry and has more than proved his level of bad judgment and ability to screw things up for everyone."

"I can take care of myself, Detective," he assured her as he opened the door again. "Hey, is it alright for me to go to Geri's apartment and start packing up his things?"

Reightman recognized his need for some kind of closure. "Yes, the crime techs are finished." At his inquiring expression, she shook her head. "No, they didn't find anything."

He ushered her out the door and Reightman watched as he locked the door and double checked it by pulling on the handle a couple of times. When he finished up with the door, he walked her to her car and waited until she was settled inside. He leaned into the open door. "Let me know when you have a picture of the coroner for me to look at, and please, call me when you know when they'll release Geri. Grams and I need this part to be over." As he stepped away to allow her to close the car door, he added, "Take care of yourself and watch your own back, Detective."

Reightman found it disconcerting he'd echoed Jackson's warning of a few hours ago. "I will, Toby. You can count on it." She pulled the door shut and buckled up. He stood watching her as she backed out of her parking spot, and as she drove away, he still standing in front of the dark and empty window of the Time Out Spa.

John Brown watched from his rear view mirror in a vehicle parked in the lot across the street as the detective drove away. He watched the young man standing in front of the window until the man looked both ways and jogged across the street. *"Good looking guy. Too bad I don't swing his way – usually."* He watched as the young man went up a stairwell. *"Probably has an apartment upstairs,"* he decided.

Once he was sure there was no one around to take note of him, John Brown got out of his late model black SUV and locked the doors with the key fob. Then he strolled down the sidewalk, looking in an occasional window, and studying the roofline. There wasn't much to see on the first side of the street, so he crossed at the corner and made his way down the other side. He stopped in front of the door to the spa and, after looking around again, he tried the door. He wasn't surprised to find it locked. He turned away from the door and glanced across the street. He noted the roofline from that side as well.

Then he returned to his SUV. He unlocked the door, giving the warm air a minute to escape. He slid into the vehicle, started the engine and waited until the interior had cooled. He drove away. It was time to get back to work. He had a problem to solve.

Once she arrived back at the station, Reightman stowed both her purse and the elegantly wrapped package in her desk drawer and proceeded to work through the messages that had accumulated while she was out meeting with Toby Bailey. Moments later, Jackson sauntered over, removed his jacket and hung it carefully over the back of his chair, and took a seat. "Any luck with Goldbleum?" she asked without looking up from the never ending piles of pink paper slips.

"No, not a lick of luck. He didn't recognize Helliman."

"I'd hoped he would. That would have tied things up neatly."

"Rather too neatly, I'd say. As much as I suspect Helliman knows far more than we've discovered, and is probably up to his thick red neck in something, I don't think he's the actual killer. He doesn't have the balls for it."

She looked up and gave him a reluctant nod of agreement. "I know you're probably right about Helliman. I was just hoping we'd catch some sort of break."

"How did it go down on Capital Street?"

"Alright, I guess. Bailey took the news as well as could be expected. He was –I don't know, somehow different today."

"Different in what way?" Sam asked.

She considered for a minute, trying to put her finger on Toby's mood. "I can't quite pinpoint it, but he was more removed from the situation. It's almost like he's stepping back and looking at it from a distance."

"He probably is. There's no way this incident didn't hit him right in the gut. Stepping back emotionally is likely just a coping mechanism to help him get through it all. He still has a lot ahead of him."

"Yes, he does," she agreed. "And we just keep handing him more delays and excuses to accept and accommodate, delaying the grieving process. I'm surprised he hasn't had a complete breakdown."

"Mr. Bailey is a man of hidden depth and resource, Reightman. Regardless of how young he seems, I think he has the right stuff inside to see this through." She didn't respond to his observation, so after a few seconds he tossed out another comment. "You seem to be growing kind of attached to him, Reightman."

"Yeah, Jackson, I guess I am."

He'd wondered if she'd admit it, but now it was out on the table. "Do you think that's a good idea?"

Melba thought about it and shrugged. "Probably not, but I am anyway. It's almost involuntary. He seems almost like a..."

"Son?" Sam suggested

"No," she disagreed, and searched for the right words. "He's like a little brother I didn't know I had until just recently." Reightman moved the pink stack of messages around on her desk, not really paying attention to what was written on them. "I don't know what to make of him sometimes, but something about him makes me want to protect him and help him and give him some extra support when he needs it." She looked over to where her partner sat across the desks. "I know it's not a good idea to get involved with anyone tied to this case, but I can't seem to help it. Is that wrong?"

"No, it's not wrong. It's human, and very, very tricky." He gave her a minute more to consider the situation and then changed the subject. "Did you get your shopping done?"

"Yes, I did, and I intend to try and make amends for *whatever* I did to ruin Nancy's life right after I go down and meet the new team in the morgue."

"May I suggest that you don't include the 'whatever I did to ruin your life' part when you see Nancy? Otherwise you might find yourself wishing you were a part of the morgue team, the permanent one – if you catch my drift."

"Suggestion approved, and point taken, Sam. Speaking of which, it's probably time to head on down there. You want to come with?"

"Sure, I don't have anything better to do." Jackson pointedly ignored his own stack of messages and pulled on his jacket. "What?" he asked when he caught her looking at the way he was tugging it into place and smoothing the lapels. "I just want to make a good impression, Reightman. Someone around here has to uphold our professional image."

She rolled her eyes and smoothed down her own jacket, trying to ignore the new wrinkles which had popped up since morning. "I knew we kept you around for a reason, Jackson." They walked to the elevator bank and she pushed the button. "I hope I don't have to pressure this guy too much to get some progress. Have you heard anything about him?" Reightman asked as they waited on the elevator.

"I may have heard a little."

"Well?" she prodded as they stepped in and she pushed the down button.

"You'll see. I wouldn't want to spoil the surprise." She noticed him rubbing his hands together in anticipation. She gave him a disgusted look and they exited the elevator and walked down the hall to the doors of the morgue. He pointedly ignored her.

They entered into the small waiting area and Reightman walked up to the woman sitting at the desk formerly occupied by Riley. The woman's head was bent over a stack of files and she was making rapid notations inside the file on top. She didn't look up at Reightman's approach. "Excuse me," Reightman said after a moment or two had passed. "I hate to bother you, but if he has a moment, we'd like to speak with the new acting coroner."

The woman looked up and gave Reightman the once over before looking back down at her files. "Who are you?" she finally asked as she continued writing.

"I'm Detective Melba Reightman, and this is my partner, Detective Sam Jackson."

The woman kept writing. Reightman waited for a couple more seconds, feeling her irritation beginning to rise. When the woman continued to ignore them, she took a deep breath and launched in. "Look, I realize things are a mess down here, and the coroner probably has his hands full, but really it's important for us to speak with him. We can go on back to his office if you're too busy to help. I know the way."

The woman flipped a page in the file and looked up briefly before she continued writing. "The coroner's not back in the office."

Reightman looked over at Jackson, noting his lopsided smile. *"He must be enjoying the show,"* she thought before turning back to the woman at the desk. "Do you know when he will be back?"

"No, I don't know when he'll be back," the woman answered, her thin lips wrinkling slightly in amusement.

Reightman reached the end of her patience. "I've had about enough of this!" she snapped. "I don't know what you find so amusing, but I doubt the coroner will find it half so funny when I tell him just how unhelpful you've been. You're wasting our time and we're here on important business."

The woman looked up at her, regarding her with a full faced smile. "He may not find it amusing, but I'm certainly enjoying myself." She went back to her writing.

At that, Reightman finally lost her temper. "Okay, that's it! We'll leave, but first I want your name."

The woman twisted her curly iron gray hair into a sloppy bun, jabbing in her pencil to hold it in place. She closed the file and stood up holding out her hand. "Certainly, Detective. I'm Doctor Patricia Evans, currently the Acting City Coroner."

Reightman regarded the hand in front of her and finally took it, noting the firm grip. "I'm sorry, Doctor, I didn't realize…" she trailed off.

"That the new coroner is a woman, and one with an odd sense of humor?" Dr. Evans finished for her. "Hello, Detective Jackson," she smiled at Sam. "It's good to see you again. I believe you owe me five dollars."

"What? Happy to see him *again*? And what's this about five dollars?"

"I met Detective Jackson this morning. When he saw me struggling to open the door with my hands full, he was kind enough to open it for me and we spent a few minutes getting acquainted."

"Wasn't he just the perfect gentleman?" Reightman narrowed her eyes in her partner's direction. *"Payback's coming,"* she thought, *"and it is going to be a doozy – long, slow and painful."*

"Detective Jackson and I spoke briefly about the Guzman case," continued the doctor. "He mentioned you'd both be coming by this afternoon and I warned him he'd likely find me up here in front since I wanted to make some progress on reviewing these files. Dr. Bridges, the new assistant coroner, has an offsite appointment this afternoon and won't be back until later today. Under the circumstances, I thought it best not to leave the front area unattended."

Reightman shot another glare in her partner's direction, planning evil and mayhem.

"When he heard that, he came up with the most brilliant suggestion," Evan's continued. "We made a small bet around how long you'd be able to hold your temper if I came across as somewhat uninterested and, shall we say –unhelpful? I'm happy to say, I won."

"Let me get this right. Detective Jackson bet I'd be able to hold my temper longer than I did?"

"No. He bet you'd reach the end of your patience at about the second or third exchange. I took the opposite position. He didn't think it was totally fair, since I'd be the one trying to push your buttons. He was afraid I might not do everything above the board, but I assured him I'd do everything possible to really get your goat." Evans looked toward Sam. "So, Jackson, did I play fair?"

"As much as I hate to admit it, you did indeed, ma'am." He pulled a roll of bills out of his front pocket and peeled of a five. He carefully sidestepped Reightman – anticipating a sharp kick – and handed it over to the coroner. "I wish you'd kept it up for a few more minutes. Reightman is a sight to behold when she flat out lets it rip."

The doctor pocketed the bill with a smile. "I'm sure she is, Jackson, but even though I'm new here, I've already heard of the Detective's rather formidable temper. I wanted to avoid possible injury."

"Alright, alright," Reightman broke in with attempted good humor, "now that you two have had your fun, can we talk about Guzman?"

"Certainly, Detective." Evans quickly gathered up the stack of files. "Why don't you both come on back, and I'll share my preliminary findings." Jackson opened the door and allowed the doctor to precede them.

"You've already started?"

"Yes. Thelma-Louise and I started as soon as we got in this morning."

"Thelma-Louise?"

"Yes, Doctor Thelma-Louise Bridges is my assistant coroner. We've worked together many times in the past and I suppose I forget the formalities where she's concerned. She served her internship under me several years ago. I was very pleased she was available for this assignment. She's brilliant, and someone I enjoy working with."

"Does she share your somewhat unorthodox sense of humor, Doctor?" Reightman asked wryly, as she took a seat in one of the chairs facing the Evans' desk.

'"No, not at all. She's perfectly nice – I'm not." Evans took her own chair, and motioned for Jackson to take the one next to Reightman.

Once everyone was settled, Evans pulled out a file from the stack and opened it. "We still have some work to complete, but I do have preliminary findings," she began, looking over her notes briefly. "To start with, Mr. Guzman's death was indeed the result of massive blood loss due to the multiple wounds he received. I've confirmed the wounds are consistent with those the knife in custody could have made. I have a couple more measurements and cut patterns to check before I'm certain it's the same knife, but that shouldn't take too long." She looked up at Reightman and Jackson and smiled grimly. "However, there are some other contributing factors I've found, and I suspect we'll find more before we've finished."

"Such as?" Jackson pulled out his notebook.

"Such as the markings on Mr. Guzman's neck area which suggest he was lassoed."

"Lassoed?"

"Yes, Detective Jackson." Evans considered her words carefully before continuing. "The markings lead me to believe someone restrained him about the neck, although there have been attempts to obfuscate the markings."

"Someone tried to cover up the fact that he was…lassoed?"

"Yes, Detective Reightman. From the state of the tissues, I suspect the cover-up happened sometime after death. In fact, I suspect it was done here, by my predecessor."

"You're saying Lieberman tried to hide it?"

"Yes, and he did a very clumsy job of it, given his training and background."

"Excuse me?" Reightman was not sure she'd heard the Doctor's words correctly.

"He took a very ham-fisted approach to it, Detective. Let me see if I can put it a different way." Evans folded her hands on the desk in front of her and searched for the right words. "Although members of our profession don't practice surgery in the traditional sense, coroners are usually fully trained and qualified medical professionals. The exceptions are instances where the coroner is an elected position, rather than an appointed or contacted one. Elected coroners are often medical professionals, but there are still a few instances when they're not. Thankfully, those are becoming increasingly rare as advances are made in forensic science, and proof of guilt is often reliant on facts found in the morgue." She checked to make sure they were following her explanation before she continued. "Any of us trained and qualified by today's standards are perfectly capable of covering up a wide variety of evidence." She paused for a moment, considering the best way to explain. "Detectives, if I were to choose to muddy the trail, so to speak, I could very well do so, and in a way difficult for anyone to discover, or even suspect. Given his background, I feel Doctor Lieberman would've been able to do the same. Why he didn't, is puzzling."

"Maybe Riley was watching him too closely," Jackson suggested.

"Ah, yes, the unfortunate Dr. Riley. A man of honor, it appears, but very little sense. Dr. Riley may in fact have stymied some of Lieberman's efforts, but his presence doesn't fully explain it. Perhaps there was a subconscious block preventing Lieberman from doing his best work in this instance. I understand that he was involved with the victim in a personal, presumably physical manner."

"That's correct, or at least the evidence suggests it," Reightman confirmed.

"Well, if it's indeed the case, there will likely be more evidence. As I mentioned, there's still some work to complete before I'm satisfied we've learned all there is to learn from Mr. Guzman's body."

"You mentioned contributing factors, Doctor Evans. What are they?" Jackson asked as he reviewed his notes.

"I suspect the toxicology results will show that Mr. Guzman was drugged with some substance before the attack. There are very few signs of defensive wounds. Usually, a victim fights back with significant force if they're able, and in this case, Guzman was a heathy man in excellent shape. I find it surprising he didn't and suspect we'll find he was drugged with some substance which rendered him unable to defend himself."

Reightman thought back to the original impressions she'd received at the crime scene and the notes she'd reviewed since, and nodded her agreement. "That would be consistent with the evidence at the scene. There was a lot of blood, but it was fairly well confined. Even the spatter patterns were remarkably controlled. If Mr. Guzman had put up a fight, there should have been more of a …."

"Mess," Jackson finished.

"Not quite the word I was looking for, Jackson, but it'll do. Anything else, Doctor?"

"Not at this time. Doctor Bridges and I will continue work this afternoon when she returns." She considered for a moment. "Why don't you join us?" When they both shifted uncomfortably in their seats, she added, "I think it may prove to be enlightening, and it'll give you a different perspective on things. However, it's only a suggestion."

The two detectives exchanged a quick glance and Reightman turned back to the coroner. "What time would suit, Doctor?"

Evans consulted the no-nonsense watch strapped to her wrist. "I think Dr. Bridges should be back by 2 PM, so why don't we plan for about 2:45?"

"We'll be here shortly before then," Reightman confirmed as she and Jackson rose to their feet. "Thank you for your help, Doctor Evans."

"That's my job, Detective. And about the little introduction earlier…"

"Yes?" Reightman raised a brow.

"Don't be too hard on your partner. You'll think of some appropriate retribution, but don't go to extremes. I don't want to find him wheeled into my morgue."

"Oh, I don't want him dead, Doctor – I just want him suffering." Jackson flinched slightly and she smiled all the way back to their desks.

Once seated, Sam cleared his throat uncomfortably. "Hey, Melba…"

She smiled brightly. "Yes, Sam?" Syrup wouldn't melt in her mouth.

"Uh, never mind." A few minutes later he cleared his throat again. "You feel like grabbing a bit to eat?"

Reightman glanced at the number of emails awaiting her attention and decided she better knuckle down and try to make a dent in them. "No, I don't think so. I need to get through some of these, but you could bring me back a ham and cheese sandwich."

After Jackson left, Reightman's fingers flew over her keyboard as she worked through her email. From time to time, she smiled as she thought about all the ways she might get back at him for the little stunt he pulled with the coroner. *"There are so many good choices,"* she thought as she finished a reply and hit send. She intended to consider all of her options before she settled on the perfect one, but she did have a few ideas she could put into motion right away.

Sam returned about thirty minutes later carrying a white paper bag and sat it on her desk. "One ham and cheese sandwich, just like you ordered."

She smiled up at him and opened the bag, digging out the sandwich and other tissue wrapped object. "You brought me a cookie!"

"I thought you might like one. They looked pretty good."

"Yes, it does look good," she agreed and picked up her mug. "I'm going for some hot water. You want me to get you some coffee?"

"Sure, that'd be great, Melba." As she started to walk away, something awful occurred to him. "Uh Melba…?"

"Yes?"

"You wouldn't, uh, put something in it or...do anything to it, would you?"

Bingo. "Now why would you think of something like that? Don't worry; I'll fix it just the way you like it...partner." Reightman returned a few minutes later and placed the cup on the corner of his desk, and sat back down, putting a tea bag in her cup and unwrapping her sandwich. She took a hearty bite. "I was getting hungry. Thanks for bringing this back."

"Yeah, sure thing. It wasn't any problem – I was getting lunch anyway."

She smiled around her sandwich when she saw him looking at the coffee with suspicion. "Something wrong?" she asked with apparent concern.

Jackson narrowed his eyes at her, trying to get a read. "Nope, not at all." He took a small testing sip, and cradled the cup carefully, waiting.

"It doesn't work that fast, Sam."

He sat the cup down quickly, sloshing a few drops on the desk. "What doesn't?"

"The caffeine, of course." She dunked her tea bag a couple of times and then removed it. She took a big drink from her own mug. "I really like this tea Zhou gave me." He nodded distractedly and picked up his cup, cut then set it down again without taking a drink. "Sam, I'm sorry if I didn't fix it the way you like it," she said in a sorrowful little voice.

"No, no, it's just perfect," he said taking another drink.

"I thought it should be. After all of these years I ought to know how you like your coffee." She took a final bite of her sandwich and brushed the crumbs off her hands. She then took a bite of the cookie. "Yum...this is great," she mumbled with her mouth full.

Sam finally pushed the coffee away from him on the desk and turned to his own computer. "What's the plan for the afternoon?"

"Well, I think I'll walk over and see Nancy." She stuffed the wrapping paper and napkin into the bag then tossed it in the trash. "Want to come?"

Sam considered it, thinking about all of the possible fun he could have if fireworks went off between the two women. Then he reconsidered, and decided he was already in enough hot water. "No, I think I'll see if I can get through some of my own email."

"Okay." Melba pulled the wrapped package from her drawer. "This shouldn't take too long." She took a deep breath, preparing for the worst. "Wish me luck. I'm going to need it."

"Luck," he answered distractedly, staring off into space.

When Melba was several yards away, she turned back to watch him. He picked up the coffee cup and held it carefully between thumb and finger and poured the coffee into a small potted plant behind him. Then he threw the cup into his trashcan and wiped his hands and mouth carefully with his handkerchief. He folded it and started to put it back into his pocket, but stopped. He looked it over carefully and then placed it into the trash along with the cup. *"Tomorrow morning I'll replace that plant with a dead or dying one,"* she thought gleefully. *"Operation Reightman's Revenge is underway!"*

Nancy was at her desk typing away with a pair of headphones plugged into her ears. *"She's either transcribing something, or listening to country music,"* Melba guessed. *"Probably listening to music."* She approached the front of the desk, holding the present hidden behind her back, and waited for Nancy to notice her. Nancy kept typing, but Melba saw her glance sideways in her direction a few times. Melba kept waiting patiently. She'd expected this kind of cold shoulder treatment.

Finally Nancy took the earpieces out and glared her way. "What do you want?"

"I've brought you something." Melba moved the package out from behind her back. Nancy didn't respond except to sniff disdainfully and turn back to her work. "I thought maybe it would make up, at least a little bit, for the other night." Melba held the package out towards the admin.

Nancy stopped her typing and eyed the offering. "Just because you give me something doesn't mean I won't still be mad."

"I know, but I want you to have this anyway."

Nancy took her time in considering the offering and then reluctantly took the package. "The wrapping's real nice," she grudgingly allowed.

Melba detected a glimmer of interest in her face. "Go ahead, open it," she encouraged.

Nancy looked it over, and gently placed the small, wrapped box on her lap. She untied the ribbon and laid it aside. She took off the wrapping paper and folded it and placed it next to the ribbon. Then she opened the box and moved aside the tissue paper. She stared for a minute and then took the scarf out and unfolded it. She didn't say anything.

"If you don't like it, I'm sure you can exchange it."

Nancy petted the delicate silk and touched one of the flowers. She then traced the outline of one of the butterflies. "It's the most beautiful thing anyone's ever given me," she whispered. She looked up at Melba and gave her a watery smile. "Thank you."

"You're welcome. Go ahead, put it on."

Nancy draped the silk around her neck and tied a loose knot, fussing with it a little. "Well?"

"It looks terrific," Melba replied, because it did. The beautiful scarf glowed against Nancy's pale skin, and raised the caliber of her otherwise down market dress by several degrees.

Nancy pulled a large compact from her desk drawer and opened it, tilting it first one way and then another to get the full effect. Nancy closed the compact and replaced it in her drawer. She petted the scarf again, affectionately. She gave Melba a considering look and turned back to her typing. "I'm still kind of mad," she informed her, fingers moving steadily. "Just not nearly *as* mad."

Melba quickly suppressed her grin and said gravely, "Well, that's an improvement so I'll have to be happy with that. I really am sorry Nancy. I hope you'll think better of me in the future."

Nancy popped her gum, never turning away from her computer. "It'll probably be at least until tomorrow until I get totally past it."

Melba knew when to make her exit. She figured she'd made good progress, and anyway, the look on Nancy's face when she saw herself in the compact mirror had been worth the full price of the scarf.

"Did the ice thaw any?" Sam asked when she returned.

"I think so, but only time will tell." Melba glanced at the time display on her phone. "Jackson, it's almost time to go downstairs. We don't want to keep Dr. Evan's waiting."

"No, we don't," he agreed. He put his hand to his stomach and then reached down and opened his desk drawer, pulling out an anti-acid tablet which he popped into his mouth.

"Not feeling well?" she asked sweetly as he chewed.

"Just a little heartburn I think."

"Gee, I hope it wasn't the coffee." She enjoyed his expression and nearly burst out laughing when he felt his stomach again and quickly chewed another tablet. Once her expression was under control, she motioned impatiently, "Come on, Jackson. Let's go."

He glared at her as he put on his jacket. She nearly lost it again as he put the entire roll of anti-acids in his pocket. "Have you heard anything from Jones or Mitchell?" she asked while they waited for the elevator.

"Yeah, Jones called in while you were with Nancy. Said they haven't found anything yet, but they're going to try to track down names and addresses of any possible relatives and see if they get a trail from there."

"Sam, this is taking too damned long," she said as they entered the elevator car. "Every minute that goes by works to Lieberman's advantage and not to ours."

"Yes, you're right but they'll find something, Reightman. Jones is a good detective and Mitchell will be working extra hard – hoping he gets a chance for a permanent promotion."

"I know, but I have a feeling we're almost out of time."

"Out of time for what?"

"I don't know. It's just a feeling I have. Like something bad could happen any minute."

"It could," Jackson agreed as they exited and headed to the morgue. "I hope not, but you may be right."

As they went through door, they were greeted by a woman in a set of scrubs. "Hello! You must be Detectives Reightman and Jackson." She practically bubbled as she held out her hand. "I'm Thelma-Louise Bridges, Acting Assistant Coroner for the time being."

"Pleased to meet you, Dr. Bridges," Reightman shook the offered hand and Jackson did the same. "Thelma-Louise is an unusual name."

The Doctor rolled her eyes and shook her head ruefully, dislodging a few wisps of baby fine white blonde hair from her pony-tail. "You're telling me," she giggled. "My momma really loved that movie and couldn't decide which character she wanted to name me after. In the delivery room she finally decided to just name me after both." She turned and shook hands with Jackson. "We'd better get back to the examination room. Dr. Evans is kid of picky about staying on schedule. Come on back and I'll help you get suited up."

They followed Bridges back into the depths of the morgue, pausing just outside the larger of two examination rooms to put on loose fitting smocks and plastic booties. At the doctor's instruction, they pulled on surgical gloves and placed clear plastic shielded masks over their faces. Once appropriately attired to Bridge's satisfaction, they followed her into the examination room. Reightman felt her stomach give a little flutter. Lieberman hadn't been one to allow cops back into this part of the morgue, so it'd been a while since she'd been present for an autopsy. She wasn't sure how she'd handle it. She steeled her nerves and looked over at Sam. His face was stoic beneath the clear plastic of his mask. *He'd probably be fine.*

Doctor Evans looked up as they entered and motioned them forward. Dr. Bridges took a position across from Evans and the Detectives approached and stood a short distance away.

Geraldo Guzman was laid out on the stainless steel table positioned under the middle of the room under a set of bright lights. There was a small cloth folded across his groin, and a small rolling cart with various implements arranged on top was placed at one side. There was also a large rolling magnification device positioned close to the top of the table. Reightman noted the ashy, pale color of his skin, and the numerous gashes and cuts scattered across his neck area and chest. There were many more cuts around his neck than on his chest, and if Evans was right, those were probably a result of Lieberman's handiwork.

"Detectives, come on over here. I want you to see this," They moved to stand next her and Evans positioned the magnifying frame over the neck are and motioned them to take a look. Jackson went first, and then Reightman followed suit, peering through the lens. She noted what she thought was bruising around the neck area and what appeared to be slightly abraded skin, almost hidden beneath the series of cuts.

As Reightman stepped back, Evans explained what they had seen. "The abraded skin suggests that an object with a soft, almost smooth nape was used to restrain the victim from the neck. Something similar to silk I would guess."

"Silk?" Jackson asked, itching for access to his notebook.

"Or something very like it," Evans confirmed.

"Like a scarf?" Reightman immediately thought of the scarf she'd given Nancy. It didn't seem like something so delicate would be sufficient to hold someone as well built and strong as the victim.

"No. The abrading suggests something much wider than the typical scarf, Detective, although silk fabric is incredibly strong regardless of its size. However, a swath of fabric the size of a scarf would've damaged the flesh more as it constricted and gathered in on itself. Whatever was used to do this was slightly thicker in texture and significantly wider than a scarf." Evans bent down and examined the neck area closely, and then reached for the magnifier. "There are what appear to be a few very small fibers in the skin, but they may be too small and incomplete to use as a sample. Silk doesn't usually shed, unless it is cut, and the presence of these particles suggests the fabric used was pulled and, perhaps slid or twisted, as it restrained Mr. Guzman. Such activity may have caused the material to shed these tiny fibers."

Evans took a pair of calipers and measured the length and depth of each of the cuts on the neck, calling out her results to Bridges who made careful note of each. "You can see almost precise pattern left by that whatever cutting device was used," Evans continued. "The cuts don't match the other wounds on the body or the neck, and don't match those made by the knife. Also, there's no sign of bleeding, which tells us these cuts were made after death."

She moved further down the body and took a series of additional measurements which Bridges also recorded. Evans moved back toward the neck area and felt the throat area carefully. She removed a scalpel from the cart and made a series of incisions, and rolled the skin away from the underlying structure of the throat. She nodded and rolled the magnifier slightly and positioned the lens. After a minute, she looked up. "The trachea hasn't been crushed, although there's evidence of pressure. Whatever object was used to detain this man wasn't used with enough force to crush the throat. Whoever wielded it had some sort of leverage and may have braced them self somehow or perhaps held on to something while they pulled and twisted."

Evans then removed the cloth from Guzman's lap. "I've compared this penis to the photos provided to me by Tom Anderson. I believe it's the same as was depicted in the photographs."

Reightman forced herself to examine it closely and then shook her head. "No, it can't be the same." She swallowed and then added, "Mr. Guzman was uncircumcised, as was the…specimen in the photo."

"That is correct, Detective. Guzman was circumcised," Evans confirmed. "His foreskin was removed after he was in the morgue's custody. Lieberman's work again, I believe." Jackson took an involuntary step back. "There are other signs of mutilation in the genital area, although none as egregious as that."

"Where…where is the missing foreskin," Jackson asked, clearly uncomfortable with the discovery.

"We haven't been able to locate it. Perhaps it's been incinerated, or maybe Lieberman kept it as some sort of souvenir."

Reightman felt her gorge rising, and suppressed her reaction with some difficulty.

"That sick bastard!" Jackson turned away for a moment, trying to calm himself down.

"I'll have to tell Toby about this," she said almost to herself.

"Yes, Detective," Evans having heard, agreed. She motioned for Dr. Bridges to replace the cloth. "Ethical practice demands it and I will of course, be including this in my official report. Mr. Bailey will have the perfect right to sue this department and this city for damages and if he has a halfway competent attorney, he'll likely win if he decides to take such action." Reightman thought about Zhou Li's well-earned reputation and hoped the city had very full coffers. "There is one more thing, Detectives. I have examined each of the knife wounds carefully. There is no trace of fabric fiber of any sort, except that we identified in the neck abrasions. I believe that was an outstanding question from the crime team. The slashes on the clothing found at the scene do not match the placement of the wounds on the victim's body. They were made after the clothing had been removed."

The two detectives mulled the finding over in their minds. After a moment, Evans caught their attention. "I still have some work to do, but I don't think you need to be present for the next set of activities, Detectives."

"Why?" asked Jackson.

"I feel it would be unnecessarily unpleasant for you, Detective Jackson. I'll be removing the internal organs and the brain for weighing and examination." She paused and then smiled invitingly. "You're welcome to stay if you'd like."

Jackson quickly raised both hands "You're right. There's no need for us to stay, Doctor."

"In that case, Dr. Bridges will show you out. I think I'll be finished in the next couple of hours, so I'll be in touch tomorrow."

"Will you be able to release his body soon? Mr. Bailey is anxious to know when he can proceed with burial."

"Release will have to wait until we get back the toxicology report, Detective Reightman. When is that expected, Thelma-Louise?"

"We should have it tomorrow by end-of-day, Doctor Evans." At Evans's surprised look, Doctor Bridges made a face. "I briefly dated the lab director at one time. Believe me, I was owed a favor."

Bridges motioned for the Detectives to follow her out of the room and showed them where to place their smocks and masks, and in which bins to dispose of the gloves and booties. Once they were done, she escorted them to the front.

"Thank you, Doctor Bridges." Reightman said.

"Sure thing, Detectives. This is a weird one for sure. I've never seen a victim treated this way before. Sometimes morgue work is a little sloppy, but this is just disgusting."

"I agree with your assessment one hundred percent, Doctor," Jackson replied shaking her hand.

"You'll call when the toxicology reports are back?"

"Yes, I will. I'd better get on back. We still have a lot to finish up on this one, and we have a freezer more awaiting our tender attentions." Dr. Thelma-Louise Bridges laughed at her little joke as she left the room.

Reightman and Jackson went out the door and headed for the elevators. "How are you going to break this to Mr. Bailey?"

"I don't know, Sam. Any suggestions?"

"Just tell him straight up." Sam pushed the call button. "There isn't any other way to share this kind of news."

"You think he'll sue?"

"He might." The elevator arrived and the door opened. "He'd have every right. I know I would. What do you think he'll do, Melba?"

She leaned against the back wall of the car as it carried them upward. "I don't know. We'll just have to see. I know I'm not looking forward to the discussion."

They were silent as they walked to their desks. "I think I'm going to get out of here for the night, Sam. You?"

"No, not yet. I'm going to try to get an update from Jones and Mitchell before I leave, and see if they've come up with anything new. I'll give Mitchell some pointers for tomorrow since your favorite Detective is going to be out for the day – dentist appointment for a root canal I think. Jones has to keep his pretty smile in top form." He turned off his computer. "Have a good night, and call me if you need anything."

"I will. Hey, Sam?" she asked looking at the plant behind him.

"Yeah?"

"Is it just me, or does that plant look sick?"

Sam paled and turned to look at the plant in question. "I...uh...it looks fine to me."

"Hmmm. I don't think it looks to good, but it's probably just the light." She pulled out her purse and slung it up on her shoulder. "See ya' tomorrow."

"Yeah." He was still checking out the plant.

Reightman walked away. When she turned the corner and was out of sight, she looked around to make sure she was alone. Then she broke into a gleeful little jig. *"Revenge is sweet!"*

CHAPTER TEN

JOHN BROWN SPENT his day productively hanging out at a few of the coffee houses and cafés located near Police Headquarters and listened to the chatter. He heard about how various kids and grandchildren were doing, about assorted plans for the upcoming holiday weekend, the chances the college football team had of making into the play-offs, and quite a lot about the volume and frequency –or lack thereof in some cases – of extracurricular activities certain people were enjoying. Frequently, he heard speculation and gossip about the man he was hoping to find. After a reasonable mid-morning breakfast, two small lunches and about twelve gallons of coffee, he finally hit pay dirt.

"I wonder where old Lieberman has run off too?" the middle aged man at the next table asked his two companions.

"Who the hell knows, and who the hell cares?" replied the slightly younger man across from him. "I sure don't."

"Frank, watch your language please," admonished the older woman seated next to him. "You know I don't like it!"

"Sorry, Gloria. I'm just really sick of hearing about Lieberman. Seems that's all anyone has been talking about the last day or so."

"That may be the case," Gloria replied, "but you have to admit this is quite the scandal. You know I don't like gossip, but the things people are saying are very *salacious*." She rolled the word around in her mouth. John Brown thought she sounded delighted with both her choice of word, and the topic of discussion.

"Really?" asked the first man eagerly.

"Yes. But I won't repeat them no matter how many times you ask, so save your breath," Gloria replied primly. "His poor old mother is probably turning over in her grave."

"Good thing the old woman's dead then," Frank offered. "She must have been ancient. How old was Mrs. Lieberman, Gloria?"

"Well, let me think. She was about seventy-five when she remarried. Rosenfeld was his name, I think. He was a car salesman over at the Buick dealership." Gloria patted her lips with her napkin and checked her reflection in a spoon. "I always figured he was marrying her for the money. That's what the ladies at Temple said anyway. He moved right in to the house she'd shared with her deceased husband and she changed the title to both of their names. It's a nice little ranch over on Chutney Street. I never knew why Lieberman didn't put it up for sale when she died. I could have used the listing." John Brown decided that they were realtors.

"Yeah, but how old was she?" Frank asked again, wanting to get back on topic.

John Brown picked up his check and started to the register. He didn't even pay attention to Gloria's answer.

After he settled his bill, John Brown drove himself to the county tax office. After waiting in line for a few minutes, he found himself face to face with a Ms. Janet Norton. He smiled ingratiatingly at her round, plump face. "Ma'am, I know it's a long shot, but you look like you might be able to help me."

Janet brightened at his big smile and fluttered her eyelashes at him. "Well, I can do my best. What kind of help do you need?"

"Well, you see, I just started work with a new real estate company and I'm supposed to meet a client at a possible listing. I'm afraid I must have mixed up the address. I've tried calling, but there hasn't been any answer and his voicemail system doesn't seem to be working. I really don't want to mess this up, it being my first week and all." He gave her his very best shy and helpless southern boy look.

"I'll need a name and the street on which you think the house is located," she said, taking pity on him, "That should get us started."

"I know the house is located on Chutney Street," he supplied. He glanced at the nameplate on the counter to be sure, and then added, "Mrs. Norton, I really do appreciate how nice you're being." He widened his eyes and gazed deeply into hers.

Janet Norton blushed. "It Miss, actually. I'm not married."

"How can a nice, good looking girl like you still be unattached?" he asked in surprise.

She bit her lower lip, emphasizing her already apparent overbite. "Just unlucky in love, I guess." She was obviously embarrassed and distressed by her lack of success in the matrimony game.

"This is like shooting fish in a barrel," he thought as he looked down at the counter and then moved his long-lashed eyes slowly back up to her face. "I'm sure your luck will change, Miss." He smiled shyly and added, "Maybe it already has."

Miss Norton's eyes fluttered closed for a brief minute. She opened them to drink in his handsome, rugged face and stared into his eyes.

"The name is Rosenfeld."

"Nice to meet you, Mr. Rosenfeld."

He looked down at his feet, shuffled them a bit, and then back into her eyes. "No, the property title is in the name Rosenfeld."

"Oh," her eyes clouded with disappointment

"My name is Smith, Joe Smith," he added with an engaging smile. "Maybe we could go out, sometime."

She smiled in delight and hope. "I'd like that. When?"

"Sometime soon. If you'd give me your number, I'll call you. But right now I'm afraid I really am going to be late."

"Oh yes, of course." She scribbled down her phone number and pushed it across the counter to him, then turned to her keyboard and typed a few things. "I think I found it for you, Mr. Smith."

"Call me Joe. May I call you Janet?"

"Yes, of course you may, Joe," she gushed. "I don't want you to be late though. I'll jot down the address."

Once she handed it over, he asked, "Do I owe you anything?"

"No, Joe. Since you already had the name and street, we didn't have to do a full records search." She fluttered her eyelashes and gave him a little pout. "Just don't forget to call – you have my number."

John Brown, aka Joe Smith, picked up the slip of paper with her number, and gave it a kiss before putting it in his front shirt pocket. "I'll keep it right here next to my heart so I won't forget," he assured her with tender smile. "Thanks for your help, Janet. I'll be talking to you soon."

A minute later, he was punching the address into his navigation system. He reached into his front shirt pocket and pulled out the slip of paper. He rolled down his window and tossed the paper out, watching it flutter across the asphalt parking lot. "I'm sorry, Janet Norton. I have a feeling we just aren't meant to be." He didn't feel badly about playing on her emotions and insecurities to get what he needed. After all, he was a working man with a job to do, and a man did what he had to in order to get the job done. Emotions just got in the way.

That evening he drove down Chutney Street checking house numbers. He spotted the house he was looking for and drove past slowly. *"Garage door closed,"* he noted, *"and there's a tiny bit of light coming through the gap in the closed drapes. Looks like someone's home."*

John Brown drove around the block and parked the next street over. He opened the glove box and took out a baseball hat, pair of glasses, and a gun. He reached in again and removed a silencer and attached it to the gun. He checked the safety, slid the revolver into the back waistband of his jeans, and picked up a red and black backpack from the passenger seat. From out of the backpack came a clipboard complete with a few blank forms. The name printed on the top of the forms matched the logo on his hat. He got out of the SUV and slide one arm through the backpack and closed and locked his door. He put on the hat and the glasses, sitting them slightly off-kilter on his face, and started down the street.

Every couple of houses, he marched up to the front door and knocked or rang the bell. "Good evening, ma'am. My name is Bill Jones, and I'm with Citizen's Action for Better Local Government. Could I ask you a few questions? Your answers will help make our city and state government more effective."

Most of the people he talked to told him they were busy and shut the door in his face. A few answered the questions he asked, and a couple invited him into their homes. An hour and a half later, he walked up the sidewalk to the house he'd targeted. He lifted the door knocker and gave it a couple of bangs against the door. While he waited, he unbuttoned the top three buttons of his shirt and took off the glasses, placing them in his shirt pocket. He knocked again, louder this time.

A short while later, the door opened slightly and a fleshy face peered through the gap.

"Good evening, sir," said John Brown, aka Bill Jones. "I'm with Citizen's Action for Better Local Government. Could I ask you a few questions? Your answers will help make our city and state government more effective." He smiled his very best smile.

The man hesitated. "I don't have time this evening."

He started to close the door, but Bill Jones spoke up quickly. "I don't blame you for not wanting to waste your time on this crap. I wouldn't be doing this, but I'm trying to do *anything* I can to make ends meet." He slid his hand around his neck and underneath his shirt, rubbing his palm over his pecs and causing the shirt to gap open considerably. "It's really hot and humid out tonight. Can I maybe come in and get...cool for a minute?" He unbuttoned his shirt the rest of the way. "Please? I promise I'll only stay a minute or two," he flexed his chest muscles, noting the man's interest, "unless you wouldn't mind if I stayed longer."

The man at the door moistened his thick lips. "I really shouldn't."

"Oh! I'm sorry. I just realized I must've interrupted you and your wife at dinner."

"I'm...I'm not married."

"Oh..." Bill Jones put a lot of effort into making the tiny word sound as suggestive as possible.

The man opened the door a little further and looked him up and down. Bill noted that although fat and flabby, the man looked pretty strong. He was going to have to play this right to avoid a struggle. Plus, his client wanted this to be special. Picking exactly the right moment to interrupt the man's perusal of his body, Bill Jones adjusted himself in his pants. "I'm sticking to myself," he apologized. "I didn't wear underwear today."

The man opened the door a little further. "Uh, I guess it'd be okay for you to come in for a minute or two. Just to get cool. You can even take your shirt off if you want...to let it dry out."

"That'd be real nice," Bill sighed at the thought. As he entered the house he winked. "I'll just have to try real *hard* to thank you properly for your kindness."

The man turned and quickly shut the door, locking it and fumbling to attach the door chain. When he turned back around, Bill Jones was leaning over, digging through his backpack. He straightened slowly and then looked over his shoulder with a sexy smile. "You don't happen to have an extra t-shirt I can borrow do you? I thought I had one in my backpack, but I don't. This shirt is really getting damp."

"I might, but it won't fit you. It'll be way too big. I'm kind of...a big man."

"I like big men," Bill Jones said with a wink.

The man took a deep breath and gave himself a little shake, not believing the good fortune that had come knocking at his door. "I think I know where there's a clean one. Hang on just a minute." The fat man hurried from the room, and returned a few minutes later. "Here," he offered, thrusting a folded white t-shirt at Bill.

"Thanks, much appreciated. Hey, I didn't get your name."

"It's Ben, or Benny, if you like."

"Oh, I like, Benny." Bill shrugged his shoulders and his shirt dropped down, draped on his elbows. He rubbed his stomach. "Could I get a glass of water, Benny? My throat feels really dry, and I need something to…wet it." He caressed his throat and let his hand travel down his chest until it came to rest at the top of his jeans. When you get back, maybe we can have some fun."

Benny licked his lips as he watched the fingers slid under the waistband. "I'll be right back. I'll fix us something better than water. Just relax and make yourself comfortable."

After he'd scurried away, Bill Jones walked further into the room and knelt down in front the recliner and pulled the revolver from the back of his waistband. He placed it under the front right side. He then stood and unbuttoned the fly of his jeans and removed his shirt. He took the white t-shirt and tied it into a knot about the same size as his fist then placed it on the floor to the left of the recliner. He stood and picked up his shirt, holding it loosely in one hand.

Benny entered the room carrying two highball glasses filled with light red liquid and a few ice cubes. "It's vodka and cranberry juice," he said, handing Bill one of the drinks. "I hope you like it."

"Oh, I'm sure I will, Benny." He took the glass in the same hand that held his folded shirt, carefully to keep his fingers covered. "My hands are all…damp and slippery. I guess I'm nervous or excited, or something. I don't want the glass to slip." He took a drink and ran the chilled glass across his neck and chest, leaving a trail of moisture. "Ahhh…that feels good."

Benny's hand shook, rattling the ice in his glass. Bill went to a small table near one of the plastic covered sofas and set down the glass. And then he wiped his hands with the shirt before folding it neatly and placing it on the sofa. He turned back to Benny and ran his hand up and down the open fly. "I hope you don't mind, but I undid these buttons. You did say I could get comfortable." He sat on the edge of the sofa and slipped off his shoes and then pulled off his socks. "Benny," he suggested, "why don't you put down your drink and get comfortable in that big comfy chair? I'll join you over there in a minute. Then we'll have some fun."

Benny placed his shaking glass on a coaster his mother had brought back from her last trip to Israel, and walked over to his chair and sat down heavily. He watched as Bill Jones carefully folded his things and then stood.

"You look comfortable, Benny. Are you comfortable?"

"Yes," Benny answered, eying the half-dressed man in his dead mother's living room.

"Good, I want you to be comfortable." Bill Jones took a few items from his pocket and set them on the table. He then turned and pulled the jeans down his hips and lifted out each leg. He folded them and placed them next to the other things on the couch and turned to Benny and framed his crotch in his cupped hands. "You like?"

"Oh... God....yes..."

"I'm glad. Now just unzip your fly and lean back in your comfy chair and close your eyes. I have something planned that you'll remember until your very last breath." He watched as the man complied, unzipping his pants and leaning back in his chair. Lieberman quivered with anticipation.

Bill Jones aka Joe Smith aka John Brown picked up the large heavy duty zip ties he had taken out of his pocket and threaded them together making a larger, continuous tie. He pulled on it a few times, tugging it to test its strength.

"What are you doing, Bill?"

"Why Benny, I'm making something...longer," he answered, satisfied with his work. "I'm coming over there to start taking care of you right now." He walked over to the man lying back in the chair with closed eyes. He placed the augmented zip tie on the floor within hand's reach and knelt on the floor in front of the chair. He ran his hands up and down Benny's heavy legs moving from knee to upper thigh. "Lift your hips a little. I can't do this by myself. You're such a...big...boy."

Benny quickly obeyed, straining to lift his big hips off of the recliner. Bill Jones grabbed the waistband and pulled the pants past the buttocks and then down the legs to just above the ankles. He held his body completely still as Benny ran a large, white, damp hand down his lower ribs to his hip. As the hand started to quest further, Bill stepped back. "Not yet, Benny. I've still got work to do." He knelt at the foot of the chair again, and picked up the zip tie and knotted t-shirt in one hand and the revolver with another. He worked his way up the fat man's body, grazing his skin along Benny's flesh. He placed his knees on each of the recliner's armrests, trapping Benny's arms. He braced one hand on the side of the chair next to Benny's head. He lifted his body up, rubbing his flesh against Benny's chin. He leaned in slightly and softly whispered, "Open your mouth, Benny. I have something special for you."

Benny groaned and opened his mouth wide. With one smooth, fast movement, Bill Jones shoved the knotted cloth into the gaping mouth and lowered his body, setting all of his weight down on his knees and butt. He placed the gun against Benny's temple and clicked off the safety. Benny's eyes opened wide in shock. "I told you I had something special for you, Benny. You need to be very still and not move. Understand?"

Benny tried to spit out the wad of cloth in his mouth but it was wedged too far back into his mouth. He tried to talk, but couldn't do anything but make weak, grunting sounds.

"Nod if you understand," Bill Jones instructed as he put more pressure on the temple with the silencer end.

Benny nodded quickly with wide fear filled eyes.

"Good job," Bill told him approvingly. "Now, I'm going to remove my knees from the chair and you are going to remain completely still. You wouldn't want the gun to go off accidently."

The man nodded quickly and Bill removed his legs from the chair one at a time. "Benny, I want you to lean forward and put your arms behind your back. Do it slowly," he instructed, holding the gun steady. Benny moved his arms behind him, struggling to do so. Sweat poured down his face and he was fighting to breathe through his nose. Bill used the zip tie to secure Benny's wrists and then stepped away. Benny followed the gun with his eyes as Bill held it slightly away from his head. "Stand up."

The sweating man tried to find his balance as he stood. He attempted to move away, but his legs caught in his lowered pants and he wobbled and fell. Bill quickly adjusted the arms behind Benny's back and tugged the tie tighter. He left him beached on the floor and quickly dressed in his discarded clothes. He ignored the whimpering man and pulled on a pair of tight black leather gloves. He went into the bedroom, where he found Benny's bag and removed some cash. He spotted Benny's cellphone and slid it into his pockets, figuring someone might find it handy. Then he went to the kitchen where he located Lieberman's laptop, sitting opened on the table. He leaned over and opened a blank document and quickly typed a few lines. He saved the file and left it open on the computer. He fetched the open bottle of vodka, added a little something to make the job easier, and set it on the table.

He returned to the living room, put his backpack on one shoulder, and knelt at Benny's feet. He used both hands to tug the trousers up the legs. When he got to the hips, he instructed, "Lift up, Benny." The terrified man complied and Bill pulled the pants up to his waist. He then rolled the man over on his back and fastened the pants. "I'm going to help you stand up. Don't do anything stupid. Remember, I have the gun."

He heaved the man to his feet. "We're going to the kitchen, Benny. I'll bring your drink." He picked up the man's drink and placed the gun in the middle of his back. "Lead the way."

Benny walked slowly to the kitchen. Tears rolled down his fat quivering cheeks and a small drip of snot hung from his nose. Once in the kitchen, Bill directed him to a chair. "Take a seat." When Benny was settled, Bill fished another couple of zip ties out of his backpack and fastened them around the man's ankles, restraining him to the sturdy chair legs.

"You want your drink, Benny?"

The man nodded weakly.

"Okay. I'm going to remove the cloth from your mouth. If you make a sound I'll shoot you right in the gut." Bill said pleasantly. "You know how much that will hurt, don't you? Being a doctor and all…"

Benny's eyes widened in shock that the man knew his profession.

"Open your mouth."

Bill pulled out the wet cloth and laid it on the table. Benny gasped for air and Bill let him recover for a sec or two. "Ready for a drink?" Bill asked, lifting the glass. When the man nodded, Bill held the glass to the moist lips and tipped it. Some dribbled out the side of Benny's mouth. Bill waited until he swallowed, then slowly poured the drink into Lieberman. He reached for the vodka bottle and poured a large amount into the empty glass.

"I know your nerves are pretty shaky, so I want you to drink everything in this glass. We'll take it slow and you will feel a lot better when you've finished it off." He lifted the glass and raised it to the lips. Benny turned his head away slightly. Bill removed the glass. "Benny, don't make me mad. You won't like me mad." He put the glass up to the lips again, "Open up," he instructed. He fed vodka to the man, waiting for him to swallow. Finally the glass was empty. He sat it next to the vodka bottle and waited about twenty minutes.

"Benny, we're going to play a game now. I am going to let you ask me one question – just one. I plan to answer it truthfully. If I like the question, I might let you ask another. Speak softly and don't make any loud noises. If you do, I promise I'll shoot you."

Benny looked up at him with drugged eyes. He swayed slightly in the chair. "W-w-why?"

"Benny, I'm disappointed in you. That's such an average question. But, I'll answer it. You became a problem – a problem to be solved. That's what I do. I'm a problem solver."

Benny dropped his head on his chest, his eyes squeezed shut. "I'm going to ask *you* a question now, and then I'll let you ask another, even though your first one wasn't very original." Tears ran down Benny's cheeks and his eyes were still closed. He did, however, nod. "I appreciate that, Benny. Here's my question. Are you right-handed or left-handed?"

"Left." His voice was so quiet his answer could barely be heard.

"That's so cool, Benny. Many talented and creative people are left handed. I used to be primarily left handed, but I taught myself to use both hands equally. It gives me more options." He walked behind the man's chair and pulled it back from the table about two feet. He then leaned him slightly forward in the chair and tied just the right arm to the chair back, threading the zip tie between the already bound hands. "Since you were so cooperative and answered my question, I'll let you have another go." When Benny didn't respond, he slapped the man lightly on the cheeks. "You must have another question. Come on, ask. I'll answer it."

Benny's words were slurred. "Why… thish way?"

"That's a much better question! You see, the person who hired me suggested something like this, but I added my own special touches just for you. Based on what I was told, you like your boyfriends naked, willing and eager to please. We wanted to make sure you were getting exactly what you like, and at the same time, getting everything you deserve. Did you enjoy it, Benny?" Bill crooned the question into his ear. "Wasn't I willing to please? I even got naked for you. I figured you deserved a little treat before I finished you off. Did I make it good for you?"

Benny sobbed silently, his rounded shoulders shaking with each breath. Terrified and helpless, his bladder and bowels loosened. "Poor Benny, you messed your britches." Bill pushed his head gently and it wobbled side to side, slack and listless. "Don't worry about it – it happens all the time. I think you're just drunk. In fact, you're about to pass out."

Bill pulled an army knife from his pocket and used it to cut the arms free. Then he refastened Benny's right arm to the chair back. The left arm hung free, motionless at the man's side. Bill surveyed the man for a moment or two and then suddenly remembered the other glass in the living room. *"Good thing you remembered! Everything has to be perfect."*

When he left the room, the man in the chair marshalled his last bit of strength and painfully reached his left arm out and over as far as he was able. Reaching the keyboard, he was only able to type two small letters into the open document. His reserves depleted, and overcome by the alcohol and sedatives that he had been fed, he collapsed back into the chair with his left arm hanging limply at his side.

Bill walked back into the kitchen and looked Benny over to determine what progress the booze and drugs had made. Satisfied, he went to the table and used the wet cloth from Benny's mouth to wipe the gun down carefully. He then stood behind the man and lifted the left arm. He positioned the hand exactly as he needed and wrapped the plump, pliable fingers around the handle and raised the gun to the man's left temple. Using his own gloved hand, he guided the chubby fingers just so, and pressed the end of the silencer firmly to Benny's head. With firm steady pressure, he caused the man to squeeze the trigger.

The gun made a sudden muffled noise, much like an air compressor shutting off. Blood and brains spattered out the right side of the man's head, splattering the walls and the lace curtains hanging over the mini-blinds.

Bill Jones, aka John Brown, critically regarded his work. He made a slight adjustment to the computer and then lowered the screen half way. He cut the zip ties securing legs and arm to the chair and pocketed the pieces, and briskly rubbed the wrist and ankles to manipulate and puff the skin, removing most, if not all of the marks made by the bindings. After one last sweep of the kitchen and the living room, he put on his hat and dug the clipboard out of his backpack.

He opened the front door and adjusted the locking mechanism. He walked through the door and pulled it shut after him. Standing on the small front porch he took off the leather gloves and put them into the backpack. Whistling softly, he walked down the sidewalk and continued until he was two houses down. He walked up to the door and rang the doorbell. "Good evening, sir. I'm with Citizen's Action for Better Local Government. Could I ask you a few questions? Your answers will help to make our city and state government more effective."

He stopped at five more houses before he went back to his vehicle. One nice, grandmotherly lady invited him in and gave him a glass of sweet tea. He thanked her graciously before he left.

He got into the SUV and removed the hat and stowed it in the glovebox. He unzipped the backpack and stowed the clipboard inside then placed it on the passenger seat. He opened the console between the seats and pulled out his phone. He typed a short message: PROBLEM SOLVED

He sent the message and put the phone in his back pocket.

John Brown started the SUV and drove out of quiet middle-class neighborhood. *"This is a pretty nice area,"* he mused, *"there probably isn't a lot of crime."* He thought about his day. *"It was a hard job, but you did good work today, John Brown,"* he congratulated himself. *"You should be very proud."*

On Wednesday morning, Reightman went into work early, intending to go over all of the crime scene evidence yet one more time. She and Sam had been through them a couple of times already, but it couldn't hurt. There just wasn't much else she could do at this point. Until Lieberman was found, it looked like things were coming to a standstill.

On the way to her desk, she spotted a sad looking plant and stopped to investigate. It was yellowed, and the few remaining leaves had brown, dried edges. *"Perfect!"* She picked it up the pot, hoping Sam wasn't in yet. When she reached her desk, she looked around then shrugged off her purse and snatched up the healthy looking plant from beside his desk and replaced it with the sick and dying substitute. She stashed the healthy plant a few desks away. She hurried to the break room and rinsed her hands under the sink. After filling a mug with hot water she strolled back leisurely. Her day was off to a terrific start. She booted up her computer and dropped a tea bag into the mug to brew. She'd worked through the first electronic file of crime scene photos by the time Sam arrived.

"Good morning, Reightman. How's things?" he asked, as he took off his jacket and hung his jacket over the chair.

"Morning, Jackson. Things are good. Just going through the crime scene photos again."

"Again?" he asked as he started up his own computer. "We've been through them about a dozen times already. What are you thinking you'll find this time?"

"I don't know, but it can't hurt to give them another pass. I got a good night's sleep last night so maybe my fresh, rested eyes will spot something new."

"I'm glad *you* got some rest. I tossed and turned all night. Must have been something I ate."

"You never know about food...or drink these days, Jackson." She carefully didn't look at him. "You can't be too careful." She felt his eyes on her as she moved to the next set of photos.

"I'm going to get a cup of coffee," he said rising from his chair.

"You want me to get it for you? I'm almost ready for another cup of tea."

"No!" he answered emphatically. "I'll get it. You keep working on those files. You want me to bring you back some hot water?"

"No thanks," she smiled up at him, "I'll get some in a little while. I'll need a stretch anyway after I get through a few more of these." She turned back to her monitor. Reightman flipped through a few more pictures, making an occasional note. She stopped on a photo of the break room. "Hmmm, I don't remember that door."

"What door?" Sam asked, overhearing her as he returned with his full cup.

"This door," she said as Jackson looked over her shoulder. "This one, right here."

"Oh, that's to the stairwell leading up to the roof. Since it is painted the same color as the walls, it kind of blends in, I guess. That's probably why you don't remember."

"Did the team check it out?"

"I'm pretty sure they did, but I'll check." He put his cup down and pulled opened a paper file with handwritten notes. After reviewing the notes, he confirmed, "Yep, they checked it out. As I said, it opens onto a set of stairs leading up to the roof. There's a door at the top for roof access, and about halfway up there's an access panel to the ductwork. Laurie said there was nothing to be found either in the stairwell, or on the roof." He closed the file and picked up his coffee. "Satisfied?"

"I guess I am," she said, disappointed she was back to square one. "I'd hoped for a minute that I'd found something new to check."

"You know better than to find clues where there aren't any," Sam chided her gently.

"You're right, I do." She reached for her tea as her desk phone rang. "Reightman, here."

"Hey, Melba," Nancy's cheerful voice came through the connection. "Two things: the first is the Chief wants to know if you can drop by his office in a couple of minutes so he can get an update. He also said he had another thing he wanted to talk to you about. He didn't say what."

"Sure thing, Nancy. I'll be over in about five minutes."

"Okay, good. The second thing is, I've decided I'm not mad anymore. That's it. See ya' in a few minutes." Nancy hung up.

"I guess my gift worked. Nancy's no longer out to get me."

"That's good. You better be extremely grateful."

"I am, believe me!" She hunted her notes, and finally found them under her mug. "The Chief wants to see me as well."

"About what?"

"Not sure," she admitted as she stood up and pushed her chair back under the desk. "Hey, Sam?"

"Yeah?" he didn't move his eyes from the file he was looking at on his screen.

"What's wrong with that plant? It looks like it's dying. I don't remember it looking like that before."

"Oh my God…"

"Are you alright?" she asked as he stared at the dead and dying foliage.

"Yeah, this just really…bothers me for some reason."

"I wouldn't worry about it too much. Someone on the night cleaning crew probably spilt some sort of toxic chemical on it, or something like that. You didn't water it with anything did you?" she asked, enjoying the stricken look on his face. He didn't respond, so she gathered up her things and departed, firing her final shot. "Loosen up partner, it's just a plant. It's not like you're the one dying."

Chief Kelley's office door was open and Nancy was at her desk typing away.

"Good morning, Nancy."

"Hey, Melba. The scarf looks good, don't you think?" Nancy fingered the silk around her neck.

"It looks beautiful," Melba agreed. "Is he ready for me?"

"He sure is. He said for you to go on in when you got here. I'm going to get him a coffee. You want anything?"

"Thanks, but I'm good right now." Reightman knocked on the door frame. "Good morning, Chief."

"Detective Reightman. Grab the door, then grab a seat."

She closed the door and then settled herself into one of the chairs in front of his desk. "Nancy said you wanted an update."

"Yes, I do. With the crazy schedule I 've been keeping the last day or so, I thought this morning might be the only time for us to catch up," Kelly leaned back in his chair. "Tell me where you and Jackson are with the Guzman case."

"Well, let me start with the discussion we had yesterday with Doctor Evans, the new coroner." She proceeded to give him the details from the day before, including the facts relating to the body's mutilation by Lieberman.

"I never did like him, Reightman, and I didn't care who knew it. But this seems extreme, even for that SOB. Still, Evans is highly regarded, and if she says it was done after the body was brought in, then it must be the case." There was a knock on the Chief's door and Nancy entered with the Chief's fresh coffee and a couple of forms for him to sign. "Any progress in locating Lieberman?" He took a sip from the cup and scowled at the forms Nancy thrust his way.

"No, sir. Jones and Mitchell are trying to track down any possible lead but they aren't having much luck."

'Have they tried checking on relatives in the area?"

"Yes, but there doesn't seem to be any they can find."

"How about his mother's place?' asked Nancy to both Reightman's and Kelly's surprise.

"His mother's place?"

"Yeah. She was a really sweet old lady. I'd see her at bingo." Nancy frowned for a second, remembering her aborted bingo outing which was still tied to Reightman in her mind, but then her face cleared. "She had a funny name. It reminded me of a field of flowers or something."

"Her name wasn't Lieberman?"

"Nope, she remarried. I'd see them both once in a while, and occasionally Doctor Lieberman was with them." Nancy screwed up her face in thought, and finally gave up, shaking her head. "Sorry, but I can't think of her name. I thought I had it for a minute." She took the signed forms from the Chief and started to leave.

"Thanks for the tip, Nancy. Even if you don't remember the name, we have another piece of information to track down. That's a big help."

"You're welcome, Melba. But don't worry – I'll remember the name eventually."

The Chief waited until the door closed. "That just goes to show information can come from the most unlikely places, and I can't think of a more unlikely place than Nancy." He took another sip of coffee and then leaned his elbow on the desk. "I suppose you've heard about Greggs' retirement?"

"Yes, Sam filled me in. Assistant Chief Greggs will be missed around here."

"Yes, he will. Probably time for him to head to greener pastures though, while he can still enjoy himself."

"Any idea's on whom his replacement will be, Chief?"

"Funny you should ask, Reightman," he leaned back in the chair causing the usual squeals and groans. "Have you thought about tossing your hat into the ring?"

"Maybe a little, but not seriously."

He eyed her intently. "Give it some thought. You might find you have more support than you suspect."

"And more detractors."

"That comes with the territory, Reightman." He took another drink of his coffee, and placed the cup down on the desktop. "Think about it. Seriously think about it."

"I will Chief. Thanks for the encouragement. If I did consider it, who'd pick up the Guzman case?"

He hedged for a minute, and shuffled a few things around on his desk. "Well, I don't know, but I could probably find someone to handle it."

"Speaking of supporters and detractors, how was the meeting with the Mayor?"

"Which meeting? Seems all I do these days is attend meetings with the Mayor, members of the city council and bureaucrats of various shapes and titles."

"I was wondering how the meeting was after Councilman Dameron's..." she searched for the appropriate word.

"Prophecy of Doom?" Kelly suggested sarcastically. "It went about as well as you might suspect. She ranted and raved a little, told me she hoped we made more progress, and then suggested, ever so politely, that I might try and show a little support for Dameron."

"Support for Dameron? That's really something coming from her. She hates Dameron!"

"She's certainly not a fan of his, but if I read things correctly, she's worried. Dameron has a pretty big war chest and she can't afford to alienate him, no matter how he castigates the current city structure and leadership of various city departments – this one included." He sighed tiredly and rubbed his eyes. "She is smart enough to know he has strong backing from some quarters and she's waiting for the election to play out."

"She can't seriously think he might win."

"I think she does. He's the incumbent, and incumbents have a natural advantage. He's stepped on his own foot a few times, but even with that, he still has a better support base than his opponents. One is too young and unexperienced, and in the other is as left-winged as Dameron is right-winged. If you put Sutton Dameron and that one together, you'd almost have a bird that could fly without wobbling." He chuckled for a brief minute and then shook his graying head. "As much as I hate to admit it, Madame Mayor has a point. If he wins, he could completely upset the voting balance on the council and hamper every department that provides critical services to the city. He'd do it too, just to prove his power. Add that to his track record of changing his horse mid-stream and he's totally unpredictable and a threat. As long as he can claim what he terms the moral and righteous high ground, he can make things very unpleasant for us all."

Reightman considered everything the chief said and found that, although she didn't like it, she had to agree. "That whole scenario is too depressing for words, sir, but your read is probably spot-on."

"I've been wading through the trash for a long time. I've learned to bend when I need to in order to survive and keep this department running the best I'm able. I do what I need to do."

"What can I do to help?"

He looked at her from beneath his brows and then told her flat out. "Find Lieberman, Detective," he said. "Button up this case. And hope to hell that it will pacify the beast without upsetting too many of its handlers."

On that happy note, she stood and made her goodbyes

"Roses, Melba," Nancy said as she exited the Chief's office. "Lieberman's mother's name had something to do with roses."

"Are you sure, Nancy?"

"I think so. You see, she used to wear this little rhinestone brooch of a rose. I complimented her on it once and she said her new husband had given it to her for her birthday. She said it was supposed to represent their name."

"Hmmm. You said in the office her name had something to so with a field of flowers, Nancy. Maybe you meant it was a field of roses?"

"That's it, Melba! A field of roses! Her name was Rosefield," she said with complete confidence before furrowing her brow and adding, "Or something like that."

"We'll check it out, Nancy. I'm sure it'll turn out to be just as you remembered. I'll talk to you later," she called over her shoulder and went to tell Sam to get Jones and Mitchell hunting down property owned by the Rosefields – or something like that.

Toby spent his morning gathering up a load of packing boxes and tape before driving to Geri's apartment to begin sorting through things. He dreaded it, but knew it had to be done. He stopped for a couple of bottles of water and ten minutes later pulled up the driveway of the three-plex. He got out of the car and gathered up an armful of stuff from the trunk, looping the plastic shopping bag around one hand. He trudged up the stairs leading to the second floor unit and fumbled with the keys as he tried to unlock the door. Giving up, he set the boxes down, inserted the key and opened the door. He picked up the boxes and stepped into the apartment.

"The police might have been thorough, but they sure weren't neat," he thought as he surveyed their handiwork.

Books were stacked on the floor by the makeshift shelves and there was a cushion off of the old tattered couch. He made his way into the small open kitchen and noted opened drawers and cabinets. He sat the bag of water on the counter and flipped on the lights then opened the blinds before walking down the hall to one of the small bedrooms. The door was open, and from the doorway, Toby could see blankets and pillows haphazardly thrown on the floor. He pushed open the door to the other bedroom across the hall. It was empty, and had probably stayed empty ever since he'd moved out six months earlier. He walked to the closet and pulled open the bi-fold doors. It was empty as well, except for a few hangers on the wooden rod.

He looked around the empty space and then went into the bathroom at the end of the hall. The medicine cabinet was opened, and the doors to the small vanity were ajar. The shower curtain had been pulled back and he could see a couple of bottles of bath gel and shampoo were missing their lids. He shut the medicine cabinet door and went out of the room.

Back in the living room, he placed the cushion back on the sofa and took a seat, taking it all in. The room, and the whole apartment, wasn't very large, but had been the best they could afford when they had moved to the city. It was close to the college they attended together and for some reason, they'd never moved.

"Where to start?" With a depressed sigh, he got up from the couch and began putting together a few boxes, strapping the bottoms with the roll of clear tape. He began tossing books into a box, not even looking at their titles. He'd taken everything he wanted when he left. After he finished with the books he started on the kitchen, emptying the drawers and cabinets into another few boxes. He cleaned out the fridge, bagging most of the stuff to carry to the trash later. He drank some water and then moved the boxes out into the living room. He decided to get someone in to clean later.

He filled more boxes with a few knickknacks, CDs and the things from the coffee table, separating a few things out for Grams, and then taped and sealed them. He took down the paintings and prints from the walls. He unhooked the small television and the speakers to the stereo system and carried them down and put them into his back seat. He forced himself up the stairs. *"Just a few rooms more."*

He carried a box and some trash bags into the bathroom and filled them, consigning more to the trash than to the boxes. He considered the shower curtain, and decided to leave it. The bathroom wasn't dirty, just messy. Geri always kept it clean. He carried the filled bags and boxes back to the living room and stacked them with the others. Then he picked up a few of the remaining empties and headed to the bedroom. He folded the sheets and blankets from the floor and set them on the mattress. The room was heating up, so he took off his shirt and turned on the ceiling fan. Then he opened the closet doors.

One by one he took down shirts and trouser and lightweight coats and folded them and stowed them into boxes. *"I'll donate them,"* he decided. *"Someone will want them."* He packed up Geri's shoes. He opened the dresser drawers and emptied out the socks and then the underwear, not looking at any of them closely in case he should recognize a pair. He cleaned out the small nightstand and packed the alarm clock from its top. *"Almost done, Toby."*

He carried the filled boxes into the living room and placed them next to the others, and grabbed the last box and a bottle of water and headed back down the hall. Sitting the water on the dresser, he started taking items from the dresser top and putting them into the box on the floor. He straightened and stretched his back, and then reached for a picture that was lying face down on the dresser surface. He picked it up and turned it over, and his heart stopped.

He forced himself to breathe again. Stumbling backwards toward the bed, he sat down on the edge and closed his eyes. After a minute, he looked at the framed photo in his hand.

The picture had been taken by Grams the day they moved in to the apartment. Geri was seated next to him on a step near the top of the stairs, and had his arm slung across the back of Toby's shoulders. They both had on ratty t-shirts. Geri was wearing sneakers and Toby's feet were bare. They smiled down at the camera held a few steps below and their eyes were filled with happiness and pride.

"Smile," Grams had said as she took the photo. "Hold still, boys – especially you, Toby Bailey! I want to get one more – just in case."

Toby wiped a speck of dust from the glass and lifted the photo toward his face. After a moment he pulled it to his chest and lay down on the bed, his eyes trained on the whirling ceiling fan above. He heard the click, click, click, as the silvery pull chain hit the glass globe below the blades. Light from the window sparkled off the tiny round spheres of the chain.

"Hold onto the chair steady, Toby! I'm almost finished." Geri stretched to tighten the remaining screw on the ceiling fan light.

The boys had spent the day hauling up boxes and belongings to the new apartment, while Grams scrubbed the kitchen and organized things in there. The day before the movers had dropped off the collection of hand-me-down and garage sale items meant to furnish the place, and the mattress company had delivered two new full-sized beds, complete with metal frames. Grams left soon after, but not before getting one last picture of them both sitting on the steps to the new place.

There were just a few things they needed to finish before they could quit, and hanging the fan in Geri's room was third to last on the list. They still had to make the beds and find something to eat, but the hard day was almost over, and they were well satisfied with all they'd done.

"I think that's got it." Geri gave the globe a soft tug to make sure it was secure and then hopped down from the chair and looked up.

"The chain's too short," Toby observed critically. "You'll never be able to reach it."

"Sure I will," Geri disagreed and reached upward to prove Toby wrong. "Ouch!" He rubbed the side of his neck.

"What happened?"

"Nothing. I think I just pulled something." Geri rolled his shoulder and then tilted his neck from side to side, wincing as he did so. "I think you're right, Toby. That chain is too short."

"Told you so. We can get an extender chain at the store tomorrow. Just don't forget to put it on the list," Toby said, referring to the list they'd started that morning which was categorized into important things, kind of important things, and things that would be nice to have sometime in the future. "Are you ready for some food?"

"That's a dumb question! What did Grams leave us?"

"She put a lot of stuff into the freezer, probably casseroles for later. I'm not sure what all's in the fridge. I think she left something on the counter too."

"Let's go see and then we can wash up."

"You gonna' shower before we eat?" Toby asked as they made their way down the hall.

"No, I'll just wash my hands and face real good for now. I'll shower after we eat."

"Why don't you go do that and I'll see what we have for dinner? If nothing else I could make tuna casserole or spaghetti."

"Oh no! Anything but that!"

"Stop being a smart ass and go clean-up – and turn on some music when you come back." Toby opened the refrigerator and dug around among the things Grams had left. 'Geri!" he called, "She left chicken! And a cobbler on the counter!"

"Great!' Geri hollered from the back.

Toby pulled out the plate of chicken and a container of green beans and hunted around for a pan to warm them. He found the plates and glasses right where they should be, and grabbed some silverware. He carried it all into the living room and placed the plates and silverware on the middle of the coffee table, and went back for the glasses of water. He made another trip for the food. He'd almost finished when Geri came into the room and turned on the stereo, crouching down to fiddle with the dials. When he had it adjusted just the way he wanted, he stood and turned around. "We're eating in here?"

"Since we don't have any chairs for the table yet, this will have to do," Toby shrugged and then settled himself on the floor. Geri did the same.

"Pick up your glass, Geri. I think I'll make a toast."

"With water?"

"Sure. Why not? Grams says it isn't what's in the glass that matters, but what's in the heart."

"Grams has a saying for about every occasion," Geri commented as he raised his glass.

"Yes, she surely does." Toby raised his own glass solemnly. "I'd like to toast our first night in this apartment, the good food, and my good friend."

"I'll drink to that!" Geri clinked his glass to Toby's and then took a swallow.

The boys started on their dinner, listening to the music and talking about the things they had to do the next day. After they finished with the food, they carried the dishes into the kitchen and Geri said "Go on and take your shower, Toby. I'll clean up. Just don't use all the hot water!"

"You sure?"

"Yes I'm sure – you're smelly."

Toby laughed and went down the hall. A few minutes later he came out of the bathroom with a towel wrapped around his waist. "It's kind of steamy in there," he said as he rubbed his wet head with another towel. "You might want to leave the door open when you shower.

"Good idea. I'll keep it open a little." He went into his room and as Toby went into his own room, he saw Geri walk in the bathroom wearing only his briefs. Toby pulled out a pair of draw-stringed sleeping shorts and hung both of his towels on the knob of the bedroom door. He combed his hair and went into the kitchen for some more water.

"You want to watch TV?" he asked as Geri came out of the bathroom, towel tied around his waist.

"No, I don't think so," Geri replied as he rolled his neck. "It's getting kind of late and I think I'll go on to bed."

"I guess it is late," Toby agreed as he carried the glass of water back with him to his room. "Good night," he said.

"Good night, Toby."

After a while Toby put down the magazine he'd been reading and got out of bed, headed for the bathroom. When he finished, he started back to his bedroom but heard a groan from Geri's room. "Geri?" he asked knocking on the door gently, "are you alright?"

"I don't know. My neck and shoulder are really hurting. I must have pulled something."

Toby pushed upon the door and went into the room. There was a faint light coming in through the window and he could see Geri sitting up in bed rubbing the space between neck and shoulder. He went back out of the room and grabbed a bottle of lotion from the bathroom and then returned. "Here, let me rub it out. It might help."

Geri lay back down on the bed. "Okay," he said, rolling over onto his stomach.

Toby climbed onto the bed and poured lotion into his hands. "This may be a little cold," he said as he placed his hands onto Geri's skin.

Geri jumped a little when Toby's hands made contact. "Jeeze! That is cold."

Toby continued to rub the area between the shoulder and neck. "Does that help?"

"Yeah, I think so. You know, you're pretty good at this and you haven't even been to school yet."

"I've been reading a lot." Toby poured a little more lotion into his hands. This time he rubbed them together a moment to warm the lotion. This time, when he placed his hands back on skin, Geri didn't jump, but did give a sigh of appreciation. Toby worked the lotion in and then changed sides. "The books say you are supposed to do the same thing to both sides," he said. As his hands massaged the muscles, he could tell Geri was beginning to relax. He worked between the shoulder blades and down the middle of the back. When Geri stretched up to meet his hands, he continued downward.

"Ummmm...that feels great, Toby."

"Good. It's supposed to." Soon, he reached the place where the sheet met the swell of Geri's ass. He kept his hands in motion while he tried to decide what to do. He knew what he wanted to do. He moved the sheet down a little further and touched the soft firm skin right where the ass met the lower back. When Geri didn't protest, he moved the sheet down a little more, discovering Geri was naked beneath the cover. His throat went dry, but he kept his hands moving. He needed more lotion, but he'd finished off the small bottle. He didn't want to stop and get more from the bathroom in case Geri pulled the sheet back up, but he didn't have much choice. "I need to go get some more lotion."

For a minute there was no response and Toby was sure Geri would simply tell him not to worry about it since his shoulder and neck were done. To his surprise, Geri softly said, "Okay, Toby."

He climbed off the bed and had to stop himself from running to the bathroom. Once there, he looked through the cabinet until he found another bottle. He turned off the light and opened the door, letting his eyes adjust to the dark. Then he entered Geri's room, hoping he hadn't changed position or decided the massage was over. Toby stopped cold in the middle of the doorway when he looked at the bed.

Geri was now on top of the sheets, his skin glowing in the light. His strong thighs were slightly spread and one knee was bent, making a muscular curving line of skin and muscle between ass and calf. " Toby?"

He swallowed deeply as he took in the sight of the beautiful nude body stretched on the sheets. The muscles of Geri's ass flexed as he shifted slightly, and Toby hoped desperately that nothing would disturb the magic spread out before him. "I brought more lotion."

"Good," Geri whispered, "because, I want you to finish what you've started here. I… I think we've both waited long enough."

Toby felt his heart quicken with something he couldn't describe. He stood trembling in the doorway while he made his decision. "I'll be right back." He turned and went across the hall to his own room and rummaged around in a drawer until he found the box Grams had given him early that summer. He took out a few and went back into the other room. He laid the condoms on the nightstand and then untied and dropped his shorts, standing naked under the whirling fan. 'Click, click, click,' the silver chain chanted on the glass globe of the light.

He placed his knee on the bed and as he moved, Geri rolled over.

Toby's blue eyes met those of the man he had fallen in love with months before, and traveled slowly down the defined chest and smooth planes of the stomach. He drank in the sight of Geri's hard arching cock, with its foreskin pulled back slightly from the reddened head glistening with a single drop of moisture. He felt himself swell and lengthen, and as he leaned inward toward the body on the bed, Geri's strong arms pulled him down into a kiss. Their mouths met and explored and learned each other, and then pulled away to take mingled breaths.

Geri pulled him close to his body again. "Took you long enough, Toby Bailey."

"Click, click, click…"

Toby set up on the bare, stripped bed. He looked at the happy picture once more, and then, with all the anger he'd been holding in, he threw it against the far wall. When the glass shattered in the frame, he stood on unsteady feet.

"Damn you, Geri! Damn you!"

He walked out of the room without turning off the fan. He grabbed his keys and locked the door before taking the stairs two at a time until he reached the car. He slid into the seat and buckled the belt across his naked chest, and then pulled away from what had been *their* home.

In the empty bedroom, the shirt hanging on the door knob swayed in the air, moved by the whirling fan.

"Click, click, click," cried the chain, shedding tears of reflected sunlight across the broken glass which had once sheltered the two faces smiling up from the floor.

After her meeting with the Chief, Melba went back down to her desk and told Sam about the 'lead' Nancy had provided.

"Might as well have Jones and Mitchell check it out. It's better than anything else they've managed to scrounge up," he said with disgust as he pulled out his phone and dialed.

As she listened to his conversation, she noticed the sick plant had been removed and replaced with a very sturdy looking ficus.

"Dr. Bridges called from downstairs," Sam said, holding the phone slightly away from his mouth. "She said to head on down as soon as you got back. I think she has the toxicology panel back from the lab." He went back to his conversation with Jones.

She quickly checked through her phone messages and listened to a couple until she came to one from Toby. "I was just wondering if you have any update about the release of Geri's body. I'll check back later. I'll…be out for a while."

She motioned to Sam that she was leaving and made her way down to the morgue, taking the stairs instead of the elevator. She'd notice her pants were a little snug in the hip area this morning and decided the exercise couldn't hurt.

Dr. Bridges was seated in the small desk in the front area of the morgue. "Hello, Detective," she said cheerily as she rose from her seat.

"Jackson said that you might have some news?"

"Yes, we got the results back from the lab. Come on back with me and I'll tell you what they found floating around in the samples we sent."

Reightman followed the doctor back through the door that lead to the depths of the morgue until they reached a smallish office, next to the one occupied by Dr Evans. Reightman peaked through the glass office window and Bridges said, "She's out for a couple of hours trying to hunt down an apartment. We've been staying at one of those extended stay places the last day or so, but Dr. Evans said it was already driving her crazy."

"You think you'll be here long enough to go to the trouble of an apartment?"

"Yes, I think so. Evans said we would probably get a least a six month contract – probably longer."

Bridges went behind the desk and picked up a file, and then came around and took a seat in one of the chairs placed in front of the desk. "Take a load off, Detective, while I share the grisly details." Melba found herself puzzled as to why Bridges didn't seat herself behind the desk.

The doctor followed her train of thought. "I never sit behind the desk, unless there are too few chairs or if I don't like whomever I'm talking to." She smirked and added, "I just think this is cozier." She opened the file and read over the notes for a minute. "Okay, here it is in layman's terms. There were significant amounts of sedatives in Guzman at the time of death, along with a nasty, but relative small dose of some sort of date rape drug."

Reightman raised her brows in surprise and whistled under her breath. "Could the drugs have killed him if he hadn't been attacked with the knife?"

Bridges shook her head, causing her ponytail to bounce. "No, they'd have worn off eventually if they'd been able to run their course, although the victim would've had the mother of all hangovers and needed a couple of days to get back to normal. What this *does* mean is he would've been very groggy and his response time would have been severely compromised."

"Therefore making it harder to fight back effectively?"

"Exactly, although why someone added the date rape drug to the mix beats me. The sedatives would've done that on their own."

"Any idea of what specific drug mix they used in the date rape drug cocktail?"

Bridges consulted the file again before answering "No. The results show a group of markers consistent with that type of drug, rather than a specific named drug. The sedatives were also somewhat of a mixed bag. Looks to me like someone simply cleaned out a typical yuppie's medicine cabinet. That would've done the trick."

"So what we need to look for is a method and an opportunity to introduce the drugs into him before the actual attack."

"That's right. Based on the levels found, I'd guess he was given the date rape drug a little earlier than he was given the other stuff , or it was a substantially weaker dose, or both," Bridges postulated as she twirled a strand of hair from her ponytail. "There's one thing more."

"This isn't enough?' Reightman asked wryly.

"Oh, this is the real icing on the cake! Guzman had an erectile enhancer in his blood."

"You mean he –"

"Took a little blue pill a few hours before he was killed," Bridges quipped, completing Reightman's sentence.

Reightman leaned back in her chair, confused as she tried to understand the implications. "But, why would a young man, in excellent physical condition, need to do that? Most twenty-eight year old men are always…"

"They always rarin' to go, you mean?" Bridges suggested with a cynical smile and then shrugged. "Given what I know about the nature of his activities, I'd hazard a guess he felt he needed some help to perform as expected. Maybe he didn't feel any desire for whomever he was meeting."

Reightman nodded slowly. "That makes sense, although it's the only thing about this case that does."

"Glad I could help," Bridges said as she stood. "I need to get back out front in case we get a customer."

Reightman rose from her own chair. "When will you be prepared to release the body?"

"We've done all we can. I tidied him up as much as possible earlier today. Dr. Evans said we can release him any time tomorrow, after she finishes with the forms."

"Thank you, and extend my thanks to Dr. Evans as well. Mr. Bailey will be relieved."

"Is he aware of the little impromptu bris performed by Lieberman?"

Reightman decided not to characterize it that way to Toby. "No, not yet. I'll tell him at the same time I give him the news the body is ready for release. It might help soften the message. I'd better try to tracking him down now. Thanks again, Bridges."

"Sure, Reightman. I'll see ya' around. That's almost a certainty."

Bridges escorted her to the front of the morgue and Reightman made her way to the stairwell, thinking over all she'd learned. She stopped by her desk to pick up her things and found a note informing her Sam had gone to help Jones and Mitchell. She felt a pang of disappointment – she'd hoped he'd go with her to meet Toby and help deliver the news. She scrawled a note for him, and left it taped to a leaf of the ficus tree.

CHAPTER ELEVEN

TRAFFIC WAS LIGHT so Reightman made it to Capital Street shortly after noon. After knocking on the door of the spa and getting no answer, she called Toby and left a voicemail. Her stomach growled and she wandered over to Earth Fruits to grab a bite to eat. She was warmly greeted by Bernice, and Lindsi was her normal doleful self as she took Melba's order. Melba read the paper, catching up on the news while going out of her way to avoid reading an editorial written by Councilman Sutton Dameron. She felt guilty as she recalled her earlier meeting with Kelly and entertained the idea that she should at least see what the jerk had to say. Ultimately, she decided enjoying her lunch out-classed her need to know what crap the good councilman was spewing today.

After lunch, she paid the bill and following Zhou Li's example, left Lindsi a generous tip, although not the princely sum Madam Zhou felt appropriate for the grudging service. She checked her phone, hoping to find a message from Toby. Finding none, she stood on the blazing hot sidewalk and looked around.

On a whim, she strolled over to Passed Around. She stopped and looked in the window, and was surprised to see most of the fluffy prom dresses were gone, along with several slutty cowgirl ensembles. She smiled, thinking of the collegiate young women who'd be wearing the silly outfits, and then went into the shop.

Moon was behind the counter and brightened when she saw Melba. "Good afternoon, Detective! It's extremely pleasant and nice to see you again. Did your friend like the present you so astutely selected?"

"Yes she did, Moon, and it looked beautiful on her. Although you know as well as I do that you did the lion's share of selecting."

"What's most important is your gift brought unencumbered joy and delight to the recipient. Are you in search for another?"

No, not today. I have a few minutes and thought I might hunt for something for myself."

"Oh! That makes me so overwhelmingly pleased, Detective. Allow me to point you to the appropriate area with your size." Moon glided around the counter and led Melba to one of the circular racks in the center of the store. Once there, she carefully studied Melba's figure and indicated the appropriate section.

Melba looked at the size indicator hanging on the rack. "Moon, I don't think these will work. I haven't worn that size in a few years."

"Detective, well-made, beautifully constructed clothing is quite different in fit compared to the more pedestrian clothing found in so many plebeian places these days. Try a few things and see. I think you'll be surprised. If not, we can move to another section."

Doubting her chances for success, Melba flipped through the clothing. She pulled out a few things which might help expand her current wardrobe and held them up to see them better in the light.

Moon hurried from her place by the counter shaking her head emphatically. "No, Detective, those will not do. The fabric although wonderful, is not in the colors your complexion demands. They'll wash you out completely, not make you glow like the beautiful, successful woman you are."

"But these are…"

"Very similar to other things already in your closet, Detective Reightman," said a voice Melba recognized immediately. She turned to greet Madame Zhou as the lady made her way into the store.

"Good afternoon, Madame Zhou," Moon fluttered forward. "Have you come to examine something new and exquisite today?"

"Unfortunately not, Moon. I had a quite astonishing shopping expedition yesterday and must wait until next week if I'm to remain disciplined. I saw the Detective enter the store earlier, and my curiosity led me here to see what she might be shopping for today."

"She is shopping for herself today, Madame, but I fear she has selected some items which will not enhance her countenance as splendidly as wonderful clothing should. I'm almost overcome with despair."

Melba was starting to feel like they were ganging up on her, so she held up the garments in her hand and explained. "I thought these would expand the current things in my closet and allow me to –I don't know –

mix things up some." She laid the draped the items over the rack as Zhou Li approached.

The small elderly lady peered closely at the selection, occasionally feeling the fabric with the palm of her delicate hand. "You have an excellent sense of good fabric, Detective," she said approvingly. When Melba smiled at the compliment, she added, "However, your sense of color and cut is not so inspired."

"But I thought–" Melba stopped mid-sentence when Zhou Li placed a gentle hand on her arm.

"There is nothing at all wrong with your usual clothing, Detective. However, I think you deserve a few special things to brighten your everyday black, navy and brown. In addition, I suspect there are many clever examples of European tailoring which, when added to your existing wardrobe, might transform your everyday things into something a bit more polished." When Melba failed to respond, Zhou Li added cajolingly, "What can it harm to try something different? Moon will not steer you wrong, I promise. If she does, I will personally acquire these," she indicated the draped clothing, "and present them to you as a gift." She studied Melba's face. "It's a win/win situation."

"Madame Zhou, I'm happy to try on whatever Moon suggests, but I wouldn't allow you to purchase any of this clothing for me, as crafty an offer as it is. I recognize your approach, you know. I used the same tactics on my daughter often enough!"

Zhou Li grinned in appreciation of Reightman's partial capitulation, and waved her tiny hand. "As you will, Detective."

Moon hurried forward and removed the draped garments and laid them to the side. She then rapidly worked her way through the remaining selection, pulling out three blouses, a few pairs of slacks and two jackets. "We will start our consideration with these. Please follow me. The dressing rooms are near the back."

As Melba followed, trailed by Zhou, she wondered what she was getting herself into with this hijacked shopping expedition. Considering the opposition aligned against her, she resigned herself to the fact she wouldn't be taking the original garments home. *"I might as well just accept my grim fate."* Moon showed her into the first dressing room and hung the items on a series of hooks placed within easy reach. She considered the choices Moon had carefully placed on the hooks in groupings, and was glad none of the items were too bright or too boldly patterned. *"In fact,"* she conceded, *"they're all good choices, just different from what I'd normally wear."* Melba undressed and then pulled on the first pair of tailored trousers, nonplussed that Moon had been correct in her assessment of the appropriate size. The trousers even had pockets. She bent her legs and then stood before reaching down to touch her toes, testing if she could move in them. She pulled on the blouse Moon had coordinated with the trousers and found it was actually a tiny bit too large. *"Hmmm, maybe good clothing is different."* She took a jacket off of a hanger and slipped it on while looking in the mirror. Her jaw dropped open.

"Do you need my expert and entirely sophisticated help with anything?" Moon asked from outside the door.

"No, I'm doing fine," she answered, still enthralled with her reflection.

"Since that is the case, Madame Zhou requests you kindly come forth so she may examine the magnificence of the selections."

She opened the door and stepped out. Moon led her to the small sitting area where Zhou was ensconced like a benevolent queen surveying her domain. Melba stood for inspection, feeling uncomfortable and self-conscious as the two women surveyed her critically.

"Please stand up straight, Detective. I've never seen you slouch until now." Melba straightened her spine and glared down at the imperious old woman, who laughed delightedly. "That's much better." Zhou Li glanced at Moon who nodded her head.

"What do you feel concerning the appropriateness of this beautiful ensemble, Detective Reightman?"

"I like it, Moon."

The proprietress shook her head, causing her dramatic hair to sway slightly. "That is not *exactly* what I meant. Let me rephrase, please." She looked straight at Melba and asked, "How, or what, do you feel while wearing those clothes?"

Melba had never been asked that sort of question before. She wrinkled her brow, trying to decide what she felt. It was an unusual exercise to say the least. "I feel strong and confident, but also attractive and well dressed. I feel like I'm ready for about anything."

Moon looked at Zhou, who inclined her head. "That being the case, I would say you should purchase this specific selection."

Melba worried over her very meager clothing allowance and finally decided it would stretch a little.

The process was repeated a few times more, with one blouse making her feel fussy, and one pair of trousers proving to be an excellent fit, but too trendy for work. Moon carried the approved garments up to the counter and prepared to add the total. "A dress perhaps, Detective?"

"No, I'd never live down wearing a dress to work," she said with a small snort. "Jackson would give me all kinds of grief, and one of us would have to be dead and buried before I'd chance that scenario." Moon gave her a disappointed pout, so Melba quickly added, "When I need a dress for a special occasion, I promise I'll ask you both to help me to select the perfect one." Moon arranged her face in a pleased smile and bent to collect prices off of tags.

"Could you let me see the total before finalizing everything, Moon? I need to make sure I'm not overextending my non-existent shopping budget."

Moon agreed and Melba turned to talk with Zhou Li about her lunch at Earth Fruits. A short while later Moon handed her a slip of paper for her "consideration, adjustment or approval." She winced. The total was not nearly as large as she'd expected, just larger than she'd hoped. After giving it more thought and remembering how she'd felt wearing the garments, she decided to take them all. She smiled and handed Moon her credit card.

She was struggling to hang her loot on the small hook in the backseat when her phone rang. Struggling with both the hanging bags and her purse, she finally grabbed the phone and managed to answer before the caller went to voicemail.

"Hello," she answered, "this is Detective Melba Reightman."

"Hello, Detective. I'm returning your call from earlier today." Toby sounded odd and distant.

"Hi, Toby. I'm right outside the spa. Would it be convenient for you to meet?"

"I can meet, but not at the spa. Not today, please."

"Is something wrong?"

He hesitated, and then answered, "Just a rough day." After another hesitation, he suggested, "Why don't we meet here at my apartment? I'll meet you downstairs on the sidewalk out front."

"I'm not sure, Toby," she replied while thinking about Sam's worry that she was becoming too close to this young man. She needed to rebuild some distance. "I think it would be better to meet here."

"I can't," he told her, with weariness in his voice. "Not today. Please."

He sounded exhausted and upset, and against her better judgement, she felt the urge to help however she could. "Okay. I'll meet you over there." She hung up the phone wondering what had gone wrong with Toby's day. She locked the car and headed across the street.

At about the same time she stepped on the sidewalk, Toby stepped off of the lowest step coming from the stairwell. "It's just up here – a couple of flights straight up." Once at the top, he opened the door and ushered her into his apartment.

She stepped into the room. *"It suits him perfectly,"* she decided as she looked over the décor and glanced through the French doors that opened onto the terrace.

"Just take a seat anywhere in the living room while I fix us a couple of glasses of iced tea."

"Please, don't go to any trouble. I can't stay very long."

"It's not any trouble at all. It's already made."

She took a seat on the edge of a sofa and less than a minute later he walked over and handed her a glass of tea. "Thanks," she said, taking a sip before placing it on a coaster at the edge of the coffee table. "The reason I called is, I have some news."

He took a seat on the chair which was angled slightly toward and nodded before taking a drink from his own glass.

"The acting coroner will release Mr. Guzman's body first thing in the morning, Toby."

He sat silently as he gazed down into his glass then placed it on the table. "Thanks," he said quietly. "I'll make arrangements for it to be picked up by the funeral home and transported for burial."

"There's one more thing."

"What?"

His despondent tone worried her. "Are you okay?" When he didn't answer she tried a different tact. "You're very subdued today." When he failed to answer her for the second time, she tried a more direct approach. "Toby, I know you're grieving, but this isn't like you."

"I'm sorry. I told you I've had an upsetting day. I went to pack up Geri's apartment and I guess it was just too much." He picked up his glass, but set it down before drinking. "You're right, I *am* grieving. I'm just not sure *what* I'm grieving for right now." He picked up the glass again and took a deep swallow before looking at her. "You said there was something else?"

"Yes." She decided just to barrel through. "Toby, this might be hard to hear, but I decided you need to know." She proceeded to tell him about the things done to Geri's body by Lieberman, and that the missing piece couldn't be located. When she finished, she was reluctant to meet his eyes.

"Did I hear you correctly, Detective? He – he circumcised him?"

"Yes."

He stood and walked to the French doors. For a moment he looked out onto the terrace. "How could someone do that?" he whispered.

"Toby, you have every right to be angry and perhaps even to take legal action against the city and the department."

He whirled around to face her. "Would that help, Detective? Would it return that... piece of flesh to me so I could have it buried with him?" He walked toward her, his anger and hurt clear to see. "Would hiring Madame Zhou to sue this city for every nickel I could get make me feel better?" He stopped abruptly behind the chair, and gripped its upholstered back tightly. "Maybe I *would* feel better," he told her once he had his emotions under control. "Maybe I *should* make myself rich off of this act committed by some evil, criminal man, but...I don't think I will."

"Toby, that is very..." she struggled to find the right word.

"Kind? Generous? Charitable, forgiving, or Christian of me?" he asked mockingly. "Pick a word. I can't. Not today."

"I don't know what to say." She couldn't tell what he was thinking, but could sense something running just underneath his surface. *"I've never seen him in this mood."*

"There isn't anything for you to say, at least not today." He walked over to where she sat on the sofa and took a seat beside her with his hands folded loosely in his lap. He tucked one bare foot up underneath him. "Let me tell you what I know, not you as the Detective, but as the woman I've started to think of as a friend." When she didn't respond, except to hold his eyes, he continued. "Look around this room," he directed, watching her face as she did. "Almost every item in this room, and in the kitchen, and in the bathroom and in the bedroom is *new*, at least to me." She turned her confused eyes to his, and waited for him to explain. "Six months ago when I walked out of the apartment I shared for many years with Geri, I only took four things with me. I took my clothes. I took some photographs that were important to me, and I took the dishes my Grams gave me when we moved in."

"You said four things, Toby," she quietly reminded him.

"Yes, I did. The fourth thing I took with me was...my pride." She watched his very still and expressionless face. "It would have been better," he continued, "if I had left my pride there in that apartment, and had brought Geri with me instead. I should have forced him to come, however I could." He looked at her with his eyes, the dark rings around the pupils very stark against his face. "A piece of flesh in a coffin or a million dollars in the bank won't reverse the choices I made then, no matter what I feel, or don't feel, right now. That's what I'm telling the woman who might be a friend." He studied her a moment and sat up straighter on the sofa. He firmed his jaw and his eyes blazed with burning intensity. "Now, I'm speaking to the Detective. There's only one thing that matters now." He waited. "Do you know what it is?"

"Yes, I do."

"Then tell me."

"The only thing that matters now is finding the person or persons who murdered Gerald Guzman and bringing them to justice."

He held her eyes for a minute more, and then unfolded himself from the sofa and rose to his feet. "Got it in one, Detective. You got it in one."

As she drove back to the station, she thought of nothing but his pale, blue eyes, rimmed in black.

Christina Dameron hurried to finish dressing for dinner. The sitter would arrive shortly and she didn't want to keep Sutton waiting. He'd probably worn a hole in the carpet with his anxious pacing. She reached behind her to fasten the clasp of a large diamond solitaire necklace and looked in the mirror. She regarded her tired eyes and wondered if a more vivid lipstick might distract from the lines of strain at their corners. She shrugged at her reflection and decided she didn't even care. She walked out of her bedroom and down the entryway stairs.

Sutton looked up as she descended, but didn't comment on her appearance. "Ready?"

"Yes. Is the sitter here?"

"She is," he nodded, and opened the front door as she picked up her small purse. They walked down to the car and got in on their separate sides. As she buckled up, she considered their destination. Tonight they were dining, for the third time in six weeks, with the Reverend Brother Ephraim Sawyer and his wife, Marilyn.

Reverend Sawyer was the founder and CEO of the largest conservative evangelical church in the entire southeastern United States.

He was also one of Sutton's key supporters and the major financial contributor to the Dameron's war chest.

Sutton turned off the main street out of their historic neighborhood onto the thoroughfare that would eventually become the interstate taking them north, toward the lake. After about twenty five minutes, he took the appropriate exit and moments later, turned into the gated residential neighborhood where the Sawyer's twelve thousand square foot home was situated. He pulled the car into the circular driveway and parked. He then got out and made his way around to her side, and opened the door. "This evening is very important," he reminded her as she stepped out onto the imported Italian stone paving the driveway.

"I'm aware of that, Sutton!" she snapped as he escorted her to the imposing front door.

He rang the doorbell and Christina could hear the resonant chimes sounding throughout the house. A moment later the Reverend himself answered the door. He was a tall thin man, with narrow lips that widened in what passed for a smile as he greeted them. "Sutton and Christina, how delightful for you to join us this evening." Christina thought she might have misheard him, and then decided she hadn't. He clearly felt it *was* a delight for them. He ushered them through the marbled foyer and down a few steps to the immense living room.

Marilyn rose from an antique couch positioned at one side of the room. She smiled in welcome and moved her lush, designer-clad self to take Sutton's hand in one set of her bejeweled fingers, and Christina's in the other. "I'm just so happy you two could join us tonight! It seems like it's been ages since we had you out for dinner. Come into the family room and I'll have my lazy husband whip us up some drinks." Christina and Sutton expressed their combined pleasure at the invitation and followed their hostess.

The offer of a drink in the home of the founder of a very conservative church didn't surprise Christina, She'd learned one basic truth of the South many years ago: everyone drank. The only questions were *what*, and whether they chose to hide it. With drinks in hand, they all made themselves comfortable on the big over-stuffed couches and chairs placed around a huge natural wood topped coffee table that was in turn, placed in front of a fireplace large enough to stand in.

They made pleasant conversation, talking about their respective children. The Sawyers had two children together and Marilyn had an additional son, born after a hasty marriage to a man she had divorced soon after meeting Ephraim Sawyer. That man was never seen again, and the previous marriage was never discussed. In addition to the aforementioned children, there was a single Sawyer grandson.

"He's just the cutest little thing!" Marilyn gushed as the Reverend told a rambling story of the two year old's exploits.

"He is a little terror," Sawyer commented before adding proudly, "He reminds me of myself at that age!"

"Because of that, Sawyer spoils him terribly, always buying him things with his name on them. 'Toby' this and 'Toby' that! He has more stuff with his name on it than you can imagine." Marilyn shook her head fondly at her husband's foibles.

"Your grandson's name is Toby?" Christina asked with interest. "You don't hear that name much in this area."

"Yes, but his real, Christian name is Tobias. It's an old family name. My father was christened Tobias and Toby will carry on that name for his generation," the Reverend replied. "Besides, he can't say Tobias yet. He pronounces it as 'Tobus', which won't do at all! We all decided Toby was acceptable until he was older."

Marilyn laughed and confided, "The other reason we call him Toby is because it's really hard to find anything with the name Tobias on it, while there are things for a Toby almost everywhere. We've picked up t-shirts and caps and little mugs and even license plates from about everywhere we've been. Ephraim even found a bunch of hunting and fishing stuff for him with his name engraved right on them."

"Isn't he young for hunting and fishing equipment?" Sutton asked.

"Not at all! Before too long, he'll be firing the rifle and using one of the hunting knifes to skin a buck." Sawyer clapped his hand on Sutton's shoulder and added, "You just wait – he'll be five before you know it. We'll get your boy out there with us. You can't start them hunting too young."

They all laughed appreciatively at the Reverend's wisdom and wit, although Christina worried her own laughter sounded hollow.

Soon, Marilyn indicated that dinner was ready and they all went into the small dining room, which only seated ten, instead of the twenty-four the formal room could handle. The conversation was varied, ranging from the extremely hot weather the state was experiencing to new residential developments underway on the lake. Eventually, dinner was over, and Marilyn leaned toward her, "Christina, if you'd help me clear the plates,

I'll put together dessert. We'll leave the men alone for a while. I'm sure they won't get up to too much devilment while we're gone."

The woman cleared the plates and Christina followed Marilyn into the giant kitchen. Marilyn motioned for her to put the plates down on one of the counters. "Emeline will take care of those in the morning. There's no need for us to ruin our nails doing dishes."

Christina set the dishes down as directed.

"You look like you could use another glass of wine," commented Marilyn. "I know I could!" She poured a couple of large glasses and handed it to Christina. "I wanted a chance to talk to you alone – just us girls. I've noticed you're looking tired. Not that you aren't still lovely, dear, but I did wonder if something was the matter.'

"Thank you for asking, Marilyn. Everything's fine. I am tired, but there's just so much to do with the campaign and the kids. I'm afraid I'm just worn out and haven't been sleeping much."

"I'm sure the campaign is a bugger, but it appears Sutton is doing very well."

"Yes, he is doing well. We're all very proud of him and his progress."

Marilyn took a drink of her wine and confided, "I think that we women are severely underestimated. We put up with things no man would."

Christina lifted her own glass and tilted a stream of deep red liquid into her mouth. "What do you mean?"

"Well, to put it simply; we cook, take care of the children, manage the home, do most of the shopping, engage in whatever business we must to get ahead in the world, and then we are expected to look as fresh as a rose all the time. On top of which, no matter what is going on in our lives, we're supposed to be ready to spread our legs and fuck whether we feel like it or not."

Christina was so shocked by Marilyn's word usage she almost dropped the fragile crystal glass.

"Oh honey, close your mouth. I know you've heard that word before and have probably used it frequently yourself." Marilyn took another swig of her wine and then poured some more from the bottle. She held out the bottle to Christina who took it and refilled her own glass. "Now, I wanted to ask you, are things are fine in the bedroom?"

"I beg your pardon?"

"You know what I mean. Are you and Sutton bouncing the headboard or has all the stress and campaign nonsense messed that up as well?

"We're fine in that respect, Marilyn, not that it's really any of your business."

"Christina, of *course* it's my business," Marilyn corrected her in a no-nonsense voice. "My husband and I have invested a whole lot of cold, hard cash into you and your politician husband. In order to get our investment back, you and Sutton have some work to do. You need to appear happy, rested and well satisfied. So, I'll ask you again, are you two tangling up the bed sheets on a regular basis?"

Embarrassed, Christina looked down at the wine glass in her hands and the trembling wine inside of it. "Not as much as we used to, before."

"That's what I thought! I can usually tell these things just by looking. Let me tell you a hard truth: the more a man conceives a need for power, the less interested he is in keeping the woman at home satisfied. You need to add some excitement to keep his engine primed."

Part in horror at the nature of their conversation, and part in curiosity, Christina took another big swallow of her wine and asked, "What would you suggest, Marilyn?"

"I can't tell you what will work in your personal situation, but I'll tell you what I did about twelve years ago. I got myself a tattoo."

"You what? You have a tattoo?" No one would believe the wife of the very respectable Ephraim Sawyer had a tattoo. It was beyond belief.

"Yes, indeed I do. I got it in Vegas when we were there for the national convention of evangelical churches. I went right down to the tattoo parlor and picked out the prettiest flower you ever did see, and had it done."

"W-Where?" Christina asked trying to control the mirth bubbling up inside her at the thought of the Reverend's wife in a seedy Vegas tattoo parlor, baring her skin for to get her some ink.

"Right down here," Marilyn pointed to her crotch. "Right near my magic cave." As Christina Dameron struggled to control herself, Marilyn continued. "Every time I'd want some attention, I'd inform the Reverend that he needed to stop by and smell the flower."

"Oh my goodness! Did that work?"

"For a while it did, but eventually, every novelty wears thin." Marilyn took a slow drink and put her glass down. "I ultimately turned to extra-curricular activity. There are plenty of willing men, and women – if you know where to look."

"You had an affair?" Christina probed carefully, waiting for the answer.

"I wouldn't call it an affair. It was more of a-rent-a-stud arrangement." Marilyn gave a throaty laugh and fanned her face. "And it was worth every penny. He really had it going on, if you know what I mean." Marilyn spread her well-manicured hands apart a considerable distance. "Unfortunately, Ephraim is a thin man, in all areas of his anatomy. I've discovered I like some meat on the bone and prefer a lot of chorizo in my taco."

Christina Dameron didn't allow even a tiny bit of expression to cross her face. "Are you still…?"

"No," Marilyn answered sharply, and then sighed, disappointedly. "Ephraim found out about my arrangement ten days ago. He's allowed his activities, and I'm allowed mine, but this particular arrangement proved to be less discreet than I hoped. Ephraim was enraged over the whole thing. There was quite a lot of blood on the floor before it was all over."

"Blood on the floor?" Christina's head was beginning to buzz slightly, maybe from all the wine.

"Figure of speech. It is a pity it had to end, but I was spending a lot more than I'd ever imagined, and was probably going to keep on paying the piper."

"He was that good?" Christina asked cautiously.

"Let's just say he'd devised a technique to keep his clients on the hook." Marilyn finished off her wine and set her glass down by the other dishes on the counter. "Would you help me dish up the pie, Christina? I'm sure our husbands are wondering just what we are up to in here."

While the ladies were preparing dessert, the men were deep in discussion over after dinner drink. As their time together wound down, the Reverend Sawyer finished off by saying, "That damned place has to be closed down, Sutton. I can't allow it to remain open any longer. When I think of the scandal that —" Sawyer broke of his comment and took a drink of his fifty year old brandy. "I'm depending on you to make sure it happens."

"I'll take care of it, sir. But with all of the attention on the event, I feel the need to be cautious right now."

"There is a time for caution, Sutton, and a time for brutal action, but I take your point." Sawyer swirled the brandy around in his glass and took another fortifying swallow. "Make sure it is handled within the next few days, even if you have to use an intermediary. There's funding for things like that readily available."

"I'll take care of it. You can count on me, sir."

A buzz sounded from the pocket of the Reverend's jacket and he reached in and pulled out a phone. He read the incoming text and then laid the phone face down on the gleaming mahogany table top.

"Something important you need to handle, sir?"

"Just the Lord's business. I'll address it later." Sawyer smiled piously with his thin lips and watched Dameron over the rim of the brandy glass he cradled close to his face. "I have big plans for you, son. I like you, and Marilyn likes your wife. If you play your cards right, you'll see yourself sitting in that big house on Pennsylvania Avenue one day. My backing, and the backing of my various associates, can make great things happen for you, Dameron. I've helped many of the important people in this city and this state get to their current positions and they in turn, help me. Do you understand what I'm saying to you, son?"

"Yes, I do, Reverend. You're looking for me to progress our agenda."

"Shit, boy! I'm telling you to keep your dick clean and out of a vise, and to follow my lead exactly!" The Reverend slammed his hand down on the table to emphasize his point. Sawyer waited until a shocked Dameron bowed his head in acquiescence of the Reverend's superiority and might, and then reached into his breast pocket and pulled out a letter-sized envelope which bulged enticingly. "Here's a little token of esteem from me and the congregation. There's a lot more where that came from. The collection plate's full every Sunday. You'll get another *offering* from me when – and if – you win this pissant election. Just remember where it came when it's time for a reckoning." Sawyer drained the few remaining drops of brandy remaining in his glass and said, almost dismissively, "Don't fret over the other thing. That problem's already being dealt with – this evening as a matter of fact."

As the door opened from the kitchen, Dameron picked up the envelope and put it into his own breast pocket. Marilyn and Christina joined them, each carrying perfectly portioned slices of pie on lovely heirloom china.

"You boys ready for the sweets?" Mrs. Sawyer asked as she placed a slice of pie in front of her husband.

"No, but we're ready for dessert!" the Reverend quipped and the table once again filled with laughter in appreciation of his wit

Later in the car on their way home, Christina asked, "Did you get the money?

"Yes," Sutton answered as he turned the car into the drive. "Did you get the information?"

"Yes, I did," she told him as she stepped out of the car.

Sutton walked up the steps and went inside to pay the sitter. Christina went up the stairs to her room, thinking about the night. She heard her husband in the hall, talking on his phone. She couldn't quite make out the words.

Sometime between 11 PM and 2 AM, the Time Out Spa received additional negative attention. Lurid, hot pink spray paint decorated the façade of the building with hateful slogan and the sidewalk below boasted a collection of crudely drawn penises and testicles, with the words "Bleeding Dead Faggots" artistically placed among them.

The vandal never saw John Brown in the black SUV across the street, sitting behind the dark tinted glass.

Reightman arrived at the office after a night spent tossing and turning. Her visit with Toby bothered her more than she'd realized, and she found herself playing their conversations over in her mind. His words hadn't disturbed her as much as his demeanor. He was evolving from the young, shaken man she'd met the night of the murder, but who he was evolving into had yet to be determined. All she knew was at this point, was he was different. He seemed more sad these days than grieving, but she knew the sorrow would come. *"He's still in shock,"* she reasoned, *"and when the pieces fly apart, Toby, I hope you have someone to help you pick them up and put them back together again."*

Reightman booted up her computer and found herself contemplating the ficus tree and wondering where Jackson was this morning. He was almost never late, and was usually in the office collecting gossip from his spot by the coffee pot well before she dragged herself in to work. She pulled a packet of jasmine tea from her purse and stowed the bag in her drawer. She had just started to make her way to the breakroom for her morning cup of hot water when Jackson came striding down the hall, walking much faster than he normally did this time of morning.

"Reightman, get your things! We know where Lieberman's holed up."

"Thank God!" she exclaimed as she opened the drawer and grabbed her bag. "How did you find him?"

"It wasn't me who found him. It was our Junior Detective and his trusty sidekick Mitchell who dug up the address," he told her as they jogged to the parking area. "I helped point them in the right direction by giving them suggestions about where to look in the county deed records, but they did the digging." As she climbed in the car he added, "Nancy was almost right about her Rosefield idea. Lieberman's mother married a Mr. Rosenfeld a few years before her death."

"Well, I'll be damned." Reightman buckled herself into the front seat of Jackson's always pristine car. "Way to go Nancy!"

"Glad you made up with her, Reightman. If Nancy hadn't gotten over her hissy fit, we'd still be chasing wind. Mrs. Rosenfeld amended the deed right after their marriage, so it took longer to find the right record. I wish the county would move into the present century. Their system's pretty convoluted and requires a lot of manual searching. Even our shoddy, cobbled together mess of databases is a damn sight better."

They didn't exchange much more chatter on the drive, and their usual banter was non-existent as each thought about what they might find at the address the team had unearthed. Reightman hoped this would be the break they needed. About twenty minutes later, they pulled up at a well-kept ranch house on Chutney Street. Detective Jones and Mitchell were waiting, along with two additional teams in police vehicles.

Reightman and Jackson stepped out of the car and approached the house. Jones and Mitchell stepped back, deferring to her and Jackson, although she could read the excitement on their faces. The other officers were waiting a few steps away, awaiting instructions from her as the senior official on the scene.

Reightman greeted her two team members and they nodded respectfully back.

"We don't know if we've found anything yet, ma'am," Mitchell said with a trace of nervousness in his voice.

"It's better progress than any of us have made in the last few days," Jackson assured him. He looked over the two junior members of the team. "Are you two suited up with vests under your pretty clothes?"

"Yes, sir," they both assured him.

With a nod from Reightman, Jackson went into action. "Since you two found the house, you get to be the first visitors through the door." He quickly turned his attention to the other waiting officers. "Officers, I need two of you to provide entry backup. The other two of you circle around to the back of the house and remain in position until I give the word. Keep your handhelds ready, and be ready for hostile fire."

Jackson watched the officers round the corner of the house and gave them a moment to get into position. "Alright, gentleman," he addressed Jones and Mitchell, "when you're ready."

Jones and Mitchell pulled their weapons and the other officers followed suit. As Reightman started to follow suit, Jackson put a restraining hand on her arm. "Reightman, let the boys here start the festivities – you'll get in on the fun soon enough." She stepped back from the door and Jackson gave her an approving nod. "Thank you, Melba," he said under his breath, before motioning for the team to proceed.

Detective Jones rapped sharply on the door, and waited. He repeated the process, with additional emphasis, "Open the door! We're with the city police and need to speak with you."

There was no response. One of the accompanying officers confirmed, "There's no movement from the front, sir."

A moment later a voice came over the handheld, confirming there was no sign of habitation from the back either.

Jackson moved toward the door. "Time to bring it down, gentlemen." With a couple of sharp staccato kicks, Mitchell opened the door.

"The kid's pretty impressive, Jackson."

He shrugged. "He's young and excited about his first action role. He'll learn there are easier ways to open a door, Reightman. Give him a few years."

They both watched as the two moved slowly through the door, with weapons drawn. A second or two later, the other officers followed suit. After what seemed like hours, Mitchell came to the door looking disconcerted.

"No one home, Mitchell?"

"Yes, ma'am, someone's home, and it's Lieberman. But he's not up to entertaining visitors."

With a grunt of acknowledgement, she moved forward, followed by Jackson. They entered the house, noting the tidy interior and the outdated furniture. Mitchell gave a directional tilt of his head and they moved further into the house. Reightman stopped at the entry way into a kitchen and small dining space. Sitting in one of the chairs with his back slightly to the door was Doctor Benjamin Lieberman, obviously very, very dead.

After taking a minute to note the blood spattered wall and curtains, the other team members stepped back out of the room. As she moved aside to let them pass, she looked at Jackson. "You'd better call it in."

While Jackson made the call, she dismissed the uniformed officers from the area. "Alright, guys, you can head out front. I suspect the neighbors will catch on that something's happening, if they haven't already. Firmly, but politely, discourage their curiosity. Let me know if the press shows up. We're going to be here for a while."

Jackson passed the retreating officers as he came back into the house. "The crime team will be here shortly and Doctor Evans won't be far behind."

"Thanks for the update." She said made her way to the doorway into the kitchen and stood just outside the door, taking in the scene and letting her mind process information. She was interrupted by Mitchell's excited voice from behind her.

"Hey! Look what I found!"

She turned to see him holding a pair of glasses and as she watched, he settled them on his face.

"How do they look?" he asked and grinned goofily at the rest of them.

"Dammit, Mitchell! Give me those!" Detective Jones pulled the glasses off of Mitchell's face. "Don't you know better than to touch potential evidence without wearing gloves?"

"I could ask you the same thing, Detective." Reightman stared pointedly at the item he held in his own ungloved hand.

"Shit!" he exclaimed as he followed her gaze and realized what he'd done.

"The senior crime tech is going to take you both out to the woodshed and whip your asses," Jackson commented drily.

"He certainly is," Tom Anderson agreed as he walked into the front door, followed closely by Laurie. He gave both of the culprits a disgusted glance as he reached into his overall pocked and pulled out a pair of plastic gloves. He snapped on the gloves and pulled a clear evidence bag from his kit. "Put them back exactly where they were found," Tom instructed harshly.

"Where were they, Mitchell?" Jones asked.

The embarrassed officer pointed toward the plastic covered couch and offered, "Right under the front leg of the couch."

His fellow partner in crime walked to the indicated spot and put the glasses on the floor. "Here?" he asked.

"A little to the left." Mitchell directed, and then unfortunately added, "I think."

"What in the hell do you mean, *I think?*" Tom barked at him. "You'd better remember – real fast – exactly where they were before you're assigned to parking detail for the next twelve months."

A white-faced Mitchell walked over to the sofa, followed by Tom. Mitchell indicated a small adjustment was needed and Tom moved the glasses slightly to the left. "Here?" the crime tech asked sharply.

"Yes, sir."

Tom stood and handed the evidence bag to Laurie and directed, "Get a picture of these and then bag and label them."

Laurie hurried to comply as Mitchell stammered, "I'm...I'm sorry sir. I wasn't...wasn't thinking. It was getting so intense in here I just thought I'd...try to...break it up some."

"You know what, Mitchell? "Anderson asked in a deceptively soft drawl.

"What, sir?"

"Crime scenes are supposed to be intense!" Tom hollered in his face, before adding in a more restrained and reasonable tone, "Since this is your first time in your current role, I might – *might* eventually find some way it in my soft-hearted soul to overlook your little transgression. At least *you* have the excuse of being new to this." Tom looked over at the other offender and gave a disgusted shake of his head. Jones stared at his shoes, and shifted uncomfortably.

Tom broke eye contact and walked to where Reightman and Jackson were waiting. "Sorry. Tom," she offered.

"I had to chew both you and Jackson out a time or two if I remember correctly. You learned, and so will they." He jerked his head toward the two, still standing at parade rest in by the coffee table. Then he grinned at her and winked. "I was young, dumb, and full of cum once myself." When he saw her blush at his crude comment, he looked toward Jackson. "Detective Jackson, I believe you said someone has hurt themselves in the kitchen?"

"Yes, I did, Tom."

"Then point me in the right direction. I'll see if the poor bastard needs a Band-Aid."

Jackson escorted him and Laurie toward the kitchen and Tom stopped mid-stride to address the assembled group. "All of the rest of you get your asses out of this house until I tell you it's alright to bring your clumsy butts back inside."

The small party of three headed back to the kitchen and Reightman shook her head at the two other members of her team. Looking pathetic, they slowly walked to the front door, heads held in shame. A minute later, Jackson came walking toward her indicating the front door. "Ready?"

"Tom didn't mean I should leave."

"You might be right. Let me think." Jackson paused only a split second. "Okay – I'm done. When Tom said for everyone to get out of here, he didn't say 'all of the rest of you, except for Detective Melba Reightman, get your asses out of this house,' did he?" She reluctantly shook her head. "That's what I thought. Now, let's just stroll ourselves right out that door until he tells us to come back. I'm not looking to get *my* ass chewed today."

Tom was a great guy and did his job amazing well given his limited staff, budget and overall resources, but he did have his intimidation technique honed to a razor-sharp edge. "Okay," she reluctantly agreed. "Let's go." Once outside, she informed him she was going to call Chief Kelly and give him an update. "Do you think I should mention the Bobbsey Twins' itty-bitty misstep?"

"Nope," Jackson answered, one hundred percent sure of his answer.

"Why not?"

He stared off into the horizon, absently noting the curious neighbors beginning to come out of their houses and huddle together across the street. "I remember back when I was a young, fresh cop, Melba." At her questioning look, he continued, "I made more than my fair share of mistakes, and someone older and wiser blistered the skin right off of my ass." She nodded her understanding. "No one told the then present Chief, and I remembered that kindness. It made me a better detective, and I've remembered that older and wiser person kindly for his forbearance. You never know when a little gratitude will serve you well in the future."

"Who was it, Sam? The person who chewed your ass out back then?"

"Senior Homicide Detective Ernest Kelly, our current Chief of Police."

Neither of them spoke while they walked back to the car to call in their update, they simply enjoyed the thoughtful silence.

A very long hour and a half passed, and Reightman and Jackson occupied themselves in different ways. While Reightman updated the

Chief, Jackson spent time giving his own version of a tongue-lashing to Jones and Mitchell. Although he didn't ever raise his voice, Reightman knew the two chastened men wouldn't soon forget his words. As she hung up the call, she saw him nod a dismissal to Jones, and walk away with Mitchell. The two leaned back against a patrol car and Jackson leaned over and spoke with the young cop.

She could tell by the officer's face that Sam was giving him a pep-talk to follow his earlier pointed words. *"Sam is one-of-a-kind. The best mentor and partner anyone could wish for. Mitchell will realize how lucky he is one of these days – just like me."* As she watched from her seat in the car, she eventually saw the young officer smile as Jackson clapped him on the shoulder and walked away.

One of the intensely curious neighbors brought out a tray of coffee in styrofoam cups and the entire contingent of officers accepted the offering gratefully, while sidestepping the accompanying questions. A few minutes later, the coroner's van showed up, and Drs. Evans and Bridges stepped out followed by an extra, very strong looking officer.

As Evans and Bridges made their way up to the front door, Laurie exited the house. She stopped and spoke briefly to the coroner and assistant, and headed over to Jackson. Reightman eased herself out of the car and walked over to meet them.

"Tom said he's ready for you all," Laurie said by way of greeting. "And he said to remind your team the boots and gloves right inside the door have already been paid for, so everyone better damned well use them." Laurie ducked her head a little shyly. "The last words are his, not mine, Detectives."

Jackson grinned at Reightman and she hid her own smile at Tom's acerbic reminder. "We'll tell them, Laurie," Jackson assured her and the young woman turned and went back into the house, stopping to take a couple of coffees from one of the officers manning crowd control.

"Round up the posse, Jackson."

He put two fingers into the side of his mouth and gave an ear splitting whistle. Jones and Mitchell came running.

"We're cleared to go in. Tom has placed booties and gloves by the front door. Use them."

Both of the junior members of the team punctuated their understanding with an instant, "Yes, ma'am." As they donned the gear, Tom came from the kitchen and watched as they completed their contamination prevention measures as per his instructions. "Why don't we start here and I'll walk you through the house, explaining what we've found and haven't found at each stop of my little specially guided magical mystery tour?"

"Sounds good, Tom," Jackson agreed. He mimed his request to pull out his notebook, and raised his eyebrows in Tom's direction. The crime tech rolled his eyes and chuckled. "I guess I made quite an impression earlier. Yes, sir, Detective, you may remove your notebook and write down all of my educational comments while I show you the sights."

Reightman waited until Jackson retrieved his writing gear. "Looks like we're ready to play follow the leader, Tom. Lead the way."

Tom led them to a small hall off of the living room and directed them to the two small back bedrooms. "In these two rooms..." he waited until they looked at him expectantly, "we didn't find a damn thing." When he saw they weren't overly impressed with the tour thus far, he walked through their hallway huddle and directed them into the larger bedroom at the front of the house. When they had all filed inside the doorway, he continued. "In here on the other hand, we did find some vewy, vewy intewesting things. "

Jackson cracked an appreciative smile at Tom's very bad imitation of the famous Elmer, while Reightman waited patiently for the goods.

Tom preceded them through the door and walked to the end of the queen sized bed positioned on the largest of the room's walls. At the foot of the bed sat an opened bag and a briefcase. Reightman could see several stacks of cash sitting in the bag's interior.

"We have a large amount of cash in the bag. It's been disturbed as if someone, perhaps Lieberman – perhaps not – removed a couple of hundred dollars sometime in the recent past. We did manage to remove a few prints from both it and the briefcase. I won't know whether they all belong to Lieberman until I have time with them back at the lab. We'll see if they hold any helpful surprises. Wouldn't get your hopes up any, for reasons you'll soon learn."

Next, Tom led them out of the bedroom and into the living room. "In this room, there's evidence of numerous footprints in the thick, cushy, harvest gold carpeting, but they're fairly mundane in my opinion. A man the size of the late, great Doctor Lieberman can't help but leave an impression in a carpet like this. The texture, fiber makeup and thickness of the padding preclude us from establishing anything more than somebody walked across the floor quite recently. Since the house has been empty for some months, my hypothesis is the somebody in question was probably Lieberman."

He motioned them toward the coffee table near the sofa. "A glass filled with liquid of some sort was placed on the coaster near the edge of the table. The slight dampness still remaining on the coaster indicates the liquid was probably chilled, and condensation formed on the glass and ran down onto the coaster." Tom turned and indicated an end table near the recliner. "There's another coaster with similar evidence of condensation on that table."

"Is that significant, sir?" asked Mitchell hesitantly.

"That's a good question, Officer Mitchell," Tom responded encouragingly to the young man he'd blasted earlier. "In this case, the answer is, I don't think so. All it really tells us is someone was thirsty and had something to drink. While doing so, they placed the glasses on these nice coasters and the glasses sweated."

"Isn't it odd there were two glasses, presumably sweating at the same time?" Reightman asked.

Tom considered her question seriously for a moment. "I don't know, Detective. Without further supporting evidence indicating there's a reason for the separate glasses beyond Lieberman's having two different things to drink during the same evening, I don't know what to say, other than I've got some sweat marked coasters." Tom walked to the sofa and pointed down at a spot near its left front leg. "Here we have the little item which provided such amusement and hilarity earlier today – the pair of dark plastic framed glasses which apparently looked so fetching on Officer Mitchell, and were so inviting Detective Jones felt the need to take them away from him."

Reightman noted that to their credit, neither of the two gentleman mentioned flinched or reacted in any way other than to give serious, professional nods.

"That's it for this part of the tour," Tom advised. "Let's head on over to the main attraction."

When they reached the kitchen and small attached eating area, Reightman noticed the two doctors from the coroner's office were standing slightly to one side, as was the beefy officer who'd arrived with them. Laurie was waiting across the room.

"I'm going to let Laurie walk you through this room, lady and gents. She needs the experience and I'm getting the distinct impression you didn't find my portion of the show all that interesting."

Laurie gave them a small nervous smile, which reminded Reightman that she was fairly new to the job. It was good of Anderson to put her into the line of fire, since it was the only real way to grow her experience and confidence.

Tom nodded and Laurie stepped forward. "As you can see in this room, there are a lot of things to see…" she started, faltering briefly when she realized how inane she sounded. She cleared her throat and continued, "As you can see from the blood spatter on the far wall, the victim was apparently shot with a weapon held close to his head. In fact, the evidence shows the weapon in question was held to his head, on the left side, and fired, causing the blood….and other matter, to project from his right side. The weapon in question is on the floor beneath his left hand, with attached silencer." Laurie stopped and looked to Tom, who gave her a nod of approval.

He stepped forward. "At this time, I think we'll let the coroner's team remove Dr. Lieberman's body for transport. I didn't want the exhibit to be disturbed until all of the paying customers had the chance to view it."

Reightman had never known Tom to be so showman like, and as the others present in the room shuffled a bit in response to his callousness, she tried to analyze the reason behind his demeanor. Perhaps this was getting to him more than anyone knew. Lieberman had been disliked by almost everyone, but still, he'd been a colleague of sorts.

At Dr. Evans' indication, the large officer left the room and returned a few minutes later wheeling in the gurney with an extra-large body bag on its top surface. Most of the room turned away as the three members of the coroner's team managed to get Lieberman's body onto the gurney and zipped into the bag. The officer began to wheel the gurney out, assisted by Bridges who helped steer the heavy load.

Catching Reightman's inquiring glance, Dr. Evans stopped and answered the unspoken question. "By the end of the day." Reightman acknowledged the indicated timetable and Evans followed her team out to the waiting van.

After the somewhat unwieldy exit of Lieberman and the coroners, Tom indicated Laurie should resume where she had left off.

"On this table, there is a mid-sized bottle of vodka which is almost empty, as well as a glass, which is empty." She directed their attention to the right. "In the kitchen area is another glass which has been washed and placed in the draining rack. We will, of course, be taking it to the lab for testing. There is also a bottle of cranberry juice, which we'll test, and a small bottle containing a variety of prescription sedatives."

Tom interjected at that point. "Dr. Evans is aware of the implications of those, Reightman, and will be testing them for a match to the sedatives found in Guzman"

"Thanks. You anticipated my question."

"Great minds think alike," Tom replied, and then inclined his head to Laurie.

She picked up where she'd left off. "To continue, there's a small vial of some sort containing what looks like a …a piece of… flesh, floating in some sort of liquid we assume is meant to act as a preservative." Laurie visibly faltered at the same moment Reightman and Jackson made sudden eye contact. Jackson looked hurriedly away and Reightman closed her eyes briefly, remembering the shock and disgust she had felt at Evans' detailed description of what had been done to Geri Guzman.

Tom answered before she could ask. "The Coroner is also aware of the need to test the specimen for a match with Guzman."

"The final items in question are the laptop computer on the table and the items found on the screen when the laptop was opened fully. When we arrived, the screen had been partially lowered," Laurie explained as she beckoned them forward. "As you can see from the position of the laptop on the table in relationship to the positioning of the chair, marked in tape on the floor, the laptop was in reach of the victim, although not an optimal distance for ease of typing." When all had nodded their understanding, Laurie added, "We assume when the victim was ready for….ready to take the presumed suicidal action, he pushed himself slightly back from the table."

"You said presumed action?"

"Yes, Detective Jackson, although I only used those words because Tom said I should, until we're certain. In my opinion, it looks like Dr. Lieberman just blew his own head off, but until the Coroner substantiates it, it's just conjecture."

Reightman spared a glance toward Anderson to see his reaction to Laurie's little speech. She wasn't surprised to see him covering his mouth to hide his own grin at her textbook response and very non-textbook extras.

"May we see the words he typed?" Jones asked. Tom affirmed that they could indeed, and one at a time they stepped forward to read what someone, presumably Lieberman, had left for them.

Reightman noticed Mitchell took his time, this being the first chance he'd ever had to participate in a case of any magnitude, much less this magnitude. The rest of the team quickly read the letter and moved on. Jackson scanned it pretty rapidly after first checking to make sure his still pressed pants weren't in any danger of collecting blood or gray matter. He knew Tom would provide them all copies later, when he had the laptop back in his lair. Jones read it equally fast, only to turn back to read it again. When it was her turn to step forward, she approached the laptop and bracing herself with her hands on her knees, she leaned forward. The text on the screen was fairly straightforward.

I, DR BeNjamIn LIEberman am tHE 1 who KILLED GUZMAN I LUVed hIM BUTt He DDn't rETUrN MY LOve EvEN ThO hE Gave mE HINTs THaT He DID i KILEd hiM AT ThAT sinful sPA ANd THeN TrYED 2 CoNFUsSE mMY tRAIL. I AM SorRY… I aM rEAdy 4 mY deATh

At the bottom of the short note were two lower case letters, bj.

Reightman frowned at the out-of-place letters beneath the main body of the confession and turned to Anderson. "Tom, what do you make of the small letters near the bottom?"

"I'm not sure. They may not mean a thing – just last minute finger fumbles as he contemplated what he'd done, and was about to do. The overall structure of the confession indicates he was in some mental and emotional distress. The blend of upper and lower case letters and the absence of most punctuation support that hypothesis. Another thing to consider is the placement of the letters on the keyboard." He stepped forward to illustrate his point. "Look where the letters H, B, and J appear on the keyboard. The last letter typed in the main body of the note is the letter H. The letters J and M are next to and directly below the letter H respectively." He paused to check her understanding of the explanation he'd provided before he continued. "If Evans confirms quantities of alcohol and drug in his system, we can also assume those substances affected his cognitive ability and manual dexterity, adding an additional explanation for the jumbled typing and poor spelling."

When no one in the room offered additional comment, Tom wrapped things up. "We still have work, Detectives, so I'd recommend you all return to the mothership. Laurie and I understand the urgency of this, and will do our best to have preliminary findings, to be confirmed and verified against the Coroner's findings, by tomorrow mid-day." Laurie groaned at the proposed timetable, but cut off her noise when she caught the look her superior was directing her way.

Reightman stifled her own smile, knowing she and the boys were likely to be burning some late night oil as well, once they received the reports from Tom and the ruling from Evans.

"We'll get out of your hair, Tom." Jackson spoke for all of them and they started to leave the room.

"Hey, Laurie?"

"Yes, Detective Reightman?"

"Tell your boss I said you did a good job walking us through the findings. I know he's a hard-assed, egotistical jerk, so tell him I'll be including my appreciation for your work in my own report."

Laurie flushed with pleasure at Reightman's unexpected praise and snuck a little look toward her boss. His grin confirmed that he agreed with the Detective wholeheartedly, and was proud she'd noticed and publicly commented.

"Thank you, ma'am," Laurie responded before she turned back to start finishing up the remaining onsite work.

Tom Anderson shot a wink Reightman's way as she and her three musketeers – or stooges – depending on your viewpoint, headed out of the room to take off their booties and gloves, and beam back to the mothership.

CHAPTER TWELVE

TOBY FORCED HIMSELF out of bed early Thursday morning and struggled through his normal morning routine. The coroner and the police were releasing Geri's body a little after 10 AM and he needed to be at the city morgue to sign the release forms. The body would then be transferred to the local funeral company for burial on Saturday.

He forced himself to shower, shave and dress while working his way through a couple of pots of coffee. "*I hope the caffeine kicks in soon.*" He poured the last of the second pot into his mug, feeling tired and sluggish as he looked out the French doors of his apartment.

From where he stood, Toby could only see blue sky and small pieces of the rooftops across the street. There weren't any clouds to mar the perfect, flat blue expanse arching above the roof tops. If he concentrated, he could identify the collection of buildings which combined old with new, and made up the downtown business and entertainment district. After contemplating the sky and the rooftops for a few minutes more, Toby drained his mug, and put it in the sink.

He gathered up his belongings and the paperwork he'd need, put his phone in his back pocket and picked up his keys. Taking one last glance out of the French doors, he left his apartment. As his foot hit the bottom step, he noticed the crowd gathered in front of the spa. He couldn't tell what they were doing, but saw they were all looking toward the big front windows. As he crossed the street, he noticed a few onlookers breaking off from the crowd and walking hurriedly away. He recognized Moon and Bernice standing at the back of the group and he adjusted his path to come up behind them. As he neared the building, he thought he saw bright pink...spray paint? *"Oh shit! It is spray paint,"* he realized as he pushed his way through the gawkers.

Moon reached out to touch his arm lightly as he brushed past her. "I'm so very terribly sorry this horrible thing has happened, Toby."

A few people in the crowd noticed him and moved out of the way so he could have access to his business. When he reached the front, he stopped and took in the artwork now decorating the entrance of the Time Out Spa. The hateful words sprayed across the façade and the crude, childish renderings of penises were shocking to many of those present. Yet for some reason, instead of flying to pieces, Toby found himself analyzing the method behind the vandalism.

"Whoever did this was slightly above average height." He looked up at the highest point of the first letter, and decided whoever had done this, they probably hadn't used a ladder. The job would have been too hurried, and even in the middle of the night there were often people returning home from a late night at work, or from the last call at a neighborhood bar.

The lettering started about six feet from the ground, and began at a point just to the left of the entrance door. The sprayed block letters continued across the old brick of the building, occasionally bleeding onto the metal frames and the glass of the door and front windows. Where the paint had hit glass, it ran, before drying to a shiny, glossy finish. The lettering angled downward in a slight arc, with the final word just about three feet from the ground. *"The painter was probably right handed,"* Toby reasoned. *"Based on the curve of the lettering, he must have started spraying the paint while reaching slightly above his head, and then lowered the arm as he walked to the right."*

There was less to learn from the sidewalk ornamentation. There, the painter had satisfied his artistic urge by simply spraying brightly colored, hugely exaggerated cocks and balls doing a happy little tango down the concrete. There were a couple of smudges in the paint. *"He probably stepped in it as he was leaving."* Toby continued his inspection, noticing all the little penises were facing the same direction. *"If he had added smiling faces,"* some detached and amused part of his mind observed, *"they'd look just like those animated hot dogs advertising concessions at the movie theater."*

Behind him, he heard Bernice's voice. "Toby, I've called the police. They're on their way." He turned to thank her and saw her bending slightly to help Madame Zhou step up onto the uneven curb.

"Toby, are you all right?" Zhou Li asked as she took small steps toward him.

"I'm fine, Madame Zhou." As he answered, he realized he really was doing pretty well – all things considered. "I'm mad as hell, but this is nothing compared to the last several days."

Madame Zhou peered up at him through her lenses, and then moved closer to the building so she could better view the damage. She tilted her head sideways as she read the lettering, and then stepped back to look down curiously at the renderings on the sidewalk. "Our budding artist is not very original," she remarked. "He has a warped sense of perspective. These are all rather disproportionate." She waived her hand to indicate all of the large, misshapen body parts and looked up at Toby with a grim smile which displayed her tiny white teeth. "His parents should have provided him art lessons at an early age. Although if they had, he may have found better things to do with his time than to deface private property."

Her use of the word *property* set off a trigger in Toby's mind. "I need to call the property management company and report this."

Madame Zhou pursed her lips for a minute and turned toward him. "I will be pleased to make the call for you, Toby. The police should be here soon, and you'll have your hands full with them. It seems to take longer to complete their forms and reports than it does to commit an actual crime."

"Police are here," Bernice interrupted and grunted toward the marked squad car. "I've got to get back across the street. The lunch bunch will be showing up before I know it and I've a truckload of turnips to peel between now and then." She cuffed him on the shoulder lightly. "Keep your shoulders up, Toby. Don't let the rat bastard's artistic expression get you down."

The next hour passed quickly. As one of the uniformed officers completed his four-part form, Madame Zhou commented, "I'd anticipated Detective Reightman's presence, given her ongoing investigation."

The officer looked briefly at his partner before replying, "She's been informed of the incident, ma'am. I was unable to contact her directly, but I've left a message. I think she and Detective Jackson are out on another call."

"Thank you, Officer. That explains it." Zhou Li snatched the completed copy of the form directly from the officer the minute he tore it off from the original. "I'll take that!" Responding to his surprised look, she added, "I am Mr. Bailey's attorney and will be handling things with the property management company and the insurance people."

The officer looked from her to the business owner, and quickly decided whose side he'd take. "Yes, ma'am." He signaled his partner and they went back to the patrol car.

"Madame Zhou, I appreciate your help, but I can't let you handle all of that."

"You will let me handle this. If I am not mistaken, you have other, more pressing matters to take care of today. I am quite capable of handling the property management company. I have a small amount of influence with them, so you don't need to worry about a thing. Now, why don't you call SarahJune, and ask her to round up the rest of the staff and start the clean-up? If she should have questions or require instruction on the best way to remove paint, she need only ask. I will be just across the street." Before Toby could think of any reply, much less a suitable one, Zhou Li turned her back and solicited Moon's help to step down from the curb.

Three hours later, he was up on a step stool scraping the last of the pink paint from the windows, and thinking about his earlier trip to the morgue. The transfer of Geri's remains had been seamless and he'd watched as the funeral company staff respectfully loaded the bag-covered body into the waiting hearse. When the doors closed on the transport and it drove away, he followed its progress until the dark vehicle made a right hand turn and vanished from view, providing him only one brief, last glimpse of sun gleaming off the chrome. He raised a hand in farewell. "You'll be home soon, Geri."

Bright sparkles reflecting off of small water droplets caught on the window brought him back to the present, where he stood on the stool with a paint scraper in his hand. Toby looked into the window's reflecting glass and caught sight of SarahJune and a couple of the spa gang finishing up their work on the sidewalk. All that remained of the dancing dicks was a mottled swirl of soft color which reminded him of a child's chalk drawing partially washed away by rain. "I think we've done all we can here, boss," SarahJune advised him as she stood up from her handiwork.

"It looks much better." Toby stepped back to the curb in order to view the entire façade of the spa.

The windows were clean and the sidewalk was colorful, but better than it had been. The brickwork still needed work, but there were only a couple of legible letters left, along with a pieces and parts of others. "At least you can't make out what it said this morning," he commented, bending down to help SarahJune gather the wash bucket and empty spray cans and catching a whiff of the orange scented detergent they'd used. "And it smells good"

"Bet that's the first time you've ever said a downtown sidewalk smells good!"

They all laughed, a little, and headed inside to wash up.

Grams called a few hours later to tell him the local funeral home had received the body and was preparing it for the burial on Saturday. "I told them it would be closed coffin," she said. "I want to remember Geri as I last saw him, not as he must look now. I hope that was okay, Toby."

"You did exactly right, Grams," he assured her as he began to turn off the lights in the spa. "I should be there a little after noon tomorrow."

"I'll be waiting for you. You be safe on the drive down here."

"Yes, ma'am, I will. Love you."

He hung up the call and put the phone back into his packet. *I haven't left my phone anywhere this week,* he reflected as he locked up his office. *"Maybe I'm cured of that bad habit."*

As he exited the front door he was met by Detective Jackson. Toby could see Detective Reightman talking on her phone by the side of the car. "Mr. Bailey," Jackson greeted him. "We heard about the incident and thought we should stop by to check on things."

"Thanks, Detective Jackson. I think we've done about all we can to put things to rights. There's still some work to be done on the brick, but the cleaning crew will take a stab while they're working on the rest of the place."

"Any idea of who might have done this?" Jackson asked.

"No, I don't have a clue who he might have been."

"He? Why do you think it was a man, Mr. Bailey?"

Toby thought over all of the observations he'd made to himself that morning before he answered. "Because of the height of the paint. I figure whoever did this was a little over the average height of a full grown man. There are a few women who might be that tall I guess, but not many."

Jackson smiled in response to the explanation. "That's a sound observation, Mr. Bailey. Anything else you noticed?"

"Well, I think he – the person who did this – was right handed."

Sam was curious now. "Why did you come to that conclusion?"

"Well, Detective Jackson, I noticed the way the writing kind of sloped down like – here let me show you." Toby walked to the door and demonstrated: "See, if I was holding the paint can in my right hand and started here," Toby indicted the remnants of the first letter remaining on the brick, "and then walked to the right while spraying the paint, my arm naturally lowers." Jackson watched carefully as Toby demonstrated how he envisioned the painting was done. "But," the young man walked back to his originally position from the door, "if I was holding the can in my left hand and walked to the right while painting, my hand holding the paint wants to lift slightly because of the angle that I would have to use to write the letters."

"That's an interesting observation, Mr. Bailey."

Toby hesitated before asking, "Do you think I've got it wrong, Detective?"

Jackson gave him a measured look before offering a smile. "No. In fact, I think you're exactly right, and that's what makes it interesting. Most people would have never thought it out the way you did." Jackson continued his appraisal of the earnest young man. "Did you pick up on anything else? Anything from the sidewalk?"

Toby answered more quickly this time, having more confidence in his deductions after Jackson's comment. "Other than illustrating – sorry for the bad pun – the sidewalk artist's exaggerated importance of the male anatomy, everything about the pictures on the sidewalk makes me suspect the person was a man. First of all, few women would draw a di…a penis that big, and the…members were all facing the same way, pointing to the right. A left handed person would've made them face the opposite way." Toby thought of something else, but then decided he'd already shared more with the Detective than the man was likely to find entertaining,

Picking up on Toby's thought pattern, Jackson asked, "What just went through your mind, Mr. Bailey?"

"I may be wrong, but I don't think the painter was gay." Jackson raised his eyebrows and Toby added, "Now that I think about it, it sounds stupid. But, I think a gay man would've used a little more judgement in where he placed the penises."

Jackson burst out laughing. "Mr. Bailey, I think every man– regardless of his sexual orientation – could occasionally use a little more *judgement* about where he places his penis." As Toby grinned, Jackson added, "But I take it that you're speaking of the artistic placement in this case." When Toby nodded, he asked, "Isn't that a tad stereotypical?"

Toby thought over the Detective's unexpected question. "Maybe, but gay men are all kind of picky about where things are placed."

When Jackson chuckled again, Toby felt his ears getting hot.

"What are the two of you finding so funny?" Reightman asked as she joined them on the sidewalk.

"Detective Jackson and I were just exchanging our views on artistic placement, Detective Reightman."

Toby caught Jackson's eye and had to quickly cover his grin. Reightman looked from one of them to the other, and then shrugged. "If you don't want to share the joke, that's fine. It was probably about something I'd find too hard to handle anyway." Toby thought he heard Jackson stifle a laugh before Reightman added, more seriously, "We stopped by as soon as we could, Toby. I had a message this morning alerting me to the situation, but Detective Jackson and I were both handling something else."

Toby keyed into something in her tone. "It's related to Geri's murder isn't it?"

"Yes, Mr. Bailey, it is related." Jackson answered for them both. "This morning Dr. Lieberman was found dead, by apparent suicide."

When neither of the detectives offered more information, Toby asked, "Is there anything more you can tell me?"

"No, there isn't. There are a lot of things we're trying to confirm at this point in the investigation, and we can't share anything else."

"Of course you can't." Toby eventually replied. "Thank you for coming to tell me."

"To tell you the truth, we probably shouldn't have told you that much, but Detective Reightman and I both thought you had the right to hear it from us before it made the news. I don't know when or if we'll be able to share more, but this is something."

Toby looked at the façade of the building, and the reflections cast by the dark windows. He took in the remains of the paint on the brick – paint which had cruelly announced this was where queers died. He contemplated the colored sidewalk, and recalled the words and images he'd seen there this morning. With a flare of blue, he raised his eyes and met each of theirs in turn.

Reightman was struck by the notion his face seemed to have been carved from the light of the afternoon sun, and his pale, unreadable eyes glowed in contrast to the deep shadows cast onto the pavement by the buildings on Capital Street.

"Yes," Toby Bailey said to Detectives Reightman and Jackson. "It's something." He turned without another word, and Sam and Melba watched him as he crossed the street, and vanished up the stairwell hidden, from their sight.

"Mr. Toby Bailey is an interesting young man," Sam observed on their way back to the office.

"That's an unusual thing for you to say." Melba struggled to adjust her seatbelt, wiggling to find a comfortable position which would afford her a better view of her partner, and provide at least the minimum level of safety that was required when riding anywhere when Sam drove.

After a couple of minutes had passed without a response, Melba considered reaching across and slapping him. "Jackson, would you mind sharing what you mean by that comment?"" When Sam didn't answer, she estimated her reach. "Before I slap you."

"I think he's changed a lot since the murder. He's waking up, or something, and starting to really see the things around him."

Melba remembered the look which had kindled in Toby's eyes earlier. "You may be right, Sam. I've noticed he's been different, but haven't been able to put my finger on exactly how he's changed. If he's waking up, as you put it, it's a good thing, right?"

Sam turned into the precinct's parking lot and pulled into the marked space. He pulled his keys from the ignition and turned to her. "I don't know. I guess it depends on what he sees when he wakes up, and what he decides to do about it."

They headed down to talk with Tom and Laurie. Tom was just closing the computer found positioned in front of Lieberman that morning, and looked up when Reightman knocked on the dividing partition of his work area. "I thought I would be seeing the two of you about now."

"Find anything interesting, Tom?"

"Not much beyond what I expected. The computer seems pretty mundane in terms of any additional evidence. All of the prints on it are Lieberman's, and there doesn't appear to have been any tampering with the system."

"Any unusual files or saved images?" Jackson asked, as he pulled out his notebook.

Tom smiled as he took in the sight of Jackson leaning against the partition with his pen poised over a fresh empty page. "Not really, Detective Jackson. It's the usual stuff you'd expect, along with some pretty explicit man-on-man porn featuring middle-aged men and nubile younger hunks. Mostly, it featured a lot of role playing and light bondage, and one or two scenes where the young handy man or college student 'accidently' lost his clothes. Pretty tame stuff by today's pornography standards." Tom paused for a moment, looking down at his notes. "The only thing of possible interest is a spreadsheet detailing a number of financial transactions, both credits and debits. It doesn't have much in the way of identifying markers, just numeric entries."

"Have you managed to get your hands on his bank records? We might be able to cross reference the entries with the deposits and withdrawals in them with the spreadsheet." Reightman suggested.

"They've been requested. I think we should have them in our possession by midday tomorrow."

Reightman nodded. "What about the other items; the drinking glasses in the sink, and the liquor and juice bottles?"

"We've finished with them as well, Detective. Nothing much there either. The one in the sink had been washed so there is nothing there. The bottle of vodka had Lieberman's prints, as did the glass on the table." Tom paused a minute thinking through something and then added, "The prints on the glass were pretty smudged, almost like something had been placed on top of them – like they'd been blotted."

The two Detectives let that run through their minds for a moment or two and then Reightman had a thought. "Could it have been–"

"Hey, Detectives," interrupted Laurie as she came around the corner and stepped into the space. "I think I've found not just one, but two things you need to be aware of."

Reightman tried to recapture her thought, but finally gave up. "We're all ears, Laurie. What've you found?"

"Well you know those eye glasses Mitchell found?"

"We do indeed, Laurie," Jackson answered while all three of them remembered the hijinks from the morning. "Did you pick up a print?"

Laurie shook her curly head. "No. Well, there were prints, but they all belonged to the two goobers caught horsing around while not wearing gloves. The thing about the eyeglasses is, they're not prescription. The lenses are just glass set into the frames."

"They're not real eyeglasses?" Tom asked as he stood from his chair.

"Nope. They're what are referred to as a fashion accessory."

"Why would anyone wear something like that?" Reightman asked. "And why were they at the scene?"

"People wear them to look smarter or more corporate, or just to go with an outfit, I think. I don't know why they were at the scene. In fact, based on where Mitchell found them, they could've been there for some time – maybe since Doctor Lieberman's mother still lived in the house. Maybe someone just dropped them while visiting."

"Was there dust on them, Laurie?" Jackson asked, looking up from the notes he was taking.

Laurie considered his question. "No, Detective, they didn't appear to be dusty. They are a little scrapped up like they have been worn a lot, but no dust. Why's that important?"

It was Tom who answered. "Laurie, the Detective asked because if they've been sitting in the house for several months, they should have some dust on them, even if they were under the sofa all this time."

Laurie nodded as she considered Tom's explanation, storing it as a good piece of ad-hoc training. "But nothing in the house was dusty."

"Maybe Lieberman cleaned," Reightman suggested. "We did find that rag in the kitchen."

"That's the other thing, ma'am. The rag's actually a t-shirt and it's a really large one, but what's really unusual is that it was also knotted up, and…." The young crime tech paused dramatically to make sure she had their attention. "The rag was covered in saliva."

"Like someone spit on it?"

"No, ma'am, unless someone spit and then just kept spitting. It's like it's been in someone's mouth."

"Is the saliva Lieberman's?" Jackson was writing frantically.

"I don't know, sir. I have taken it down for Doctor Bridges to determine if it's a match. We'll see what she has to tell us."

"Thank you, Laurie. Let us know what she determines." Jackson turned a page in his notebook and continued writing.

"Tom, why would there be so much saliva on the cloth?"

"Who knows, Detective Reightman?" Tom answered. "It may have had some connection to Lieberman's little movies. There were a couple of scenes where one man put a handkerchief or cloth into another's mouth while he then proceeded to 'ravish' him. Maybe Lieberman was imagining himself in a starring role."

"Thanks for the visual." Reightman tried to erase the image of Lieberman being ravished and focused on his explanation. "I guess it's possible." She thought through other scenarios which would explain the wet cloth and offered the only one that made sense. "What if someone came into the house, or was let in by Lieberman? What if they engaged in a little roleplay? "

Jackson looked up from his notes. "Tom, you indicated money was missing from the briefcase in the master bedroom."

"That's right, it did appear some amount was missing," Tom confirmed, "although there's no way to determine how much was actually in it to start.

"Maybe he hired a hustler," Reightman suggested as she tied the missing money to her theory of why the rag was wet.

"That sounds almost plausible, Reightman," her partner said, jotting down the thought. "And if I accept that, the next question is, could their roleplay have gotten out of hand?"

"Are you suggesting Lieberman died while engaging in some fun with a hustler, Detective?"

"I'm not suggesting anything yet. But, now that you mention it, is it so far-fetched?"

Tom leaned back in his chair and looked up at the ceiling while he thought about Jackson's question. "I can buy the idea he hired someone to tickle his fancy, and maybe I can accept the idea of things getting out of hand. But, I don't see how an average, garden variety hustler managed to cover up an accidental death and make it look very convincingly like suicide."

"Stranger things have happened, but I guess I'd have to agree with you right now, Tom," Then she had another thought. "Lieberman's private entertainment might explain the glasses. Maybe they belong to the person he hired."

"Detective Reightman, as tempting as you make it sound, we've been over the entire scene very thoroughly. There's no evidence suggesting anyone was in the house when Lieberman died."

"Then how do you explain the glasses?"

He shrugged. "There may not be anything to explain. They could have been there for a long time."

They were back at square one. For some reason, the lack of dust on the glasses continued to bother her. "Jackson, can you have the Wonder Twins canvas the neighborhood and see if anyone saw somebody new in the area that evening? I want to make sure we've covered all the bases on this."

Jackson looked up from his notes. "I think it's a longshot, but I'll have them ask around."

After Jackson had moved away from the cubicle to carry out her instruction, Reightman moved to the next item on her mental list. "Anything related to the gun?"

"I've confirmed the bullet came from the gun found at the scene, Reightman, and prints on the gun match Lieberman's."

"So, it appears he pulled the trigger himself, then." Her theory about an unknown person being present when the doctor died seemed even more remote, but there were still a couple of unanswered questions in her mind. "Tom, did you draw anymore conclusions from the suicide note?"

"Not really, Detective. It appears to be pretty cut and dried."

"How about the extra letters?"

"You're referring to the lowercase 'b' and 'j?'" he asked before shaking his head. "I really think it was a finger-fumble."

"It could be a clue Lieberman left about the identity of a killer."

Tom turned and picked up his printed copy of the note from his desk. "It could be, I guess. It could also be a two letter description of his best gift of the evening, which he received from the mysterious hit-man hustler." When she raised an eyebrow in his direction, he toned down his sarcasm. "It's possible, but I think it's just a case of his fingers hitting the keys inadvertently. By all accounts, he was pretty out of it."

Jackson returned from making his call and after listening to the last part of Tom's commentary, added, "Sometimes the simplest possible explanation is the right one. You know that as well as any of us."

Reightman sighed heavily and rolled her shoulders to loosen the tension. "You're right, Jackson. I guess I'm not ready to buy Lieberman just upped and offed himself, and I'm sure not ready to accept it as the whole explanation."

"I think it may be the whole explanation," Jackson told her firmly. "Lieberman knew we were going to find him sooner or later, and he didn't have many options. He probably arranged a little evening entertainment for himself and once that was done, he decided he might as well go out with a –"

"Don't even finish the thought, Jackson," Reightman said with a grimace. "I get your point. I think we're done here, so we should head downstairs and see what the coroner has to tell us."

Dr. Bridges was just coming through the doors from the examination room when Reightman and Jackson walked through the door to the morgue suite. "Detectives, you have perfect timing. Dr. Evans is ready for you. Do you remember the way back to her office?"

"We know the way," Jackson answered before he and Reightman walked through the door that Bridges held open for them.

Evans' door was open as they arrived and catching sight of them she waved them in. "Come on in. Let me just finish up with my last few notes." Reightman and Jackson each took one of the chairs in front of the desk and waited for her to finish. "I've just finished up with Lieberman," she began, looking up from the notes in front of her. "Let me summarize what I have found, and you can ask about anything that comes to mind as we go along."

Reightman and Jackson signaled their agreement with her approach and waited for Dr. Evans to begin.

"Let me start with the basics. Doctor Lieberman – although grossly overweight – was in fairly good physical condition otherwise, although there was a slight enlargement to his liver. That indicates he probably consumed a lot of alcohol on a regular basis and would've eventually suffered from health issues as a result. There were no indications his other organs were anything but healthy." She looked up to check that they were following, and then continued. "My examination did find Lieberman had ejaculated a few hours before his death, although there are no other indications of sexual activity."

Reightman was curious as to how the doctor had come to her conclusion, but decided it wasn't germane. She didn't really want to know, anyway.

"Lieberman did have a large quantity of alcohol in his system at the time of death," Evans noted, "and significant levels of sedative as well. That wasn't unexpected, but there was one item of interest."

"What was that, Doctor?" Reightman asked.

"Although there was a lot of alcohol in his system, not all had made its way into his bloodstream. It appears he finished a significant amount only twenty to thirty minutes before his death, and it had not fully metabolized into his bloodstream."

Jackson looked up from his notetaking. "Why is that of interest, Doctor Evans?"

"Because, given his size, the alcohol in his system was not enough, in my opinion, to account for his presumed lack of motor skills which could explain the state of typing present in the suicide note."

"You mean, he wasn't drunk enough to be that inept or clumsy?" Reightman suggested.

"That's exactly what I mean. There may have been other contributing factors; among them poor typing skills, or perhaps despondency or maybe even fear. Of course, the sedatives he ingested would have contributed as well."

Reightman could hear Jackson's pen scratching on paper as she tried to form her next question. "Could he have been afraid of something or someone, Doctor?"

"Perhaps, Detective. I suppose he could have felt fear, regret, apprehension about the means and the process of taking his own life, depressed, or even excitement as he realized the end was near. The options are limited only by his unique and unknowable mental and emotional boundaries. Does that answer your question?"

"Yes, it does."

"There's not much more to add. Death did occur from the shot to the head. The entry and exit paths, and the way in which the matter left the side of the head, suggest the gun was placed to his left temple and fired once. The angle of entry suggests Lieberman pulled the trigger himself."

Reightman set in silence reviewing all she'd learned from Tom and Evans. "Was there anything at all about Lieberman's death you feel is out of the ordinary?"

The doctor hesitated before answering. "The only thing which caught my attention was a small mark on his right wrist. It appeared to have been caused by a binding of some sort. I dismissed it when there were no similar markings on the other wrist. It may have been caused by a too tight sleeve cuff or something of that nature."

"Could it have been caused by a restraint, Doctor Evans? A restraint used in some sort of bondage roleplay?" She saw Jackson give a slight roll of his eyes.

To her credit, Evans didn't dismiss the idea. "It could have been caused by any number of things, Detective Reightman. As I said, it did cause me to re-examine the marking and to check elsewhere."

"What was in the vial of liquid found at the scene, Doctor?" Jackson asked. "Tom Anderson indicated that he was going to turn it over to you."

"He did," Evans confirmed. "The vial contained a preservative solution and held Geraldo Guzman's severed foreskin. Unfortunately, it confirms what I'd suspected about Doctor Lieberman. I'm only sorry it wasn't retrieved sooner so it could've been included with the body when I released it earlier today. Please let Mr. Bailey know it's now in our possession, although I won't be able to release it until we've finished up with the case."

"I understand Dr. Bridges was given a cloth from the scene to test for a saliva match to Lieberman." Reightman replied after a moment. "When will she be done determining if the saliva is a match?"

"She is currently concluding the work on Lieberman. I think she'll be able to finish tomorrow. I'll make sure she notifies you of the result."

"Thank you Dr. Evans. I suppose my last question is, when you will be ready to rule on the cause of death."

"I'm going to have one more conversation with Tom Anderson, and I'll make sure Dr. Bridges doesn't have anything to add to the findings. However, as of this moment I'm intending to rule the death as self-inflicted, by gunshot wound to the head. In other words – suicide."

Reightman leaned back in her chair, thinking of her earlier theory. Evans sounded sure of herself, and so had Tom Anderson. Still, there were unanswered question and she wasn't willing to let things rest yet. "I understand why you've reached your decision, Doctor, although as Jackson knows, I'm not yet satisfied it's all as straight-forward as it seems. I intend to investigate further."

"That is, of course, your prerogative and has to be decided between you and Chief Kelly. If additional evidence does turn up and warrants further consideration, I'll be happy to amend the ruling." After a moment more, Evans stood from her chair behind the desk. "If that's all, Detectives, it's been a very long day and I hope to get out of here as soon as possible."

They thanked her, and went back to their desks. They worked on updating the files of both Guzman and Lieberman, making additions based upon the last day. After about an hour, Reightman's desk phone buzzed and after glancing at the caller ID, she answered.

"Hello, Chief."

"I'm glad you're still here in the building. Is Jackson with you?"

"Yes, Chief, we're both still here."

"I'd like you both come on over so we can talk about the Guzman case, and Lieberman's death as well."

"We'll both be there in a just minute, sir." Reightman hung up the phone and looked over to her partner. "The Chief wants to see us in his office, Jackson." He was entering notes into an electronic file, while swearing softly under his breath. He remained focused on his task so she nudged, "We'd better head on over there. You know how he gets if he's kept waiting."

"Yes, I know," he grunted as he struggled to finish his entry. "I'm about sick of this new notation system anyway. It keeps sending me back to add something to a field, even when there is nothing appropriate to enter." He stood and pulled on his jacket.

Once seated in the Chief's office in the very familiar pleather chairs arranged in front of his desk. Reightman noticed the circles underneath Kelly's eyes and the slightly clamped way that he was holding his jaw.

"I've spoken with Dr. Evans and with Tom Anderson," he started without any greeting or preamble. "I wanted to talk with the two of you about how we finish up."

"What do you mean, Chief? I wasn't aware we're ready to close the files," Reightman said slowly, surprised by Kelley's words.

"It seems to me like we've reached the end of the line on this one. Unless you have something to add that I'm not aware of."

Reightman considered her words as she eyed the Chief's expression. "The thing is, I'm not sure we *are* at the end of this. There are still unanswered questions, and I have reservations about calling it a done deal right now."

"Perhaps you'd better explain yourself, Reightman," the Chief directed as he paced his hands on his desk.

Reightman proceeded to detail the open questions, including the glasses, the cloth, the marks on Lieberman's right wrist, the missing cash, and the two letters at the bottom of the suicide note.

When she'd finished, Kelly leaned back in his chair. "Let me see if I understand what you're telling me. You think Lieberman was killed by some hired hustler, who arrived at Lieberman's house wearing a pair of dorky, non-prescription glasses, and then proceeded to simulate a suicide so professionally he didn't leave a single trace of himself behind, and just slunk out the door with no one any the wiser."

"When you put it like that, I guess it does seem far-fetched, sir. But I do think we need to close the loop on a few things before we just accept it was suicide."

The Chief chewed the inside of his check and fiddled with a pen on his desk. "Doctor Evans sounded pretty sure of herself and Anderson didn't seem to feel there was any need to dispute her ruling. I appreciate wanting to tie everything up with a neat little bow, and can almost understand your reasoning. Hell, I can even accept the idea Lieberman hired a trick and engaged in some kinky fun. I can get behind the theft of some cash. What I can't buy into, Reightman, is the rest of the scenario. That kind of thing only happens in the movies, Detective, not in real life." The Chief watched Reightman's face, seeing doubt appear after his last comment. "Jackson, what do you think about your partner's wild ass suppositions?"

Jackson squirmed in his seat before answering, "Sir, I think Reightman's concerns have merit and should be investigated further." Before Reightman could brighten at his response, he added, "But, I agree the scenario she suggests is not probable." He turned to his partner and shrugged. "I'm sorry, Melba, but I have to agree with the Chief."

Kelly leaned back in his chair, pleased he and Jackson were in agreement. "I think there's more than enough evidence to tie Lieberman to Guzman's death. The suicide note coupled with the little vial of…skin is pretty damning. It's pretty clear Lieberman was the person responsible for Guzman's death."

"But, Chief, that's impossible!" Reightman objected. "I agree Lieberman is somehow tied to Guzman's murder, but he was a huge man and he certainly wasn't coordinated enough to exit the murder scene without leaving a trace."

"Maybe his hired hustler hitman helped," Kelly mocked and grinned at Jackson.

Reightman heard the ridicule in his voice. "Sir, regardless of your personal view of the situation, I don't think making fun of me or my reservations about the closure of these investigations is warranted." As the Chief's grin faded and his jaw clamped tight, she added in a more conciliatory tone, "Give us just a little more time before we close this case. I can't accept the idea Lieberman killed Guzman, at least not directly."

Kelly directed his gaze to Jackson. "What do you think, Jackson?"

Jackson was uncomfortable at being put on the spot again, especially since this time he agreed with his partner. "Sir, I think you should consider what she's saying."

"What I should consider is up to my judgment and discretion, Jackson, not yours!" the Chief snapped. "And you didn't answer the question."

"Yes sir, I believe I did," he replied calmly, although there was a hint of steel in his voice.

"I'm disappointed in your answer, Jackson," the Chief replied tiredly. There was also an undercurrent of some other emotion in his voice. "I'll take it under advisement and give your position some thought. You'll know my answer tomorrow."

As they left the office and headed back to their desks, Reightman nudged Jackson with her shoulder. "Thanks for backing me up, Jackson – there at the end. I'm glad you agree we need to investigate this further."

He stopped in the middle of the aisle running between desks. "I don't know if I agree with your theory, Melba. But I've learned to trust your gut. If something's bugging you I have to give you the benefit of the doubt, at least for a while longer."

Arriving back at their desks, they turned off their computers and left the building for the night.

Melba made herself some dinner and then had a cup of tea while looking through a couple of magazines. She finally turned out the lights and called it quits. She had a restless, dream-filled night. She finally climbed out of bed and stumbled to the shower. Clean and dressed, and feeling better after the hot shower, she started the coffee pot. When she turned on the television and saw a live action feed of several people standing behind microphones on the steps of City Hall, she frowned, recognizing some of the faces.

She turned up the volume in time to hear Chief Ernest Kelly announce they'd closed the murder of Gerald Guzman. The murderer, former City Coroner Benjamin Lieberman, had been found yesterday, he announced to the crowd and the cameras, dead from a self-inflicted gunshot to the head. The case was now closed. He gave credit for solving the murder to her and to her team and generously praised Anderson's staff and to the Coroner's office for their work. Then he stepped back from the microphone, and turned and accepted the congratulations of the Mayor and members of the City Council. The last person he spoke with was Councilman Sutton Dameron, who heartily shook Kelly's hand and leaned forward to whisper something near his ear.

A moment later her phone rang and she picked it up, recognizing it was Sam.

"Melba, did you see?"

"Yeah," she said in a stunned voice. "Just now, when I turned on the TV." She mentally ran through what she had just witnessed. "Kelly sold us out, Sam. He caved to pressure from somewhere or someone."

"I'm sorry."

"Me too, Sam. Sorrier than you'll ever know."

❖ ❖ ❖

An hour later, Reightman pulled into the precinct parking lot and got out of her car. Her mind was still processing the image of Chief Kelly shaking hands and exchanging polite words with the Mayor and the City Council, and most vivid in her mind, with Sutton Dameron.

She stowed her purse and headed to the breakroom for a mug of hot water and discovered the usual collection of characters waiting on the coffee pot.

"Congratulations, Reightman," one of the gang greeted as she entered the breakroom door and pulled a mug from the cabinet. "Bet you're glad that one's over," another coffee addict called from his place near the back of the line. "Yeah, and even happier Lieberman got his!" another added.

She pasted a brittle smile on her face, and responded to their comments as politely as she could before making her escape. Back at her desk, she placed a bag of tea into her mug and the picked up the phone and dialed Kelly's office.

"Good Morning, Nancy." Reightman inhaled the jasmine scent rising from the cup. "Is the Chief in?"

Nancy hesitated before answering, "No, I'm sorry, he isn't. He hasn't made it back from City Hall yet."

"He's probably still glad-handing and slapping backs," Reightman's inner cynic suggested. "Does he have any time open on the calendar today?" She gave the teabag a gentle squeeze while she waited for Nancy's response.

"No, he's gonna' be really busy today."

"Okay, if he gets a free minute can you–"

Nancy cut her off. "Look, Melba I probably shouldn't say anything, but he asked me not to put any of your calls through, and said he for me not to find you a spot on his calendar today, even if he *had* an opening." Nancy made it clear that there was no way Reightman was going to get in to see Kelly any time soon.

"So, that's the way it's going to be," Reightman's inner voice acknowledged. The outer voice took longer to respond. "I understand. Thanks anyway." Reightman hung up the phone.

She sat with her elbows on the desk as she sipped the tea. *"I wonder where Sam is this morning?"* She turned on her computer and waited for it to boot. She was working through her new email when the phone buzzed.

Without looking at the display she absently picked up the receiver. "Reightman," she answered.

"Good morning Detective." She recognized Doris's voice as the clerk continued, "I'm calling to let you know I have some things over here for Mr. Bailey, from the Guzman case. Since you picked them up for him last time, I was wondering if you wanted to do the same with this batch of stuff?"

"I thought I'd already picked up and returned everything."

"Well, there are another couple of things here," Doris replied as she rustled something near the phone. "Looks like an earring and a necklace of some sort. Word came down from on high this morning that these items are cleared for return."

"Sure, Doris. I'll be down shortly to pick them up."

"Don't forget to take a release form with you, Detective," Doris reminded her before hanging up.

"Now isn't that interesting? Kelly must be anxious to sweep out everything related to this as quickly as possible." Reightman finished the last swallow of tea and then picked up her cell phone and dialed Toby. "Good morning, Toby, this is Detective Reightman."

"I wondered when you'd get around to calling. You must have been busy cleaning all the files off of your desk." Reightman could hear the anger in his voice, hidden underneath the harsh sarcasm.

"You must have seen the news this morning."

"Yes, I did, and it was quite a surprise. I thought you would've had the decency to call me first and give me some kind of warning. That's what you told me you were going to do."

"I didn't intend for it to happen that way, Toby. It was as big of a surprise to me as was to you. I'm sorry you heard about it the way you did."

She heard him blowing out a breath of air before he spoke again. "What do you need, Detective? I have a busy morning ahead of me. I'm trying to get things under control so I can leave town. Tomorrow is Geri's funeral."

Try as she might, Reightman couldn't find anything to say in response. Finally, she simply told him the reason for her call. "I have some items of his that I'd like to return to you – the jewelry he was wearing the night he...that he was..."

"I think the night he was murdered is what you're trying to say, Detective. The night Geri Guzman was stabbed and sliced until he bled to death on a massage table. Is that it?" His anger was no longer hidden, but was now front and center in his voice.

She took the only road available, and asked, devoid of emotion, "Mr. Bailey, would it be convenient for me to drop the items by this morning before you leave? I can be there in about thirty minutes."

"Yes," he answered, as cool and detached as she'd ever heard. "I'll be here at the spa. I think you know the location. The front door will be open. The cleaning company is working here today." He disconnected without saying goodbye.

Twenty-four minutes later, Reightman pulled her car up in front of the Time Out Spa. As she stepped out of the car and positioned her purse, she noticed a man on a ladder wielding a small handheld tool of some sort, blasting fine particles of fine, gritty sand against the old brick work to remove the graffiti. Another man was working a few feet to the right, dipping a brush into a small bucket and applying some unknown liquid around the window.

Reightman stepped up on the curb and walked to the door. "Excuse me!" she shouted, "I need to get in. Can you hold up for a second?" The man obliging turned off the blaster so that she could open the door.

She recognized SarahJune, the spa receptionist, seated behind the front desk talking on the phone. "*Sounds like she's trying to reschedule appointments,*" Reightman thought as she waited patiently in front of the desk.

SarahJune looked up at her and smiled while rolling her eyes. "One sec," she whispered. "Sorry, Detective," she apologized when she finished the call. "I've been trying to reconfirm clients all morning. Between handling that, and the dealing with the cleaning crew, this place has been a zoo."

"I'm sure it has," Reightman sympathized. "I'm here to see Tob…Mr. Bailey. Is he available?"

"Yeah, he's in his office. You can go on back," SarahJune told her with another smile before picking up the phone again and dialing another spa client. Reightman brushed past a man coming from the back of the building carrying a container marked with symbols indicating it held hazardous waste. When she reached Toby's partially opened office door, she knocked on the doorframe.

"Come on in," his voice called.

She entered and saw Toby seated at his computer, back to the room. "Are you done in the breakroom?" he asked without turning around.

"He must think I'm part of the cleaning crew," Reightman realized before she cleared her throat and answered. "Mr. Bailey, it's Detective Reightman."

His fingers stilled on the keyboard and he slowly turned around and then stood up. "Detective Reightman," he acknowledged coolly.

"Good morning, Mr. Bailey." She reached into her purse and pulled out the small brown envelope and its accompanying form. "I have Mr. Guzman's things." She placed them into his outstretched hand. "I'll need you to sign the form as well." She watched as he unfolded the form from around the envelope and laid it on the desk. He picked up a pen and signed it before handing it back. "Aren't you going to check the contents?" she asked, taking the paper from him.

"No," he replied as he sat back down in the chair and turned back toward his computer. "I think things are wrapped up completely now, Detective," he said as he typed.

Reightman stood watching his back as his fingers moved over the keys. "Goodbye, Mr. Bailey," she finally said, turning and leaving the office. She softly closed the door behind her.

When Toby heard the door click shut, his fingers stopped their typing. He stared at the screen in front of him, realizing he had typed nothing but a mess of unintelligible letters. He turned in his chair and picked up the envelope from its place on the desk, holding it gently in his hand. After a moment of sad consideration, he reached down to the floor beside the desk and opened his satchel, dropping the envelope inside. Toby turned back to his screen and erased the nonsense of mixed capital and lowercase letters he'd just typed. He then placed his fingers on the keyboard and resumed his work.

On the way back to the station, Melba tried to reach Sam by phone. Getting no response, she left a brief message for him letting him know her plans for the day. She contemplated lunch, but decided against it. When she pulled into her parking space she simply sat in the car for several minutes, trying to decide what to do next. Finally, she punched a number into her phone. "Nancy," she said when the call was answered, "If anyone should be looking for me, tell them I'm unavailable. I'm taking the rest of the day as personal time." She turned the phone off and dropped it into her purse. She drove home to find what comfort she could in a pair of sweatpants and comfy t-shirt, and her ratty old couch. *"The rest of the world can just get screwed!"*

CHAPTER THIRTEEN

THE SOUND OF BIRDSONG and the smell of frying bacon pulled Toby up from his deep, dreamless sleep. He blinked open his eyes and looked around him, finally recognizing he was in his old room at Grams' house.

He lay there for a minute, comfortable under the sheets and thin quilt, before slowly sitting up and putting his feet on the floor. He ran his finger through his sleep tangled hair and then stood and shuffled to the bathroom. He turned on the shower. Unknotting his sleep shorts and dropping them to the floor, he stepped under the spray of hot water. Twenty minute later, he made his way to the kitchen – clean, shaved and dressed for the day ahead.

"Breakfast will be ready in a few minutes," Gram informed him from her place at the stove. "Why don't you fetch us each a glass of orange juice? I just made some this morning – it's in the fridge."

"Sure, Grams," he replied, getting down a couple of juice glasses and then retrieving the cold juice. He poured a couple of glasses and then carried them to the table and set them down at the two places already set.

"The birds are sure busy this morning," he commented as he placed the pitcher back in the refrigerator and then took a seat at the table.

"They know summer's almost over," Grams replied as she turned the stove burner down and dished up some eggs from the skillet. She added a few strips of bacon to their plates and then carried them to the table and took her own seat.

They didn't speak much as they ate, each of them caught up in their own individual thoughts and feelings. After they finished, Toby took the plates and carried them to the sink. "I'll take care of cleaning this up, Grams. You go on and get yourself ready."

She walked over to him, and brushed a stand of hair away from his eyes. "Thank you, Toby. I won't be long. We're supposed to be there a little before ten." He nodded sadly and turned back to the sink.

A few minutes later, he folded the dish towel and laid it across the edge of the porcelain sink and then poured another cup of coffee. He listened to the sounds of the dishwasher, and watched the sunlight slowly move across the counters and floor. Grams came back into the kitchen, wearing the somber dress she only wore to funerals, and carrying a small black pocketbook. She opened the bag and placed a white lace trimmed handkerchief inside.

"Ready, Toby?" she asked, watching him with her red rimmed eyes.

"Yes, ma'am, I suppose I am." He carried the now empty coffee cup to the sink, rinsing it and placing it in the drain rack.

Grams placed her arms through the loops of the handbag and opened the refrigerator, removing a foil covered plate. *"She's probably going to want to drop off some food for someone on the way back,"* Toby thought as he held the door for her and then locked it.

Toby drove and they rode to the cemetery in silence. He parked the car and helped her out, waiting while she opened the door to the back seat and took out the plate. She closed the door and took his arm before they began the walk toward the small white awning that he could see in the distance. As they approached the tent, he was surprised to see a small group gathered under the canvas, sheltered from the bright morning light.

As he escorted his grandmother to a seat in the front, he recognized all his friends and neighbors from Capital Street: Bernice, Moon, Herman, SarahJune and a couple of others from the spa staff, and in their midst – tiny, but dignified – Madame Zhou. He felt the tears well up into his eyes and hurriedly brushed them away with a trembling hand. He managed a short nod of greeting as he took his seat next to Grams. "They wanted to come," she said, taking his hand. "They wanted to show their respect, and say their own farewells."

A moment later, a black clothed Pastor Donaldson from Grams' church stood at the front of the small gathering. "Let us bow our heads in respect and silent contemplation for a moment," he suggested gently, and then he began to pray.

Toby found himself focusing not on the words of the short service, but on the simple spray of flowers laid across the plain coffin that sat near them in the morning sun. In the distance he could hear birds singing, and he felt a gentle breeze on his wet cheeks. He lost all sense of time and place, until Grams patted his hand and brought him back to the present. "Toby, it's time."

He stood and escorted her to the side of the grave, and when the others had gathered the funeral home workers lowered the coffin into the grave. As Toby watched, he saw the cemetery workers begin to fill in the hole with spades and shovels, until eventually they rolled new sod over the top of the newly turned earth. Eventually he realized it was over, and that the others had gone. He turned and watched them walking away, huddled closely together with Moon lending her arm to support Madame Zhou across the grass.

"I didn't even tell them goodbye," Toby said quietly.

"They understand," his grandmother assured him before going to retrieve the covered plate from underneath her chair. She carefully unwrapped it, and placed it near the head of the newly filled grave.

"What's that, Grams?" he asked.

"A piece of fried chicken and some cherry cobbler," she answered, as if those few words explained everything in the entire world. And to Toby, they did.

He stood by her side in the quite peaceful place and watched as first one bird, and then another, and another, investigated the offering. "Perhaps they'll take him a bite," Toby ventured as he watched them sample from the plate and then wing their way up into the vast blue sky.

"I expect they will, Toby Bailey," Grams said. "I expect they will."

The rest of the weekend passed slowly and quietly. Toby slept in his old bed and gratefully ate the meals his Grams prepared. They fell into a fragile semblance of their old routine: Toby drying the dishes his Grams handed him, and she swatting him occasionally with her towel as he made a half-hearted attempt to sass her. She watched him intently, wondering when he'd start to grieve. He pretended not to notice her worried glances, and so they went on.

On Sunday evening after dinner, they sat at the big kitchen table, finishing up the last of an apple pie that Grams had baked the day before. "What happens to us when we die?" he asked suddenly. "Do you think we go to heaven or to hell depending on how we lived our lives?"

She put her fork down gently by her plate. "No," she said, "Although Pastor Donaldson would probably rather I did." She pushed back her chair in turned to face him, her face gentle in the evening light. "I do think that our souls go somewhere," Grams said gently, "but not to some kind of Heaven or Hell. I think we go somewhere the good Lord has prepared for us, and that *we* have helped to prepare. There, we get to think our lives over and learn from both our mistakes and triumphs, and then rest and recover from our time in this world until we're ready to move on."

"Move on?" Toby asked quietly from his chair.

"Yes, when it is time, we leave that place. I think some souls wait a while before moving on, until they're joined by the people they loved and who loved them in return. Others can't want to take the next steps through whatever doorway awaits them. Regardless, I think whenever they resume the journey God has planned for them, they do so with wiser souls and lighter hearts than before." Grams watched him work through her words, and then added, "I also know it is not for us to worry too much about in *this* life, Toby – other than trying to cause the least amount of pain to others as we can, and to do as much good as we're able. In the end, I think if we simply love, it will all be fine, even if it doesn't seem like anything will ever be fine again, and as we struggle through the rough patches." She gave his hand a pat and then rose from her chair and left the room. When she came back into the kitchen, she laid a white envelope in front of him on table.

"What's this?"

"It's something I was keeping for you. Geri drove down here to see me about a week before he died. He said if something were to happen, I was to give it to you after he'd been laid to rest."

Toby fingered the envelope edges, but didn't pick it up. "Why didn't you tell me, Grams?"

"Because he asked me not to, until he was put in the ground. He asked me to please respect his wishes and I promised I would."

Toby looked into her shadowed eyes as she stood behind the chair, hands tight on the wooded backrest. He searched her face for some hint of what she was feeling. "What if I choose not to open this, Grams?"

She turned to leave without answering, but when she reached the doorway she looked back. "Open the letter, Toby Bailey. I know you're not a coward. "

He sat in his chair, stunned, as she left the room.

Eventually, Toby lifted the envelope and turned it over a few times, running a finger across the seal. He could feel folded paper and something hard inside – something made of metal. He finally opened the flap and pulled out the paper inside. As he did, a small silver key fell to the table, making a small ringing sound as it hit the hard top. He picked up the key and examined it before placing it to the side. He unfolded the note.

"*Toby,*" the handwriting read, "*if Grams has given this to you, then I guess some really bad things have happened. I'm sorry.*"

Toby laid the letter down because his hands were shaking so much that he couldn't hold it any more. His mind flashed back to the night he had discovered Geri murdered, his body laying white and still on the soft blue sheets while blood dripped to the floor. He could see Geri's green eyes staring, their bright, vivid, green lifeless and dead. After taking a long, shuddering breath he forced himself to smooth the paper on the table and read more.

"*I tried to make sure things were handled, so you wouldn't have to worry about anything, and the business would be fine. I know it was always your dream, and it also became mine. Not because I wanted it, but because you did. I tried to help the only way I knew how.*

I thought that I'd finally figured out how you wouldn't have to worry about money or small-minded individuals – and for a while things went according to plan. But, if you're reading this letter, things went terribly wrong and the things I did hoping to help must have not worked out so well after all.

I could probably write pages and pages about the things I did and the reasons I did them, but they wouldn't matter now, and so I won't. I don't know what words to use anyway. What's important is what you do next. This key fits a small lockbox on Justice Street – you know the place. I rented it a couple of months ago and it's been paid in advance. The box number is on the key. Inside is everything you need to figure things out.

I only have one more thing to say. Regardless how things turned out between us, I knew wherever you were, was my home – the only one I ever had. I know I didn't tell you much, or maybe ever, but I said it to myself often enough.

I loved you, Toby Bailey, as much as I could – Geri."

Toby traced his fingers over the words, pausing when he came to the last few Geri had written. He picked up the key. The number '529' was engraved in a small raised space on one side. After considering the letter for a moment he slid it back into its envelope. Then he stood and pocketed the key. He turned out the light over the sink and went through the doorway. His grandmother was in the living room,

"Grams?" he asked.

"Yes, Toby?" she answered, from her favorite chair.

"I'll be going back in the morning. I need to get back to the city."

"I thought you would." she said, rising to turn off the small lamp. "Are you alright, Toby?" The worry in her voice was plan for him to hear.

"No, but I will be." He walked over and gave her a hug, holding her tightly in his arms.

"You read his letter," she said both in question and in acknowledgement.

"Yes, ma'am. I did."

"What are you going to do now?" She stepped slightly away from him and looked up at his face.

"Why, Grams," he answered, surprised she had to ask. "I'm going to do what you taught me to do. I going to do what comes next, and keep on doing it until I'm done."

Melba crawled out of her bed on Saturday morning, well before the alarm went off. She stretched sleepily and to her surprise found she was actually ready to start her day. She'd worked off some of her dismal mood from the day before by cleaning her condo from top to bottom, and she'd also sorted through the clothes in the closet; replacing a couple of particularly old and drab items with her new purchases from Passed Around. After she finished with that chore, she spied a couple of boxes lurking beneath her hanging clothes – things she'd never unpacked after she'd divorced Stan and left the martial home for good. She unpacked the boxes, discovering a reasonably good pair of shoes, three plastic containers full of bras and stockings, and a hand-held mixer, along with a few other things she'd forgotten she had ever owned. Satisfied with her progress, she treated herself to a partial bottle of good red wine while she caught up on a couple of shows she'd recorded. After a cup of her special tea, she called it a night and hit the sack.

She sat on the bar stool at the kitchen counter and dug her phone out of her purse. She turned it on as she nursed the remains of her second and final cup of coffee, and after it powered up she checked her voicemail. There was only one message and it was from Sam, telling her that he, too, had decided to take a personal day. *"Maybe he was as surprised and disillusioned as I was by the announcement yesterday."* She rinsed out her cup and placed it in the sink. She finished dressing, gathered up her things, and headed out the door to meet at the designated check-in point for her official morning of parade duty.

Sam was standing near the check point, slightly off to the side as she stepped up to the table and signed in. She and Sam would be working the crowd near the front of the parade route, hoping to spot and head off any potential trouble before it got out of hand and ruined the weekend's festivities.

"Morning, Melba," her partner greeted her as she finished with sign-in and joined him at his place near the table.

"Good morning, Sam," she said in return, trying to determine if she should mention anything about their unplanned personal day. Deciding against it, she settled for asking, "Are you ready to get this show on the road?"

"Sure am," he replied as he tossed his empty paper cup into a nearby trash receptacle. "Let's get our butts in gear."

They walked in companionable silence to their assigned starting position, noting the large size of the crowd and pointing out a couple of interesting characters along the way. Soon they were in place and Reightman could tell by the excited comments from the people around them that the parade was getting ready to kick-off.

One of the area high school bands was the first down the street, and Reightman could see the sweat running down the faces of the marching players. The baton team high-stepped down the asphalt, with a few minor mishaps, and then the main body of the parade began to pass by.

There was the usual contingent of volunteer fire-fighters and civic organizations interspersed with another couple of bands. Brightly decorated floats passed by, filled with local dignitaries and the occasional beauty queen from somewhere in the state. Reightman and Jackson changed position frequently, keeping their eyes open for trouble spots as they navigated through the crowd.

They paused about a half a block down from their last viewing spot just in time to see a bright blue vintage convertible pass by, with a waving Dameron family seated behind the driver. Banners with Dameron's campaign slogans draped the sides of the vehicles and his two children were holding aloft a banner which asked the attendees to "Bring Back the Good Old Days." Reightman noticed Sutton Dameron occasionally look behind him from his seat in the car, scowling and whispering furiously to his wife at her place beside him. He'd quickly remember where he was and what he was supposed to be doing, and then he would slap a big fake smile on his face and resume his waving motion.

A few seconds later, Reightman was able to see what was causing the Councilman such agitation. Directly behind Dameron's car was a float decked out in brightly colored balloons, which Reightman eventually realized were actually condoms in various colors, blown up and attached to the float. Riding on the float itself, and tossing individual condom packages to the crowd, were several popular drag queens wearing pastel colored poufy prom dresses. Reightman recognized the dresses as those formerly displayed in the window of Passed Around. Escorting the drag queens in their netted splendor were several muscled and oiled down men, clad in only small pastel bikinis made from sequined fabric which left very little to the imagination. A banner was hung from the back of their float proudly proclaiming everyone should "See the World in a More Wonderful Way – Support Equality for All."

Reightman was pleased to hear the crowd cheer and shout good naturedly at the float occupants, and jostle to catch the thrown condoms. Occasionally, one of the foil wrapped condoms hit the back of Dameron's head as the parade moved down the street. She suspected, but wasn't totally sure they were being thrown by Dameron's liberal opponent, who was positioned in the front of the drag queen's festive ride.

A split second later, an altercation broke out a short distance away and Reightman and Jackson hurried to step into the fray. As they parted the crowd to make their way to the disturbance, Jackson asked in a loud voice "What are the odds of this, Reightman?"

Sprawled out on the ground was the familiar and unwelcomed sight of former Officer Helliman, with his hands held up to a bleeding nose and a busted lip. Standing in front of him was a good looking, busty redhead, wearing a questionable example of cowgirl attire. Reightman recognized it as coming from the same shop as the prom dresses. Aligned by the redhead's side were several other young women, dressed in similar fashion.

"What seems to be the problem here?" Jackson asked. Reightman already had a good idea of what the problem was as she looked to Helliman sprawled on the ground.

"That bitch hit me!" Helliman answered, shaking his head in disbelief that anyone would dare.

"He started it by calling my brother a goddamned fucking cock-sucking fag," the redhead said defiantly. "And then the tubby-assed, redneck dickwad said my brother should be strung up by his heels and beaten to death!"

"Well, well, well, Helliman," Reightman drawled, "I can see you are still spreading love and goodwill all around you."

"You're a fuckin' bitch, Reightman," Helliman retorted as he struggled to rise to his feet. "Arrest her!" he demanded, pointing an angry finger at the redhead.

"For what?"

"For assaulting an officer!"

Reightman searched the areas with her eyes and turned back toward him. "I don't see an injured police officer, Helliman. I just see you."

Helliman's eyes narrowed in rage and he launched himself toward her. As he neared, she braced herself for the impact and readied her fists. He suddenly stumbled and fell, tripped by a dainty, pointed-toed cowboy boot. Helliman gave an astonished gasp and then shrieked as he landed face down, adding additional damage to his bleeding nose.

Two uniformed officer's reached them through crowd. They took a look at the man on the ground, and one of them turned to Reightman. "Need any help, ma'am?"

"I don't think she does, Jarvis," Jackson offered from her side. "Looks like the trouble's over." As the other officer helped Helliman to his feet, Jackson added, "I think it'd best for you to escort Helliman away from here. Make sure he leaves. We don't want any more trouble."

"Yes sir," Jarvis replied, as the other officer took hold of Helliman's arm.

Once he'd been led away, Reightman turned to the redhead. "I know he insulted your brother by calling him those names, miss, but you probably shouldn't go around hitting people."

The young woman looked a little shame-faced as she turned to Reightman. "He didn't make me mad with the names he called my brother. Gary *is* a fuckin' cock-sucking fag and he's damn proud of it! It was when the stupid ass-wipe said he needed to be beaten to death that I lost my temper and decked him."

"I'd say you were justified then, miss," Jackson commented. "But please, don't start another incident today. I'd hate to have to take you in for assaulting folks during a parade."

The rest of the morning passed uneventfully and around lunchtime, Reightman and Jackson stopped to grab something to eat from an enterprising street vendor. "Where are we supposed to be next, Sam?" she asked as she wiped mustard from her chin. She knew Jackson had already memorized their schedule for the day.

"Founder's Park – one o'clock," he mumbled through his chili-dog.

"If I tried to eat that, I'd be wearing about half the chili on my blouse." Jackson didn't have a single spot on his light blue shirt. She watched as he carefully wiped his hands on a napkin and tossed it into a bin. "Ready?" he asked.

"Might as well be," she shrugged as she quickly finished her own hot-dog. "What's happening at Founder's Park?"

He shot her a sideways glace before answering "Dameron's giving a speech."

"Great."

"I thought that'd make your day." Jackson chuckled as they made their way on foot to the park a few blocks over.

"Did you see him getting hit in the back of the head with the flying condoms?" Reightman asked, savoring the memory of the foil-wrapped projectiles finding their target. "I was surprised so many of them actually hit."

"Not me. The guy on the float was aiming at the Councilman's bald spot."

Reightman snorted loudly. "I wonder how much horse crap the Councilman will unload today."

Jackson seldom commented on city politics or the major players. To her surprise, he laughed. "Probably a whole stable full," he answered, in a thoroughly disgusted tone.

"Jackson, I'm surprised at you. You *never* comment on the bigwigs in town or any of the city's brass."

"In this case, I'll make an exception," he said as they turned the block. "When it stinks – it really stinks!"

They found places on the outer edge of the crowd that had gathered to listen to the speech. A small platform was erected near the center of the park and the set-up included a podium with microphone. A few portable speakers where mounted on stands near each side of raised area. Along with Dameron's usual supporters, Reightman saw a few people huddled together a few feet from her and Sam. She noticed several holding protest signs. Her favorite was the one that played off of Dameron's campaign slogan: "Vote for Dameron and HE will lead the way – right back to the dark ages".

"You think this'll get ugly, Jackson?" Reightman pointed out the protestors standing to the right of them. "Looks like some unexpected citizens have turned out for the Councilman's speech."

"I don't think that group's going to give anyone any problems, although Dameron might not be exactly thrilled to see them. However," he tilted his head toward the far side of the crowd, "I am worried about the group just now making their way over to join the fun."

Reightman looked the direction her partner indicated and saw a frothy swirl of pink netting approach the crowd, along with the briefly attired body builders. The oiled men had sensibly added some footwear to their ensemble. *"Those black leather lace-up work boots look very sturdy."* Several of the near-naked men picked up one gowned, be-wigged, and jeweled member of the party and carried her to the front of the crowd. The hunks positioned their delighted burden right in front of the podium and its attached campaign poster.

"Oh…my…God." She calculated the chances for mayhem and grabbed Jackson's arm. "Come on, Sam! We need to get closer to the front. This may get *real* ugly."

They moved through the closely packed people, apologizing and occasionally discreetly flashing their badges. Two or three minutes later they were near the front of the crowd and about six feet from the potential trouble spot.

They didn't have to wait long before a commotion at the back of the crowd signaled Dameron's arrival. Reightman and Jackson observed the Councilman's progress through the crowd, ready to intervene if needed. Dameron was followed by the Reverend Ephraim Shaw, who looked as if he had just stepped away from a funeral in his expensively tailored black suit. Dameron hesitated when he spotted the front row spectators, but lifted his chin and stepped up to the podium. Reverend Sawyer took a position slightly to his right, his thin, pale face stoic in the afternoon sun. To Reightman's surprise, Chief Kelly also joined the two men on the platform, although he stood slightly back from them. Jackson eyes widened, and then narrowed in speculation when he also recognized Kelly.

Dameron took a moment to gaze out into the crowd. She knew the exact moment he spotted the protest signs – now held aloft in the back. He glanced quickly at the Reverend, and then cleared his throat.

"He's kind of cute," the drag queen in front commented. "I just love, love, love, all that dark red hair!" Then sotto voice, she added, "It's a shame how thin it's getting on top. By Easter he'll look like an egg wearing red fringe!" A few folks in the crowd laughed at the sharply pointed comments. Reightman saw Dameron flush and noticed he had to make a visible effort not to lift his hand to his head. He cleared his throat again.

As he started to speak, one of the muscled escorts broke in, right on queue. "Oh honey! Bald men are sexy! All that smooth skin gives me something to play with when they're on their knees in front of me." The laughter was louder this time, although to be fair, there were a few shocked gasps.

The Reverend stepped forward and leaned into the microphone. "Let's all welcome Councilman Sutton Dameron," he instructed and brought his hands together to led a scattering of applause. When the clapping died down – after a shorter time than he'd hoped – Dameron lifted his arms and leaned into the microphone. "Fellow citizens, thank you for joining me on this, the first day of our glorious Labor Day celebrations. I won't take too much of your time today as I know you are all anxious to attend the various entertainments the city has planned for the weekend. However, there are a few things I thought it was important for me to share with you today."

The crowd waited expectantly for him to continue. "As all of you are by now aware, the recent murder that occurred in this beautiful city has been solved, thanks to the efforts of Chief Ernest Kelly and his responsive team. Let's show our appreciation to our City Police Chief." Dameron turned and motioned Kelly to the front of the platform when he shook hands with the politician, while those gathered applauded politely.

"Sister, I could eat that one up like good cake!" Reightman heard from the front of the crowd. "You know I do love me a man in uniform." She couldn't interpret the expression on the Chief's face as he stepped back to his spot at the back of the small stage.

"Although the horrific crime has been solved, and the murderer is now known to have been a degenerate and depraved homosexual," Dameron shook his head sadly at this revelation, "I'm sad to report the business where this terrible event occurred is now planning to reopen, instead of quietly closing for good in respect for the soul slain on its premises. But I've come to realize that men and women who share the perverted lifestyle of the owner, and indeed, of the poor man butchered inside the very walls of that business, have no respect for the proper behavior. Soon those doors will be open again, and others of similar persuasion may enter the doors and disrobe for the pleasure of having strange hands linger on their flesh."

"What's he talking about?" one of the oiled men asked.

"Toby's spa. You know – where Geri was killed," answered a member of the entourage.

Dameron was momentarily distracted by the question and answer session taking place right under his nose. With effort, he regained his focus, and increased the volume of his voice. "We must end this type of behavior!" He exclaimed as he brought his hands down sharply on to the podium. "We must remove all temptations of this kind for the sake of all the good people of our city! We must band together to make sure that these types of businesses and degenerate people cannot flourish among us! We must use every means at our disposal to –"

"What's it to you anyway?" shouted a protester from the back. "Who made you our morality police, Dameron?"

Dameron smiled; delighted he'd been given the perfect opening for his next agenda item. "I serve the will of the people who put me in this office, and you, the people who will bring me back for another term to finish the work I've started! By popular vote, I was made a custodian of this city and by the vote I'll return for another term and prove I can continue to make a difference. I Will Lead the Way!"

"If you're a custodian, why don't you improve the city's trash pick-up service and make sure all of the potholes on our roads are filled?" shouted a woman from the other side of the crowd.

"I hear your concerns," Dameron assured the woman. "And I pledge to work –"

"Your pledges aren't worth a damn, Sutton! I voted for you last time because you convinced me you were a fair and tolerant man and understood how difficult it was to make a living here as a business owner. You didn't do a damn thing for me over the last few years! You just changed your position and your politics every time the wind blew!"

Reightman couldn't identify where the voice originated, but tensed as she felt the mood of the crowd start to change.

Dameron tried valiantly to bring the assemblage back under control so he could continue his planned remarks. "I know many of you are frustrated by the city's complicated and sometimes acrimonious governmental process. And all of us, as elected officials, must take responsibility for what doesn't work. Those issues can and will be addressed. I know how important these things are to each of you. Yet many of my supporters have shared with me their serious concerns about the degradation of the moral standards within the city, and many more have expressed their disgust and outrage at the recently adopted city policy that forbids us to single out the deviants among us."

"What gives you the right to judge anyone, Dameron?" a man from the crowd asked in a loud but reasonable voice.

"Why sir, the bible does. It says plainly in the Book of Leviticus such behavior is an abomination in the eyes of God," Dameron declaimed. "The Bible is the word of God and as such, must govern our behaviors and actions."

"Dameron, I was with you up to now because I agreed with your conservative approach to taxes and city government," a matronly lady said loudly from the second row back, "but the Book of Leviticus also says not to eat shrimp or wear blended fabrics – and I do love a good plate of shrimp. It's all outdated and foolish. Besides, the New Testament trumps the old. You should keep in mind the good book also says, "Thou shalt not judge", but that's exactly what you and those up there on the stage with you are doing. I could believe that from Sawyer – he's always had a stick up his butt! But I must say, seeing our Chief of Police standing up there just breaks my heart!"

"You tell him, sister!" "Hear! Hear!" "This is not Nazi Germany!" Assorted people chimed in loudly after the lady finished, and they continued to speak their minds for a considerable time. Reightman noticed Kelly wasn't looking so comfortable in his place on the platform now.

Jackson comment quietly from her side, "Looks like some of the dyed-in-the-wool supporters are slipping away."

Reverend Sawyer moved to the mic to try to salvage the situation. Before he could speak, another voice near the front rang out, "You can save your breath, Sawyer. My daddy told me to never trust a man wearing a five hundred dollar suit and the one you have on today must have cost double that!" The Reverend surveyed the crowd for a moment with narrowed contemptuous eyes before pressing his thin lips together and speaking into Dameron's ear. The Councilman listened intently and his own lip compressed in annoyance. He started to say something to Sawyer, but the Reverend abruptly turned his back and stepped off of the back of the platform. Reightman could see him talking furiously into his phone as he circled around the crowd and stalked away.

Sutton Dameron looked out to the crowd, his face pinched with anger. He smoothed his tie down the front of his shirt as he tried to think of what he could say to salvage the situation.

"Sutton, honey!" one of the drag queens shouted. "Somebody needs to do a better job of picking out your clothes. That yellow tie is so last year!"

The crowd laughed again and began to disperse, leaving Kelly and Dameron standing alone on the platform. Sutton turned to Kelly, hoping to share his frustration with his new supporter. He approached Kelly, but the Chief held up his hand and shook his head, before walking right past the shocked City Councilman without another look.

"Well doesn't that beat it all to hell?

"What do you mean, Sam?" Reightman asked distractedly as she tried to figure out the meaning behind what she'd just witnessed.

"I never thought I'd see the day when both Councilman Sutton Dameron and the almighty Reverend Ephraim Sawyer were run out of a park by a bunch of drag queens, almost nekkid men, and a handful of left-wing protestors." He turned to her with his eyes wide with amazement.

Reightman grinned. "It turned out to be a pretty good day, huh, Jackson."

"One of the best I can remember in a long while."

Reightman and Jackson walked past a small group of men beginning to take down the podium. As they headed toward their cars, Reightman stopped and picked up something from the grass.

"What's that, Melba?" Sam asked.

She held up a small piece of pink prom dress netting for him to see. "It's just a little memento of the day, Sam. I think I'll keep it to remind myself the most unexpected things can turn the situation around, at least temporarily." She folded the delicate wisp of fabric and put it carefully in her pocket, and then joined her partner to finish their walk back to their cars through the shady and now empty park.

On Sunday, Melba enjoyed her morning, and made herself a decadent breakfast of fried bacon and waffles – something she rarely indulged in. She changed into a pair of jeans and a loose cotton shirt and pulled her hair up under a hat.

She wasn't officially on duty today but was still on call. After thinking through options for her afternoon, she decided that she'd head out to the shooting range to brush up on her skills. Her firearm recertification was coming up in a few weeks and she knew she'd better get in some practice while she could. *"You never know when you'll have to be prepared,"* she reminded herself as she retrieved her weapon from the small gun safe and gathered up the rest of her things.

She called Sam on the off chance he'd tag along and brush up his own skills, but he happily informed her he was planning to spend the day with his wife, grilling some steaks and maybe getting in a little afternoon nap. Thirty minutes later she walked onto the shooting range and, after a few rounds, began to find her groove. After another thirty minutes she checked her results with satisfaction, convinced her re-cert would be a piece of cake.

She left feeling a mellow sense of satisfaction with her day. On a whim, she made a slight detour on her way home to drive down Capital Street. All the businesses appeared to be closed, but she did notice the brick façade of the Time Out Spa looked pretty good, although she could tell work had been done.

Reightman returned to the condo and locked up the gun then tried to decide what to fix for dinner. She finally pulled out some defrosted chicken and started up her small charcoal grill. Soon she was settled in front of her TV enjoying an old movie she remembered as being fun. She had an early night and fell asleep quickly.

Monday morning she woke with a slight headache, but powered through a shower. She poured herself a cup of coffee and turned on the outdated stereo to keep her company.

A few minutes later she checked her voicemail and discovered to her disgust and disappointment that she and Sam would be needed to cover the crowd that was expected to attend the fireworks display planned for that evening to close out the Labor Day celebration. "That shoots the joy right out of the day," she muttered into her coffee, thinking about the amount of money the city was spending. *"I guess they've gotta give the people bread and circuses, especially during an election year."* She called Sam to coordinate where they'd meet, and to verify the time. She then dug out an old paperback crime mystery and amused herself with the improbable story to pass the afternoon. Around six o'clock, she put down the unintentionally hysterical book, and pulled some comfortable clothes from her closet.

She checked her phone and discovered a call from Toby Bailey. Melba frowned as she recalled their last meeting and then dropped the phone in her jacket pocket. *"I'll call him tomorrow."* She retrieved her gun and picked up purse and keys and went to meet her partner.

❖ ❖ ❖

Toby Bailey stopped by his apartment just long enough to drop off his clothes and make a sandwich. He hurriedly wolfed down the pimento cheese and hunk of bread, taking an occasional drink of lukewarm water to wash it down. "*Slow down*, Toby," he told himself after he choked on a piece of the bread. "*It'll still be there in another few minutes.*" He couldn't explain the sense of urgency building inside him, but he knew it was steering him to the lockbox, and whatever answers Geri had left for him. He checked his ring of keys to make sure he had the lockbox key and then ran down the stairs to his car. Ten minutes later, he pulled into the parking lot of a small shopping center and ran to the door, his satchel slapping lightly against his hip. The place was deserted, with iron bars pulled down between the after-hours access area and the small section of the store that sold office supplies and made keys while you waited. He eventually located the banks of metal boxes in a small hallway, and after a convoluted search he located the one he needed. He knelt on the floor in front of box 529 and inserted the key.

Toby pulled out a large brown envelope, containing paper of some sort, and another envelope he could feel held another key and something else, small and hard with a thick, short metal wire on one end. He reached back in and pulled out a small ledger notebook which when he flipped quickly through the pages, appeared to have numeric entries and dates with names listed beside the rows of numbers. He reached in one more time, and pulled out a small note with his name printed on the front. Checking with his outstretched hand to make sure he'd retrieved everything, he then placed his face to the opening and looked inside to double check. Satisfied he had everything, he stuffed the items into his satchel and locked the box. He stood slowly to his feet, and reached out a hand to steady himself against the bank of boxes. His heart was racing, and he stood in the empty hallway as he tried to catch his breath. "*Slow and steady*, Toby," he breathed. "*You have what you need now.*"

He exited the building after checking to be sure no one was watching, although why he felt the need, he didn't know. "*It's probably just nerves.*" He unlocked his car and got in, pulling out of the space to drive to the other end of the parking lot. There, he placed the car into idle, and reached for the satchel. He opened the small envelope that was addressed with his name, and read. Toby closed his eyes for a moment and then quickly stuffed the note back in the envelope before pulling out the larger one made of brown paper. He looked through the images it contained. After recovering from his shock, he carefully slid the photos back in between the brown paper covering, refastening the brass brads with shaking hands.

Suddenly overcome by what he'd seen, he opened the door and heaved a few times, before slowly sitting up and pulling the door closed again. Toby leaned his head on the steering wheel as a series of sharp, painful sobs racked his body. After a couple of minutes he wiped his face and then pulled out the ledger book. He carefully read through the entries, noting some familiar names. He stuffed the brown envelope and the book back into the satchel. He didn't open the envelope containing the key and the other object. He already knew what one of the items was, and the other could wait. He sat in the car, letting the cool air wash over his face. He finally opened the door, and got out to lock the satchel and the information it held in the trunk.

Toby got back in and fastened his seat belt. After driving a block or two, he was shaking so badly he could barely drive. He pulled over to a small diner and got out of the car, locking it before making his slow, labored way to the door. He paused just outside and worked to control his breathing before entering the diner. A sign near the front indicated he should feel free to seat himself, so he searched for an empty booth. He located one and made his way to the back of the space, not even glancing at the people seated near him. When the waitress handed him a menu he ordered black coffee before understanding that if he was going to occupy a booth, he was expected to order something to eat. He asked for the special.

"Breakfast special, lunch special, or dinner special?" she asked. "We serve all three, all day." He ordered dinner, and watched as she walked away. Once she was gone Toby pulled his phone from his pocket and opened his contact list. He located the name he needed and pressed the button to make the call. When the call went to voicemail, he left a message. "Detective Reightman – please call me back as soon as you get this message. Geri left some things for me and I think…I think that they're tied to his murder. There are a lot of pictures and a list of financial transactions tied to some really important people. He was messed up in some really dangerous stuff and I think someone had him killed because of the information and pictures he had. Please – it's really important. I'm going to the spa soon and I can meet you there any time tonight, no matter the time…and… I'm sorry – for the way I acted last week." He hung up the phone and put it back into his pocket before picking up his coffee and gulping down the hot liquid, not bothering to add cream and sugar.

Toby waited for the food he didn't want, and never noticed the man sitting alone in the booth behind him. He wouldn't have recognized him if he *had* noticed, because he had never seen the man before.

After listening to Toby's conversation, John Brown pulled out his own phone and typed a few words. A few minutes later, a text came back:

POP HIM 2NITE

John Brown exchanged a few more texts, eventually agreeing on a price he could live with to take care of this particular problem. After all, it was in his best interest to do so.

A short while later, he counted out some money and laid it on top of his bill. He included a good tip for the waitress. He was a regular here and he knew she'd appreciate it. After all, everyone had to make a living these days.

John Brown walked out of the diner, wondering who he could convince to help him. *"Better have back-up on this one. The timing is going to be tricky."* He started his vehicle and drove away, looking at the early evening sky. *"Time to get to work. The fireworks are about to begin."*

CHAPTER FOURTEEN

R EIGHTMAN MET UP with Jackson near the entrance of Riverfront Park. Unlike the park in the center of the city, Riverfront Park sprawled long and lean along the river, with both sides connected by a series of pedestrian bridges, as well as by two four lane vehicular crossings, one at each end. The park was popular with the locals, who enjoyed the numerous walking and biking trails as well as the opportunities the slow moving river afforded for canoeing and kayaking during the warmer months.

Reightman appreciated the park's many offerings and the city did a fine job keeping it maintained, but she hated patrolling because of difficulties presented by the multiple bridge crossings.

"Where do you want to start?" Jackson asked, as he eyed a group of college-aged partiers who looked like they'd stop to sample the wares at every beer truck and booth operating along the river since late afternoon.

Reightman considered the options as she gave the crowd a once over. "Why don't we start with the far side and work our way back as the evening progresses? That way, we'll be over here and much closer to our cars when this shindig is over."

"That's why you make the big bucks, Reightman – always thinking of the exit plan." Jackson led the way to a nearby concession booth and purchased a couple of bottles of chilled water. "I think we can take our sweet time making it to the other side," he observed as he handed her one of the bottles. "We still have a couple of hours before the big show starts." She took the water from him and saw him sniff the air. "What's that smell?"

Reightman unscrewed the cap of her water and took a long drink. "Bug spray. I figured since I'm so sweet, I'd need extra protection from all the hungry mosquitoes. I'd just as soon not be their evening buffet." Jackson grimaced and took a drink of his own water while she thought over his comment about the starting time of the show. "You're right. We have plenty of time. Let's walk down to the second footbridge. We can cross there as well as anywhere."

As they made their way through the small but growing crowd, Reightman noted the generally pleasant mood of the attendees. A few celebrants had obviously been well served, like the college students they'd spotted earlier. Thankfully, the party gods were apparently spreading good cheer tonight, rather than the mixture of anger, aggression and just plain meanness liberal alcohol consumption sometimes engendered. *"I'll take the good cheer and mellow vibe,"* she decided. *"And I hope those capricious deities don't get bored and decide to send us some trouble – just to liven things up."*

She noticed groups of families and friends starting to spread blankets on the wide grassy banks, and unfold chairs and open coolers containing cold beverages and munchies. Everyone was getting comfortable before the show stated. While they strolled toward the agreed upon crossing point, Reightman remembered the times her own family had attended similar events, and found herself smiling at her recollection of those happy days when Abby was still young and untouched by life's little surprises.

Jackson noticed her reflective mood. "Penny for your thoughts."

"They're not worth much more than a penny," she replied with a smile. "I was just remembering when Abby wasn't much older than those two over there." They stopped to watch a couple of young children being herded back to their safe spot among the rest of their family. "Abby loved outings like this, and it was always such fun to see her discover new things. I still remember her surprised face the first time we took her to see fireworks." They continued walking, now just a few yards from the second bridge. "It seems like those days were such a long time ago. I forget Abby is all grown up and has little ones of her own."

"How are the girls doing, Melba?"

"They're doing great and giving their mother a run for her money!" They stepped up to the bridge and started across. "Abby has a new romantic interest. I'm going to meet him over the weekend if things work out."

"Good for her," Sam approved. "How long has it been since she was serious about anyone?"

"Abby hasn't really been serious about anyone since her divorce, and that was nearly four years ago." Melba stepped aside to allow an elderly couple to pass. She smiled at the sight of them making their way across the bridge arm-in-arm, providing support to each other on their evening stroll.

"It's about time for her to be stickin' her toe back in the water then. She'll do just fine."

They reached the other side of the footbridge and met Jones and Mitchell beginning to cross back over to the other side. Reightman noticed the younger man was in plain clothes rather than suited out in a uniform. *"His provisional promo must be sticking,"* Reightman thought with approval. *"Good for him! I hope he'll get the right training and mentoring to go as far as he wants."*

"If it isn't the terrible twosome," Jackson greeted them. "You headed back to work the other side?'

"No, thank the good Lord," Jones replied. "We were on duty all of yesterday, and most of the day before. We got fairly light duty today – just the early hours. We've now officially done our time."

"Are you staying for the show?" Reightman asked the both of them.

"I think I'll hang around. I don't have anything better planned for the night," the younger cop said. "You mind if I hang with you two?"

"Not at all, Mitchell," Jackson assured him. "You can help me keep old lady Reightman in line."

Reightman shot him an evil glare before turning to Jones. "You want to stay with us old, broken-down geriatrics?"

Jones laughed. "As pleasant as it sounds, I think I'm going to hunt down a cold beer or two on the way home. I've had about all the crowds I can take." He started across the bridge and added, "Try to keep Mitchell in line. I think he has all the makings of a proper hell raiser."

"We'll do our very best," Jackson assured him as they waved him off and started down the other side of the river. "Has there been any trouble over on this side, Mitchell?"

"No, sir, not a bit. We did help one very out-of-it frat boy find his friends. That's been all the excitement so far."

Their party of three walked the river's edge for the next hour as the evening began to turn to night. They only had to intervene once: a rapidly escalating family argument was quickly settled when Reightman gave the mouthy mother-in-law, who was fanning the flames of discord, the option between calling it an evening and heading – quietly—home. The alternative she offered was spending the next several hours enjoying the fine hospitality of the city jail. The woman wisely chose to pack up her folding chair and go on home.

Reightman looked up river and could see the fireworks barge in the distance, moored about a hundred yards upstream from the dramatically lit bridge arches. From the activity on board, it appeared they were almost ready to start the show.

"Looks like they are about to begin," she pointed out to her two escorts.

Jackson located a position near the back of the grassy riverbank, where they could observe both the show and the attendees. Moments later, the first rocket launched from the barge, painting the sky with hot, fiery bursts of color. Another followed in quick succession, and then another, punctuated by loud rumbling booms and the 'oohs' and 'ahs' of the crowd.

"There goes next year's raise," Jackson grumbled as sparkling light illuminated the area. "Blown all to hell in the sky."

"I think it's pretty cool," Mitchell said.

Reightman and Jackson turned to him and said, in unison, "Of course you do."

They laughed at his feigned expression of hurt as another burst of light spread trails of red and gold and silver across the sky. Just as another rocket launched, the phone in Reightman's pocket buzzed and vibrated, indicating she'd received a voicemail. She pulled it out and looked at the number, frowning.

"Who could possibly be calling that puts that scowl on your face?" Jackson asked.

"Toby Bailey. He left another voicemail."

"Another voicemail?" At her nod, Jackson asked "Has something else happened at his business?"

"I don't know," Reightman admitted. "I haven't listened to his first one. I thought it could wait until tomorrow. Given his attitude the last time we met, I didn't feel obliged to immediately respond."

"It won't hurt anything to see what he has to say."

Reightman thought about just putting the phone back into her packet and dealing with it tomorrow. But as Jackson continued to look her way, she decided she might as well see what Toby wanted and turned away slightly to shield some of the noise. She accessed voicemail and listened to the message, straining to hear over the sound of fireworks and crowd noise. She played through both messages and then listened to the first again, making sure that she had heard correctly.

"Detective, you look like you've seen a ghost!" Mitchell exclaimed as she turned around.

"In a way, maybe I have or at least received a message from one." Reightman took another look at the phone in her hand and then turned to Jackson. "Toby says he found something, or rather, Gerald Guzman left him some things he thinks tie directly to Guzman's murder. He says there are photos and an account ledger, complete with the names of multiple clients." When Jackson didn't respond, she added, "He wants to meet tonight if possible."

Mitchell, of course, had listened in to the conversation. "But isn't the case closed?"

"It is closed, and Chief Kelly will be after our asses if we start stirring things up again." Jackson answered, continuing to study his partner. Resigned to the inevitable, he sighed heavily. "I correct my statement, Mitchell. The case *was* closed. Looks like I'm not going home after the fireworks. Alice may skin my hide."

"You don't have to come with me, Jackson. You can head on home. I'm perfectly able to meet Toby Bailey by myself." Reightman started to walk toward the nearest bridge.

"Yes, you are," Jackson agreed readily. "You're perfectly able to head off this time of night to meet with Mr. Bailey. You're perfectly able to review and possibly take into custody any evidence which may open this can of warms again. You are perfectly able to do that, Reightman." Jackson walked by her side as she placed her foot on the bridge with Mitchell trailing slightly behind. His voice was calm and measured as he continued. "You are also dumb as a bag of rocks if you think I'm going to let you go down there by yourself." He held up a hand as she started to object. "Now, I have no reason to suspect Toby Bailey himself of anything but a certain level of naiveté, but think about it. This could be a set-up. It's probably just a wild goose chase, and I almost hope it is. I'm not worried about that. It wouldn't be the first time we went chasing after something that turned out to be a load of crap. What I *am* worried about is it could be something worse. You better reconcile yourself to the fact that there's no chance in hell I'm letting you drive down there by yourself and maybe step right in the middle of a bigger mess than you can handle."

"Jackson, I'll be fine," Reightman assured him. "I'm not exactly a helpless damsel in distress." He didn't say a word as they continued to walk toward the main exit to the park.

"I could go," Mitchell suggested after a minute of uncomfortable silence.

"No!" Jackson and Reightman both answered.

"I appreciate the offer," Reightman added when she saw the disappointment on the young officer's face. "But you've put in a few long, hard, thankless days and what you need is to find yourself a cold beer or two before getting some rest. I'll be fine."

Mitchell gave her a couple of token nods, but Reightman didn't trust the speculative look on his face. "I mean it, Mitchell. Don't make me pull rank because I'll make you cry like a baby." Her threat elicited a small, grudgingly given grin and, after weighing his expression, Reightman started walking again, confident at least the matter of Mitchell's participation was settled.

Once they reached the parking lot, the young man reached out and shook their hands. "Thanks for letting me tag along tonight, Detectives. You old people are alright, no matter what anyone else says."

"Old people, my ass!" Jackson growled, but the twinkle in his eyes took away any sting, just as he'd intended. "You better get yourself home and all tucked in, sonny-boy, and don't forget to brush your teeth!"

Mitchell grinned and looked down at his feet, thrilled that Jackson was giving him hell. "See ya' later." He turned and jogged across the lot to where he was parked.

"I like him," Reightman told her partner as she watched Mitchell crossing the lot at a lope. "He reminds me of the stray puppy I conned my parents into letting me keep when I was a kid."

"He's a good kid," Jackson agreed, making no move toward his own car.

She tightened her lips and gave him her very best evil eye. When he didn't react, she forced of exasperated stream of air through her mouth. "I thought I'd park in the lot on the corner across from the spa. It would attract less attention."

"Sounds like a good plan, Reightman. Glad to see you're thinking for a change," Jackson said with a wise-ass grin. "I'll meet you there."

She rolled her eyes and started to walk away, but was brought up by a guttural roll from the back of his throat. "Yes, I know that I'm supposed to wait for you if I get there first." She stomped off to her own car. "Men!"

she exclaimed in frustration. She could hear Sam's shout of laughter behind her as she opened her truck and stowed her gun. She could still hear him as she walked around to her door and got in. She took some satisfaction in slamming her door shut and cutting off the obnoxious noise.

Reightman dialed Toby from the car and he picked up before the first ring had finished sounding in her ear. "Detective Reightman?" he answered. She could hear the relief in his voice.

"Yes, Toby...er...Mr. Bailey," she responded. "I'm sorry I took so long to call you back, but I just picked up your messages." She listened to Toby's reiteration of his message as she backed out of her space, waving gratefully to the driver who had slowed behind her. "Yes, that's what you said...Yes, Detective Jackson and I are just now leaving the fireworks show at Riverfront Park." She pulled into the line of traffic waiting to exit the parking area. "I think it'll probably take us thirty or forty minutes to get down there. Traffic is pretty bad and will probably be backed up all the way downtown."

As she inched forward, a thought occurred to her. "Does anyone else know you have those things?...Good. Are you at the spa now...Do you have the door locked...Okay, here's what I want you to do. Turn off all of the lights except the ones in your office. Stay there and don't come out until I call you to tell you we're both out front, okay?" She carefully navigated out on to the small two-lane road that led in and out of the park. "No. I don't, but it's better to be cautious.... Alright. We'll be there soon." Reightman hung up and tossed her phone on the passenger seat, watching as it slid off and wedged between the seat and the door. She tried to reach for it, but discovered that her arm wasn't long enough. After another try, she decided to just leave it where it was until she got out of the slow moving mess. She crossed her fingers, hoping that no one else called.

John Brown slid into the passenger seat of the pickup truck pulled alongside his vehicle. He situated the black bag he carried from his SUV and placed it at his feet. Before he fastened his seat belt he handed an envelope full of cash to the driver. "I guess you know where we're going?"

"I sure as hell do," Helliman said, almost quivering with excitement. "I had some business of my own down at that queer-ass fag place a few nights ago."

"Yes, I heard about that," John Brown responded without much inflection. "You did quite a number on the place, from all reports."

"You better believe I did!" Helliman said proudly. "I hate all those queers! It would serve 'em all right if all them businesses just burned right to the ground. That prissy ass faggot's just lucky I didn't torch his place!"

John Brown didn't respond to Helliman's hate-filled rant. He sat completely still in his leather bucket seat until they turned on Capital Street. "Park across the street in one of the parallel parking spots near the end of the block," he instructed.

"What now?" Helliman asked as he parked the car and turned off the engine.

"Now we wait. I already know the target is in the building. I confirmed it about thirty minutes ago. I drove down the street before you picked me up and saw him standing in the lobby talking on his cell phone. He had a satchel strapped to his body which I recognized when I saw him at the diner. I bet the items he found are in there."

"Why don't we just break in and take care of him?"

John Brown didn't answer immediately. "We may have to," he agreed reluctantly, "but I want to avoid that if possible. It would give him warning something was happening and time to call the police. I think it'd be better if we wait here a while and catch him when he exits the building and starts to walk across the street to his apartment."

"What if that bitch, Reightman, shows up before we do it?"

"Then we will have to adjust the plan accordingly. Regardless of who shows up and how long it takes for him to leave, we have to do this tonight. My instructions are very clear."

"But if he hands the stuff over to that goddamn bitch before we hit him, won't there still be a world of trouble? She can make life hell. I've watched her do it."

Helliman's question made John Brown uncomfortable. "With the kid dead, it should be easy enough to discredit her," he eventually answered. "After all, the case is closed and she'd have to explain how she just happened upon new evidence. It could be made to appear a little too convenient and maybe even staged. That would throw some doubt on her credibility. Without Bailey's testimony it would be messy, but not insurmountable for the boss. Evidence has been known to disappear before and all it takes is the right incentive." John Brown glanced at his driver. "You should know – you've helped with a few such instances yourself."

"Money talks and shit walks," Helliman agreed.

The two men settled back in the dark interior and watched the front of the store. About ten minutes later John Brown set up straighter in his seat to watch a car pull into the small lot on the corner. Another car pulled shortly after. From his current position he couldn't see who got out of either car.

"You think something's up?" Helliman asked nervously.

"I don't know yet. It may be nothing other than someone coming home from dinner or from the show down at the park."

Barely a minute later Helliman whistled softly through his teeth. "It's Reightman and Jackson," he said. "What now?"

"I don't know," John Brown conceded, as he watched the two detectives cross the street and walk to the door of the spa. He observed the woman make a call on her phone and then wait with her partner until the door was opened and they were ushered into the building. "I'd better double-check our instructions," he said, pulling out his phone and typing a few lines. He watched the screen until a text came through. "No change in plans," he told his companion. "We're supposed to proceed."

"You don't sound too damn happy about that."

"It's a lot more complicated now," John Brown said quietly. 'I don't like it when things get too complicated." He typed another line or two into the phone and sent the message. Almost immediately the reply came through. He read the text and then turned off the phone and put it back in his pocket without saying a word.

Uncomfortable with the man's silence, Helliman asked "How you liking that there phone?"

"Other than the scratch on the case, it's fine," John Brown replied. "You must've made a mint when you so helpfully snagged it that night."

"First on the scene skims the cream," Helliman said smugly. "Thought it might have something good on it, so I swiped it. When it didn't, I was told to have it wiped and then hand it over to you. It's kind of ironical and all – given what we're doing tonight." Helliman laughed and added, "It serves the fuckin' queer right for us to be getting the confirmation on his own hit over a phone that used to belong to him."

"Yeah…ironical," John Brown grunted in reply. He settled back into the seat for a moment and thought about the new complications. "Drive around the block and park on the other side near the corner." Once they were parked in the new position, John Brown reached into the bag at his feet and pulled out a gun and a piece of black fabric.

"What's that?" Helliman asked, eyeing the cloth.

"A mask," John Brown answered as he unfolded it.

Helliman thought it over. "Did you bring one for me?" he asked.

"I just have the one," John Brown answered, as he settled back into the seat, making himself comfortable for the wait. "Sorry," he shrugged, not really meaning it.

Helliman gave the black fabric one more look before he, too, leaned back into the leather bucket seat.

Reightman and Jackson entered the spa door. "Thanks for coming," Toby said gratefully as he locked the door again. "I didn't know if you'd come after the other day, but I didn't know what else to do or who to call."

"That's alright, son," Jackson assured him, "If you've gotten your hands on what Reightman says you have, then you did the right thing."

Reightman stood by the door in silence for a moment looking out into the dark streets before turning to the nervous young man. "Well, Mr. Bailey, we better take a look at what you've found."

Toby turned and led the two Detectives back to his office. Jackson gently closed the door. "Better safe than sorry," he commented before he reached out and took a seat. "Let's see what's got you two all worked up."

Toby handed him the ledger book and the photos. "Geri left these for me at a lockbox down on Justice Street. He gave a letter to Grams –my grandmother," he explained to Jackson, "and asked her to give it to me if something bad happened. The letter had a key in it and told me where to go to find this stuff."

"May I see the letter?" Reightman asked as she watched Jackson open the brown envelope.

Toby flushed slightly, but handed her the letter. She took the paper from Toby's hand and unfolded it to read the words that Geri had written.

"Damn son!" Jackson exclaimed, looking up at Toby in shock. "These photographs could just about set fire to the whole city, even if they aren't directly tied to your friend's murder." Jackson looked through the photographs one more time before handing them to Reightman. "You'd better take a look," he said. "You're not going to believe your eyes."

Reightman put down the letter and reached for the stack of photos. She flipped through them, noticing that a few were similar to the photographs Tom had recovered from Geri's phone. There were many more images in this stack, and unlike those images, several of the photos included the clearly visible faces of – as Jackson had indicated – several of the city's leading citizens, powerbrokers and officials. The subjects completely nude and in some cases were shown engaging in a variety of sexual acts with a well-built man Reightman recognized as Geri Guzman. The one without recognizable features included the tattoo she recalled from the photos retrieved by the crime tech.

Reightman arranged the photos in groups, shuffling her placement a few times to find any common themes – besides the obvious. She turned to Jackson, who was examining the small ledger. "Find anything in there?"

"Yes, I did," he replied thoughtfully. He turned a few more pages, and then looked up. "It appears Guzman was not only providing a varied set of services to the city's elite, but also managed to get photos of the interactions. From the entries in this ledger, not only was he collecting some pretty hefty fees for service, but also blackmailing them with the photos." He turned a couple of more pages. "Hand me those photos again. I want to check something."

She handed them over and watched as he checked a few and then turned back to the ledgers. "What are you looking for?"

"Each of the photos has a date and time stamp indicating when they were taken. See here?" Jackson indicated the small print on the photos. "Those little numbers cross reference to the entries in this book." After checking a few more examples he handed the book and the photos to his partner. "Were you aware of any of this Mr. Bailey?"

Toby's pale eyes were steady. "No, not until I saw these." He sat down in his chair and studied the desk top, moving a pencil and then picking up a paperclip and placing it back down. "Geri had been engaged in providing those kinds of services for a while. I told Detective Reightman about it when she interviewed me on the night of his murder." He waited until Reightman nodded her confirmation and then continued. "At first I thought he was just doing normal outcalls, and when he finally told me what else he was doing with his clients, I was shocked and hurt and tried to get him to stop. He said he needed the money, and this was the only thing he'd ever been good at doing. He told me it wasn't so bad, and convinced me to go with him once. I got here, and discovered once things got started I just...couldn't go through with it. I got dressed and left. Geri told me he'd find his own way back to our apartment once they'd finished. He laughed and said I shouldn't wait up."

Toby shifted around in his chair and finally stood to lean against the wall with his head hanging down. "You see, this place was just getting started and things were tight financially after all the start-up cost had been paid. I had some money left from mom's insurance and the sale of her house, but not much, and we needed to be really careful." Toby let out a breath of air and then looked up at the two Detectives. "I asked him to stop and he asked me how I thought we were going to get this place open without a source of steady cash. When I told him I didn't know, but we'd find some other way, he said he'd make sure we didn't have to worry. After arguing about it for several weeks, he told me to just shut up and mind my own business. He said he liked doing it, and didn't care what I thought anymore."

Reightman watched as the young man visibly prepared himself to say what came next. "I couldn't take it anymore," he said in a dead, lost voice. "I told him he needed to stop what he was doing or I was going to leave." He paced a few steps, confined in the small space until he went back to his chair. Once seated, he gave a sad shrug. "He said he'd see me around when he came in to work, and to give him a forwarding address when I had one." Toby reached across the desk and picked up the letter Geri had written. He looked over the words and let it drift back down to the table. "I had no idea he was taking pictures in order to blackmail these people. I know who some of them are, and I don't like what they stand for in many cases. But they didn't deserve to be held hostage for what they were doing in private – no matter what."

Reightman handed the folder and the ledger book back to Jackson. He looked through them one more time and then set them on the edge of the desk.

"Was there anything else in the lockbox?" Reightman asked.

Toby bent down and pulled another sealed envelope from his satchel. "Just this."

She took the envelope from him and felt the items inside.

"I think one of the things in there is a safety deposit box key," Toby said as she carefully pulled open the flap. "I think it is probably for the box that we shared and where we kept our birth certificates, and the original papers for the business, and a few other important documents. I don't know what the other thing is."

After the flap had been pulled open, Reightman looked inside and then carefully tilted the envelope over the desk and gently shook it. The key hit the desk and was followed by the other item. "This looks like the earring Mr. Guzman was wearing the night he was killed." The large diamond reflected the light in the office as it sat on the desk.

"But I already have that! This can't be the same one," Toby said as he started to reach for it.

"Don't touch it!" Reightman commanded sharply. Toby slowly withdrew his hand, and she explained, "It may have evidence on it and I don't want to chance contaminating it."

She gently used the end of a pencil to herd it back into the envelope. "Is this your safety deposit box key?"

Toby stood and came around the desk, stepping between the two Detectives in the chairs. He leaned in to look at it, keeping his hands well away from it as it lay on the desk. After recognizing the small numbers, he stood and said, "Yeah, I'm pretty sure it is."

Reightman pushed it into the envelope with the end of the pencil and then tore of a piece of tape from the dispenser on the desk. She sealed down the flap and placed the envelope on top of the ledger.

"What now, Reightman?" her partner asked as soon as she was finished.

"Now I am going to call Chief Kelly. Those photos just moved all of this way above my pay grade."

John Brown continued to watch the entrance to the spa, occasionally checking the time on his phone. Helliman was nodding off in the driver's seat and once he had started to snore, John Brown jostled his shoulder to wake him up. "Helliman, you need to stay alert!" he hissed.

Helliman jolted upright. "Sorry," he mumbled. "What's happening?" he asked after a minute.

"Nothing yet, but they've been in there a long time. We need to be ready." He picked up the mask and pulled it carefully over his head and then tugged it into place, arranging it until the eye holes and mouth opening were properly aligned.

"That's going to be hot as hell."

John Brown shrugged and didn't bother to comment.

Reightman shoved her phone back into her pocket. "I went right to voicemail," she said with evident frustration.

"You're not going to leave a message?" Jackson asked.

"No, I want to talk with him directly. He's been avoiding me the last few days and if he still is, he might not even listen to it. I'll try again later. If that fails, we'll just camp out by his office in the morning." She ran her fingers through her hair and then stretched to relieve the tension building in her neck and shoulders. "Let's take these and get out of here. Tomorrow's going to be a doozy and we need to try and get some rest." She stood and reached for the items on the desk, but before she could pick them up, Toby laid his hand on them.

"I don't think so," he said firmly.

"But, Mr. Bailey...Toby...I'm going to need them to show Chief Kelly."

He softened for a minute at the use of his first name, but just when Reightman thought he was going to agree, he shook his head. "No." She looked at him in disbelief. "No," he said again firmly, before she could try and argue with him. "I'm not letting them out of my possession. I'll keep them and bring them down tomorrow." He picked them up, making it clear his position was non-negotiable.

"That's just stupid! They'll be much safer in police custody."

"Like Geri was safer in the morgue, Detective?" He focused his blue eyes on her and drove home his point. "The same morgue where some sick, obsessed city official sliced the foreskin from his penis? Or did you mean safe, like the jewelry he was wearing was safe, before it was misplaced and couldn't be found?"

"But, that was all Lieberman —"

"And Lieberman had inside help." Jackson reminded her regretfully. When Reightman turned her shocked face to him he continued. "Those things might be safer with us and I think they would be. But you have to agree Mr. Bailey makes a good point. He's kept those items for this long and a few more hours won't matter." The photos he'd viewed along with the ledger entries made him very uncomfortable. "Some really important and powerful people are going to be dragged into this, and they're going to do everything they can to prevent, or at least delay, any of this from seeing the light of day. All things considered, I think the best thing would be for Mr. Bailey to turn these in – very officially and very publically – tomorrow, with his attorney present." Jackson took a minute to enjoy the thought of how well that was going to play down at headquarters. "With Madame Zhou involved, it's going to be more difficult for someone up top to let things slip, and it'd be much more noticeable if something in that folder was *accidentally* misplaced."

She considered who his definition of someone up top included. "Jackson, surely you don't think the Chief would…?"

"I don't know Reightman. I didn't think he'd rush the announcement that this murder had been solved, and I didn't think he'd agree so quickly with the verdict Lieberman offed himself without letting us dig around some more." He held her eyes and she read the disappointment he felt in his. "The Chief I thought I knew wouldn't have acted that way, and he sure as hell wouldn't have made a public announcement without being doubly sure all the loose ends were tied up. But he did, Reightman. He did."

Reightman ran her hands through her hair again, and rotated her neck a couple of times while she thought. "Toby, do you have a safe place to put this stuff until tomorrow?"

"I could put them back where I found them – back in the lockbox."

Jackson looked up at him in approval, a slow smile spreading over his face. He looked at his partner. "I told you he was turning out to be interesting." He turned back to Toby with a suggestion. "Why don't we escort you to that lockbox and make sure everything gets tucked in where it can spend the night, all safe and sound? You can stop by and get it when you and Madame Zhou come to the station in the morning."

"Alright," Toby agreed.

"Let's get the show on the road then," Reightman suggested. "Put those things into something secure until we can get them locked up."

Toby picked up the satchel and stuffed the items back in, and secured it by draping the bag across his body. Reightman opened the door and let the others precede her. She turned off the office lights and pulled the door behind her.

Toby locked the front door and the three of them stepped out onto the sidewalk. As she looked up and down the street she noticed they had company. "What the hell is *he* doing here?"

Jackson looked across the street toward the small red sedan and groaned. "I should have known Mitchell couldn't leave well enough alone."

"You two stay here – I'll be right back." They watched as she hurried across the street and pounded on the driver's side window. "Get out of the car, Mitchell."

The young cop jerked awake, startled and disoriented. When her words registered in his foggy brain, he opened the door and stepped out.

"Now!" John Brown commanded. "And make it fast! Get me as close to the kid as possible."

Helliman quickly pulled away from the parking space as the other man rolled down the window.

"I thought I told you to go home, Mitchell!" Reightman stepped up into his face. "Did you think it was just a polite suggestion?" she asked, reaching out to shake his arm. Mitchell dropped the keys he was holding and crouched down to pick them up. Behind her, Reightman heard a large engine revving.

She turned and saw a glaring set of bright headlights headed in their direction – tires squalling as the vehicle picked up speed. She shielded her eyes from the unexpected brightness, trying to regain her vision. She blinked and squinted across the street to where Jackson and Toby were standing and noticed them stepping away from the building to see what was causing the noise.

"Hold it as steady as you can, Helliman!" John Brown shouted as he reached out of the open window and sighted down the barrel of the gun.

Reightman saw the arm and screamed across the street "Sam! He's got a gun!" She reached to her side and realized that her weapon was still locked in the trunk of her car.

She knew the moment Sam made sense of her shouted warning. He reached for his own gun and turned to Toby. "Get down!" he shouted, pushing Toby to the ground. Reightman saw a series of bright flashes from the pick-up window and heard the loud, deafening sound of gunshots. She watched in disbelief as – in slow horrifying motion – Sam grabbed his chest and looked down to where he'd been hit. His right arm jerked twice, and she saw his hand open and his gun drop to the pink, stained sidewalk. The truck's tires squealed again and she turned in time to see it headed directly toward her and Mitchell. He tackled her and carried her to the ground.

"Get off me!" she screamed as the truck zoomed dangerously close and then sped away. She dragged herself up off the ground, using the side of the truck for support. "I've got to get to Sam!" She ran across the street, shouting over her shoulder, "Call it in, Mitchell! Call it in! Tell them to hurry – Sam's been hit!"

She heard him shout into the phone as she ran: "Officer down! I repeat officer down!"

Reightman ignored the swelling of her knee and propelled herself up the curb, where Toby had propped Sam up. He was frantically trying to do something about the blood already soaking the front of Jackson's shirt. Toby tore off his own shirt and ripped open the buttons of Sam's. He frantically pressed the balled-up fabric to the wound on Sam's chest. Reightman knelt down and pushed Toby's hand aside. "Let me see!" she demanded. Toby lifted the cloth and she saw blood gush from Sam's chest. "Put it back and keep applying pressure!" She positioned herself along Sam's side to support his head and shoulders.

"Stay with me, Sam!" she ordered the terribly wounded man, as she cradled him with her arm. "Look at me, dammit!"

Jackson tried to focus on her face, fighting against the pain and shock. "Melba…" he groaned.

"That's right, Sam," she told him. "It's Melba and I've got you – just hold on. I hear the sirens now. Help is coming."

No…" he gasped weakly, and she saw his eyes start to droop again. He struggled to force them open. "Tell Alice……I ….love her…."

"You can tell your wife your own damned self, Jackson!" Then gently – insistently, she crooned, "You're going to be fine – they'll fix you right up, Jackson –you'll see. Just hang in here with me a little longer… I've got you, Sam – you hear me? I've got you." She held him, talking the whole time. She felt him spasm and fear rose up within her and then ran down her spine. She looked into his face and whispered to him desperately "Hang on, Sam. Don't you dare give up on me!"

She was vaguely aware of the ambulance pulling up behind her and the shouts of the first responders as they jumped from its cab. She heard the back doors open and the crash cart hit the ground.

"Melba…" the man she held said, so weakly she had to strain to hear him. "Get the…….bastards……."

She saw a tear hit his cheek before she realized she was crying. Before she could reassure him, his eyes glazed over…. and she felt herself falling from a great height. Then abruptly her soul hit the ground and she was being pushed out of the way by the EMS team.

"No!" she screamed with great, terrible hurt and helpless terror. "I have to stay! I have to help him!"

"Get out of the way, ma'am, so we can do our job!"

She barely registered the presence of Mitchell and Toby as they half-dragged, half-carried her away.

"Let me go!" she screamed. "Please..." she pleaded as she fought against the arms holding her with everything she had inside. "Damn you to hell!" she fought. "I said let me goooooooo..." Her painful heartrending wail was cut off as Toby slapped her, open handed across the face. Her head snapped back and she screamed again and desperately kicked out at the two men holding her.

He slapped her again.

She shook her head in surprised shock and blinked her eyes a few times, noticing the bright glare of whirling red and neon blue lights surrounding her. In the distance she could see the crash cart team step away from the body and shake their heads. "Oh, Sam.........." she cried, the sound grinding low and mournful in the back of her throat. "Oh, Sam......." She felt her wounded leg start to give and she sagged against Mitchell. He held her tightly against his chest. "Shhhhh....." He held her while the sobs racked her body. "Let it go," he told her. "Let it go...."

As the truck careened around the corner John Brown pulled of his black mask and jammed it into the bag at his feet. "Take the back streets and head north. I'll tell you when to pull over."

Helliman's hands gripped the wheel tightly and were white across the knuckles to match his pale face and he started to laugh hysterically. "Toby Bailey's been done rubbed out! That'll teach the cocksucker!" After another pleased shout of triumph, he recalled how terrified he'd been. He cast a nervous glance to the man next to him. "I didn't think it would be like that. It was kinda' out of control."

"Shit happens," John Brown said as he reloaded the gun.

"You're expecting them to catch up to us, aren't you?" Helliman asked, worried for the first time of the night.

"You just never know." A couple of blocks later, John Brown instructed his driver to make a left, and then to take the next right. "Pull over here."

"I can take you on over to your vehicle," Helliman offered, not wanting to be left alone yet. "It's just a couple of blocks from here."

"Thanks, but this is fine." When the truck eased to a stop by the curb and Helliman put it in park, John Brown gathered up his bag and opened his door.

"What I'm I supposed to do now?" Helliman asked uncertainly, turning to face John Brown as he stood outside the opened passenger door "What if they find me?"

"Well, I've been thinking about that," John Brown assured him. "I think the best thing for you to do right now would be to just …take a nap."

"What do you –?"

John Brown raised the gun in his hand and fired once. The bullet only made a small hole in the front of Helliman's forehead, but it did break the glass of the driver's side window as it exited the back of his head.

John Brown looked around to see if the shot had caught the attention of anyone in the area. Then he opened the black bag and took out the dark cotton mask and a small spray bottle of cleaning solution. He sprayed the cloth and wiped down every surface he'd been in contact with on his side of the truck. Wrapping the cloth around his hand, he reached over and turned off the truck with the key in the ignition switch and closed the passenger-side door. He dropped the cloth and the bottle back into his bag. As he started down the street he could hear the sirens in the background.

Mitchell held Reightman for what seemed like a very long while she cried herself out, and he felt her stiffen against him. "Mitchell…." Her voice was very small and sad. "Let go of me – please."

Mitchell cautiously loosened his arms, ready to hold tight again if she lost control. When she didn't, he slowly released her and dropped them to his side. Reightman roughly rubbed the tears from her face and then stepped away. She turned and slowly hobbled to the gurney where Sam was lying, stumbling on the first couple of wobbly steps. She looked down at the man who'd stood by her side for so many years, and she reached out and gently touched his face.

She traced his face with trembling fingers and then pulled her hand away to place it over her heart. "I'll get the bastards," she promised his white and still face.

She forced her swollen knee to obey her, and walked by his side as they wheeled him to the emergency van, and then stood silently a few feet away, watching with dead eyes as they loaded him in the back. She turned around and dully observed as Toby Bailey's arm was cleaned and then bandaged. She realized he'd been hit as well, although it looked as if it was just a graze.

Mitchell stepped up beside her. "Detective, I saw the driver." Her eyes drilled his face. "It was Helliman." He flinched at the look on her face, and knew the crooked ex-cop would never survive if she found him.

"And the shooter?" she asked, in the coldest and most terrible voice he'd ever heard in his life.

Mitchell shook his head. "I couldn't tell. It looked like he was wearing some kind of mask."

She didn't respond, but her eyes were dark and thoughtful in her face.

"They've got a couple of teams out there trying to track him down. They'll find them, Detective."

"If they don't, I will." Reightman promised, grimly.

A couple of uniformed cops came over to where they stood. "Ma'am," the taller of the two said, in a voice which almost disguised his own sorrow. "I'm sorry, but I need to get your statement." He looked toward Mitchell. "And yours too, Mitchell."

Reightman started to follow waiting cop to the relative isolation of the patrol car's backseat, but stopped. "Officer Mitchell has something he needs to do first." When the officer started to argue, she snapped at him. "Don't make me pull rank." She felt her eyes starting to fill again. "Please, not tonight…" she almost pleaded as she brushed new tears from red rimmed eyes. "Mitchell, come with me. I need you to do something." She led him to Toby Bailey and said through her tears, "Mitchell will take you to finish the errand we started….before……."

Toby looked toward Mitchell, weighing and considering. "You trust him?"

"Yes, I do. And so can you."

"Are you going to be alright?" Toby asked her, his voice thick with the emotion he was feeling.

She turned away as grief rose up again. "I'll let you know...." She spoke so softly he strained to hear the words. Reightman limped away to answer the questions that would be asked about the evening.

He watched her go, following her painful progress, and then faced the young officer. "If she says I can trust you, I will." His eyes flashed an icy blue and the black rims seemed to enlarge to engulf their color. He blinked and turned his head to look toward Reightman where she stood, head bowed, as the uniformed officer spoke with her. "If she's wrong about you," he said still watching the Detective, "I promise I'll make you wish you'd never thought of betraying her trust."

Mitchell had only heard one voice as cold and as dangerous as Toby Bailey's in that moment, and that voice belonged to the woman who'd just watched her partner shot down in cold blood. He looked into the other man's eyes for a just a moment, and felt the intensity and determination in their depths. "She's not wrong."

Toby closed his eyes, as if in prayer, and when he opened them they were a little warmer. "Lead the way," he said simply, and followed Mitchell to his car.

A couple of blocks from where he had stepped out of the pickup, John Brown stopped into a small neighborhood bar, located just across the street from where he had parked his SUV. He strolled up to the bar, and pulled a couple of twenties out of his front pocket. He laid them on the counter and climbed up on a stool. "Bourbon, straight up," he ordered from the bartender. He slugged back the drink and ordered another.

"Did you take in the fireworks tonight?" the barkeep asked as he set the fresh drink down.

"Sure did. They were something special." He nursed his second drink for a while, and then counted out a tip and placed it under his empty glass. He folded the remaining bills and put them back in his pocket. John Brown picked up his black bag and waved at the man behind the bar. "Have a good night," he said.

He walked of the door and noticed the patrol car driving slowly down the street with a small spot light sweeping the area. As the car approached, he raised his hand in a friendly salute. The cop nodded back and when the car passed, John Brown walked to his vehicle and opened the door. He threw the bag into the passenger seat and eased himself in.

When he pulled out and headed down the street, the patrol car slowed and the officer in the passenger seat motioned him past. John Brown gave an appreciative wave from the steering wheel as he drove by. He watched the lights in the rear view mirror until he reached his turn. John Brown headed home.

Reightman sat huddled in the backseat of the patrol car which was taking her home. She kept her tear-ravaged face turned toward the window and watched the city slide past. She never noticed the black SUV which shared the highway beside them and it wouldn't have mattered if she had. Her thoughts were turned back to the moment when she'd held Sam in her arms, and to the promise she'd made to him, and herself, as his blood flowed from his body, staining the sidewalk beneath.

"Melba, get the bastards," he told her weakly; his eyes beginning to glaze with death.

"I'll get them," she promised him as she looked down on at his white, still face while walking by his side, escorting him to the emergency van which took him away from her, forever. "I'll get the bastards."

And she would.

ACKNOWLEDGEMENTS

Writing this book had been quite a journey. This started out as a simple little murder mystery, but when I started to put the words down, the characters had their own ideas about how things should unfold. My simple little mystery has turned into a series of adventures that will unfold as the Reightman & Bailey series continues.

I have learned more about the changing world of publishing in the past several weeks than I ever thought I'd need to know. There are a variety of traditional routes to follow: both traditional, and less traditional, emerging paths. Being the person I am, I of course, took the less traditional route. Thanks to the fellow writers and editors who provided feedback and shared their experiences so I could make the best choice for me.

Books might get written in isolation, but they don't make it out of the computer and into a reader's hands without the writer getting a lot of help and encouragement. I need to thank two dear friends: Dr. Rhea Ann Merck, and Julia Prater.

Rhea graciously read a couple of drafts and provided a lot of honest, constructive feedback. She read multiple versions of the draft and always had great suggestions which she shared with kindness and enthusiasm. Character developments related to the twists and turns of the human mind owe a lot to her.

Julia was also one of my first readers, and provided me with good food for thought. She made sure I didn't have any dropped threads and pointed out those times my characters made awkward, unrealistic choices! They didn't always listen, but when they did they become better than they would have been otherwise.

I'd also like to thank other good friends and supporters who listened me talk about this book, and the series, far more than I should.

Special thanks to Kathy LaLima of LaLima Design for the outstanding cover and for her patience with me during the process.

I need to thank mother for giving me a life-long love of reading. When I was very young she read to me and allowed my mind to stretch and grow until I was reading on my own, and indulged my lifelong passion for reading – sometimes to the detriment of other things.

Finally, I have to thank my husband and partner, who lets me read when I want, and write when I need to. He solves my technology and formatting problems and is the best friend and supporter I have. I couldn't have done it without him.

ABOUT THE AUTHOR

JEFFERY CRAIG is the writing pseudonym of the author and is used for fictional works. Jeffery resides in the southeastern United States and shares his life with his husband and partner, and a menagerie of much loved pets. For several years he worked an executive providing technology and consulting services to help clients meet their business needs. He's an avid supporter of the arts and co-owns a local art gallery/gift store that provides an outlet for area artists and craftspeople to showcase and sell their work.

When he isn't writing, he might be found working on a painting or enjoying the covered porch of his historic southern home with a good book in hand. He can be contacted via his webpage (www.jefferycraigbooks.com) or on social media.

COMING SOON
HARD JOB
REIGHTMAN & BAILEY BOOK TWO

JOHN BROWN DIDN'T sleep after he made it home from the botched hit on Toby Bailey. He cleaned his gun and sat down in his favorite chair and just thought things over. *"Everything got too complicated, too fast,"* he told himself. He'd known it was risky, and he hated unnecessary risks. He didn't like it when there were too many pieces in play, and right now there more than he thought wise. Last night had unfolded very differently than planned, and a simple drive by murder went to hell because of it. He wished they'd just called it off and waited for another opportunity. He wondered if he'd even hit the man he was supposed to take out. He got his answer when the phone in front of him buzzed.

U KILLED A COP

He stared down at the phone as he digested the words. He wasn't sure what to say. It was unfortunate, but the screw-up wasn't his fault. If his employer had listened to him, none of this would've happened. He was inclined to ignore the message, but if he did there'd be a high price to pay down the line. He thought it over some more, and decided he should at least respond.

SORRY, he eventually typed, adding a sad, frowny face after the word. When he didn't receive a response, he typed a question. THE MARK? He waited.

ALIVE

Now John Brown was worried he wasn't going to collect his pay, and that wouldn't do at all. He'd done his best, and he wasn't about to let himself get screwed again by the person who'd hired him.

WHAT NOW? He typed, after thinking though the possible impact to their already hostile relationship.

The response wasn't long in coming. WAIT

John Brown could do that. He put down the phone and got up from his chair. He had plenty of other things to do today, and there wasn't any point in worrying about what might happen next. He didn't like worry. It made things complicated.

He locked up his gun in the safe and headed for the shower. A shower always made him feel better. He emerged from the steam a few minutes later, fresh and clean, and took a look in the mirror. He liked what he saw.

His hair was a medium brown, neither to straight or too curly. His hazel eyes picked up the colors around him, but never caused comment. His body was good, but not overbuilt and or worthy of immediate notice, at least with his clothes on. He wasn't model handsome, but that suited him just fine. Being too good looking wasn't an asset in his line of work.

He changed expressions a few times and then grinned. He could be whoever he needed to be, and that was perfect. His grin turned into a smile as he studied his reflection. John Brown was ready for a new day.

Tuesday morning, Melba sat on the edge of her bed staring at the alarm clock. She tried to summon up the inner strength to move, but she just couldn't. She'd been sitting and staring at the clock for forty-seven minutes.

When she finally dragged herself into the apartment the night before – hurt and distraught over Sam's death – she forced herself to walk painfully to the kitchen, where she pulled a bag of frozen peas out of the freezer. Needing something to dull her aches, she poured herself a glass of wine. After the first taste, she found she didn't want it. She poured the liquid down the sink and slowly lowered herself to the floor of her small kitchen. She dug around in the cabinets until she located a dusty, old bottle of scotch – a holiday present from a few years ago. She pulled herself up from the floor using the edge of the counter for support. She filled the wine glass with several fingers worth of dark, smoky liquor and drank it down, choking once as it burned a trail down her throat. Then she filled the glass again.

Melba stuck the bag of cold peas under one arm, lifted the bottle with one hand and the wine glass in the other, and hobbled to her bathroom. There, she undressed, dropping her clothing to the floor and leaving the pieces where they fell. She eased herself onto the side of the tub and propped her injured leg up on the toilet, and applied the peas to the swollen knee. While the cold penetrated the puffy flesh, she slowly finished her second drink. After twenty minutes, she tossed the peas in the bathroom sink then carefully stood up and tested her knee.

She filled the tub and managed to maneuver her body into the water. There she sat, slowly washing herself as tears slid down her cheeks and eventually dropped, one by one, into the soapy, hot water. She stayed in the tub until the water cooled then pulled herself upright and placed her good leg on the bathmat. She lifted her other leg, using the back of the toilet for balance. She reached for a towel and wrapped it around her wet body and sat down.

She poured another inch or so of scotch into the glass and lifted it to drink. Before it touched her lips, she set it down on the bathroom counter. She heaved herself up from her seat and stood by the sink looking into the mirror. "Not much of a surprise, Reightman," she said dully to the reflection in the glass, "but you look like absolute hell." She considered her tear-ravaged face and her rat's nest head of hair. She picked up a hairbrush and gave the graying strands a few half-hearted swipes before deciding she really didn't care. She dropped the brush to the counter and picked up the wine glass and poured the scotch down the sink. She'd never cared for scotch.

Melba dried herself off and pulled her faded blue bathrobe from its hook on the wall and eased it around her body. After knotting the belt, she picked up the bottle of scotch and the wine glass and looked down at the now thawed bag of peas, trying to figure out how she could manage all three items. After giving the problem more consideration than it warranted, she wedged the wine glass in one pocket and the floppy plastic bag of vegetables into the other. With the scotch in one free hand she half hopped, half limped, back into the kitchen.

She filled a sandwich bag with ice from the freezer and looked at the peas. "What the hell?" she asked before pulling a plastic cereal bowl out of the cabinet. She ripped open the bag and poured the peas into the bowl, which she then carried, hobbling, to the sagging couch. Propping her leg up onto the coffee table, she balanced the bag of ice on her swollen knee and ate the peas with her fingers, one at a time from the bowl on her lap.

She sat on the couch for a couple of hours, staring at the empty cereal bowl and occasionally looking up at the dark screen as if there was something on that caught her interest, although the television was turned off. She felt like crying, but didn't have any tears left. She took the melted bag of ice off of her knee and placed it into the cereal bowl, which she left sitting on one of the old couch cushions. She tested her knee, and decided the swelling had gone down a bit. She stood up and went into her bedroom and eased herself down on top of the covers.

She stared up at the ceiling in the dark room for the rest of the night, thinking about everything that had happened. She recalled the night she'd answered the dispatch call, and had walked into the Time Out Spa for the first time to discover Geri Guzman arranged on a massage table, his naked body marred by multiple cuts and slashes across his chest and around his neck. She remembered Toby Bailey has he'd been then, his innocent pale blue eyes, floppy hair and deceptively slight frame causing him to look younger than his actual years. They'd all been bewildered by how the murderer had made their way in and out of the room without leaving a trace. She was still perplexed, because that puzzle had never been solved. She reflected on the next day, when she'd met Madame Zhou, Toby's seemingly ancient, incapable attorney, who'd surprised them all with her brilliant mind and inscrutable demeanor. She replayed the discovery of Lieberman's involvement in a case that had since spiraled out of control, and the discovery of his death, by apparent suicide. She'd never believed the former City Coroner had taken his own life, but had yet to disprove it. Finally, she reviewed the last several hours, from the moment she and Sam had rushed to meet Toby and review the new evidence he had found in the lockbox Geri Guzman had rented and filled with a set of ledgers and photographs implicating some of the most prominent social and government leaders in the entire city. Try as she might, she couldn't erase the image of bright lights rushing down the street, blinding her for moment as the gunman fired at Toby, but instead killed Sam Jackson, her partner of many years.

Over and over again, the image replayed in her mind, until she sat up and turned on the bedside lamp, and swung her feet off the bed. There she stayed; staring at the alarm clock on the nightstand, counting down the minutes until it would sound its wake-up call, signaling it was time to begin the day.

An hour later, and only through grim determination, she managed to wrap her knee to give it extra support, then dressed herself and hobbled to the kitchen. She poured a cup of extra strong coffee. Her phone buzzed in her purse and she reached across the counter to retrieve it.

"Hello," she croaked, her voice rough and gravelly from screaming and fighting to get to Sam the night before.

"Detective Reightman, I am sorry to be calling you this early, but there is something we need to discuss." Melba recognized Zhou Li's voice, although the old woman sounded uncharacteristically gentle this morning.

"Yes?" Reightman's voice was a bit clearer this time. Zhou Li continued to speak and Reightman listened carefully to her words, answering the few questions she was asked. "Alright," she responded when the woman paused. "I'll see you both at headquarters a few minutes before eleven." Zhou uttered a few more words, and then ended the call.

Reightman stuck the phone back into her purse, smiling a grim, wintery smile. She finished her coffee slowly, waiting for the caffeine to hit her tired, shocked system. She rinsed the cup and gathered her things. Thirty minutes later she walked through the glass side doors of Police Headquarters.